CU00688752

William Wordsworth
A Conflict of Love

By the same author

Adult Poetry

Amphitheatre

Steel Wings

Solving Atlantis

Selected Poems

Anthologies

An Enduring Flame:
The Brönte Story in Poetry and Photographs

Poetry in the Parks:
The National Parks of England and Wales
in Poetry and Photographs

Journeys: Poetry and Literacy for
the National Curriculum

Novels

The Other Concerto

Branwell Brönte's Creation

Wordsworth in Chains

The Passions of Mary Wollstonecraft

William Wordsworth
A Conflict of Love

Wendy Louise Bardsley

Methuen

William Wordsworth

A Conflict of Love

First published in 2019 by Methuen

1

Methuen
Orchard House, Railway Street
Slingsby, York YO62 4AN

www.methuen.co.uk

Copyright © Wendy Louise Bardsley

Wendy Louise Bardsley has asserted her right under
the Copyright, Designs and Patents Act, 1988
to be identified as the author of this work.

This is a work of fiction.
Whilst many of the people and events are real,
the characterisation and story are from the
imagination of the author.

All rights reserved.
Without limiting the rights under copyright reserved above,
no part of this publication may be reproduced, stored in
or introduced into a retrieval system, or transmitted,
in any form or by any means (electronic, mechanical,
photocopying, recording or otherwise), without the
prior written permission of the both the copyright
owner and the above publisher of this book.

A CIP catalogue record for this book is available from
the British Library.

ISBN: 978 0 413 77826 0

Typeset by SX Composing DTP, Rayleigh, Essex.
Printed and bound in Great Britain by Clays Ltd, Elcograf S.p.A.

This book is sold subject to the condition that it shall not, by way of trade
or otherwise, be lent, resold, hired out or otherwise circulated in any form of
binding or cover other than that in which it is published and without a similar
condition, including this condition, being imposed on the subsequent purchaser.

For Imogen, Spencer and Miranda

Acknowledgements

M y thanks go to Julian Hitner, specialist vineyard owner in Southern Ontario, for enormous help with the ways and wonders of winemaking, and for acquiring academic information from Harvard University to attest to the fact that persons of bourgeois extraction would seem to have owned vineyards in the Loire Valley before the French Revolution.

Thanks also to Dr Richard Gravil, Chairman and Winter School Director of The Wordsworth Conference Foundation, for reading and commenting on the manuscript, and for his grace and patience with my flights of fancy. And I must not forget the ever generous Fay Weldon who gave of her precious time to help me get started with the novel.

Books I have found particularly inspiring are: *Wordsworth, A Life*, Juliet Barker, Penguin Books Ltd, 2000; *A Preface to Wordsworth*, John Purkis, Routledge, 2000, *The Collected Poems of William Wordsworth*, William Wordsworth, (Author), Antonia Till, (Introduction),Wordsworth editions, 1994, *Lyrical Ballads: With a few other poems*, William Wordsworth (author) and Samuel Taylor Coleridge (author) Penguin Classics, 2004. *William Wordsworth*, Hunter Davies, Frances Lincoln, 2009, *The letters of William Wordsworth*, editor, Alan G. Hill, OUP, 1990 and *The Journals of Dorothy Wordsworth*, edited by Mary Moorman, OUP, 1988.

1

Yearning

"Bliss it was in that dawn to be alive,

But to be young was very heaven."

William Wordsworth: *The Prelude*

His uncle's words that Christmas echoed in his mind as he made his way through the woodland: "My dear nephew, why do you go on these dangerous escapades and worry us? The French Revolution is nowhere near over, there is worse, far worse to come. – And it could happen here, oh yes. The Gordon riots put the fear of hell into the government. You were only a boy at the time, you won't remember. Newgate prison was attacked and the prisoners set free." And his uncle had held forth zealously, asserting his esteemed position as the Reverend William Cookson, Rector of Forncett St Peter and St Mary and speaking with priestly authority. "Now let me tell you, William, when hell breaks loose there is no knowing its intentions. – Oh, I know you like travelling, but travelling is sometimes dangerous and someone must pay for it too. It is your uncles who turn out their pockets to help you. – We had hoped you might work at Cambridge, find a profession, do something useful, but all you do is write poetry . . ." Then he'd wrung his hands as if he held the devil by his neck determined to throttle him. "Had that 'Jimmy Grasp-all' paid your father his dues, you and your siblings would never have been forced to leave home. Why, John would turn in his grave if he could hear how your sister still weeps in the night. She has never got over it . . ."

William felt the struggle again in his soul as he strode along the lonely pathways. It had started to rain heavily. *"She has never got over it ... She has never got over it..."* the rain sang out in the trees. He'd never got over it himself. First the death of their mother, followed soon by the death of their father who had lost his way in a storm while returning from work. The horse had found its way home, but wet, tired and fatigued his father had died soon after, and William along with his siblings had been cast out on to the winds and made to live in different places. It had happened too fast. He'd felt dismembered and scattered, like the Egyptian god Osiris, waiting for Isis, his goddess sister and wife to discover his parts and put him back together. Dorothy could always do that; just a choice few words could re-assemble his being. – "I doubt we'll ever see that money," his uncle had sighed. "Not in a million years." William's father had been a lawyer to the Earl of Lonsdale, James Lowther, but wages had been left unpaid.

William pulled his frockcoat closer about him. He was feeling depressed. His visit had ended badly and he'd left silent as a shadow. Once again he'd annoyed and disappointed his family. But he had no choice; he must go on yearning, yearning for life, yearning for understanding. He did like to go on escapades that much was true, and he *was* sort of escaping. Some words from Rousseau came to him through the trees: *"Man is born free and everywhere he is in chains."* As life was chained to breath, his soul was chained to poetry. And what a powerful chain it was, it connected him with the whole of life about him.

Lightning flashed before him like a sword battling the wind and rain. The woodland glistened with wetness. He heard the branch of an aged beech cracking above him. It fell with a thud beside him. He quickened his pace. Storms could be lethal; a storm had killed his father. It was winter 1791 and he was twenty one years old. What must he do with his life, he wondered, his passionate, throbbing life? He bent his head and trudged through the rain. How could he earn some money? For now, his uncles helped him out; he never went hungry and most of the time got by, if that meant being entertained and writing things down. Over the last few weeks he'd been enjoying the city of London. But wherever he'd gone, whatever he'd done, his mind turned seaward towards France, and despite his family's misgivings he would soon be taking a boat. He'd been in France last year on the first anniversary of its 1789 revolution, and now he would visit again. Weary of exploitation and poverty the peasants had taken up arms and rebelled most savagely. Now it seemed the whole of France spoke with a different voice.

Back in his London lodgings, he looked in his purse. His uncle Richard had sent him his autumn allowance, though it was less than usual this time. He hated begging for money, but it was better than doing work that made him feel ill. He hadn't enjoyed university and was glad to get away. He might have worked harder, but he hadn't been one of those clowns either who clambered up the college walls at weekend besotted with drink. In any case, he was quite familiar with beggars; there were plenty of beggars in Lakeland, often interesting fellows, vagrants by cruel chance. But they were free. And how he believed in freedom! He would not see himself captured by a life that destroyed him.

He felt for his notebook in his pocket. Now where were his pencils? Ah yes, he had three. He needed to check his thoughts too. Sometimes they went too fast if he got anxious, as if Time raced away in his head and he must catch it before it disappeared. He'd seen how life sprang up from the earth then very soon withered and died and how his parents had breathed their last too soon. He wrote things down and talked to people, trying to discover truths through his thoughts and senses. Sometimes he'd muse for ages then try to write poetry hoping for those celestial words that delivered the best of his feelings. Richard, his older brother, a lawyer in London didn't read very much poetry, but John who was younger and worked for the East India Company as a sailor, claimed to hear poetry in the weather, especially in storms. There were fearsome tales about the sea. Cutthroat pirates roamed the oceans, ships sank from colliding with rocks, and some said mermaids lured sailors to their deaths with beautiful seductive songs. "To be serenaded to death by a mermaid is an excellent way to die!" John had laughed, when Dorothy had voiced her fears. He liked telling stories, especially the one about the American colonists who'd jettisoned shiploads of taxed tea into Boston harbour. Taxation without representation would not do and they'd shown their anger unambiguously. It had ended in large-scale rebellion, war, revolution, and the birth of a new nation.

William recalled his visit to Forncett that Christmas which in the main had been to call on Dorothy who helped look after their Uncle William's children and assist their aunt with the house. Uncle William understood how things were in the family and had taken her away from her miserable life in Penrith where she'd lived with their maternal grandparents, a tyrannical pair she couldn't get on with. Indeed it was a great rescue.

His thoughts moved on to Mary Hutchinson, a friend of theirs since childhood who he'd met with again that holiday. In his youth her laughter and the sight of her long dark hair flying out in the wind had confused him and made him awkward. There were things he'd wanted to say to her, questions he'd wanted to ask, but she'd gone in a flash of sunlight over the fields, and alas, the moment was over. She, her four brothers, and Sara, her sister, had also been orphaned in childhood and as time had passed they'd all become devoted friends. But it was more than friendship he felt for Mary Hutchinson. She was always there within him and had stirred his youth into manhood. There was a richness in her, a voluptuousness he wanted, but he would not affirm it yet.

He thought again about Dorothy. How good it was to see her so happy; she hadn't been happy in ages. She'd been learning too. Uncle William was something of a scholar and she'd made good use of his library. The Rectory of Forncett St Peter was a fine Georgian house beside the church of St Peter and St Paul. Dorothy had taken him to places she'd written of in her letters; the graveyard that flowered so profusely in spring, the great passionate trees that danced so wonderfully in the wind, and the footpath that led to the river Tas, where they'd listened to the voice of the water, just as they'd listened to the voice of the Derwent as children on the death of their mother and heard its soothing consolations.

But he'd known he would cross the channel. The hardships of a country constantly at war had made French peasants savage and he needed to see for himself what was happening. "Liberté, Égalité, Fraternité, ou la mort!" was their cri de cœur. The crops had failed; they were starving and taxed to the hilt. Émigrés who had fled to England brought stories of slaughter and plots, constantly repeating the horrific tale of how revolutionaries searching for arms had stormed the Bastille prison and hacked off the governor's head with a knife parading it through Paris on a pike. Justice? Was that justice? What of the governor's horrified eyes and agonised screams, his blood soaked carcase? And that had only been the start. A bloody message had been sent to the government, the ancien regime was over; the poor of France had had enough.

And what of the horror now? Without doubt the world needed justice, but need there be so much bloodshed? There was a feeling of disquiet in England too; the whole world was changing and learned people were discussing those changes and putting their thoughts into writing. "These are the times that try men's souls," the English radical, Thomas Paine had said at the start of the American Revolution. Paine's revolutionary ideas spoke to peasants and scholars alike. Anyone reading his work did so with vigour and passed on his messages urgently. But his sympathies with the French Revolution were constantly marked as anti-monarchist. Paine was a man to be watched. At the London Revolution Society yesterday, where an elderly fellow had allowed him in without a card, William had listened to the scientist and philosopher, Joseph Priestley. In 1782 Priestley had published *An History of the Corruptions of Christianity* causing restless anger in the country, whilst his scathing criticism of the government's treatment of the colonies had made them nervous. Monarchs of the future, Priestley claimed, with the advent of the French Revolution, would be first and foremost servants of the people, and accountable to them as well. No wonder he disturbed the authorities. There were no doubt officials in the gathering listening and reporting back.

William opened the door of his lodgings and stepped out on to the street, then he walked for a while glancing about for a café where he thought to take an early morning breakfast. Finding one he liked the look of, he went inside and sat down. As he ordered his food and drink, he saw that Joseph Priestley was seated at a corner table.

'Ah, the dark angel who pursues me,' Priestley said with a laugh.

'Good morning,' William said quietly, gathering himself together. 'I do not pursue you, sir, and I assure you I am no angel.'

Priestley bit on a slice of toast and chewed it slowly, holding William with his eyes. Then he wiped his mouth with a napkin. 'I saw you yesterday at the Society. Weren't you at the back?'

'Indeed I was,' William replied nervously. 'But I was only there as a guest. You might say I begged my way in. What a stimulating gathering it was. I very much enjoyed your address.' He felt as if he were dreaming. He had hardly expected to be remembered by someone like Priestley. Priestley had animated eyes and dark heavy brows; there was so much power in his features, it was almost as if the man had been created for a purpose. His clothes were old and well worn, strange for the son of a cloth dresser from Yorkshire, but William liked his attire. The shapes of the man's elbows were impressed into the sleeves of his coat.

'Good,' said Priestley. 'I like to think my words might be useful.' He folded his arms and sat back. 'The year 1789 is indelibly carved into our souls. – Tell me, my friend. What is your opinion? Do you think the fall of the Bastille was a great historic event or do you think France is now on the verge of collapse?'

The waiter brought William hot steaming coffee and toast. He saw that Priestley watched him with interest, waiting to hear his reply. William's mind sped in every direction. What did he think, really? The truth was he did not know, not properly, his thoughts were a melange of colours and shapes, feelings and ideas. He listened a lot to others, he read the best works he could find, including Priestley's, and was deeply interested and concerned for the future. But his thoughts were often in disarray, as if he were sorting through a ragbag of absorbing ideas, some of them jewels, others just pieces of clay. And as he thought on it more, it came to him clearly, that this was the reason he must visit France once again. He wanted to discover how such great events like the fall of the Bastille came to be. What had made the people revolt, finally? What had been the final straw? 'Yes,' he said slowly and thoughtfully, 'I believe the fall of the Bastille is a great historic event, in the sense that it has changed things for good.'

Priestley waited.

'But those changes,' William continued, carefully choosing his words 'would seem to have been totally necessary. And if France were on the verge of collapse, I believe it is because there is a need for a certain equilibrium in the way matters are dealt with, a certain essential balance, or a country cannot be sustained, and collapse it must. I believe . . . from what I have heard and read . . . that . . . and I also visited recently . . . France has not ministered such a balance.'

'Quite true,' said Priestley sagaciously. 'There are many who believe that hereditary monarchy is essential to harmony and peace and they will not budge from that opinion.' Priestley braced himself and stared around the walls of the cafe. 'But absolute power is fatal, and Louis, as we know, is an absolute monarch.' He sniffed. 'Aye, and other things too.'

'I am deeply sorry for it,' William murmured. Louis XVI was known for his extravagance, and what appeared to the world as an uncaring attitude to the poor. Though there were many who said that the nobles who surrounded him had rebuffed his ideas for reform, they did not want to damage their own vested interests. The queen, Marie Antoinette, was loathed and ridiculed; obscene and mocking cartoons about her circulated the world. Some had found their way to coffee houses and taverns in England. People told of how she'd built herself a pretty little village where she might 'play' at being a peasant. The fact of their queen seeming to make jokes about their poverty had enraged the poor even more. William took a drink from his coffee, all the time thoughtful. Yes, matters were becoming clearer.

Priestley frowned and pursed his lips. 'Oh, do not be sorry for it,' he said low and good-humouredly. 'It is rather the way things go, when people are unsparingly exploited. And if a king is treated godly, will he not think himself a god?' He gestured with his hand. 'Whether the god be good or bad is by the way, he will still think himself a god.'

'And the poor have been made into demons,' said William, carefully slicing his toast into four perfect portions. He saw that Priestley still listened, though he knew he was talking too freely. 'I do apologise, sir,' he said, quickly. 'I had a very odd dream last night. It is still in my mind.'

Priestley sat back and stared at William with interest. 'A dream, you say? Oh, I will not tell you mine. And they won't go away either.' He touched the sides of his head. 'They stay with me day and night. There are those who laugh me to scorn, and there are others who fear me. I like to believe that there are some who value what I say – and who knows, perhaps like me a little.'

Priestley's heavy eyebrows rose and fell as he spoke, and William perceived that the prodigious writer and speaker appeared unhappy. 'There are probably more who admire you than scorn you,' said William. He glanced about. The café was relatively empty. It was strange sitting with Priestley like this having breakfast, as if they had known each other years. 'I know that your pamphlet incensed people. It does not do to defend the revolution, of course. Men like yourself and Paine are brave to speak your minds.'

'The revolution has heralded great changes in the role of monarchy,' said Priestley. He shook a finger in the air. – 'I have offended King George . . .'

'Yes, I heard.' William lowered his voice. 'Though you only say what you believe, and from such an immense perspective. You are very learned.'

'Am I?' Priestley laughed quietly. 'I have offended the church too by rejecting the Trinity. And so, you see, I am despised.' His shoulders lifted and fell. 'I am despised for this, despised for that – I fear I shall be found with a knife in my back in the Thames ere long.'

'Oh, sir, do not think of it,' said William. He bent his head as he spoke.

'You say I am brave,' said Priestley, finishing the last of his coffee. 'But my friend, you are even braver. You dare to talk to a man whose house has been ransacked and who cannot put his head down to rest.'

William listened in sympathy. Priestley had been made to suffer for what he believed in. It was amazing how men like him continued to offer their thoughts through lectures and books, regardless of consequences. 'I believe that leaders should be moral leaders,' William said with emphasis, 'not just political leaders. There is great distress among the poor in England too. They are also beset by poverty – as you know only too well – and need help.'

'Oh, for an ideal world,' sighed Priestley. 'My readings and observations show me that human behaviour alters very little with time.'

'But you have hope, sir; it is there in your writings. You believe things can change.'

'I would like to think so,' said Priestley, with a long intake of breath. 'Though I doubt it will happen in my lifetime. Power, power, you must not tread on its toes or it will turn and devour you!'

'You are a man of great feeling,' said William. 'You are good. I feel intensely myself, but I am far from good.' He frowned and lowered his voice. 'In fact, I am rather selfish.'

Priestley shook his head in bafflement. 'We have no idea of what we are. We are full of our own pretensions, constantly trying to water what we think are the best of our seeds, but they often grow into monsters.'

'Human life has a mystical quality,' William replied in earnest. 'A certain grace that as far as we allow, can guide us. Getting and spending we waste our strength, and our lives too in the bargain. I would rather have a springwood bursting with flowers than a chest full of money.'

Priestley looked at him curiously. 'Are you a student?'

William put out his hand. 'William Wordsworth – it is good to meet you, sir. I have just completed a course of study at Cambridge.' He rubbed his nose, for he could hardly say he'd "completed" his course; he had quite neglected it.

'Ah,' sighed Priestley. 'I fear I shall have a book in my hand when I am lowered into my grave.'

Well, at least humour assists him, thought William, for it seemed Priestley was doomed. Words were weapons as surely as guns and spears and a free thinker like him was in a dangerous position. Priestley put on his hat and dragged down the rim. 'I thought I'd get out into the city early,' he said, 'before my enemies are up.' He gave a low little chuckle. 'Who will know me with my collar turned up and my hat pulled down like this, though I might just as well be murdered for my pocket watch as my name out there?' He stared ahead for a moment and folded his arms.

William glanced outside. The street was becoming busy. 'Yes, you are probably right; there are beggars and drunks everywhere it seems at night-time. I am not used to it. I come from the Lake District. It is all so silent in Lakeland.' He sat for a moment thoughtful. He loved to think of his Lakeland home and the oneness he felt with the land. He told Priestley about his early home in Cockermouth and the early deaths of his parents, and how the family had been torn asunder. He told him about The Earl of Lonsdale and how he owed money to their family. 'A lot of it too.'

'But you studied at Cambridge University, a rich experience, surely?'

'I might have worked harder,' said William, in a tone of familiar regret. 'The course wasn't to my taste.' He felt like firewood that would not burn, he said, if his reading didn't inspire him. 'Just now I am eager to travel, though I have little in the way of money.' He glanced downwards embarrassed. His poverty always reminded him he ought to be working. 'I intend to stay in London a little longer, then I shall sail to France.'

'Right to the action, eh?' said Priestley frowning 'Do think carefully about that.'

'I must practise my French,' William said intently, determined not to be discouraged.

'Of course,' said Priestley. 'By all means practise your French. Though much of what you hear over there will be fierce and obscene.'

'A system that relies on exploiting others cannot survive,' William said flatly. 'Nothing has a right to last except reason and equity.'

'Ah, Locke – you have read him,' said Priestley looking at him straight. 'Despite what you say about your course, you are obviously quite well-read.'

'I learn what interests me,' William said firmly. 'It cannot be otherwise. Much learning is forced into the heads of students like the pain of a bullet.' He felt young and inexperienced now as he talked to Priestley, though he knew there were parts of his mind that could rise to great heights. But how could he speak of such things when he couldn't quite grasp them? How could he talk about the exquisite patterns Nature allowed him to see, the great expanse of beauty it laid before him? He spoke again, quietly. 'I am very imaginative . . .' He drew a breath and wondered what to say next, eager to get his thoughts across to this man who listened so carefully. 'I can see the importance of science, but it is not a path I wish to follow.' He recalled the statue of Isaac Newton close by his window at Cambridge, most proud in the dying light. 'The exact precision of science is somehow comforting. Yet it leaves something wanting for me, a certain freedom of thought and emotion. I prefer to think on the Arts.'

'So you see them as definitely separate?' said Priestley, making to rise. He held William with his dark intelligent eyes.

'I do at present,' said William, enjoying the stirring conversation and the feel of the rush of his thoughts. 'Perhaps in time, if such concepts become familiar, and their language is felt in the heart, then I might think differently.'

'It has been good to talk with you,' said Priestley. 'But now I must go. I hope you enjoy the rest of your stay in London, and your time in France too, if you get there. But do watch out. There is no denying the danger.' With that, he went to the door . . .

2

Elizabeth Montrose

Waiting at the harbour, he settled his bag at his feet and pulled up the collar of his coat. People were shouting from the boat and loading on luggage, others talked with their companions. The mist stayed dense. "Right to the action", Priestley had said. And it was true. He was certainly drawn to action. Though most of the people who knew him would probably call him the studious type; a man of books and contemplations, hardly the fierce fighter who lived in his soul. But his poetic and creative mind became suddenly transformed when he thought of injustice, then he was ready for battle, though the violence in France was brutal and he did not feel he could ever be part of that. Mothers rallied their sons to fight with their fathers and brothers; wives urged their husbands do the same. The revolution was their raison de vivre, or else their reason to die. Here, in England, people lived in relative peace, though men of politics kept their eyes peeled and their ears close to the ground, for the French were constantly plotting. The talk at The Revolution Society had stirred him. "If a man doesn't fight for liberty, then is he not a slave?" someone had shouted. Another had cried, "Slavery is incomprehensible!" and the crowd had applauded. William gave a sigh of relief that the state of affairs on British slave ships had now been regulated, but slavery must stop altogether! A society had been founded in England to try to abolish it, and the ideals of freedom and independence had sped through the world but the Abolition Bill presented by Wilberforce to parliament had sadly failed to get through. There was still much to be done and many brave minds were busy.

He'd enjoyed his stay in London, and had even been to the circus. Acrobats, tumblers, clowns and animals had helped lift his brooding concerns, for it was hard to break free from the tensions that often claimed him. Ships, towers, domes, the Houses of Parliament and Westminster Bridge, had fired his imagination. Gazing up at the great buildings and down at the dark brooding river, he murmured, *"Dull would he be of soul who could pass, a sight so touching in its majesty. This City now doth, like a garment, wear the beauty of the morning; silent, bare . . ."* A poem would come in time; just now he was capturing impressions.

It was hard to imagine the miserable existences of many of the city's inhabitants, living, whole families in cold damp cellars, their existence blighted by starvation and disease. He shuddered. They would probably live out their lives in those vile conditions. He was grateful for his childhood in Lakeland where he'd enjoyed the beauty of the seasons. He was a countryman through and through and loved the wide-open spaces, the chance to wander as far as his eye could see, to listen to the sounds of Nature and somehow take part. Best of all were the woods at night where silent winged creatures offered themselves up to the moon and small warm blooded beings brushed against his legs. No owls sounded in London, and only rats ran free. At times his heart spilled over with the sufferings of London's poor, but he'd seen great poverty in Lakeland too where families had lost their land and all they had worked for . . .

'How much longer?' he murmured, peering through the mist. Waiting to board the vessel was a tiresome business, especially in unpleasant weather. He'd packed Dorothy's letters and would read them again, lodgings were often lonely and it was good to have words from home. She enjoyed her life in Forncett, but he couldn't help feeling responsible for her. And he needed her too. They had vowed to get a cottage together some time. But when would it happen? And how could they possibly afford it without help from their uncles? She had worn a red winter rose in her hair when he'd left Forncett at Christmas. It had cheered him greatly to know she had worn it for him. His brothers too, were living their lives without ado. He, himself, felt like a sort of bird, flying from tree to tree, simply following its instincts, pursuing a freedom remote and secret from humans, no path charted and each route mysterious. Climbing a mountain, whenever he reached the top he felt like a great winged creature, an eagle perhaps, his Roman nose a vestige of what it had been. If he thought hard enough, he felt he could remember tearing apart the flesh of some poor doomed animal he'd slain on the hills. He sighed and straightened and tried to make light of what others called his eccentricities. He was wild, rugged and unpolished; take it or leave it that's how he was.

There was a great deal of hustle and bustle around him. People were complaining the mist was getting thicker, some said the boat wouldn't sail.

'You must find it right now!' came the anxious voice of a woman close by. 'Or I shall have to speak to your captain. Now, look for it properly. I have taken that trunk all over the world and I don't want to lose it!'

'Keep yer 'at on, Ma'am,' called a bewildered youth dashing about. 'I think I know where it is!'

'I hope you do!' the woman called back.

William moved in through the mist. She was a handsome middle-aged lady, indeed having trouble with her hat. Atop of it an assortment of feathers waved about in the wind. 'It looks like he's got it,' said William, pointing at the boy, struggling with a large trunk.

'Ah,' she said, turning. She pulled her dark fur coat closer about her person, looking embarrassed. 'You heard all that then, did you? I am so sorry, my dear. I get so worried about my things, you see. I always fear they'll get lost.' She met his eyes and smiled. 'But they are only *things* aren't they. What a fuss I am making.' She gazed at her sturdy black boots and sighed. 'My brother was drowned some years ago with his wife and daughter. They were sailing to England.'

'An awful thing to have happened,' said William, sympathetically. And he thought again about John and hoped he was safe. There were a great many tragedies at sea, but losing family was tragedy enough, however you lost them.

'The sound of the waves reminds,' she murmured.

'I'm sure,' said William, lowering his voice and leaning in closer. 'But it does not do to keep remembering something so painful.' The restless feathers on her hat constantly tried to escape. She lifted her hand to secure them.

'You are quite right, and thank you.' She stamped her feet to warm them. 'If they do not hurry, I fear we shall turn into icebergs. I doubt I shall be travelling much longer. The mind grows weary of carrying the body along with it. And I have to say, I have started to fear those waves.'

'I believe we can rest assured that our British ships are the best,' William added firmly.

'I am not normally as nervous as this,' she said, glancing about. 'But France is so divided now, and I hate the agitation. I am on my way to see my nephew, Pierre. – Oh, I shouldn't be going at all, except I worry he could die if I don't, he is so self-willed. Nephews can be very trying.' She stretched out her hand. 'Elizabeth Montrose, it is good to have your company.'

'William Wordsworth,' he joined. He laughed briefly. 'Yes, nephews can certainly be difficult.'

'Where are you going?' she asked, observing the bag at his feet.

'Paris,' he said. He took a deep breath. The thought disturbed him a little for what he might find. 'Then after that, I shall go to Orléans.'

Her eyes shone with interest. 'Ah, my nephew lives in Orléans. That is where I am staying. He is the son of the brother I lost. Oh, poor, poor Pierre. He lost a sister as well as his parents in the shipwreck. It was all too much. He was only ten years old at the time, but the drowning continues to haunt him. I stayed at the château until he was eighteen years old, then returned to England. I visit him periodically.'

'Are you French?' asked William, because of her accent.

She sighed loudly as if with memory. 'I am. But I fell in love with an Englishman from London, a pianist, and I came to live with him in England. He died from tuberculosis. Oh, I feel for the French as Pierre does. Matters are quite alarming. Nothing is certain but death and taxes, as they say.'

'He was lucky to have you with him.'

'But I love him, you see,' she said quietly. 'I'm glad I could be there to help.'

The youth came running and told her the trunk was on board. She clasped her hands with relief. The mist was beginning to lift and he glanced at the bag at his feet. 'This is the lot for me,' he said, frankly. She looked him up and down curiously. 'I don't need much,' he smiled. 'It's a very good bag actually. I have all I need in here.'

'Why are you going to France?' she asked, looking at him straight. 'Are you visiting relatives?'

He shook his head and frowned, again questioning his purpose. 'I have no relatives in France. I have relatives here in England however, three brothers and a sister. They would rather keep me here, I think, but I'm eager to find things out.'

'"Find things out"?'

'Well yes, I want to see what is happening and write.'

'You are a writer?'

He laughed briefly. 'I like to think I am a poet.'

She spoke thoughtfully. 'You have purpose, my dear. You are going your own way, whatever way it might be. What could be better?' She looked ahead. 'I can see people gathering. Do you think they're boarding?'

'I think they're still loading on luggage,' he said, watching the shadowy movements of the group in an atmosphere of noisy chatter.

'My nephew is often unhappy,' Elizabeth murmured, sighing. 'His letters are far too intense. He gets carried away with politics, you see. But of course, he is young.'

'And how old is young?' asked William, wondering as she spoke, what it was like to be young and French in a time of revolution.

'He is just twenty-seven,' she said with a smile. 'A terrible age for men. It is getting near thirty, and woe betide what the age of thirty can do to us.'

'Well, I hope to be thirty myself eventually, if I am lucky.' He laughed quietly, thoughtful.

'You are strong and healthy,' she laughed, tapping his arm. 'But the sky will darken as it wants and the sun is determined to rise each day regardless.'

They stood for some minutes listening to the sounds about them. People talked together loudly, men called out to each other as they finished loading the vessel.

'It is good that the poor have rebelled,' he said, nodding for certainty.

She looked at him sharply. 'You are a republican Mr Wordsworth that much is obvious. My nephew would like you. He is a republican too. Pierre is rich; it is just that he thinks he shouldn't be. My brother left him a vineyard in the Loire valley. It is one of the best.'

He waited.

The woman continued. 'It has been in our family many years, purchased from a French nobleman. Now it belongs to Pierre. But he cannot bear the hardships of the poor, he does not like to be wealthy while others are starving and is often quite foolish. He gives away vast sums of money to those who are needy.' She leant towards him. 'Or those who *pretend* to be needy. He is often exploited. His letters tell such melancholy stories. I wish he were less naïve.' She did not know what to expect from Pierre, she said, when she reached Orléans, he was changing so fast, and she did not like his companions either. 'The Girondins insist they are liberal republicans, but I am not so sure. Their leader Brissot, says things that suggest otherwise. Some of the Girondins try to make friends with Pierre, but I do not trust them. It is hard to know who is in charge in France just now. But that is the way of revolution.'

'And the Jacobins?'

'The Jacobins are radical revolutionaries. They have clever men in their Society who would drive the revolution into ever more fierce bloodshed. They are against King Louis.' She covered her face with her hands. 'Oh, I wish some help could come to France. Proper civilized help. It is all so hopeless.'

'Violence and bloodshed should never be used to change things,' said William. He hoped he could continue to believe it.

'The king, it seems, is all but a figurehead now.' Elizabeth continued. 'He is a prisoner in Paris with his family. They tried to flee to the border of the Austrian Empire but were captured at Varennes and the soldiers returned them as traitors. Someone recognised the king's face from a coin. Just imagine. I suppose you will know about that.' She spoke tiredly.

'Yes,' said William. He thought about what he'd heard. The king had accepted an oath on a new constitution with a warning that should he try to head an army for war or get anyone else to do it for him he might just as well abdicate. Matters were certainly bad. 'The king put his private interests before those of his people,' William said flatly. 'It was wrong.'

'His ministers do most of his work,' said Elizabeth, coming to Louis' defence. 'It is their own interests they care about, never mind the king's. Many of them would dethrone him in a flash and steal his power for themselves.'

The sea had quietened and the wind had fallen. 'I believe they are boarding,' said William, glancing towards the boat.

They both went forward.

'Why do you have the little book?' she asked, pointing to his pocket.

William touched his notebook. 'Ah this, I write in it, that's if I'm feeling inspired.'

'What do you write?' She held his gaze, curious.

'Little passages of poetry mostly,' he smiled. Her face seemed to ask for more. 'Oh, all manner of jottings.' He laughed. 'Things I must remember to do. Other people's words I've enjoyed, all sorts of musings.'

'Will you write down my nephew's address?' she asked. 'You are very welcome to visit us. The Vallons are on holiday at Pierre's château just now. Annette and Paul have been friends of his since childhood.' She frowned. 'They are royalists however, the three of them are often arguing. But do come to see us. I think you would like their company.'

He wrote down Pierre's address then pushed his notebook back in his pocket. That done they went to join the others.

3

Paris

Once on board Elizabeth had been taken to a comfortable part of the boat and he'd lost her. She'd smiled at him warmly as if to tell him not to forget her. Though there was no danger of that, he'd every intention of visiting her nephew's château and felt drawn there.

He was trying to write while crossing, but his pencil danced with the waves. From his porthole window there was nothing to see but waves, waves and their glorious liberty! But what awaited him in France? Would he be too soon afraid, forced to return to England like a young bird squawking back to its nest on discovering a dangerous world? Through his talk with Elizabeth, the problems of France were in absolute focus now. There was much to see and learn. There would be new experiences to write about, new ways of thinking to inform him. He wondered about Pierre. He was a wealthy viticulturist who liked to give money to the poor. Maybe he had a great capacity for kindness, or was he disenchanted and depressed? He had lost his parents and sister at sea. Those poor people were dead; it was bound to have affected his thinking. Did he blame himself in some tangled confused way and need to give to others to compensate? And what could be wrong with giving, especially when people were starving. He scribbled some words in his notebook, then secured it deep in his pocket. It would be interesting to meet with Pierre, he thought, if he were approachable that was, dejected people were often reserved and remote. He'd experienced such moods himself, constantly feeling guilty, always restless to a degree that rendered him acutely sensitive sometimes and difficult to talk to. He began to feel irritable. Taking advantage of what appeared to be calmer waters he decided to sleep.

The last part of the journey was slow and sluggish and the ship experienced bad weather. But they had reached the shores of France! The ship grew noisy as passengers prepared to leave the boat. Disembarking with the others, he looked through the throng for Elizabeth, but he could not see her anywhere and presumed her nephew had sent someone to take her to Orléans. Treading the French soil his body seemed still to be rocking and he was feeling quite nauseous. But, oh what joy – it was snowing! 'Ah, the dignity of snowflakes!' he murmured putting out his hands. He had always loved the softness of snow and the way it could silence the earth as if magically putting it to sleep. He stopped to enjoy the feel of it landing on his skin and wondered if it were snowing in England on Dorothy. A surge of longing filled him as he thought of his beloved Lakeland and how on days like this the waters would be frozen over and he could skate to his heart's content.

But he wasn't in England he was in France, a sleek, clean land, covered just now in whiteness without the least blemish. But that wasn't true; he was walking in a fractured country, a turbulent country, with only his notebook and pencil for company. He walked on further, looking about for a chaise. Voices around him spoke in earnest and in low tones, often foreign to his ear. But he'd determined to keep his own lips sealed on his visit, for having an English accent might cause him problems. He was though, determined to write, his resolve was strong and fresh as a new day. He wondered what new experiences he'd have in this now tempestuous country. He took so much for granted back home; the easy pace life afforded, the English countryside, and of course his family. – Just then there came the sound of a chaise nearby. He hailed the driver and climbed in, thinking through his intentions as the chaise moved off. Before he went on to Orléans, he would stay in Paris a while and explore the city. He wanted to see what was left of the Bastille prison after having been attacked by revolutionaries.

The chaise went quietly and softly over the snow, and he fell to thinking about King Louis and his hapless situation. For all intents and purposes, the king was now a prisoner in his own country. It *was* still Louis' country, wasn't it, but for how much longer? The revolution was becoming barbarous and those who opposed it were dealt with ruthlessly. William had read of a Doctor Guillotin, who was promoting a contraption of execution, "many times faster than an axe and more humane." He chilled at the thought. It might take several blows for an axe to take off somebody's head and there were horrific tales of screaming and shrieking and mouths still fluttering while the sad head hung by a thread. French Doctor Guillotin claimed this machine could slice off a head in seconds. William winced, reflecting how Charles I and Mary Queen of Scots had both met their deaths through the axe. The executioner had had to make a number of blows to remove the poor queen's head; the muscles of her neck were so strong.

He fell to thinking about Elizabeth. She had sympathy for King Louis, who was probably a good deal better than he'd been painted. But it seemed his right hand didn't know what his left was up to, and it would not do for a king. Also, Versailles was too far away from the ordinary lives of his people; their king didn't know or understand them . . .

'The snow is too slippery for the horses!' the driver called out, as the chaise slid about the road. 'Tenez votre siege!' They skidded round a corner and the horses careered down a hill. It seemed they might never stop. Presently, on flatter and easier terrain, they whinnied and slowed, struggling along through the snow.

William settled back in his seat. Was it not obvious, he concluded, that France would become a republic? The king's foreign wars had depleted the French treasury; atrocious weather had brought miserable harvests and wide scale starvation, while unreasonable taxes and constant conscription had broken the spirits of the poor. The country needed a new constitution, but to get it might be as difficult as mining for gold in a quarry of clay. The dark heart of it was the problem of the three estates into which France was divided. There had always been a problem in France with the three estates; the world knew the story too well. First came the Clergy, Second came the Nobility and the Third consisted of ninety percent of the people, who were merchants, craftsmen, bourgeoisie and peasants. With only a third of deputies in parliament, The Third Estate had been rightfully angry, arguing clergy and nobility would always look to their own interests first. But once people were starving, history had shown that the people began to talk and think. Then came the riots. The king had been forced to address the disquiet in the country, bringing together the representative body of the whole of French society, the Estates General, silent since 1614. He watched the snow, slowly stopping about him, falling on the bodies of the horses and trickling as rain down their coats. *The Estates General?* He saw in his mind old men rising from their graves, skeletons walking and shaking their fists at having been disturbed from their peace. Who were these people? Where did they come from? Louis, it was said, had felt threatened by the meeting, and the Third Estate's deputies had been locked outside from proceedings. But not to be overcome, they'd organised a meeting of their own in the tennis court next door and had declared themselves "The National Assembly" swearing to keep on meeting until there was a new constitution. Incensed and affronted, the king had responded by placing troops around Paris, an action seen by The Third Estate as the start of a royal coup. It was common knowledge that the Bastille prison held gunpowder, and revolutionaries had stormed its walls, then brutally hacked off the governor's head with a knife while Louis and his family had been taken from the Palace of Versailles to the Tuileries Palace in Paris where they might be watched more closely. Much had happened in a short space of time, but history had been waiting, just like poison in the blood erupts into a boil or the earth grows weary and pours out its pain in fiery volcanic eruptions, Time itself was well and truly alive.

Gazing from the window of the chaise, he saw that he travelled through a lovely vale with stilled high trees either side, and he imagined armies hiding, freezing soldiers contemplating their mortality, wretched and hungry. He lurched slightly forward as the driver halted his horses all of a sudden. 'I detest this snow!' he shouted. 'And so do my steeds!' He seized a shovel beside him and leapt from the chaise. For several minutes, but for the sound of his shovel grating on the snow packed track, the vale was silent. After five or so minutes, he climbed back up and whipped his horses into action cursing them as they went for wasting his time.

On the outskirts of Paris, all appeared safe and sound. White banks of snowdrift shone on the hills like waves of the sea. He thought of Elizabeth and hoped she was safe with her nephew. He thought of the travellers on the boat, some of them probably visiting relatives or coming back home. Others perhaps were writers like him, mysteriously drawn to France. There were no doubt unfortunates too, trying to evade the police. He'd occasionally gazed on sad young men with forlorn and miserable faces and had wondered who they might be and what sort of lives they had led.

As the chaise passed through the city, he caught sight of a woman on a balcony, shrieking to a man below while hurling down a large ceramic pot. 'I do not want your gift!' she shouted. 'Give it to your other woman!' The man called back in quick, passionate French as the pot crashed to pieces beside him. The driver lashed his horses and the chaise sped on.

After another forty minutes, they arrived in the centre of Paris. The snow lay heavy on the ground without the least sign of thawing. He found his hotel and was shown to his room, a small though neat little chamber with excellent views of the city. He gazed on the snow covered streets and knew there would be peasants in the alleys begging, possibly even dying or else sharpening their knives for action. He shook the thoughts from his mind and organised his books and clothes, then partook of a little light refreshment, thinking he would visit the Champs de Mars that day. It was a vast spread of lawns, taking its name from the Campus Martius in Rome, a tribute to the Roman god of War and the principle Military Parade Ground in France where the National Guard had killed fifty people that summer. He wanted to walk there, hear what people were saying and watch their faces as they talked. The event was shrouded in confusion. Reports said a crowd had gathered to sign a petition to depose King Louis, but the people had been unruly and the National Guard had grown edgy. At first they'd fired into the air and the gathering had scattered, but the people had returned with George Jacques Danton, a lawyer, and Camille Desmoulins, a writer and politician, two of their fiercest leaders. This second assembly, the papers had said, had been even more rowdy that the first, and this time the Guard had fired into the crowd.

William checked his map. What had *really* taken place, he wondered? He found his bearings and put his finger on the Champs de Mars. Within no time at all he was striding from the hotel and well on his way. He averted his eyes as he walked, for he did not want to talk with anyone as he went.

Very soon he was there. The place was eerily silent. The snow was deep and he stamped his feet to shake the excess off his boots. He stared down curiously at the shape of his footprints in the snow. Now he understood what Dorothy had meant when she'd said he was heavy on his feet; his footprints were deep, and how strange it was, to see the path he'd been treading. His footprints were like a pattern of the past, they would disappear with the sunshine, just as the blood shed on the lawns that day would have gone with the rain. If he listened hard and closed his eyes, he could almost hear the people protesting, their screams and anguish. He stood, a solitary figure, a light wind whispering in his ears. He desperately wanted to write. 'Just one or two days to wander Paris,' he murmured. 'Words, words, please find me!' But as his pencil touched on his notebook the air was so cold he could scarce keep it fixed in his fingers and the lead broke off in an instant. 'Damn it!' he muttered, reaching in his pocket for his penknife. He sliced fast into the wood, tiny wooden shavings fluttering about him like butterflies, the only movement in an otherwise still landscape. But he could feel the nervous energy of presences about him, entities without sound or substance. He drew a breath and started again, his pencil poised on the page. He wanted to write from his heart. But would his heart be faithful? Would it provide what he searched for – not just poetry for the educated classes, but a poetry for all, for did not poetry also need a revolution? He thought of the people he had spent his time with as a child, the vagrants on the hills who had shared their vivid stories and sang to him their memorable songs. He thought of the rustics, dignified in their plainness, inviting him to sit by their hearths with their families where they spoke a poetry passed through the generations, words that trembled with feeling, words throbbing with life. How could he show how Nature connected with man right from its roots? Rustics lived and breathed it, and through it had their being. It took much heart to see how the human soul could be a part of Nature. If people didn't see it, were they not in danger of simply becoming mechanical, cogs in a wheel of life they did not belong to, a life that might even destroy them?

He was shaking slightly. Moments like this he feared, when his body pulsed with feeling and his mind flooded with ideas. Did he have the strength to realise the guiding principle his heart commanded, or was he just pandering to his vanities? 'Oh, vanity of vanities, all is vanity!' he murmured. This was something he had often thought about at Cambridge; when he might write all night, then commit his work to the waste bin, only to search for it later and straighten it out frantically to see what he'd composed. His poetry was like a tenacious clay that grounded him wherever he went. Some days its persistence seemed pitiable and tired him, other days he felt magnificent. He felt he might have ideas that were new and different, thoughts that might grow into something important and healing. He scribbled some notes in his pad then decided to make his way back.

As he neared his hotel, he met with a group of sans-culottes huddled together on a corner, peasants and urban labourers, who took this name because they did not wear the knee breeches worn by the privileged and instead wore trousers. He saw they were watching and whispering and his heartbeat quickened as he reached them. They must have been curious as to why he was wandering Paris, alone, and obviously English.

'Who are you?' shouted an angry looking fellow. 'Citizen – come over here!'

William's mind turned between thoughts of addressing them and trying to keep safe. Deciding on the latter, he called back cheerily in the best French he could muster. 'I have to be somewhere in haste!'

A pretty girl shouted, 'You are an Englishman here in Paris? Do you serve King Louis?' One of the men took hold of her arm and pulled her round the corner. The others narrowed their eyes, watching William as he went. He walked on faster, the icy snow crackling beneath his feet. Then he turned quickly and saw with relief they had gone.

His brief time in Paris had been hard to endure; he had seen and heard so much. He had seen the Champs de Mars. He had felt the pain of that day. He had walked the streets of the poor, strewn with rubbish and offal and running with rats. He had seen the miserable homes of the poor, places where ragged women offered their bodies for a morsel of food, their shivering children hanging on to their skirts, while the rich hastened past in coaches away from the suffering.

He left Paris in darkness, the sound of the chaise travelling at speed and the occasional cry of a creature of the night entering his dreams. They moved on fast to Orléans. His imagination was busy, though he had yet to make sense of his impressions. He felt oddly separate from himself, mining his memories. He had to believe that justice actually existed, that the word wasn't merely a plaything. Words had responsibilities, and must not cheat or pretend. But was *justice* really possible? Wasn't there a natural preference amongst people for greed and wealth? Did they not strive for it, admire it, desire it? Greed had caused fraud and selfishness. And didn't parliaments have special interest like all systems of power? There were despots everywhere. He felt down in his pocket. Now where was that stone he had stooped for by the Bastille? He brought it out and turned it over in his fingers surprised by its solidness and weight. 'What a lonely little thing it is,' he murmured, 'but how quickly one earths with stone.' It was quite instantaneous. They were now on the edge of Orléans.

4

Annette Vallon

As the chaise passed through the forests, the sweet air of Orléans met him through the open window. The smell was more like the smell of an English autumn than a French winter. Images of floating thistledown entered his mind, colours of Lakeland trees in autumn, the splendid English trees in so many shapes and sizes. Here in the forests of Orléans the pines, like sentinels, were tall and straight, guarding the grand castles and châteaux about them.

He was glad to be on the move again, finding his way about Paris had been quite distressing. The stench of the place from waste and sewage had sickened him. And the sight of so many ghostly people wandering the streets in the snow, the shine in their eyes replaced by a dull white glare, was hard to bear. The River Seine, overflowing with debris, was a sad, diseased river and he'd decided to keep clear of its banks. He remembered the Derwent back home, where you could see the eyes of the fish, busy in the crystal water and where he and Dorothy as children had often bent over to look.

He sat thoughtful, his hands clasped in his lap. The soles of his boots, clogged with snow, were thawing into puddles on the floor. Just as his feet ached from walking his mind throbbed from thinking. He had come to France and had dared to walk amongst its people in such dangerous times. He had dared to draw close to them and had heard their anger and frustrations, hurrying back to his lodgings each day to write down his feelings and impressions. He had pondered over them intensely, hearing their music, turning them into stories, stories throbbing with pathos, metres and revelations. And he had thought a lot about home. What was happening to Dorothy? Was she content? Was John happy at sea?

All about him now as he gazed from the chaise was beautiful and astonishing. He knew he would enjoy Orléans. The fact that French royalty had resided there in the past did not surprise him; the contours and lie of the land were picturesque and graceful. He imagined the forests in springtime, clothed in a variety of greens, the trees lolling on warm summer days with an undergrowth of dazzling broom and gorse and wild colourful flowers. He imagined sitting by a table, enjoying a good French wine. The wine areas in the Loire valley extended for mile upon mile. To make a delectable wine, a French student at Cambridge had told him once, a grower had to stay within precisely observed guidelines. Even those who had the perfect soil must use a particular vine and a special way of pruning, and the wine must be kept in its barrel for the correct length of time before sale. He mused on one or two quotes. – "Beer is made by men," Martin Luther had proclaimed, "and wine by God," and "He who loves not wine, women and song, remains a fool his whole life long." For a moment the words cheered him. It was better to think of people being merry than wretched and dying.

The chaise darkened as they entered a shaded area. Then a blaze of sunlight flooded him and warmed his face. But there was so much tension within him! Could it be fear? Fear was a useless emotion. When a man was afraid, he learned nothing. He could hear the peal of church bells somewhere in the distance. Not knowing where he was, he could not predict how long it would take for the chaise to find his next hotel, but they had to be near to it now.

After another fifteen minutes the chaise pulled up by the door.

'Monsieur Wordsworth from England?' said a bald headed man at a desk. He gazed at William warily. The sun, as it came through the window, fell upon William's papers. The man looked down at them and frowned.

'I am he,' said William, attempting a casual demeanour. Apart from the sound of the proprietor shuffling his papers and the chaise moving away, all was silent in the foyer.

'If you want food and drink, I can have it sent up,' the man said coldly.

'Thank you,' said William. 'Yes, I would like refreshments.' The man lifted his head, his manner still cautious. Being English and a stranger, William concluded he was bound to arouse curiosity and resolved to think little about it.

The proprietor nodded at a heavyset youth, standing nearby. 'Arrange for some food to be sent upstairs for this man!' he called brusquely. The youth ambled across, picked up the guest's bag from the floor, flung it across his shoulder then pointed to the stairs.

William was taken to a small but comfortable room. He stood, his bag at his feet the boy waiting before him. On receiving some coins, the young man bolted downstairs. William felt deeply uncomfortable, like a criminal thrown into a cell. It was obvious he wasn't welcome. The proprietor didn't like him and it certainly showed. Did he suspect him of spying? He probably did. The English government would certainly have spies in France. What if a touch of something disagreeable were put in his food and drink? – Ah, it was nonsense.

The room itself was cheerful, with red damask curtains at the windows and a clean, cosy bed in the corner. The window looked out on the River Loire and woodland. Gazing down at his feet, he saw that his socks were soaked through and he bent to his bag to find another pair. Just as he drew them out a knock came to the door and a pretty young girl brought in a tray of tea and a small slice of bread, and more importantly, a smile. With her dark brown hair and her shining eyes, he decided she looked like Mary. He watched as she put down the tray. She smiled again and went out.

There was nothing quite like the smile of a pretty young woman, he thought, as he poured out his tea. It was certainly heartening. He bit into the bread, reflecting on Elizabeth's words and some of the savage conversations he'd heard in the streets of Paris. He had heard fierce talk about Prussian and Austrian armies coming to aid the king and his wife. Further death and destruction. He sat for another ten minutes, eating, drinking and thinking. Then he turned his eyes towards the bed. With a loud sigh he made his way across and fell on it heavily, within seconds he was sound asleep.

But he didn't sleep long. From outside the door of his room, came the sound of heavy footsteps pacing the floor. It did not sound like the youth. It had to be the proprietor! Determined to look, he braced himself and got up, but on opening the door, not a soul could be seen. Next, he went to the dresser, poured some water in a bowl and splashed it about his face. Then he gazed at himself in the mirror. His eyes were bright and alert and his skin looked healthy, but he certainly needed a shave. He found his tackle and shaved the bristle from his chin. Then he straightened his cravat and ran a comb through his hair. He was a good-looking fellow for certain, just like Dorothy had said. Perhaps he would visit Pierre's château that day? Opening his map on the bed, he was delighted to find the place wasn't too far away. After he'd sorted out his things he would walk there.

'It's a long way, Monsieur,' said the proprietor, as William went to the desk. 'I can get you a chaise.'

His manner was argumentative, William thought, but most of all it was annoying. Why was he being so churlish? 'The distance is nothing,' he told him, straightening. 'I like a good walk. – I have walked the Swiss Alps my man. Oh, such wonderful mountains!'

The proprietor scribbled on, his head bent to his work. William leant over, and murmured something he'd been trying to compose that week:

> '. . . And, headlong from the cliffs, a deafening load
> Tumbles, and wildering thunder slips abroad;
> When on the summits darkness comes and goes,
> Hiding their fiery clouds, their rocks and snows;
> And the fierce torrent, from the lustre broad,
> Starts, like a horse . . .'

'What is it "hides" Monsieur?' asked the proprietor, raising his head quickly.

William frowned and waved away his words. 'Darkness hides the clouds! It is a poem! A poem! The weather is clear and promising. I intend to make the journey on foot. – Adieu!' He laid his key firmly on the desk and went out. There was a whole afternoon to look forward to. It would be good to talk with Elizabeth again and meet Pierre and his friends.

Up and down the hills he went, the paths twisting and turning, all the while thinking about his family. Would Dorothy get the letter he'd sent that week? He hoped so, though he had no fixed address for her to reply to. He doubted he'd stay in that dreadful hotel much longer. Finding another place though would be far from easy and his uncle was paying the bill . . .

His thoughts turned to John. Was it possible he might have a sweetheart? He'd been quite dejected last time they'd met, which was strange. And no-one seemed to know where his ship was. But that was the way with John; he just disappeared. As a matter of fact, he and his brother were very much alike. They both liked escaping. And where better to escape than the sea. But at least John had ambitions, as their uncles kept saying. He aspired to be a ship's commander. Now that was what you called a *"career"*! But what did "career" mean? And in any case a life on the ocean waves could be fraught with problems. He thought of Horatio Nelson, a highly renowned sailor who had found a wife on her family's sugar plantation while sailing the Caribbean Sea. Frances Nisbit was widowed with a young son. Once they'd got married, she'd followed Nelson to England with the child. But how could a man give the necessary time and attention to a wife and family while always away?

He walked for another half hour then found himself standing by high steel gates, opening onto a long winding path leading to a splendid château, its windows flashing with sunlight. So this was Pierre's home! For a minute or two he gazed at the house, wondering what he would say to Elizabeth and what she might say in return. He straightened his clothes and adjusted his hat. He had landed in strange new territory. But strangeness always aroused him. New smells, new sounds and new ways of thinking excited him. Enjoying the scent of the air, he stood watching the sun, glistening and bouncing on the great stone walls of the building and dancing in the grounds about it. It had obviously been built in the Golden Age of France after the wars between Catholics and Protestants. The last two centuries, William reflected, had seen the Catholic Church gain ascendancy; there were convents and seminaries everywhere. But constant political instability had brought about decline in the agrarian and textile industries that had once flourished. And greater changes were afoot. In the Loire Valley, armies were waiting to fight, for it was almost certain the queen's Austrian relatives would soon invade to support her, and Orléans was central to the ferment. – He turned on hearing a sound. Someone was walking up the hill. A woman in a scarlet riding habit suddenly came into view.

One hand lifting her red velvet skirt but an inch from the snow, the other holding her whip, she gazed at him curiously and he looked back in silence. She was very lovely. Was she visiting Pierre's château? She leant her whip against the wall, then they bent together for a brooch that had fallen off her jacket. His fingers closed on it first and he smiled as he handed it back. Meeting her eyes, he saw that her features were pale and her gaze held a sadness that disturbed him. She returned his smile, then ran her finger across the shimmering pearl flower that rested in her gloved hand.

'What a splendid brooch,' he said, mainly for something to say.

'Thank you', she returned. 'You are English, Monsieur?' She lifted her head and waited.

'Mademoiselle, I am. Good afternoon!' said William, bowing lightly. 'Yes, it is true.' He stepped back, embarrassed. He'd been struggling to keep up with his laundry, his boots were dirty and needed polishing, and his shabby brown frock coat was hardly the attire of a country gentleman from England. He was though, wearing a coloured patchwork waistcoat he liked. Dorothy had made it and sent it to Cambridge last year. 'I would offer to fix the brooch back on your clothes, though I fear I might cause you an injury, the pin is so sharp.' He laughed, though a little self-consciously.

He stood quietly for a moment, watching her steady fingers work at the clasp. His eyes wandered to her lips, open with concentration. The urge to touch her soft brown hair overwhelmed him. The perfume she wore had a strong scent of roses. Roses – roses in winter! She placed the brooch in her pocket, then struck her whip on the wall. 'The leather is far too hard,' she frowned. 'I must tell Pierre. It has marked my horse. It is as hard as the heart of France!'

'And your brooch?' he asked. He glanced at her pocket.

'The clasp is faulty,' she sighed. 'It always falls off.'

'I have come to see Elizabeth Montrose,' he said. 'I believe she is living with her nephew Pierre at this château. Are you acquainted?'

She smiled and looked him over. 'Ah, you are William Wordsworth from England. We are expecting you, William Wordsworth.' She put out her hand. 'And I am Annette Vallon. I am here on holiday with Paul my brother. Elizabeth looks forward to your visit. – Come, let us walk to the château. I have been riding, but I like to return by way of the front in winter. The way by the stables can be wet and unsafe this time of year. You will enjoy your visit, no?'

'I hope so,' he faltered. 'But I am here a little too soon . . .' His tone was anxious.

She glanced at him sideways. 'Oh – why do you say so?'

'I have only just arrived in Orléans, and you see me already.'

She stopped and faced him. 'I am glad,' she said, suddenly solemn.

'I am rather too hasty at times,' he said, embarrassed.

'We can never be too hasty with Time,' she answered sadly. 'It leaves us behind so quickly.' She gazed at the château before them.

'You are right,' he said. *'"Make use of time, let not advantage slip."'*

She met his eyes and smiled. *'"The tender spring upon thy tempting lip, shows thee unripe, yet mayest though well be tasted . . ."'* She laughed into the sky, 'Your own William Shakespeare.' Again they were silent, walking the path to the château. 'Nothing is as it was in the days of our childhood,' she said unhappily. 'Everything has changed. Pierre has changed. I have changed. France is different now. Pierre never smiles. But his parents were drowned with his sister Clarisse a long time ago; he does not recover. He weeps inwardly, so much so that the tears have entered his bones. And now he weeps for our country. But he has found new ways of being. They are not always good. He is wealthy, but he is foolish. He gives away money to the poor, but they only abuse him. It is purgatory to hear how he talks. And they laugh at him behind his back. They cheat him and make up stories about lame, starving relatives.'

He saw that she flushed as she spoke. 'Perhaps he has a keen conscience,' William said, shrugging. 'The revolution has made people reassess their lives. It has caused them to think.'

'What? – Why, Pierre's *thinking* is absurd? He takes beggars into his house and gives them food and money. Within days they have told their friends and families and they are hanging around in wait by the gates. It is a fearful business.' She spoke in a melancholy tone. 'The poor can be just as ruthless as the rich.'

'Yes,' he said quietly, though her words frustrated him. 'But Mademoiselle, the poor of France have nothing. – No food, no laughter, no joy, no music, nothing. The flies are on them already.'

Her dark, thoughtful eyes surveyed him steadily. They had reached the door of the château. She put her hand on the large iron knocker and rapped it twice. Then he heard a sigh of desperation. And he wondered strangely if he might hear that sigh forever.

5

Mysteries

He couldn't remember walking down the path with her, but presumed he had done so. Her gentle oval face and soft full mouth seemed contradicted by the power in her voice and person. She gazed down intensely at the marble step at their feet as if some deep thought held her, something she couldn't get away from. Then the door opened before them.

'Mr Wordsworth!' Elizabeth smiled, with obvious surprise and pleasure. 'How glad I am that you found us. And I see you have met Annette. – Come in! Come in!' She held out her hands in welcome.

William returned her greeting, then entered the marble floored hall, watching Annette as she stood removing her gloves, her eyes still thoughtful. He felt unusually at one with her, as if he knew her already, as if he had always known her. 'I'm glad to see you are safe and sound, Elizabeth,' he said. 'The way they ushered you away, I feared you might have been kidnapped.'

'Indeed,' she laughed. 'I was well taken care of, however, and managed to get some excellent sleep.' She turned to look at Annette, who sat in a chair by the door, taking off her boots. 'The weather was worrying towards the end of the journey, wasn't it?' She wrung her hands, and for a moment looked anxious. 'Such is the way of the sea.'

A maid arrived and picked up Annette's wet boots. Elizabeth bent to her and whispered something in her ear. William gazed about the hall. It was like entering a glittering cave. His mind flashed back to his childhood and a cavern he knew on the fells where the walls had sparkled as if covered in fine gemstones, and the loose rocks about his feet were like richly decorated gold and silver objects. But the large hall he stood in now was no imagination; this glittering house was reality, the same as the even greater opulence he'd seen on his travels through France where many a wealthy aristocrat still dared to ignore the poor. This château of Pierre's was but a glimpse of what the poor had sneered at, jeered at, and killed over.

'Mr Wordsworth, you are lost in thought,' laughed Elizabeth. 'You are quite right; I might well have been captured, all that jostling about, not to mention criminals pushing up against us. What an awful commotion. A strong fellow like you though, would have easily dealt with those roughnecks.' Annette was still in her coat, though she listened and smiled, and he saw that she cast her eyes across him gently.

'Ah,' he said, laughing, "'roughnecks?"' He glanced at his boots, which were far from clean, and his old worn breeches. He probably looked a bit of a roughneck himself. He gazed into Elizabeth's face, which looked quite different from when he'd first seen her in Brighton. Without her hat and long fur coat, she looked like somebody else, relaxed and vibrant, younger than he'd remembered. Her grey silk dress shimmered as she leant towards Annette, warning her that she should take off her wet clothing. Annette excused herself and ran up the marble staircase.

He told Elizabeth he'd only just arrived in Orléans but had been eager to see her again and meet Pierre and his friends. As he spoke he heard the angry voices of two young men in a room down the hall. Through the door he could hear the sound of passionate French. Elizabeth ran her hands down a beautiful ceramic vase on the sideboard beside her and sighed. Such objects, William reflected, were almost like living things, people wanted to touch them, the sun embraced them, and they were thrown from balconies by lovers in moments of pain.

'I must talk with those howling wolves down there,' Elizabeth frowned. 'Please excuse me.' Her silk dress rustled as she went down the hall.

Standing alone, he pondered on all he saw. For a moment or two his eyes focused on a large stone eagle set above the heavy oak door, poised as if ready to fly. It was a thing of sky and stars, of cliffs and ravines, of darkness and light. In an odd way it was kin. He glanced around him. The walls of the long hall, with doors to each side, held an abundance of gilded mirrors that would no doubt dazzle the marble floors in the mornings. Powerful paintings, along with elegant tapestries, glistening in coloured silks, adorned the walls. The reign of Louis XIV, "The Sun King", had been seen in France as the golden age of culture. Though the man had weakened the country with his foreign wars, and by the time of Louis XV a lot of fiscal reforms had been forcefully proposed. Many French citizens sympathized with their present sad monarch and argued that Louis XVI had inherited "terrible times".

'I am really sorry,' said Elizabeth, returning. 'Poor Mr Wordsworth, you are always getting abandoned. Thankfully though, from what you say, you don't mind being alone.'

'That's right,' said William, who'd spent the last ten minutes in intense thought and pleasure. He laughed, 'I am quite partial to aloneness.' He was never actually *lonely*. In his homeland he heard the whispering voices of trees, the exultations of waterfalls and streams; he knew the companionship of strong stoic rocks and their stilled grandeur, while the lakes and rivers he swam in flowed in his blood. Here in France he was experiencing a new kind of life, a watchful, unquiet existence in a country rife with unrest.

'To be content with your own company is good,' Elizabeth was saying, looking him up and down with a nod of approval. 'I only wish Pierre were the same? He must always have someone to talk to, or argue with, that is. When I lived with him here in France it was hard if I wanted to travel. He despaired when he was younger if I left.' She paused, thoughtful. 'He is better now, but he talked with the servants too openly; I never liked it. – How do you know what they're thinking? Not one of them lives here now, except Henriette, the old maid.' She looked again at the door of the room she had left. 'I do not know how long Paul and Annette can keep coming to the château. Over the years, they've been regular guests and Pierre has enjoyed their company. He has enjoyed his times at their home in Blois too. But not now . . .' She lowered her voice. 'It is finished. Hear how they argue. It was never like that before, they would go out riding, take picnics by the Loire, discuss the taste of the wine each year – oh, many merciful matters.' She shook her head sadly then took hold of his elbow. 'Come and sit down.'

The room they entered was warm and comfortable. A strong fire burned in the grate and an array of luxuriant coloured velvets fell softly over a large chaise longue and a few easy chairs. She went to the window and looked towards the stables as if a visitor were expected any minute. The windows of the room were mainly to the west, she said, where the light grew weary at this time of day and felt mournful. She rubbed her arms and shivered then she turned and directed him to a seat by the fire, taking a chair opposite.

The most interesting feature of the room, he thought, was an enormous painting hanging on the wall beside him depicting a man in a loincloth lying in chains on a beach with a naked girl beside him. Her long dark hair was hardly distinguishable from the seaweed wrapped about her head. Both appeared dead. He frowned and drew away his eyes. He thought the painting looked incongruous in the sitting room, and felt as if it were somehow connected to him, as if it held a personal message.

Elizabeth gazed at him kindly, straightening the folds of her grey silk dress as she sat by the fire. He thought she looked elegant in her cream coloured slippers and pearls, her greying curls neatly arranged about her face. 'I am rather averse to my lodgings,' he told her, though a little abruptly. 'I think the proprietor distrusts me.'

'How do you know?' she asked, looking concerned.

'It's just a feeling.'

Elizabeth shrugged. 'Well, he probably would, my dear. I too am feeling uncomfortable in France this visit. It is hardly a place to relax in. I shall have to leave though shortly, a friend in Rome wants to see me. I shall return to England after that, but I . . .' She broke off then and shook her head worriedly. 'The revolution is moving so fast, and I have to admit I am frightened for Pierre – and for Paul and Annette too. It is dangerous for royalists to consort with someone like Pierre. The committees think he is plotting. They are always in fear of plots that might thwart the revolution.' She spoke intensely. 'Pierre's attitudes are known. Paul is a lawyer and understands the dangers, but Annette insists on accompanying him here. Paul is sensible, I know, though Annette can be stubborn. – Ah, she is just like Pierre. I fear so much for Pierre.'

'He is a grown man,' said William. 'He will not thank you for your fear. My own family fear for me, but I wish they wouldn't. It is quite a burden.' He stretched out his fingers and contemplated his hands. His fingers were long and strong, his hands heavy, his veins big and snake like. The skin on his palms had softened, as he'd grown older. It had once been full of calluses from climbing trees and heaving stones to dam up the streams on the hills so he could watch them swell then spill ecstatically into freedom.

'You are right, Mr Wordsworth,' she sighed.

Again they were silent. The sound of the argument in the room down the hall came to them strongly through the doorway.

'How awful,' said Elizabeth. 'I would like to have introduced you, but I doubt it would be wise today, for obvious reasons. A woman of my age can have little effect on the minds of men so disposed.'

'Disposed to murder,' said Annette entering the room and sitting down. The yellow silk of her dress, he thought, was moonlike and shimmering. She adjusted the sleeves at her elbow then fastened up a strand of hair that had fallen on her cheek. 'My brother and Pierre are fierce fighters,' she said. Her features tightened with feeling. 'Oh, that they were on the same side!' She glanced at the window towards the sound of a horse rider galloping off from the stables, then she threw out her hands hopelessly. 'Feudalism is abolished. The aristocracy have lost their rights and privileges. – Church lands have been seized. – The National Assembly has voted the Declaration of the Rights of Man and the Citizen, now everyone in France will be equal . . . What more can the revolutionaries ask for?'

'Pierre is angrier than ever today,' said Elizabeth, sighing.

'So who has made him angry?' asked Annette, gazing at the fire. She glanced at William and smiled.

'Oh, small minded officials.' Elizabeth spoke wearily. 'The bourgeoisie have vested interests in manipulating the peasants of course.' She looked at William. 'He will tell you all about that.' She spoke with an air of certainty. 'He will tell you everything.'

Annette spoke gravely. 'That would be impossible, dear Elizabeth. "Everything", is far too complex. A lot of the nobles wish to overthrow the monarchy and the peasants want to bring down the nobles – oh, and a lot of the bourgeoisie too who threaten them. In the end they will all lie in blood.'

Seated beneath a lit candelabrum, the pale yellow silk of her dress shimmered and the light of the candles danced on her soft brown hair. But he saw that her eyes were worried. What did it take, William wondered to still her fears for a while – a gentle stroke of her hair perhaps, his lips brushing her cheek?

Elizabeth braced herself and tried to sound more cheerful. 'We have William Wordsworth from England here with us today, and we must make him welcome!' she laughed. She leant back in the chair and gazed at him warmly. 'I told you how handsome he was. Do you not think so, Annette? Look at that grand Roman nose. He is a fine figure of a man. Do you not agree?'

William moved about awkwardly. 'I fear I am looking rather shabby,' he said. 'I have so little money to make myself look decent. I . . .'

'Well,' said Elizabeth, a playful look in her eyes. 'Your breeches hang very well, my dear, however long you have had them.'

Annette bent her head. 'Oh dear,' she murmured. 'Elizabeth is far too direct.'

'Not at all,' laughed William. 'I am in total agreement. I am a fine figure of a man, and I do have a rather grand nose.' He tapped it with a finger, ready to burst into laughter.

Annette laughed first, though without looking up, and Elizabeth after. It eased the tension a while. They talked about the snow. Elizabeth said how she liked the snow, and that she felt it covered much of the sadness of life, and wondered if it came for that very purpose at the close of the year. 'I am hoping you will join us for supper,' she said, looking at William directly. 'Not today, but tomorrow?' She waited. William sat gazing at the fire. Elizabeth took up a poker from the hearth and riddled the logs into flame. 'Paul and Pierre will be easier to talk with tomorrow. Though Paul may be silent. He is always cautious with strangers. But Pierre . . . Oh my poor ungovernable nephew! There is always some so and so somewhere who won't see sense. It is one thing arguing with Paul here at the château, but it is quite another to argue with people outside where his words can be misinterpreted. She rang a bell and requested sandwiches and tea. 'There is nothing I want more than that the people of France find liberty. But at what price do they gain it? – Son turning against father, father turning against son, sister turning against brother . . .' Just then the wheels of a coach were heard in the courtyard. Elizabeth went to the window then turned to Annette.

'What – right now?' Annette asked anxiously.

Elizabeth nodded. 'Please excuse us,' she said tensely. 'There is something Annette must attend to.' She rang for the maid and instructed her to bring Annette some boots and a coat.

'Yes, I must go,' said Annette, looking at William and smiling softly. 'I'm sorry.'

He held her gaze for a moment then she went out into the hall with Elizabeth. He rested his elbow on the arm of the chair, his chin on his hand. He felt as if a limb had been torn from him, a limb he didn't know he had. Where was she going? When would she return? He could hear her putting on her boots, making anguished little cries with Elizabeth. Within minutes, he heard her running down the path to the stables. Then he heard the coach move away. The loud voices of Paul and Pierre had silenced.

Elizabeth returned to the room and sat down. 'Annette's sister is ill,' she said, 'Annette has gone to talk with their brothers Charles and Jean. They are both doctors.' She shook her head concernedly. 'Françoise has a highly excitable temperament. She drives herself into delirium.'

The maid brought food and drink. Elizabeth poured out the tea. She passed William a thin china plate and offered him a sandwich. 'I have requested that Annette tell the coachman to return for you here, once he has dropped her at home.' She gazed at the painting on the wall. The naked girl, covered in seaweed was now in the mournful light. 'What a dreadful first visit you have had,' she said sadly. 'You will eat very well tomorrow, I promise. And I shall ensure that Paul and Pierre have far better manners.'

'Oh, do not worry about manners,' he said, drinking from a small china teacup. 'I do not care about manners. Good, sincere argument is my thing.'

'And I do believe you will get it,' said Elizabeth.

6

The Second Visit

He scrutinized his eyes in the mirror. They were sometimes shot with blood when he'd stayed up reading by
a candle. To his pleasure, today they were clear. And he was
hopeful, yes, he was very hopeful indeed. His meeting with
Mademoiselle Vallon had ignited his passion. The mellow
tones of her voice still rang in his ears and her smile still lived
in his mind as he glanced outside on the pleasant winter's day.
He couldn't recall his reading last night; only that she wasn't
in it. As he brushed down his coat and prepared for his second
visit, he wondered what she was doing that very moment. He
had put on a crisp clean shirt and a fresh loose linen cravat
edged with lace by Dorothy and put away for best. Today was
certainly *best*. He fell to thinking about Annette's older sister.
There was so much distress over Françoise. What could have
happened? The woman had a son, but no-one had spoken of
his father.

He opened the window and looked out. The roof had been
noisy all night and the clatter hadn't been rain. He strained his
neck and looked above. A number of pigeons quietly rested
on the guttering. Not in the least perturbed, they stayed right
where they were, their wings folded, their feathers still and

unruffled. 'Impertinent creatures', he murmured, pulling down the window with a thump.

The hotel was silent, though it was now mid morning. The place was sinister he thought, a most unpleasant abode. He intended to take a walk by the river before making his way to the château. 'Those pigeons will drive me insane,' he murmured as he pulled on his frockcoat, 'let alone that infernal proprietor sneaking about by the door.' Did the pigeons belong to him, he wondered, or were they wild from the woods? He knew that people often used pigeons as carriers. He imagined them flying hither and thither with messages all about *him*. That proprietor was certainly shifty. Did he enter his room while he was out? After all, he did have a key. But he had nothing to interest a nosey fellow like him, unless he liked reading books that was, and anyway they were all in English.

Tying the laces of his boots, he determined to find another place to live as soon as he could and wondered where he might look. For a couple of minutes he strode about the room thoughtful. What sort of talk would he share with Paul and Pierre, one of them a royalist and the other a republican? It wouldn't be easy, for they were both spirited men. Questions flooded his mind, but he would not voice them and determined to stay restrained. There was a certain safety in silence, but he wasn't a man to be silent, just like those pigeons in the night, he was excitable and needed expression. It was impossible to make an honest acquaintance if you did not speak your mind. Here in France though, speaking your mind could be dangerous.

He thought about Pierre and his life at the château and the vineyard. As a businessman, he would need to perform the normal seasonal tasks of a French viticulturist. He would employ many people. Did those people still work for him now, William wondered, or had everything changed. He took out his pen and ink, thinking he might manage a few lines of poetry, but they were not ready and would not come to his aid. He reached instead for A *Voyage Round The World by Way of the Great South Sea,* a gift from John which he'd been trying to read last night, an interesting tale where a sailor shoots an albatross perched on his ship thinking it an evil omen. He read from where he'd left off . . .

"We all observed, that we had not the sight of one fish of any kind, since we were come to the Southward of the streights of le Mair, nor one sea-bird, except a disconsolate black Albatross, who accompanied us for several days . . ., till Hattley, (my second Captain) observing, in one of his melancholy fits, that this bird was always hovering near us, imagin'd, from his colour, that it might be some ill omen . . ."

He spent a good half hour reading then rang for the maid. He asked her to bring him bread and cheese for lunch before he went out. As she left, he wondered if she might be the proprietor's daughter for her eyes and hair was similar. It was strange, he reflected, how the most unpleasant of fellows often had the prettiest daughters. After he'd eaten, he donned his hat and went out.

The river walkway was empty. He took out his pocket watch and glanced at the time. Was it only a quarter to one? Time was moving like a snail! He gazed at the pale blue sky; there was hardly a bird in sight that day and the walkway was silent. Then he looked ahead at the twists and turns of the paths, the sleepy trees, their spectral branches dark and shocked as if stilled by a winter spell. The river licked leisurely at the bank, yet for all the seeming peace of the day, he did not feel peaceful inside. He might be a million scattered stars! The sound of her voice haunted his inner ear, his eyes bent to the same French soil she walked on. He felt as if all words of poetry had left him. Today it was she who inhabited him body and soul. She was all his feeling, all his verse, all his life and breath.

He strode down the path to the château like a man with intent. What that intent would deliver, only Time would tell. It was getting quite dusky and the windows of the château glimmered with the light of candles. The tips of the trees and bushes flanking the approach glistened with evening dew and seemed to be beckoning him on. Would she be there tonight, he wondered, she who had given his heart such a plentiful gift!

A maid answered the door. Slightly disconcerted not to see Elizabeth or Annette, he stood for some minutes waiting in the candlelit hall. Finally, Elizabeth approached, followed by a tall young man, upright, stiff and aloof, who Elizabeth introduced as Pierre. A quick light bow, a critical look and a cold formal hand-shake were hardly what he'd hoped for from Elizabeth's nephew, but it seemed this was his way. Pierre was a strong looking fellow, dressed in striped green trousers, and just as William expected, his long dark hair fell free down his shoulders, resting on his black silk waistcoat, a brightly decorated garment, flashing with tiny coloured beads. 'My aunt tells me you have come to France as a visitor, Monsieur Wordsworth. So what do you visit us about?'

'I am not quite sure,' William said, as if he were talking in a dream. He looked at the door to the parlour, half open. Voices came to him softly.

'He has come to see what is happening in France,' said Elizabeth, 'and how the French are faring.' She looked at Pierre and frowned. 'My dear nephew, William is here as a friend. Please be more courteous.'

'You are a poet?' said Pierre, in a tone of amusement. 'You might write a few weary prayers, dear poet, for the poor and starving, but poetry, I ask you? What is the use of poetry? It is not poetry our country needs it is liberty!' He leant towards William, his voice almost a whisper. 'The people of France need honesty, Monsieur. If you are keen to stay breathing then I give you a warning, do not write poetry.'

Elizabeth sighed and braced herself. 'Let us go and sit down,' she said, directing them towards the parlour.

William looked at Pierre, to see if he followed, but he stayed in the hall absorbed in thought. 'Good evening, Mademoiselle,' William said smiling, as he entered. 'I am delighted to see you again.' Annette sat on the chaise longue reading. She smiled and embraced him with her eyes. It stirred him to see her waiting. She had decorated her hair with tiny pearl slides and had gathered it into a delicate cluster in the nape of her neck. It suited her well. He liked the curve of her neck and the way her shoulders lifted and fell with her emotions. There was an utter radiance about her that captured him body and soul. Elizabeth bade him sit down.

'I am really happy you came,' Annette said softly. Paul Vallon, of medium build and height, and with a quiet ponderous demeanour, stood by the fire. Pale featured, he looked like someone who had spent a lot of his time reading books. But his manner was kind and William felt at ease as they talked.

Paul suggested they took a ride in the country together. 'Pierre has a variety of horses,' he said. 'What sort of steed do you like?'

'Oh, a hot-blood, if possible,' laughed William, 'a spirited stallion that still remembers the wild.'

'I see,' said Paul, narrowing his eyes and looking at William more closely. 'I mainly travel by carriage myself, though I do like to ride when I can. My sister, you know, is a very fine rider.' He turned to Annette. 'N'est-ce pas vrai?'

'As a matter of fact, I am missing my riding,' said William quickly, looking at Annette. He saw that his cue had been received.

'It sounds delightful,' said Elizabeth, 'I have never been on a horse, though I have suffered much on account of it.' She sighed. 'All my friends ride horses, but horses frighten me a little. I ought to add though that horses can be very dangerous. Paul broke a leg when he was younger.'

'I was thirteen years old and reckless,' said Paul, in a scarcely audible voice, eyeing Elizabeth with the eyes of a child whose mother was disclosing too much.

'You are an excellent rider, Paul,' said Elizabeth, leaning and patting his arm. She turned her attention to Annette. 'I wonder what has happened to Pierre? He said he would join us.' She shook her head slowly. 'But he is perfectly capable of organising dinner and vanishing.'

As he talked with Paul, the tension in William lessened. He had a feeling Pierre disliked him and a sudden fear passed through him. Was he Annette's lover? Just then he walked into the room and lowered himself into a comfortable armchair beside her. William saw that she did not acknowledge him, and instead talked on with Elizabeth. It was easy to see there was intimacy between Pierre and Annette, probably born from companionship over the years, or so he hoped. But he did not like it and was jealous. Annette was in soft blue silk, a shimmering pendant at her throat. He saw on her dress the same pearl brooch that had fallen off her habit by the gates.

A servant entered the room. 'There are problems at the coast, Monsieur,' the man said worriedly. 'We could not get the fish you requested. The chef has prepared something else. – And the sugar sculpture you wanted has not arrived from the confectioners . . .' The servant waited, standing very straight, his manner polite and deferential. Pierre nodded, murmured something to Elizabeth, then with a nod sent him off.

William's eyes lingered on Pierre. He had furrows in his brow and an anxious look that belonged to a much older man. His hands were not the hands of a gentleman, but more the hands of a labourer. His knuckles were hardened and his muscular frame disposed to working in the fields.

'Ah, Danton! Danton!' Pierre cried suddenly, clapping his hand to his brow. 'He speaks the truth, oh he is *so*, daring. But he puts his life in danger. The revolution has allowed many of the rich to grow even richer. It is bad.' He waved a finger in the air. 'Rousseau is right; we cannot become good citizens if we are constantly striving to satisfy our own selfish needs. It is selfishness that causes the pain.'

'But you are generous with the poor,' Elizabeth interjected, frowning. 'You are known for your generosity. Why must you talk so?'

'Bah, nothing I do is right,' said Pierre, covering his face with his hands.

Paul sighed wearily. 'A system of politics is like mathematics. Once you have created the rules, there is little room left for genuine human interaction. It is a problem. Rousseau's ideas are good and just, but Just is an abstract concept. How can it enter the world of reality? – How?'

'How indeed?' said Pierre. 'Do you have an answer Mr Wordsworth?' Pierre's eyes rested on William. 'You are a son of Rousseau, are you not?'

'Am I?' said William, slightly bewildered. They all sat waiting.

'So my Aunt has informed me,' said Pierre. He glanced at Elizabeth as he spoke. 'You follow Rousseau's ideas, Mr Wordsworth, do you not?'

'I agree with much of what he says,' said William cautiously. 'Though I also have questions.' He braced himself and drew a breath.

Pierre continued to listen.

'The imagination,' William continued, because they were waiting for his words. 'The *true* imagination I believe is a part of reality, just as the romantic and rational minds belong to each other. To tear them apart is only to destroy the coin, and we are left with nothing of worth.'

'And Mr Burke,' said Pierre, holding William with sharp, questioning eyes. 'He does not like our revolution.'

'Have you read Burke's writings?' asked William, looking at him straight.

'I have them in my library,' said Pierre. He uncrossed his legs and threw back his great shoulders. 'I am quick to acquire such reading.'

'He does not give a clear enough view of his politics,' said Annette dismissively.

'I doubt he can,' said William. 'Liberty is certainly a right, of course, and Burke is all for that. But liberty with order . . .' He gazed at the red carpet. 'How is order to be instilled into liberty?' He spoke as if to himself. 'Is freedom of thought to be bound? If so, then where is its freedom? Burke argues that life's practicalities are of more importance than metaphysical ideologies. It is a fiercely debatable point.'

'Your Edmund Burke thinks he can split the coin,' said Pierre.

'These Committees are a problem,' said Annette sighing loudly. 'The men are at one another's throats. And they hate the queen.'

'Everyone dislikes the queen,' said Pierre. 'She builds herself a village to play at being a peasant in and she doesn't expect to be despised? She is also known to while away her time in the sweet smelling groves of Madame de Pompadour's gardens.' He laughed quietly. 'No doubt with lovers.'

'The king's authority is like the web of a spider in a high wind,' sighed Paul.

'He has tried very hard,' said Annette, defensively. 'He suggested changes in taxation, but there was so much whispering and threatening. He is forever blamed for our bankruptcy. Oh, how I hate liars!'

William spoke quietly from the depths of his thoughts. 'Imagination is a wonderful thing, but it is also a powerful weapon. Repeated enough times, lies can be seen as truths.'

'Even by the liar,' Paul said flatly. 'Truth and fiction can merge as one and laugh at us.'

Elizabeth braced herself. 'Well,' she said smiling, 'you will eat splendidly tonight, William, as promised. One of the things Pierre finds hard to relinquish is his food table. As a member of the vineyard elite, my brother was quite a connoisseur when it came to food and wine. Pierre has continued the tradition. His fish and game surpass all others in the area, as do his stews and sauces. Pierre can boast the finest *Lapin* à la *moutarde* in the whole of France.' She glanced at Annette and nodded. 'Monsieur Rousseau once dined here. He was an avid conversationalist and caused others to reflect. Oh a real provocateur!'

Annette shrugged. 'I despise what he says about women: *"The whole education of women ought to be relative to men. To please them, to be useful to them, to make themselves loved and honoured by them . . ."'* She blew out irritably. 'And we women should be taught such absurdities in our infancy.'

Pierre turned again to William. 'I do not understand . . .' he said quietly. 'You have come to France to write poetry? But why do you . . .' He might have continued, but there came the sound of a rider galloping away from the stables. He went to the window to look. 'Who can it be?' he murmured.

'Do you trust your groom?' asked Elizabeth, her voice steady and calm.

'But of course, Anton has served us many years.'

'But nothing is the same as it was,' said Annette. 'People are changing. Anton has changed. You should watch him more carefully.'

Pierre returned to his seat. He put his hands on his knees and leant towards William. 'You are not like Mr Paine Monsieur, that much I know. But I . . .' He paused for a moment and looked William all over. 'I can tell you now. I do not like to be spied on.'

'Why do you think I would spy on you, Monsieur?' said William, taken aback. He knew, only too well, the distress of thinking you were watched.

Pierre pointed his finger towards William's pocket. 'My aunt tells me you are often writing in your book. You say you write poetry. But ah, perhaps you only *pretend*? Perhaps it is other things you write.' He drew himself up slowly. 'That book could cost you your life, Monsieur. And mine also!'

'My book will cause you no harm,' said William. 'All it contains are pieces of poetry and prose.'

'Here in France you would be wise to keep your thoughts to yourself,' said Pierre gravely. 'It is foolish to write them down – especially in poetry.'

'Oh, please,' murmured Annette, lifting her shoulders and dropping them despondently. 'You are fond of poetry, Pierre. You have plenty of poetry in your library.' Her voice was soft and low. 'I believe the ability to write poetry is a gift from God.'

Pierre laughed loudly. 'Oh! So your poetry is written by the angels, Monsieur?' He stared at William, his eyebrows lifted in mockery. 'You can hear their songs, can you? You listen to them do you, then you write what they say in your book.'

'Who knows these things?' said William. 'Maybe Mozart hears their music, and perhaps a poet hears their words if his mind is open.'

Pierre slapped his thighs and laughed again. 'You come to this troubled country to discover the words of angels?'

William looked round at the company, wondering what to say next. He did not want to offend Pierre, and he did not want to upset Elizabeth or Annette. Paul stayed silent throughout, his face unchanging.

'I do not mean to offend you because of my writing,' William said hesitantly. 'If you saw my notebook, you would see that a lot is scribbled out.'

Pierre laughed again. 'So your angels are very poor scholars. Be careful of angels like that.'

'It is best not to talk about Mozart,' said Paul with a cough, and nodding at William. 'He is out of favour with royalists. The Marriage of Figaro is a mockery of the French nobility.' He bent his head and added quietly, 'As for music and poetry, such arts are elevating I think. I believe they take you to places of peace and tranquillity.'

'Oh, indeed,' said Pierre, 'while others are starving and dying.'

A servant entered the room. 'Dinner is served, Monsieur,' he said to Pierre.

'For now, Monsieur Wordsworth, come and enjoy my fare,' said Pierre rising. 'Though we will not eat so well at this house in future, I intend to adopt a much more frugal existence.' He breathed in deeply; it seemed with a sense of hopelessness.

'This way, William,' said Elizabeth.

7

Table Talk

They went, all five, along the long marble floored hall; Paul, Pierre and Annette in front, Elizabeth and William behind. The windows of the château, high on the lonely hill were dark with night. Bats fluttered past the window. William watched, intrigued by their mechanical movements. He was welcome to stay at the château if he wished, Elizabeth told him. It was Pierre's suggestion, she said, hotels in Orléans were unsafe just now and best avoided.

He smiled at the tantalizing thought. Outside was silent and deserted while here in this house there were interesting people to talk with, excellent food to be eaten, and a beautiful woman to look at who had stolen his heart. How could he leave without his heart? He glanced ahead at Pierre. 'How kind,' he said. It filled him with ease to think of it. 'I really must escape that dreadful hotel.' But he felt challenged. 'I have a feeling Pierre doesn't like me,' he said, biting his lip worriedly. 'It's only a feeling, of course.' He straightened his cravat self-consciously. 'I fear I am far too sensitive.'

Elizabeth smiled. 'Not at all. He brims with anxious energy. It might seem focused on you, but I assure you, my dear, it is not. You heard him with Paul yesterday and I know he loves him.

Pierre is angry all the time, most of all he is angry with himself because he feels helpless. He thinks the Jacobins will destroy the revolution and there is nothing he can do to stop them.'

The tall body of the hall seemed to engulf them as they walked and talked. As she passed by a large candelabrum, Annette's curls shimmered with life. She looked so delicate, he thought, but her determined stride suggested pride and independence. She too nursed anger, but there was gentleness and longing in her eyes, those were the spirits he would go for.

He wasn't sure what he would say when they took their places at the table. Talking at table with strangers could often be difficult, and no matter what Elizabeth said, as she charmingly offered him her nephew's hospitality, he felt torn between taking the key she held in her fingers and leaving after dinner. The key Elizabeth held was for room number three, she said, the third on the second floor, "An excellent and comfortable room", where a fire would be burning in the grate and the bed would be freshly made up. He felt truly seized in the most seductive of ways.

Pierre turned and caught his eye, though the coldness in his manner made it hard for William to respond. He nodded acknowledgement. Pierre was bound to be suspicious of him now, but his attitude was hard to accommodate, and to live in his house might be awkward. He was a difficult man to understand; his mind was like the root of a tree grown from the crevice of a rock, trees like that could split granite.

William turned to Elizabeth and took the key from her fingers, then slipped it into his pocket. He had made his decision. He'd collect what he had from the hotel next day and pay the man what he owed. The idea put him in an excellent frame of mind. He was eager to get to know Annette better and would like to have shared a laugh with Paul and Pierre over dinner, and try, if it were possible not to talk so heavily. But the two men walking before him were absorbed in the turmoil of their country and their frustrations were obvious from their gestures. Perhaps a glass of good wine, and whatever it was that delivered such delicious smells from the kitchen, would calm Pierre and make him friendly. He wanted Pierre to be friendly, mainly because he wanted Annette and must battle Pierre to reach her. The human mind was immensely skilful when it came to getting what it wanted. And he wanted Annette Vallon.

'. . . He only goes to talk to the groom, dear Aunt,' said Pierre, as they entered the dining room. 'Anton is kind to him.'

'But the boy was with him until the last of the daylight today,' Elizabeth said concernedly. 'I am not so sure he should be talking to the groom so freely.'

'Leon is the son he has lost,' Pierre said flatly, showing Elizabeth and Annette to their seats. 'His own son died from a disease of the blood, remember. He would now be something like the age of Leon had he lived. Leon likes to help with the horses.' He looked downwards and lowered his voice. 'His own father is absent.'

Elizabeth implored him. 'But, my dear, he is ten years old and the country is so dangerous. – Does Françoise know where he goes, he cannot just wander.'

'Françoise is in no condition to manage him,' Annette said with a sigh. 'I suspect he is sensible though. And my parents will know of his whereabouts.'

'But Annette, they are rarely at home. How can they know where he is?' Elizabeth turned to Paul.

'My brothers will have spoken to him too,' said Paul. 'He is spirited and intent on living.'

'But do you not believe with Rousseau, that children are innocent?' said Elizabeth.

'Leon is quite rebellious,' Annette said flatly. 'Whatever you tell him is bad for him he does all the more. He must make his own mistakes and learn. He is not as innocent as all that.'

'A couple of times I have found him in my cellars at the vineyard,' murmured Pierre. 'He likes to climb up the barrels. But if they should roll on him . . .'

'You never told me that,' said Paul. 'I shall speak to Françoise. We cannot lock him in his room, of course. That would be as good as imprisonment.'

'The king is imprisoned with his family,' Annette said sadly. 'The Tuileries Palace is horrible. It is dark and full of misery. The king and queen will always long for Versailles.'

'They can long as much as they like,' said Pierre. 'They will never go back. It was Lafayette, you know, who took them from Versailles to Paris. It was he who escorted them. But the king was wrong. To lock out the Third Estate like that from The Estate General's proceedings was an act of madness. He is a fool. It seems Lafayette is in charge of everything now. He has proved his worth in the American Revolution and as Commander of the National Guard he thinks he can help us. But ah,' Pierre shook his finger in the air. 'France is different from America. Here we are close to our king whereas they were distanced by the sea.'

'The Marquis de Lafayette is bound to be declared a traitor, one way or another,' said Paul. He shook his head at the thought.

'Lafayette is quite an enigma,' said Annette. 'According to Marat, he is responsible for the killings at the Champs de Mars. That was madness too. They say it was he who ordered the soldiers open fire.'

Paul gave a cynical laugh. 'Bah! Marat would have us all hanging from lampposts. They should commit his writings to the flames!'

For a while they were silent. The servants were bringing in food.

'I think we must give a little more thought to Leon,' said Elizabeth, returning to her previous reflections. 'Your parents are blaming him for Françoise's troubles, Annette. How can that be? They know who is to blame. The boy probably feels lonely when your parents are away and you and Paul are with Pierre. Yet he will not stay at the château with his mother. Your home in Blois is large and gloomy and Françoise walks it like a ghost.' She bent her head and lowered her voice. 'The boy must wonder why his mother is often weeping.'

William heard Annette sigh. 'I wish I could help him more,' she said, 'but I fear I too am invisible. The groom is the only one he talks to.'

Elizabeth broke in quickly. 'Yes, it is true. I went to the stables this morning to take him something to eat. "Who is the king?" I asked him. '"I do not know"', he replied. "Is his name Louis?" I asked. "I do not know," was his answer. Elizabeth threw out her hands confounded. 'Such sad, lonely, innocence.'

William was glad to be seated by Annette. If he wanted to speak with her he could do so quietly out of earshot. Though he doubted he would get the opportunity, everyone was talking at once. He looked about the room while he listened. The windows were long and wide, hung with exquisite silk draperies. His eyes wandered to a large, highly polished sideboard, where a luscious variety of desserts were displayed on silver platters. His eyes moved to a plate of darioles, a delectable sort of French custard he liked. Next he saw the marmalade tart. He adored marmalade tart! And there were pear cakes, jellies and other things lovely to look at and eat. On a glistening white linen cloth, candlelight danced on the silver cutlery and cut glass wine glasses before him. A silver rococo bowl, brimming with colourful sweetmeats stood at the centre. Smells came from the kitchen from food he knew he would relish. He saw that Annette sat gazing at a painting on the wall. Her look was one of despair. 'What is the matter?' he asked, leaning towards her.

'The paintings in this house are bad!' she whispered. 'They are all so violent.'

They gazed together at the picture on the wall opposite. The painting depicted a war at sea, cannon fire and men fighting. He did not like such works himself and said so. Candlelight was the only light in the room as the night closed in. The servants were bringing in food – vegetables, fish, all kinds of sauces, and smoking hot potatoes.

'Ah, good, we are to eat pot-au-fau!' cried Pierre, clapping his hands. 'A mere beef stew to you, Monsieur Wordsworth, though the pot-au-feu is the essence of French cuisine, a highly celebrated dish the way it is cooked in France. You must eat it very very hot though, or the flavour is lost. The best flavours are down to the skills of the chef. Each chef has his own secret.'

'And yours is wonderful,' said Elizabeth, her eyes bright with pleasure. 'You must try the wines as well, William. They are all from Pierre's vineyard. The white is excellent with pork and fish. You might want one of the reds with darker meat. But no matter, have what you want; we don't stand on ceremony here.'

'Freedom, freedom that is what we stand for!' cried Pierre. 'I drink whatever suits me with whatever cuisine I fancy.'

'Freedom indeed,' said William.

The servants brought wine to the table. William chose white. He saw that Pierre chose red. It was obvious Paul had often eaten with Pierre for the servant knew exactly his choice, and murmured that they had prepared him his favourite dish.

Pierre lifted his wine glass, gazing at the wine inside it, as if he beheld a beautiful woman in its midst. He moistened his lips and took a drink. 'Exquisite,' he murmured. The servant poured more. 'To Annette!' said Pierre. 'Let us drink to the lovely Annette!'

'Well, yes,' said Paul, also lifting his glass.

William smiled and raised his glass with the others, though Annette flushed with embarrassment.

'I hope you will like that vintage, Monsieur,' said Pierre,

screwing up his eyes to look. 'You have chosen a fine one.'

William opted to eat fish. He lifted the lotus shaped sauceboat to pour out the sweet smelling sauce, which ran a thin orange stream, settling by the white steaming fish. He placed a napkin on his lap, then picked up his knife and fork.

For several minutes they all attended to their food.

'Robespierre is stirring up trouble for the king,' said Elizabeth, dabbing her mouth with a napkin. 'The groom told me this morning.'

'Those awful Committees,' Annette moaned softly. 'Robespierre claims he is neither republican nor royalist, what nonsense. He is certainly a nuisance. He destroys what he attempts to achieve.' She looked across at her brother for confirmation.

'He grows more powerful by the day,' said Paul. 'People listen to him. The man is a skilled orator.'

Pierre took a forkful of food to his mouth, for a moment or two thoughtful.

'He's a highly skilled lawyer too,' added Paul, watching the servant as he carefully poured out the wine. 'He knows all the tricks. He knows what he wants and will stop at nothing to get it.'

'He *wants* to be rid of the king,' said Pierre, nodding at the servant to bring more wine from the cellars. He looked at William. 'You will know about Marat, of course.'

'I have heard about his press,' said William.

'He creates delirious writings, stirring the revolutionaries to even greater barbarism. He is very much valued by the Jacobins. His views would make your dinner hard to digest, Monsieur. And Brissot too, makes intense compositions that grow from undisciplined emotions. He does not think about consequences. Much of what he says is irrational. His suggestions that our country might be helped by what has happened in America is absurd, yet the man has an abundance of followers.' Pierre stopped suddenly and put down his knife and fork, then he rested his head in his hands. 'Ah, these people have a soup of ideologies, but they have no idea how it should taste.'

The sound of an approaching carriage came from the courtyard. They all stopped to listen, then carried on eating. For several moments they were silent. Perhaps a chaise had arrived for the boy, William decided. He began to wonder how Pierre was placed with his politics. He enjoyed an aristocrat's wealth, but not an aristocrat's mind. How did people like him survive in such threatening times?

'I hope you will stay in my home, Monsieur Wordsworth,' said Pierre, gazing into his wine. 'My aunt would like it.'

William was slow to answer.

'You are quite welcome,' Pierre insisted, emptying his glass.

'Thank you,' said William, swallowing a mouthful of perfectly delicious fish. 'You are most gracious. I was grumbling to Elizabeth about my hotel earlier. I do not like the proprietor. Or more precisely, the proprietor doesn't like me. I was thinking of looking elsewhere . . .'

Pierre gazed at him straight. 'Well, look no further. You will stay at my château. One of my rooms will be most grateful for your company; they are so forsaken. But I must go to my vineyard shortly. I have a great deal of work awaiting me.' He forked about in his food thoughtfully. 'I must watch my men too. Some are becoming lazy; they sit about slovenly and drink all my wine and they are often too much light hearted. It does not do to get too light hearted at the vineyard. Important things are forgotten.'

'The groom believes Robespierre is brilliant and destined for greatness,' said Elizabeth. 'I am amazed at their admiration. The man will think himself omnipotent!'

'Robespierre is a bloodthirsty fiend,' said Paul. 'He has a good following, I grant you. But for Robespierre cause is all, no matter what sacrifice.'

'He is young,' sighed Elizabeth. 'He is all emotion. He must use his common sense.'

'Common sense is not so common,' Annette said quietly.

'The trouble with politics is it kills the common sense,' Elizabeth asserted. 'Oh, I know, believe me. I have lost mine often enough. And what a dark place you find yourself in when you do. By all means believe in something, but don't . . .'

'Don't let emotion take over?' offered William, raising his eyebrows as he spoke.

'Quite,' Elizabeth said firmly. 'That is my opinion.'

'What is the matter?' Pierre asked Annette, seeing her staring at the painting on the wall behind him.

'It's that,' she said, nodding towards it. 'I find it offensive.'

'But why?' he asked, frowning. He craned his neck to look. 'It is only a war at sea. It was one of my father's favourites. You have seen it before, many times.'

'I have never liked it. It is all about death – smiting, smiting, so many dead and wounded, so much blood. Why must we celebrate war in art? I do not understand.'

'You are very irritable tonight, my dear,' said Pierre. He gazed at her curiously. His chair creaked as he turned back to the table. He poured more wine. 'You have never expressed such annoyance about the painting before. Why do you do so now?'

'Because tonight I am emotional, and I must always be rational and restrained – or that is what Paul advises.'

'I do not know that I said so, Annette,' said Paul, wiping his mouth on a napkin and with a hurt expression. 'My own work asks for calmness and reason. It must. But I do not recall that I . . .'

Pierre still looked at Annette. 'Had I known how the painting offended you, I would certainly have taken it down. You know how I like to please you.' He sat awaiting her response.

Annette shook her head sadly. 'Death, death, more and more death.'

'What passion about a painting,' said Pierre, looking confounded? He looked at William and sighed. 'Passion indeed, Monsieur Wordsworth, do you not agree?'

William cleared his throat. 'Mademoiselle Annette, it seems, is passionate about many things.' He turned to look at her and smiled. 'You are very passionate about politics.'

'Oh yes, she is passionate about her king,' said Pierre, with a laugh. 'Though the man is a fool. And you are passionate about music too, Annette. Remember when I took you to Paris to listen to Dussek? What a wonderful time we had together.'

Annette bent her head.

'Dussek, you know,' Pierre continued, 'is the queen's favourite composer. But Dussek has fled to London now. Loyalty, you see.'

'We must all preserve ourselves somehow,' said Elizabeth flatly. 'Dussek was indeed favoured.'

'Oh, the man preserves himself alright,' laughed Pierre. 'And he has got himself a pretty young wife as well.' He leant back in his chair, observing Annette with a long and steady gaze. 'A harpist, I believe. She will no doubt warm his bed at night through those cold English winters.' He turned back to the picture, then of a sudden, rose from his chair. Spreading his arms across the painting, he lifted its weight off the hook, then marched out into the hall.

William stared at the faded space on the wall. It looked, he thought, like an island in a purple lagoon, a deserted place without life.

'I fear you have upset him,' sighed Elizabeth.

Annette threw out her hands in silent reply.

Shadows fell across the room. A servant brought new candles and placed them on surfaces. They listened to Pierre's footsteps as he strode up the marble staircase. William wondered what would happen to the painting – would he destroy it?

Annette gazed into her shining dessertspoon. 'He is inebriated,' she said, feigning indifference. 'He will be better once he is sober.'

'Quite right,' said Elizabeth, adding that it was almost impossible for Pierre to entertain nowadays; he was so intent on arguing.

'But men like to argue,' said Annette, straightening. 'And then they go to war. If they cannot find a reason to kill I fear they will invent one.'

'That's very unfair,' said Paul, in his calm lawyer like way. 'I see no pleasure in fighting to the death. Arguments are different. My allegiances are with the monarchy, of course. I take the side of the king and queen and will argue all night if I must.'

'All this harassing the king is simply to get him out of the way so that others can usurp his power,' Annette said, angrily. They all sat waiting for Pierre, whose footsteps could be heard as he returned down in the hall.

'The king has more than his fair share of power,' Pierre said caustically as he entered. His speech was slurred. He made a gesture with his hand. 'Look at this table. It is so heavily laden it could sink through the floor. I am ashamed. – Ah, that the food would sink through the floor and take me with it.' He bent his head, and for a moment or two sobbed.

'You are generous, Pierre,' said Annette, in a warmer tone of voice. 'You are good. Matters must change in our country, but how can it happen? I see nothing but pain and bloodshed ahead.'

'Things are improving,' said Elizabeth. 'The National Assembly has brought about important reforms. There is a fairer system of laws. There is . . .'

'There is still a lot of stupidity about,' said Paul. 'Our finances are wrecked. There is still increasing inflation. And there is still much violence.'

'And we still have a lot of powdered idiots,' said Pierre sottishly. 'Enjoy this food. We will eat less well in this house in the future, I promise.'

'Do go easy on the wine, my dear,' said Elizabeth, seeing him reach another bottle.

Pierre rubbed his face tiredly. 'Tell me Paul. Do you think the National Assembly has been effective?' He spoke wearily.

Paul smiled wryly. 'Well, the crime of magic has been abolished.'

For a moment or two they all laughed.

'To abolish the crime of magic is a crime in itself,' laughed William, slightly more at ease and glad of a change of heart.

'I believe you went to see Versailles,' said Paul, searching his face.

'I did,' said William. 'It is the envy of the world, I should think.'

'Bah, the poor will tell you about that,' growled Pierre. 'It is testament to long-standing greed. Ah, greed, greed. Our Finance Minister should have taxed the nobles and the clergy. A cleverer king would have made them pay up. And I cannot imagine the money we have spent on financing the American wars.'

'War, war, war,' murmured Annette.

'That is all true,' said Paul. 'Let us listen to America! Rise up, rise up against tyranny! A Republic will serve us better than a monarchy! Well, let me tell you, it will not.'

'People need a chance to prosper,' Pierre said vehemently. 'There is a need for free commerce, a much more liberal way of life.' He turned his gaze on William. 'So what do you say, Monsieur Wordsworth? Have you no voice?'

William put down his napkin and braced himself. 'I can talk as well as the next,' he answered assuredly, 'once I am started. I am hearing your every word.'

Pierre nodded. 'Ah yes, you are an excellent listener, Mr Wordsworth, and it is wise to stay silent. Talk is dangerous in France. I am a slave to my talk sometimes. I need to improve. As a matter of fact, I believe the queen is far more at fault than the king. She has squandered the country's money on trivia. And she knows no more than you, Monsieur, about our politics. She desires only frivolity.'

'I doubt she will have much frivolity in the Tulieres Palace,' sighed Annette. 'You must remember Pierre; she was all but a child when she and Louis were married. Her youth was stolen away.'

Pierre shook his head irritably. 'So she is having it now, is she? She did not get her childhood in Austria, so she is having it here as our queen. And good luck to our country?' He poured more wine in his glass. 'And what's more she wears jewellery that belongs elsewhere.'

'It isn't important,' said Annette, her skin tightening with emotion. 'I am sorry for Marie Antoinette. Louis is often depressed. I am sorry for them both.'

'The king is crazy,' said Pierre. 'All kings are crazy. To live the life of a king is unnatural.' His eyes rested on William. 'King George of England is also mad, they say. And he drinks laudanum too. Is it true that your king is insane?'

William frowned. 'I doubt he is any more insane than the rest of us. But just as you say, the life of a king is unnatural. I suspect he might act a little crazy now and then. It seems like a good idea.'

'A good idea to act crazy?' Pierre narrowed his eyes, watching William intently. 'I think I might go crazy myself, if I did not do so already. I shall adopt this good idea.'

'Marie Antoinette is a beautiful woman,' said Paul. 'Mozart, you know, asked for her hand in marriage once, or that is what mother has told us.'

'It is true,' laughed Elizabeth, 'though I believe he was only a boy at the time.'

'She is certainly beautiful to look at,' said Pierre, gazing now at Annette. He breathed in deeply and sighed. 'But she is not so lovely as Mademoiselle Vallon.'

'Pierre,' said Elizabeth crossly as he poured even more wine. She put out her hand to stop him.

'My dear Aunt,' said Pierre, taking the glass to his lips. 'You have no idea of the suffering you cause me when you try to advise me on my drinking. My wines are on the tables of the world, and you tell me how much I can drink?' He waved her away. 'You are off to Rome very soon, are you not?'

Elizabeth straightened. 'So you want me to leave the country do you, then you can drink yourself into the grave.'

'I hate to be unpleasant, Aunt Elizabeth. Please forgive me. You know I shall miss you.' Pierre spoke miserably.

Annette stood up slowly. 'You will have to excuse me,' she said. 'I am tired.' Then she went to the door and walked out.

William listened to her footsteps as she went down the hall. He glanced through the open doorway. The marble hall and staircase soon became silent. Elizabeth stared into space. Pierre gazed down into his drink. Paul's eyes fixed on the flickering candle before him. They were all thoughtful.

But William was planning ahead. He would think of a way to leave the table and find her . . .

'And how is Françoise?' said Pierre. He lit a cigar and turned to Paul. 'Is she better?'

'Yes, and I am glad of it,' Paul said with a sigh. 'Love is a dangerous business. I am quite relieved he has gone. That man has caused her endless suffering.'

'He is a coward,' said Pierre, blowing out smoke and watching it rise into the air. 'The fellow always was.'

'I warned her,' said Paul. 'He was hostile and abusive to us all.

What he has done to Françoise though is unforgivable. For years he has been away, yet he returns and makes terrible demands.'

'But he did not stay very long,' Pierre said flatly.

'She ought never to have started that acquaintance,' said Elizabeth. 'And you are right, Pierre. He is a coward. You challenged him to a duel and he fled. Everyone knows that your swordsmanship is second to none.'

'Françoise is getting stronger,' said Paul, bracing himself. 'She'll get over him.'

'Love uses and abuses,' sighed Elizabeth. 'Who can know what it is up to? I met the man but once. A handsome fellow I thought. And his father, I believe, is the richest wigmaker in France.'

'He *was*,' Pierre said dryly. 'I doubt he is wealthy now. The people are throwing their wigs to their dogs as playthings. They do not like them anymore, for obvious reasons, of course. I have never liked them myself.'

'No,' said Paul, running his fingers through his own loose brown locks.

William turned, and glanced again down the hall. He felt like a tethered animal straining on a leash.

'Do take a look around the château,' said Elizabeth. 'Pierre has some excellent works of art. You might like to look at them a while.'

'Ah yes, before they are gone!' said Pierre, his features stony. 'Every last one is going.'

'But who will they go to?' asked Elizabeth, looking confounded.

'Anyone who wants to buy them, dear Aunt, I shall give the money to the poor.'

'And who do you think will buy them?' she asked sighing. 'No-one will admit of having such money now. They will be packing their art works into boxes and sending them abroad for safe keeping.'

'And packing themselves in the boxes too,' said Paul. 'Aristocrats are fleeing the country like frightened chickens.'

'Perhaps I can find a buyer from abroad,' said Pierre. 'I have contacts.'

'Don't be a fool,' said Paul. 'You will draw attention to yourself. You are stuck with them now, just as you are stuck with your vineyard and your châteaux. You can't get away from your wealth, unless you run from it like the others.'

'I have never run from anything in my life,' said Pierre, glaring at Paul.

'Sometimes running is all that is left,' said Paul with a shrug.

'Well, Monsieur Wordsworth,' said Pierre, drawing a deep breath. 'You had better go look at them now, before my château is razed to the ground. I fear it will happen very soon.'

William stood and gave a quick light bow. 'Indeed, I shall. Though your fears are a little overstated I think.' He smiled. 'Thank you for the meal. It was wonderful. I shall probably retire to bed when I have done exploring.'

'Of course,' said Elizabeth. 'You know where your room is. I will send a servant to the hotel with a note, and he will fetch your belongings.'

As he stepped out into the hall, Elizabeth called to him: 'The East Wing is always kept locked! – That part of the château is closed!'

8

God Of Desire

The flickering shadows gave life to the paintings on the walls as he walked along the dimly lit hall, stopping to look as he went. Just as Annette had said, the images were mainly of war. Guns and swords pointed towards him, tortured faces confronted him from battleships, many in flames and ready to be devoured by the sea. Had one of Pierre's ancestors been a sailor, he wondered, there was a distinct sense of maritime life in the house?

At the foot of the marble staircase, the smell of candle wax grew strong. He breathed in the scent of Annette's wandering perfume as he went up the stairs.

Arriving on the second floor, he touched the key in his pocket and noted again that his room was third on the left, a few paces ahead. Everywhere was still and silent. Where was she, he wondered. He passed beneath a curved arch and arrived by a door displaying the words "EAST WING" above it. This was the door to a place never entered, a door always kept locked. All the doors on the corridor were high, with splendid motifs of leaves, shells and blossoms carved into the wood suggestive of spring, delightful to look at and expertly done.

He walked on further, stopping by a painting of Boucher's

'*Cupid a Captive.*' The green and gold of the verdant background, the rich texture and redness of the red and gold cloth cloaked about the god of desire looked new and fresh, while the creamy skin of the naked forms seemed vital as living flesh. He stood for a moment entranced, how did a painter do that?

He moved on slowly wondering where her room was, the place where she took off her clothes and lay down to rest. Then he suddenly caught sight of a shining object lying on the floor by a door. He knelt down to retrieve it, and found he was holding the brooch that had fallen from her habit yesterday. She had worn it tonight on her dress. His heart beat fast as he held it. So this was her room! The door was slightly ajar and he could hear her singing softly:

> '*The pleasure of love lasts only a moment*
> *The pain of love lasts a lifetime.*
>
> *I gave up everything for ungrateful Sylvia,*
> *She is leaving me for another lover.*
>
> *The pleasure of love lasts only a moment,*
> *The pain of love lasts a lifetime.*
>
> "*As long as this water will run gently*
> *Towards this brook which borders the meadow,*
>
> *I will love you*", *Sylvia told me repeatedly.*
> *The water still runs, but she has changed.*
>
> *The pleasure of love lasts only a moment,*
> *The pain of love lasts a lifetime.*'

How sad her mood is, he thought. He stood pierced with longing, until the singing stopped. Ought he to put the brooch in his pocket and hand it to her tomorrow? – Or might he tap on her door? He was about to turn, when he heard her call out, 'William, why not come in?' Her tone was warm and sleepy.

He remained perfectly still and slightly alarmed, fancying she might be displeased that he had come to her room so boldly. He looked at the brooch in his fingers. The little jewel was a blessing. 'I needed to see you,' he said through the doorway in as strong a voice as he could muster.

'But how can you see me out there?' she said. 'Do come inside.'

'May I?' he asked, hesitantly.

'Did I not just invite you?' she called a hint of laughter in her manner.

He pushed the door and stepped in. The words of her melancholy song echoed in his mind. 'I wanted to ask you . . .' he faltered.

'What?' she said. She looked at him through the dressing table mirror.

Her shapely form was bright in the candlelight, her arms rising and falling as she brushed out her hair. He met her eyes through the mirror, and she put down her brush and laid it amongst an array of puffs and powder boxes, her face calm and lovely. He felt anchored. Images he had never dared have entered his mind. He stepped back quickly, watching as she carried on brushing out her hair.

'So, what do you want to ask me?' she said, turning to him and waiting.

'I'm not sure,' he answered, confusedly. He could ask her how many minutes he could spend with her. He could ask her to be with him forever. He could ask if she might stop time right there and then . . . Instead he held out the brooch. 'It was on the carpet out there . . . I thought I should let you have it.' His voice came strangely formal.

She rose quickly and went to him. Taking the brooch from his fingers, she examined it again and frowned, just as she had done before by the gates of the château.

'I doubt you can mend it by looking,' he said.

'Oh, I wish it didn't fall off,' she moaned, touching the catch and curious. 'One day I shall lose it for good. Pierre would be very angry if I did.' She waved him across to a chair. 'There, go and sit down. It was impossible to talk to you before at the table. Pierre is a heavy drinker. He is quite ridiculous sometimes.' She laid the brooch on the dressing table and went to perch on the edge of the bed where she started to take off her stockings.

He sat in the chair as instructed. She had probably had many lovers he decided; she was so natural and relaxed.

'You are embarrassed,' she murmured, lifting her face and smiling. 'But I am only undressing. I do it every night, like you do.'

He breathed in deeply and hoped he didn't break the spell. This enchanting woman had stolen him bit-by-bit, breath-by-breath, second by second. Yet somehow he felt he had always been hers, had always known her, always expected her . . . She had been in the shadows on the fells. He had seen her face in the waters of the lakes. 'Your eyes are so sorrowful,' he said.

'Are they?' she said, looking surprised. She drew her stockings through her fingers. Her bare legs shone in the candlelight.

For a moment or two they were silent.

'Why must the joy of love last only a moment?' he asked, 'while the pain of it lasts a lifetime?'

'Ah, that,' she murmured. 'My song.'

'You sang it beautifully,' he told her.

'It is true,' she said finally, her voice full of emotion. 'Love is often so hurtful. I wonder if it can help it.'

The candlelight flickered on her skin. He held to his feelings. Nothing she said would rob him of this precious moment. He had no experience of the passionate kind of love and could make no sensible reply. But the way he felt about her hurt him somehow, though he didn't know why. There was a loneliness in her, a desperate, tragic loneliness. 'Must it always be so?' he asked achingly. 'I mean, *always?*'

'I think so,' she sighed. She walked across to the dressing table and sat on the stool. Her fingers moved towards the brooch.

Then he rose and went to her. Kneeling beside her he took her hand and drew her palm to his lips. *'Annette, Annette,'* he murmured. 'Can you not see that I adore you?'

She cupped his face in her hands and held his gaze. Then she kissed his forehead gently. His hands shook as he found her waist and pulled her towards him.

At that moment, footsteps were heard on the corridor. 'It is Pierre!' she cried. She rose hastily. 'Pierre — it is Pierre!' But already he stood in the doorway.

'I wondered how you were,' he said, looking at her hard. 'Elizabeth thought you were ill.' In a flash, his eyes turned to William. 'Monsieur, you are in the wrong room? — Come, let me to direct you.'

Annette ran to him. 'Pierre! Oh, Pierre! William found my brooch on the floor in the passage. He came to return it.' She talked on breathlessly. 'See how loose the clasp is. — Oh dear, I should hate to lose it.'

'The brooch, ah yes,' said Pierre, glancing at William and Annette by turns. 'It is important, of course, it was my mother's.' He took it from her and examined it, then handed it back.

Annette gazed at it fondly. 'You let me have it as a gift on my sixteenth birthday. I have always treasured it.'

'Allow me to get it repaired,' said William, stepping forward. 'I passed a jeweller this morning. I am sure the clasp can be fixed.'

'I suspect it has perished,' Annette said sadly.

'Do let me take it,' William insisted.

Annette gazed at him hopefully. 'Very well then,' she said, handing it across.

Pierre looked on confused, then turned and left.

9

William And Annette

Encountering Pierre in his château now made William uneasy. But he had never before felt so joyful! Everything had suddenly changed. Pierre might have booted him out, but instead he passed in silence, his head bent low, his hands clasped behind his back. His dark moods, Elizabeth said, were best ignored.

William had spent a good half hour that morning talking with Paul over breakfast. Annette's brother had been pensive, pointing through the window at the sky, saying it resembled the Loire in drought it was so muddy and grey, and adding with a shrug that it was much like Pierre's mood. "If he carries on sulking," he'd warned, "I shall take Annette back to Blois, for his manner is far too tiresome." William had braced himself at that. To take Annette back to Blois would be tragic. The minutes he did not see her felt like hours. "No, no," he'd agued. "She is happy here at the château. And Pierre has a lot on his mind. – As you know, only too well, the vineyard has been his livelihood. Perhaps he must make some important decisions." "Of course, of course, you are right," Paul had replied sternly, looking embarrassed. William had seen immediately that Paul was unaware of what had happened. Yet to William it seemed the whole château understood.

The groom had brought them newspapers today, which they'd talked over avidly. Change was rife throughout Europe. Wilberforce's motion to abolish the slave trade had at last gone through Parliament and scholars everywhere were thinking about science and religion, searching for resonances between them and discussing ideas. Mozart's opera, *"The Magic Flute"*, had premiered in Vienna, with Mozart conducting the orchestra, a work condemned in the past for its Masonic symbolism. For a time it had seemed that Mozart was damned in France. But minds were changing swiftly. Pajou's marble sculpture, *"Psyche Abandoned"*, previously frowned on for the boldness of his nude Psyche, had now been presented at the Paris Salon, and admired for its passion. Singular developments rose out of social change, William reflected as he sat in the parlour at the château, pointing to a new future. But what was the future for him and Annette, a republican and a royalist, an Englishman and a French woman in love?

Over the next few days, Pierre's bad mood grew worse, announcing itself in loud thundering footsteps along the corridors, as if there were something he searched for but could not find. Much of the time Elizabeth stayed in her room. William felt they were all oddly separated now. He himself took his meals with Paul and Annette. Pierre took his meals wherever he happened to be; his library, his bedroom, even at the top of the stairs. Elizabeth ate alone in her room. The atmosphere was strained, though no-one voiced their concerns. And William felt he should leave. But he could not break the bond between himself and Annette. He could not leave her. Wherever she was, he must be. He had watched her walking the gardens that morning, in that slow melancholy way of hers where she shook her head unhappily. A republican from England and a royalist; it could not be. But he knew she loved him. Her eyes had told him whenever he'd held her close.

Paul had spoken of an English servant at their home in Blois, a woman intent on returning to England who had worked for their family eight years. The house would be without servants, he'd said, for one by one they had left. His sisters, however, were excellent cooks, he'd added resignedly, and he too could learn. There was much clattering of feet about the château, both upstairs and down. Pierre was leaving for his vineyard and Paul had business in Orléans. Elizabeth was leaving for Rome very shortly and William decided to find her.

As he passed her room he saw that the door was open, but Elizabeth wasn't inside. She wasn't in the parlour with Annette and was hardly likely to be walking the gardens while needing to pack away her things. He found her down at the East Wing of the château turning a key in the lock of the forbidden door. As he approached she gasped.

'I was wandering . . .' he said, embarrassed and sorry to alarm her.

'I shouldn't have done it,' she said shakily, looking away.

'Done what?' he asked, with an air of innocence. He saw that she trembled slightly. For a moment or two they were silent. 'Shall I go away?' he asked quietly.

'Not at all, my dear, it's just that I went into the rooms. Pierre forbids it, you see. But sometimes . . .'

Again they were silent.

'My coach will be arriving shortly,' she faltered. She slipped the key into her pocket and shook her head sadly. 'I do not know how long I can keep coming, or what will happen to this country.' She looked about her as if what she gazed at were beloved. Her throat seemed choked with tears. 'Pierre is so sick. Those rooms are filled with the past. We were able to talk about it once. Now he is out of reach.' She braced herself and took a breath. 'I always fear for him. There are informants everywhere and many officials will listen to them, even to lies. He fears for you and Annette also, but we have talked about it, and now he is thinking better. He knows that you love each other. – Ah, it is all right. He accepts you.' She shivered as if from her thoughts then took hold of his arm. 'Come, my dear. Let me tell you the charge I have been given.' They walked together down the corridor.

At that moment Annette came running. 'Elizabeth will probably have told you,' she called brightly. 'Pierre has invited you to his vineyard today. It is a special privilege.' She glanced at Elizabeth. 'You know how he promised to take William to the vineyard. He is still of the same mind.' She talked on excitedly. 'It is essential to him that you see how he makes his wines. He has always been proud of the vineyard. It has been his life, you see.' Her face became suddenly sad. 'And now it is threatened.' He saw in her eyes how it mattered.

'Today?' he said, looking perplexed. 'I know very little about vineyards, my love. And truth be told, I know very little about wine.'

'Well, soon you will know much more,' she laughed, clasping her hands with pleasure. 'It is to show that he trusts you as his friend. To him, his vineyard is sacred. You will be entering his temple. It will be good for you and I know it will be good for Pierre. He can show you better who he is.' She went on talking emotionally. 'He can tell you about his wines from the very beginning.' She threw out her arms. 'How the sun sends its messages, how the rain lets him know about the land . . .' She made a gesture with her fingers. 'He can take a grape between his finger and thumb, taste it and know its secrets.' She spoke in the voice of her childhood, a place she had shared with Pierre.

Elizabeth gazed through the window as they spoke. 'The weather is better today. I believe it is going to be dry,' she said softly. 'You can ride there. Pierre has many fine horses, William, you may take your pick.'

Still confused, he gazed at Annette. 'He wants me to visit the vineyard?' he murmured. 'Very well, if that is his wish.' He straightened and smiled.

'I shall soon be off,' said Elizabeth. 'The maid is preparing my trunk.' She gazed at them both warmly.

'Paul is off to Paris this minute,' said Annette, glancing down the staircase. 'He is standing in the hall with Pierre.' Pulling on William's arm, she urged him bid him farewell.

Paul and Pierre were in heated conversation by the door. Morning light blazed through the windows dancing on the marble floor and lighting up the intense tableau. Annette announced she would be visiting the vineyard later that day with William and Pierre looked at them both by turns nodding approval. He did not speak though there was no denying the pleasure on his face as he went down the steps of the château to his horse. William exchanged a few last words with Paul who was soon on his way. Then he turned to Elizabeth and Annette who were both subdued. The house felt strangely bereft. Elizabeth too would be leaving shortly.

'Well,' she said, looking at William with a serious determined expression. She drew a breath and hastened to the parlour, bidding him follow. 'I have something to give to you.' Annette followed in silence, though her eyes were bright with knowledge. Reaching the bureau in the parlour Elizabeth pulled out a drawer and drew out a grey cotton bag secured with a drawstring. 'There now,' she said, holding it out before him. 'It is rather heavy!'

He stood silent and bewildered.

'*Money*,' Elizabeth confirmed. 'Take it. It is yours from Pierre. You will need it.'

William stared at the bag. 'For me?' he asked, confusedly. 'But why? He wants me to visit his vineyard, and he leaves me a bag of money?' He wiped his brow with the back of his hand and frowned. 'Annette, nothing makes sense.'

'Nothing at all makes sense in France anymore,' Elizabeth murmured, still holding out the bag. 'But money is always useful.'

'Please take it,' begged Annette, as she watched him step back. 'If he does not give it to you he will give it to somebody else. – What's more, if you take it, we can go to Orléans and buy you some better clothing.'

At that he frowned. 'And what is wrong with my clothing?' he asked. The old pains of poverty returned and rushed through his blood. 'Is it shabby?'

'You have said so yourself,' said Elizabeth. She threw back her head and thrust the bag at him again. 'Take it William, Pierre wants you to have it.' Her voice fell low. 'If you have to return to England quickly, then you will need it.'

Annette's features saddened. As the sun lit the room he drew her towards him. 'I will not leave you,' he whispered. *'Never.'* He gazed down at his breeches. They were certainly old and frayed. 'Your tailor can't make the clothes we wear in Lakeland,' he said to Elizabeth, brooding.

'Our tailor can cut anything you like,' she replied assuredly. 'You can go with Annette this week and he will measure you up. Tell him exactly what you want and he will cut the cloth for you and sew it.'

'He can make you a lovely silk cravat as well,' Annette whispered in his ear. 'How grand you would look in that.'

'And I must get me a wig too,' William replied churlishly. 'I shall look like an aristocrat if it kills me.'

Annette sat down heavily. 'You are so stubborn,' she sighed. 'Take Pierre's money and be glad of it.'

William still stood thoughtful. He was relieved that Paul hadn't taken Annette back to Blois, and that Pierre had allowed him to stay. In truth, Pierre had been kind, despite his curmudgeonly manners. Slowly, he put out his hand and Elizabeth passed him the bag. 'Gold coins!' he gasped, looking in. But the coins seemed to pulse with despair. This was a world where too much wealth was a danger, like a sun too hot, a wind too harsh, a rain too forceful. For a moment he stared into space. Did Pierre want to get rid of him? It was quite conceivable.

'He will be happy if you accept it,' said Annette. She took his hand and clasped it to her lips. 'Oh mon Dieu! I am trying to please two men.'

'I believe you are,' said William, 'and Fate will decide which of us is pleased the best.'

10

Pierre's Vineyard

Chimes from a nearby church announced 10 am. It would take them an hour to reach the vineyard if they took the horses steadily. They went up the winding pathway to the stables. Were it not winter, she said, they would have made their way to the vineyard on foot rather than ride, for the banks of the Loire from spring till autumn were a haven of wild flowers and butterflies.

It was good to get out into the cool clear air. It had rained heavily in the night and the walkway had suffered; the spaces between the stones were busy with water and Annette was finding it hard to manage her skirts. But the lush vegetation about them soaked from the rain smelt wonderfully sweet.

'It is better now Pierre has changed his attitude,' she said, struggling to lift one of her heels out of the mud. 'He has been so jealous. We had words about it at dawn. I heard loud footsteps in the night, and went to see who it was. He was in the library alone staring into space by a candle. I thought he was walking in his sleep, something he has done before, but he spoke my name softly and put out his hand. I knew he was depressed.'

'To see us together in your room that evening must have been unpleasant. He loves you.'

She stopped and smiled. 'He does not love me, *like that?*' She shook her head confounded.

'I think he does,' sighed William. 'I only wish he didn't, but I see it.' He could hear the painful note in his voice as he spoke. But he did not want to discuss it. 'We ought to have come the other way,' he said, glancing about. 'This ground is sodden.'

'He loves me as a friend,' she said tenderly. 'He fears I will land myself in trouble if we are seen together at the château.' Her tone was anxious. There were tears in her throat as she spoke. And he wondered again how it had been with her and Pierre, the life they had shared, the things they had done.

'Your presence has sharpened everything about us,' she said quickly. 'It has focused our thinking. Pierre told me so many things this morning I thought he would weep. He is very sad for our country; its heart is weary and torn.' She stopped and gazed at the sky. 'Pierre's father would have enjoyed this wretched revolution. It would have given him an outlet for his anger. He despised the Estates; they made him angry at everything, even his wife and children. He took to heavy drinking and was often abusive, hurting Pierre's mother, even striking and bruising her. Pierre believed his father was in love with a married woman in Paris, an aristocrat I think. That is what we decided – some woman he could not have.' She stamped mud off her boots, then they gazed together across the estate to the woods where they would ride, the Loire like a silver snake, winding into the distance. 'Pierre's father came from a military family. Whenever I visited the château as a child, he would talk of nothing but war. I often wept into my pillow, and there were days when Pierre would hide until his father left the house. His mother and sister were often distressed and weeping.' She sighed softly. 'Pierre once said he wished his father were dead. And when the boat crashed on the rocks and sank, he felt he had killed them all. Elizabeth tried to tell him vessels often hit rocks and sank and that many people died in shipwrecks. He knew these things but would not acknowledge them. He had killed them, he said, his mind was hardened to stone.'

'He is very disturbed,' William said quietly. And he began to think about John. But John had thought it all through. If he died with a mermaid, so be it, he would die happily. But that was imagination coming to his aid, if his ship crashed on the rocks and sank, sharks not mermaids, would greet him. He thought again about Pierre. It was interesting to hear about his father, there was a great deal of violence and anger in the paintings at the château, but what a terrible legacy for Pierre. Would he ever be released from his pain?

He gazed down the grounds as they went. Narrow little paths intersected the drystone walls that divided them off from the trees. He imagined fawns hiding in the wild flowers in summer, deer rambling the woodland. And he imagined her as a child, then a woman, waiting in Time for him.

'Do you miss your family?' she asked.

'Of course,' he sighed. 'I miss my sister Dorothy most, we've been close since childhood. We haven't seen much of each other, but we've always kept in touch through letters.' He frowned at the thought. 'She doesn't know where I am just now. I have no fixed address for her to write to. I can only hope she is well.'

'How old is your sister?' she asked.

'A little bit younger than me,' he answered, smiling.

'And I am a little bit older than you,' she said, glancing at him sideways and straightening. 'So take care.'

He laughed. 'I have heard you are an excellent fencer too. Yes, I had best be careful.'

'I am,' she asserted, gazing at the forest before them. The slippery pathway had slowed them. 'And you should know we must call each other Citizen now, dear William, not Monsieur or Mademoiselle. The revolution demands it.' She pointed with her whip. 'The vineyard is just behind those trees and beside it the château where Pierre lives when he is working. The labourers live in it now. They are loyal people mostly. Il aime le penser. He pays them well and feeds them. All that matters is that the grapes are good and that the wine yields the same excellence.' She shook her head as if at a weary echo. 'The wine is his life's blood. But I do not know how much longer the vineyard can survive.'

He met her eyes, and saw that her cheeks had reddened with their talk. He took hold of her hand and kissed it. The warmth of her body came through the thin leather glove. She talked again about Pierre.

'The guilt from the drowning never leaves him. He was really quite devilish for a while, but Elizabeth helped him.' She held his gaze, her eyes filled with feeling. 'He knows that I want him to care for you . . .'

He checked his impulse to speak the words of his feelings, the words of his jealousy and fear. He was ashamed.

She looked downwards. 'You are such a grand creature, William.' She lifted her face and smiled. 'How can it be that I have only just met you, yet you have always been in my heart? Come – make speed! We are taking too long! Pierre will be happy to see you, I promise. The vineyard saves him. In the past there were many visitors, but the revolution has changed all that. The work continues, however, and that is all to the good, the workers are very busy this time of year and will be pruning frantically. The pruning has such an influence, you see, on the potential yield of the grapes, and finally the wine.' She talked on quickly as they went. 'The prunings are chopped and crushed then worked back into the soil. Nothing is lost. It is good that nothing is lost. Nothing good should be lost. He has always been proud of his wines.'

He might have been hearing about a kind of religious cere-mony, deeply intimate and threatening. It was a new feeling for him this ardour, the desire he awoke to each day. Her song returned to his mind. Had she loved and lost? Was that lover Pierre?

She glanced again at the sky, murmuring softly, 'How clear and untroubled the sky is, if only our thoughts were the same.'

He braced himself and sighed.

At the stables they chose their horses. But Anton, the groom, was nowhere to be seen and Annette felt anxious. The new groom was a stranger. 'No-one told us that Anton would not be with us,' she said to him sharply. 'Why were we never informed?'

'I do not understand,' the stranger said brusquely. 'Must you be informed?'

'But of course,' said Annette, frowning. 'You should have told Monsieur Pierre. Sometimes my nephew is here. Do you know Leon, the boy?'

The man was straightening her bridle. 'No, I have never seen him. And I did not think it necessary to tell Citizen Pierre that his groom had left for Paris.' His tone was cold and surly. 'I have taken over his duties for today. He will return at nightfall.' He turned from them then and pulled down a harness from the wall, polishing it with fast-determined strokes. Annette watched him warily.

'It will not do,' she said irritably, as they headed their horses to the Loire. 'His eyes are shifty. Anton is taking too many liberties, and he is far too much with the boy. I wonder if he has taken him somewhere today. Oh, my poor sister is lost!'

'Your sister's lover has caused her a lot of distress,' William said, as they rode slowly side by side. He tried to soothe her. 'The boy is probably safely at home and perhaps Anton has gone for provisions.'

'Yes, perhaps. But I think Pierre would have said so . . . And there is something else that bothers me . . .' She spoke quietly, still thoughtful. 'There was another stranger at the stables last week. He was talking with Anton, and they quietened their voices as I approached. I could not hear what they said. I believe he was a hotel proprietor from Orléans.'

'That's interesting,' said William pondering. 'I wonder if he asked about me.'

'Why would he ask about you?' She looked at him concerned.

'The hotel I was staying in had a very peculiar proprietor. I had a feeling I might be followed. The man didn't like me.'

'I shall ask Pierre what he thinks,' she said decidedly. 'We must guard against danger.' She spoke passionately and turned her eyes towards the great trees about them. 'We are riding through ancient oaks,' she said wistfully. 'When I was little I would ask Maman how an oak knew the way to reach through the sky in a way that was different from a pine. It is quite amazing I think. She talked to me about seeds, and told me the seed would know how its life must progress.' She shook her head as if amazed. 'Oh, the power of a simple seed and how uncomplicated their lives are.'

'Oh yes,' he laughed. 'The journey of a seed is magical.' The trees high above them were mighty. White light speared through their branches.

'We too are under a spell,' she murmured.

He stretched across and pulled on the reins of her horse, thinking he would lean to kiss her. – But just then there came a shriek from the top of a tree. They both looked up quickly.

'It is Leon!' she cried. 'See! – He is calling for help. And the branch is swaying!'

The boy clung to the branch. It creaked and was ready to break.

'Stay still!' shouted William. 'Don't move! – It's a strong bough that holds him,' he told her, as they both got down from their horses. 'It will not snap if he is still.' He threw off his frock coat and swung himself into the branches, climbing speedily.

The boy was right above him, lit by morning sunlight. 'Leon, use your arms!' he called, closing on the sobbing child. 'Stretch them and move like a snake! – Slowly, slowly. Yes, perfect!'

'Monsieur! Monsieur!' cried the trembling child, reaching for William's hand and weeping profusely. 'I tried so hard to be a snake.'

'And you *were* a snake,' said William, helping him down. 'You have done very well.'

Within minutes he fell into the arms of his bewildered aunt.

'How many times has Maman said not to climb the trees?' scolded Annette, white and emotional. 'Do you hear nothing? – Oh, my pet, you try us too hard!'

'Should we take him home?' asked William.

'Not now,' she sighed, drying the child's eyes with her handkerchief. 'He can come to the vineyard with us. The workers will calm him with their jokes.' The boy was recovering, though he breathed quickly and nervously. 'Where did you think you were going?' she asked. 'There is only the sky.'

'If a child can't imagine, who can?' said William, remembering his own days of freedom, when he had dared the heights of trees and rocks without the least fear of danger. He murmured as he buttoned his frock coat . . .

> *'Oh, when I have hung*
> *Above the raven's nest, by knots of grass*
> *And half-inch fissures in the slippery rock*
> *But ill-sustained, and almost (so it seemed)*
> *Suspended by the blast that blew amain . . .'*

'How do you find such words?' said Annette with wonder.

'How? I have no idea,' he laughed, as he helped fix the boy on the horse. And it sometimes unnerved him when lines of poetry came to him quickly eager to be written in his notebook. For a moment or two they were still, listening to the wind through the trees, the whisper of the water lapping the banks of the river.

'Will you write poems about France?' she asked him softly. 'I would like to think you will remember us with your poetry.'

He frowned. 'You speak as if I am leaving. I will not leave you, Annette, have I not said so?'

'You will,' she said with a shiver. 'You must.'

He too felt cold at the thought of returning to England and leaving her behind. She was right though, it was bound to happen. In the real world, that was. But not in the world of the mind, where so much happened for him outside of time and luxuriant with possibility, immense as eternity and fruitful as heaven. But *must* he leave her? Must he? Could he not stay? He was bold and brave when it came to mastering the elements, but fate was its own master, and he knew it would have its way.

'You *will* write poetry for us William, wont you?' she said hopefully.

He held her gaze, but he could not answer. It was important she wanted his poetry, her especially. But it was *her* he wanted, not his imaginings of her, but *her,* body and soul. Then he leapt up into the saddle, the boy seated before him.

'I promise you, Monsieur, I shall not worry the people who care for me again,' said Leon shakily.

'Don't make promises you know you can never keep,' said William, ruffling the child's hair.

They rode on slowly in the mild and pleasant weather. If Annette's family didn't find the boy an absorbing pastime soon he would land himself in serious trouble!

The early afternoon light shone lazily on the château ahead. At that moment, there came a chorus of voices from a nearby thicket. A small band of excited people emerged.

'Citizens, Citizens!' cried a man in long grey trousers, running towards them. 'See how the smoke rises from the vineyard! Ah, poor us. We might have been burnt to cinders!' The others frowned and whispered.

'What happened?' Annette asked anxiously. She strained her eyes to look.

The man talked on in a rush. 'Monsieur Pierre was in the cellars. – A crowd of visitors were following. – Then we heard a loud explosion. – Flames leapt through the cavern, high as the sky!'

'Not quite,' said a woman with long dark hair. 'We could hear Monsieur down the cave talking with the guests, then came some little explosions and a trail of smoke crept up the passage like a ghost. We hurried back and ran out.'

'And Monsieur Pierre?' asked Annette, looking alarmed.

'Monsieur Pierre is somewhere down the cave,' said the woman, turning to the vineyard.

'You left him?' cried Annette, in a tone of disbelief. 'How could you leave him?'

'There have been many fires in these parts,' shrugged the woman. 'Revolutionaries have razed so many châteaux to the ground. We were afraid. We are trying to live the old life as it was, but it seems the old life has gone. Now we have nowhere to go.' She bent her head and wept.

'Pierre ! Pierre!' cried Leon. 'What has happened to Pierre?'

'I fear he is dead,' said the man in the long grey trousers. 'The walls of the cave are collapsing. Oh, he must surely be dead.'

'I believe there is a door at the back of the cellars near the château,' said Annette. She looked at William desperately. 'It is used to take in the barrels.'

They set their horses to a gallop.

'You ought to have known better!' cried a middle-aged labourer to the distraught young man beside him. 'You are most irresponsible. And you do not know where the key has gone for that door, either. – Do you know anything?'

The young man berated was Alain, who stood looking miserable, his arm around the shoulder of his girlfriend. The girl wept loudly as they contemplated the heavy wooden door before them.

'You are paid good money,' said the older male worker. 'You ought to have checked the barrels, but all you do is make love to your girlfriend and neglect your important duties. Monsieur Pierre is probably a heap of ashes by now.' He glared at the door and clapped his hand to his forehead. 'How shall we break this citadel down?' His eyes searched about for something to aid them, and alighted on a large oak log resting by a wall. 'Brace yourself Alain!' he shouted. 'We must try to lift it!'

All three of them went to the log, gasping and shoving and heaving, but they could not budge it.

'We need to get some of the others,' said Alain, glancing about. Though the others were nowhere in sight. But for the prunings blowing about in the wind, the vineyard was silent.

'They are all in the château thieving,' said the girl flatly. 'What do you expect? – Oh Alain, what have you done?'

'What hasn't he done, you mean,' thundered the older male worker, scratching his head.

'It was just a mistake,' moaned Alain, finding somewhere to sit and covering his face with his hands. 'I forgot.'

'It was pure neglect,' said the older man exasperated. 'You did not check the temperature of the gases. Such checking is vital. Monsieur Pierre has told you so many times. – Why do you never listen?'

Alain sat down trembling.

'Let's run away,' said the girl, going to sit by his side. 'We can work somewhere else.'

Alain drew her towards him. 'We must try again with the log in a minute.'

For a moment or two they were all silent with fear. Then

they went again to the log, attempting to lift it. At that moment William and Annette came cantering into the vineyard.

'Where is Monsieur Pierre?' cried Annette, leaping from her horse.

'He is down in the cave,' said the girl, her voice trembling. 'We thought we might force the door with this, but it is far too heavy.'

William sized up the gathering, then the log they were trying to lift. It was part of the limb of a mighty oak, a dense and heavy piece of wood, but lift it they must. 'Together, I think we can move it,' he said hopefully.

'I can help too!' called Leon, jumping down from the horse.

They all bent down to the log, each of them finding a hold, and giving it the best of their strength. Then they ran at the door fiercely. – Once! Twice! And again! Until finally it screeched on its hinges and at last gave way.

Thin clouds of smoke rushed out at them as they made their way between the broken and spilled barrels, frantically searching for Pierre through the sweet smelling streams of wine.

At last they found him, moaning and coughing by a wall. A cascade of rocks had knocked him unconscious, he said. William knelt down and tried to allay his fears, telling him the maid had gone for a doctor and all would be well.

'I am still alive!' gasped Pierre, clutching at his throat. He shivered. 'Rubble has gone down the neck of my shirt. – Ah, it is cold!'

'That is the least of your worries,' said William. 'Now here, lean on my arm, we must get you across to the château.'

'My conversation with Alain will be *most* delicate,' moaned Pierre, still coughing. 'I know exactly what has happened. The man is in love, you see. He is out of his mind.' As they came to the light, he shaded his eyes with his hand. 'Is that Annette and Leon in the doorway?' he asked.

'It is,' said William.

Annette and Leon ran forward.

'I have one or two cuts and bruises, but I am sure nothing worse,' laughed Pierre as they fussed him. 'It was only a minor explosion.'

They made their way back to the château, where inside, Pierre sat down by the fire, and the maid pressed cloths soaked with healing balms against his cuts and bruises. 'Come here!' he shouted to Alain, who trembled in a corner with his girlfriend. 'You are not yet twenty and I give you such serious work. Who is the bigger fool? Monsieur Pierre, yes?' He gazed at the sad young man.

'Monsieur, Monsieur!' cried the girl. 'I am the one at fault. I yield to him all too easily. Now much of the wine has been lost, and your workers have disappeared with lots of nice things from your château. Oh, they are thieves!'

Pierre touched a cut on his brow and screwed up his face. 'Never mind. I have not been hit by a cannon ball, have I? And for that I am thankful.' He examined his injuries. His long dark hair, hung about his face, mixed with dust and little stones. 'My heart is glad that it beats just as before!' He turned to William and gazed at him gratefully. 'Thank you, my friend, you are brave.'

'He is! He is!' cried Leon bounding forward. 'Today he has saved me from the tree. I reached the top and must stay there forever if he had not climbed it and saved me. The branch had broken, and . . .' He bent his head and spoke in a guilty tone of voice. 'It was swinging and making noises . . . I would have fallen and shattered to pieces, just like the rocks in the cavern.' He covered his face with his small soiled hands and sobbed.

'But now you are safe with us,' said Annette. 'At least for now.'

'You have had something of a busy day, Mr Wordsworth' said Pierre, studying William carefully.

William blinked the dust away from his eyelids. 'Please call me William,' he urged. 'I would much prefer it.'

For a moment Pierre gazed at him thoughtfully then turned to the maid. 'Is there anything left in my kitchen or has every morsel been taken? If not, then bring some refreshments for my valiant friends.' He turned back to William and Annette. 'I have a great deal of work to catch up with now, and will need to stay longer than intended, but you are welcome to live at my château if you wish. I will be thankful. Aunt Elizabeth has gone to Rome and Paul has gone to Paris. Who else can take charge? Your family, Annette, will be grateful to William I think.'

Alain and his girlfriend were talking together about how to return the boy back to Blois. 'Poor child,' sighed the girl. 'How he has suffered.'

But Leon was biting into chocolate cake and had quite forgotten where he was. William and Annette found their horses and were soon on their way to Orléans.

11

Leaving For Blois

Returning to the château, they saw that Anton was back at the stables and the unfamiliar groom had left. Not a word did Anton divulge of his errand, nor did he greet them. Instead he stood staring at his lantern looking dejected. That something had happened was obvious, but as they grew near he looked away.

'More bad things are happening in Paris,' said Annette, as they walked to the front of the château. 'Anton was silent as the grave, and what fear there was in his eyes. He will no doubt talk to Pierre about it in time.'

'Anton doesn't trust me,' murmured William. 'He thinks I am spying for my country.'

She shrugged. 'Oh, I am not trusted either. He watches my movements constantly. I am a royalist. It is becoming increasingly difficult to visit Pierre's château. There are royalist spies, republican spies, spies everywhere you go.'

William brushed his hands down his clothes. Tiny pieces of rubble fell to the ground. They could hear the dogs from the stables barking loudly.

'The hounds are restless,' she said. 'The new groom has disturbed them; they are quite averse to strangers. And Anton's behaviour is baffling.'

'Climbing trees and wading through caves has given my clothes a thrashing,' laughed William. He saw that his frock coat was torn at the elbow. 'I had better go see that tailor you talked about for certain.' His eyes lingered on the dry stone wall as they arrived near the door of the château. 'The men in France make terrible dry stone walls,' he said thoughtfully. 'Do they not know that the earth must be excavated first before a single stone can be laid? Where are the bond stones? How can it battle the wind?'

'The wall finds a way,' she said, smiling. 'It has been there many years.' She gazed at the growing darkness. 'I do not think I can endure it . . .' she murmured wistfully.

'Endure it?' he whispered.

'Our love,' she said shakily.

He drew her close and kissed her.

'Our hearts will be broken,' she murmured.

Her words disturbed him. Was their love doomed to failure already? Moonlight lit her face as she spoke and he saw that her eyes were earnest. 'Come,' she said, taking his hand. 'I cannot see you for dust. We must wash it away.'

The maid was busily lighting candles when they entered. Seeing them arrive, she left and went to the kitchen. For a moment or two they embraced. As they went up the stairs, Annette bid her bring fresh towels and hot water to their rooms.

His room was warm and he fell into a chair by the fire and for a minute or two sat hesitant and troubled. His body felt vigorous and ready. Would she wait for him to come and find her, would she expect him, or would she lock herself away to avoid the inevitable heartache lying ahead? She had as good as suggested she might do so. Ought he to run from her now, run from her for good and save her? But his longing was fierce.

The maid came up and down bringing jugs of hot water

which she poured into the bowl in his room. He took off his clothes and washed, the light from the candles flickering on his naked limbs. He was young, strong and in love. And the love was urgent. He stood, the towel about his waist, contemplating the logs flaming in the fire. They would flame, grow cold and die. All things died. He opened the door and made his way down the corridor.

Seeing her door was ajar, he pushed it gently and saw that her stockings and corset were laid across a chair and she was washing. She sighed as he approached, and he watched with wonder as she sponged her beautiful body.

'How lovely you are,' he murmured. He turned her towards him and she pressed her lips to his chest, then with a heavy sigh of surrender gave herself up to his passion.

They loved heatedly for the whole of the next few days, scarcely eating, night merging into day and back to night. Then finding their way into the house again they discovered a note on the table left by Elizabeth. It contained her London address and suggested William might pay her a visit in Hampstead when he returned. He gazed through the library window dismayed by the fact that she believed his return was inevitable. But he had made Annette love him and the fire of their passion had burned into their souls and fused them together as one. He could not return to England now, not without Annette! But truth dictated different. Truth cared nothing for love. Elizabeth, wiser and older, had known this from the first.

Pierre had experienced a complete change of character since the explosion in the cellars at his vineyard. When he returned to the château he was more considerate, kinder, even courteous. He greeted them warmly when they met about the house, and endeavoured to see that all their needs were met. They had

contented and peaceful days, when Annette ran about barefoot
and happy, even kissing Pierre as he worked at his accounts.
He was constantly busy, reading political books and pamphlets,
writing and sending out letters. He had an admirable grasp of
German and English and kept track of important writings and
revolutionary developments. William would hear him talking in
feverish French with Annette in the library but it was all too fast
for his hearing. News grew worse by the day and Pierre grew
increasingly anxious. The revolutionaries were angrier than ever
as the king sought help from abroad. Pierre would meet with
strangers at the stables or outside the gates of the château and
might sometimes be gone for days, returning to read some newly
acquired pamphlet, all the time murmuring or cursing.

As he gazed outside, William saw that gardeners were cut-
ting the dead wood out of the shrubberies. Further beyond the
grounds, were the homes of poverty-stricken peasants, struggling to eke out a living, scavenging, begging, stealing and
seething with anger. He ought to take Annette to England he
thought, fall at her feet and beg her to depart from France, but
he knew she would never leave her family. He went to find
her in the hall. She was requesting a carriage be brought to the
gates and that a servant bring down her trunk. William had
been persuaded to live with her family, what he had done for
Leon had been noted. Paul had pleaded with his parents, Annette had sent letters and that day they were leaving for Blois.
But what would it be like for him, living with devout royalists?
And how would it be for them? He would certainly be outnum-
bered if he dared speak his mind. He might argue his opinions
with Paul at Pierre's château, but in Blois with her family it
would be different.

'And so you are about to desert me!' said Pierre, striding down
the hall. He stared at Annette's trunk and William's bags by the
door. 'You are all ready it seems. Je suis tout seul!'

William's frock coat had been washed and repaired by the maid and neatly packed away. He now wore clothes made by the tailor in Orléans, the clothes of an English gentleman. That is the way he would present himself to her family. 'You have become a dear friend,' he said to Pierre. They exchanged a heartfelt handshake.

Pierre looked at him straight. 'I give you my blessing, William. I recognise a soldier when I see one, and a soldier of life you are, as well as a poet. But you will not be content, my friend, until the sea of life has tossed and turned you, and delivered you wherever it will!'

They both glanced darkly at each other. Where would that sea deliver him, William wondered. He breathed in deeply, his eyes thoughtful. Pierre just then had the air of a sage, standing in the light of the window, his arms folded tightly. 'I've enjoyed staying in your home,' said William. 'And I shall miss our long conversations.'

'Likewise,' said Pierre. 'Such conversations are important. I do not visit the Vallon's nowadays. Our political ideologies are too far apart.' He nodded his head in a sad and final way. 'But you are mettlesome, William. And audacious too.' He looked downwards awkwardly. 'I know you must be with Annette. These matters have a life beyond us; through us they have their being.' He rubbed his face tiredly. 'It is sometimes unnerving.'

Annette pulled on her cloak, then lifted her gloves from a table by the door, drawing them on to her fingers thoughtfully.

'The coach is waiting by the gates,' said William. He touched her elbow gently.

'Françoise is still a little unstable, as you know,' sighed Pierre. 'I know she will fear you. But I doubt you will see her a lot.' He turned to Annette. 'It will be quite an event, my dear, when your father meets your English lover! – Ah, William, you will be entering a den of lions! The men in Annette's family are men of honour, however, and have great wisdom.'

'I have heard a lot about Jean and Charles,' said William. 'And I am warmly acquainted with Paul, of course.'

'I cannot emphasize enough,' said Pierre, staring at William with hard, penetrating eyes, that you manage your words carefully. You speak a different language; things can be misunderstood and misrepresented. Françoise has suffered a lot for her political opinions . . .'

'She is now back home,' Annette interjected. 'She is still unwell, but safe.' She gazed at William sadly. 'My sister voiced her thoughts recklessly, and was seized by a gang of revolutionaries. They took her to a house by the Loire and questioned her brutally. It was all because *he* had come back. No one is safe. It was all very chilling for Françoise. There is no real authority now. Who knows where our country is heading?'

The 'he' William decided was Françoise's lover, the man who had ruined her life.

'They are bound to spy on you,' Pierre said, looking concerned. 'You will be watched, known, and categorised. Though they have probably done that already. There are some strange comings and goings here. I can only caution you not to speak of your persuasions.' He pointed to William's pocket. 'And guard your notebook too.'

'And you?' said Annette, embracing Pierre. 'You will also be careful?'

'As far as I can,' he said firmly.

The trunk was taken to the coach and William picked up his bags. Within no time at all the coach was speeding down the hill. Pierre stood at the gates of the château until it was out of sight.

12

Living With The Vallons

A purple sky crowded with stars covered the city of Blois. William looked out on the night while Annette lay sleeping. Animals would be shifting about in the undergrowth; owls would be making their lonely calls through the woods. And men would be up drinking; angry at how their king had bankrupted France, how the new constitution was futile and at best a temporary affair. Many of the nobles had taken their grievances abroad. Others plotted civil war. Every level of society was on the alert. But William's concerns about life with the Vallons had eased. They had all found a way to get by, for there was much to endure for republicans and monarchists alike. He had now been with them a whole six months, and it was summer. Located by the Loire River, Blois was a fine place to live with beautiful charming terraces, long narrow streets and abundant woodlands. He and Annette had been happy that May walking through the grasses and wildflowers, blossoms scenting the air and the sound of songbirds in the trees. The family home was sunlight itself with pale lemon coloured walls, soft welcoming chairs and sofas that were good to relax in. Sometimes they argued. He never sank lower in spirit than when they argued. He could not count the number of times he had woken up in the night, wondering how to split himself in two? He needed to get back home, his presence was endangering Annette, but he needed to be with her as well.

The boy, Leon, still found his way to the château to while away time with Anton and the horses. He was rarely seen in the house. Françoise kept to herself. If ever William glimpsed her, she quickly averted her eyes and was soon away to her room, a pale ethereal figure suddenly emerging amongst them, then gone within seconds. Jean and Charles, both busy doctors, went about their business in silence, as did Annette's parents. They all worked out of the house. Paul was often in Orléans. Annette read and cooked and did other household tasks, while William wrote or went walking. He had written and sent letters to Dorothy but without an address for her to write to; she was bound to wonder where he was. He hadn't told her about Annette, not yet. He would when the time was right.

But he was sleeping badly. There was much he wanted to write, but committing his thoughts to paper made him uneasy with the constant fear of revolutionaries entering the house, turning it upside down, taking them away or even killing them. Both Girondins and Jacobins attended the Paris Jacobin club where he sometimes went to hear speakers and get word of latest events. "I do not fear the Girondins", Paul had declared. "They are moderates. But Robespierre . . . Robespierre, is different. He is a clever orator, but will not compromise. He thinks only of his own cause. How he achieves his ends doesn't matter, and the minds of the people bend to his will within minutes."

Annette slept soundly in their comfortable lovers' bed. He placed more logs on the fire, then turned to his writing. He'd a letter to finish to Mathews, a friend from Cambridge who he'd thought he might start a magazine with. The writing belonged to his life in England, a life that seemed in the past, yet a life he must somehow stay part of. Annette was stirring.

'Where are you?' she called to him softly. 'It is the middle of the night, my love, do come and sleep.' She climbed out of bed. 'My treasure, you are writing a letter. Will your mind never rest?' She went to him and clung to him like she always did at night-time. 'Was it the dream? Did it wake you?'

'No, no, not that,' he said, tiredly. He recalled the event from his youth, the dead schoolmaster suddenly rising from the water, his mouth agape as if in a silent scream. He had thought a lot about that scream. He had heard it often in his soul. And he heard it now in France. He put his arm around her waist and pressed his face to her breast. He loved Annette Vallon. And he'd followed her here to Blois, but it was selfish.

'Oh what is the use of trying to sleep when sleep evades us,' she said, throwing out her arms. 'Why not be awake in the darkness when the moonlight floods the bedroom, and sleep in the day when everything is so upsetting.' She knelt on the floor beside him, resting her head on his lap. 'Do you want me to turn against the king?'

He heard the tremor in her voice. In the still of the night her words had nowhere to go, they hovered ominously about them. He was anxious for her, she'd been brought up Roman Catholic, her conscience must serve her king. Most of the time she was total mistress of herself, other times she sought his advice, and he offered what he could. But he must always remember her allegiances. He could feel her trembling through her thin silk nightdress. What business had he to interfere with her allegiances, except he felt so strongly for the poor? Was it not possible for change to happen without bloodshed? Must there always be slaughter? England too was rife with political unrest. People were eager for reform, religious equality and better education. Burke's criticism of the French rebellion and Paine's writings on The Rights of Man had caused violent arguments in cafes and coffee houses, even fighting on the streets. The world was ripe for change.

He was slow to answer. By the light of the candle, he saw that her eyes were afraid. 'You must do as your conscience tells you,' he whispered. 'I loathe all violence, as you know, and I am just as opposed to brutal revolution as you are.' He poured her some water then watched her drink in silence. 'As regards England,' he continued. 'There is a need for a better civil policy . . . But my love . . .' His voice was quiet and serious. 'Governments led by monarchs and aristocrats are wrong.' He could hear her breathing softly.

Then she looked up sharply. 'You have been seen with Captain Beaupuy.' For a moment or two they were silent. She persisted, trembling slightly as she spoke. 'He is an aristocrat turned revolutionary. Who can know what his thoughts are. – Oh, William, there are royalists about who distrust him, and republicans too.'

For a moment they were both silent. 'So who is it spies on me?' he asked in a tone of surprise, frowning and looking at her straight.

'What does it matter, you have been seen. My brothers have friends.'

'Michel Beaupuy seeks fairness in all things,' William said irritably. 'A voice for the plain speaking poor, bread for the mouths of their children, clothes for their backs . . .' It annoyed him to think he'd been watched, and that his friendships were questioned. Michel Beaupuy, a captain in the Revolutionary Army, had energy and wisdom. William's mind went through the times they'd walked together in the woods, the times they had met at the Jacobin Club in Paris. There were bound to be spies in the shadows. Could he go nowhere? Could he say nothing? 'Must I always tell you who I talk with?' he asked gently.

She braced herself and went to stand by the window, looking out on the night. 'I know who you talk with already. And I know that you visit the Jacobin Club. My brothers know everything. Oh why do you go there? It will lead our enemies to this house.'

He sat down again by the desk and stared at the flickering candle.

'Do you go to the club with Beaupuy?' she asked, turning to him and waiting.

'What?' he said abstractedly. 'No, I go by myself. I can see Beaupuy whenever and wherever I like. We are friends, Annette. Beaupuy is an excellent man.'

'I do not want to dictate who you have for your friends,' she said wearily, covering her face with her hands. 'But can you not see how vulnerable we are? No-one trusts anyone now.'

He frowned, thoughtful.

'Will you continue to see him?' she asked. She gazed at him troubled.

William wrung his hands. 'I must. His thoughts are valuable and true. Such a mind is not often come by.'

'But does the captain know which side he is on? I am not so sure about that.' She shook a finger.

'There are many points of view,' William said flatly. 'Beaupuy considers all things. Our talks are pure in heart, and I do believe good will grow from them.'

'Will it?' said Annette, sternly. 'I do not know the answers to all this trouble. And what I am afraid of most is that no-one at all understands, not the king, not the queen, not Robespierre, not Danton, no-one. When people do not understand each other they fight, as if fighting will deliver the answers from seas of blood.'

Apart from the sound of the crackling fire, the room was silent.

'Your uncles suggest you take Orders?' she murmured. She glanced at him anxiously. 'Will you do so when your return?'

He straightened and breathed in deeply. 'So you think I will return, do you. Of course you do. I am powerless here, and if I stay I might very soon be dead.' He sighed. 'If I *do* return, I could find some work and offer you a life, Annette. . . . As it is, I am only a wanderer, trying my best to write poems.' He opened a drawer and drew out some papers, then laid them out on the desk. 'I thought I might try to sell these. They are only descriptive sketches. I wrote them walking the Alps. I thought they might start me off as a poet in England . . .'

She rubbed her arms. 'Oh let us not talk about England, William. Not now.' She shivered. He returned the poems to the drawer and closed it.

'I shall fetch us some food,' she murmured. 'Maman baked a cake today. We can eat some of that.' She crossed the room and went out.

He turned again to the letter he was writing to Mathews. He and Mathews had talked about starting a journal together, but when would they do it and how? They would need some money. He didn't think Mathews had much. He had money himself from Pierre, though that was sacred. He would need it to take care of Annette in the future. He didn't do much for her now. What did he do for anyone? He rubbed his face tiredly. They did not visit the château anymore or meet with Pierre. Apart from the tales Leon brought back, it seemed Pierre and his château had gone from their lives. He braced himself and stirred the fire. He was resolved. He would earn some money of his own in time and take care of Annette properly. He read through his letter again:

Dear Mathews,

When I look back on the length of time elapsed since my receipt of your last letter I am overwhelmed by a sense of shame which would deprive me of the courage requisite to finish this sheet . . . You have still the hope that we may be connected in some method of obtaining an independence. I assure you I wish it as much as yourself. Nothing but resolution is necessary . . . It is at present my intention to take orders in the approaching winter or spring. My uncle the Clergyman will furnish me with a title. Had it been in my power I certainly should have wished to defer the moment. But tho' I may not be resident in London, I need not therefore be prevented from engaging in any literary plan, which may have the appearance of producing a decent harvest . . .

You have the happiness of being born in a free country, where every road is open, where talents and industry are more liberally rewarded than amongst any other nation of the universe. You will naturally expect that writing from a country agitated by the storms of Revolution my letter should not be confined merely to us and our friends. But the truth is that in London you have perhaps a better opportunity of being informed of the general concerns of France, than in a petty provincial town in the heart of the kingdom itself . . . The horrors excited by the relation of the events consequent upon the commencement of hostilities, is general . . .'

He picked up his pen and wrote on quickly, then blotted the ink. He would fold it later and dispatch it as soon as possible. Annette came back in the room. 'I brought some wine,' she said, in the voice of her sleep. She settled the tray on the desk and lit more candles and they talked on quietly. She talked of how she had wept when they'd brought back the king and queen after trying to escape. 'And the children, the poor children, their feet were so tiny, such sad, sad little shoes . . .'

He glanced outside. The trees through the window grew silver with the light of dawn.

'Oh, I know you are longing for home,' she said as the fresh new light found them. You speak of your sister and brothers . . . I know how you miss them . . .'

The shakiness in her voice hurt him. Tears glistened in her eyes.

'I loathe this revolution,' she said. 'If you had seen the faces of my brothers when they heard of the fall of the Bastille, you would never have forgotten their expression. Next morning they were dumb. I went for Françoise and she made loud noises in their ears to try to dispel their madness. It was such a terror to us all. My brothers knew what would come.'

Her shawl slipped from her shoulders and fell to the floor. He retrieved it and replaced it gently. 'Do not distress yourself so,' he said, drawing her close. 'We must enjoy what we can of the present and try to stay calm.' She pressed his palm to her mouth, murmuring how she loved him. Then she looked at him fearfully. 'What is it?' he asked frowning. All the tenderness he felt for her rushed to the fore.

She slipped to the floor and leant her back against the wall. '*I am pregnant,*' she whispered, wrapping herself in her arms. 'I have wanted to tell you, but . . .'

For a moment they were both silent. He crouched beside her and kissed away her tears, all the time murmuring how wonderful her news was and how happy he would be to have a child. 'Let us not think of sadness now. This is a time for rejoicing.' He looked at her as if with other eyes. Annette would be a mother. He would be a father. They would become a family of three. 'This room is chilly,' he said, glancing about. 'I need to put more logs on the fire. Are you cold? Are you well?'

'I do not fear for my health,' she said, suddenly smiling. 'I am well as can be.' She placed her hands on her middle. 'Whatever happens, I shall always have a part of you here. Each time I look at my child, I shall think of its father. This way I shall never forget you.'

'*Hush,*' he said, holding her close. 'You make our parting sound permanent. I shall have to return to England, of course, but I'll be back with the speed of a comet – I promise!'

She pressed her palm against his mouth. 'Stop, don't speak! The wars will continue for years. I have talked about it with my brothers. There are terrible times ahead. We have been very foolish.'

'No, no, I will not hear of it,' he protested, his lips on her ear. 'What we have done has come from the wildness of our hearts. What could be better than that?' He lifted her up in his arms and took her to the bed. Then he lay beside her and held her until she slept.

13

A Gunshot Sounds in the Forest

No-one spoke of the pregnancy and William and Annette enjoyed their secret as they went out walking by the river. But William and the family had one common root; they all loved Annette and it gave them strength and cohesion. He was fully aware however, that he must make some important decisions, letters had to be written, things must be done. The old political beliefs and faiths were in ruins, the name of Paine and what he stood for sped through France like lightning, while in England his writing caused torrents of anger as evermore scorn was poured on the government through affordable and accessible pamphlets. In England his enemies burned effigies of him and he was chased for treason. The Vallon family passed anything that came their way to William and Annette. Passages by Paine were becoming increasingly familiar and William knew several by heart. Close to his thoughts one of them entered his mind out riding that day, and he spoke the words out loud, emphasized it seemed by the clopping of his horse's hooves:

"If to expose the fraud and imposition of monarchy, and every species of hereditary government—to lessen the oppression of taxes—to propose plans for the education of helpless infancy, and the comfortable support

of the aged and distressed—to endeavour to conciliate nations with each other to extirpate the horrid practice of war—to promote universal peace, civilization, and commerce—and to break the chains of political superstition, and raise degraded man to his proper rank—if these things be libelous, let me live the life of a Libeler, and let the name of Libeler be engraven on my tomb."

A powerful affirmation, thought William, as he made his way back to Blois. He had been to the Jacobin Club and burned with the intensity he always felt after listening to revolutionary politics. Some lines of poetry he'd been trying to write that week came to him again and he murmured them as he went:

> *'The world is too much with us . . .*
> *Getting and spending, we waste ourselves . . .*
> *We do not see in Nature what is ours . . .*
> *We have given our hearts away . . .'*

Not quite, he thought, not quite. He didn't have hold of it yet. He would have it though in time; he knew the poem was there. With a guilty sigh, he braced himself as he slowed his horse to a trot nearing Annette's home on the edge of the forest. As he'd dressed at dawn, he'd told her he was going to see the tailor in Orléans, a pocket needed mending on his frock coat. But she would know the truth anyway. He'd intended to visit the Jacobin Club, of course. Artisans, tradesmen and nobles gathered there to talk and Annette was right to feel anxious. But he needed to hear at source the climate of the times, not just the words of her brothers. That day he'd listened to Maximilien de Robespierre, the most fervent deputy in attendance, and much distrusted by Annette. Robespierre, his enemies maintained, epitomized the most evil potential there was in the Jacobin movement. It was important to hear what he said, thought William, and judge for himself; hearsay was often ambiguous. He was a small unimposing fellow, though immaculate in dress and manner, and greatly admired for his eloquence. His caring, sympathetic tones, when mixed with his angry certainties, could reduce a gathering to silence, and it seemed then as if the whole world was his own. Many who followed his doctrines found him exciting and respected him, while others loathed him, keeping their own counsel, until they could set their horses' manes to the wind, to repeat his latest allocution with whatever embellishments they might think of. Was it not right, William asked himself, that he heard what the man had to say just as he said it? Did Annette not want him informed? By such considerations he rationalised his covert behaviour. He was trying to think things through. He would return to England come autumn – though only for a brief visit – and he'd ensure before leaving that Annette was safe and hopeful. Once he'd reached England, he would seek out some writers in London and familiarise himself with the latest books and essays. Perhaps he would visit Mathews and see if they could start that journal. And he would visit Dorothy and Richard, though it was bound to be difficult if he wanted to talk about Annette. He sighed at the thought. He had written to Dorothy of the way things were, but as he'd folded the letter, he had feared it might never reach her. He'd made his decision though now, he would not, could not, take Orders, and had said so. She could tell his uncles if it suited. She could tell them whatever she wanted. He would make a living one way or another and support Annette and his child, but he would not make a living through the church. He would dedicate himself to poetry, for it held his impassioned life and what he knew to be his heartfelt destiny.

It was late afternoon. He watched the moths fluttering about him, softly descending and rising in the evening air. Then all of a sudden, he caught sight of a man striding fast through the undergrowth nearby. Wearing the tricolour cockade, his hands in his pockets, his sword swinging in its scabbard, he saw it was Michel Beaupuy!

William alighted from his horse quickly and led it into the woodland, calling as he went. 'Captain Beaupuy! Captain Beaupuy! I spotted you from just over there. I was riding!'

'Ah, my friend, did you? I am all too easily spotted! It is a problem. I came to relax in the woodland, but now I have lost my horse.' He glanced about worriedly.

They were almost on the path leading to the Vallon's château. But Beaupuy turned to look back into the depths of the forest.

'I had hoped to speak with you this morning,' said William, 'but you left the club quite early.'

'I did. It was Robespierre! That man gives me a headache. His voice is so loud.' Beaupuy glanced through the trees and along the pathways. 'I thought my horse was safely tethered, but I fear the beast has escaped me.' He stroked his chin thoughtfully. 'Or perhaps it was taken by a thief, no?'

They both gazed about. Nothing but the trees swaying and whistling in the light evening breeze came to them. 'My horse will need food and water,' said the captain. 'It has galloped a lot today.'

'It has probably escaped its tether,' said William trying to see through the trees. 'Please let me help you find it.' He pulled on the reins of his horse and led it along; it was a good, compliant beast.

'These trees are so alive in the wind,' said Beaupuy. 'Listen to their voices. They speak of the past and the future. Oh, what is the future for France?'

William felt at one with this man as they made their way through the undergrowth and underneath the tall trees, talking of what they had heard at the club and the way the revolution was unfolding. The woods were sleepy from the warmth of the day as they walked along the winding pathways, wandering through thick vegetation and pulling back stubborn branches. Apart from the snorting of William's horse, all was silent about them. They went on further through ferns and streams, passing by beautiful châteaux, stopping to contemplate the significance of so much wealth and how it might have been acquired.

'When I look at all this,' said Beaupuy, casting out his hand, 'I am ashamed. I have never known want in my life, except the want of peace of mind when I know that others are starving. The faces of the poor, the terrible hunger in their eyes makes me angry. And when fathers thrust out their hands, and lower themselves to their knees to beg, my heart fills with despair!'

Just then they came upon a girl sitting by a tree with a heifer tied to a branch. The beast grazed while the girl sat trying to knit. She lifted her head sorrowfully and her sunken eyes searched their faces. 'It is against that, we are fighting,' said Beaupuy quietly. He put his hand in his purse and threw some coins to the girl, who thanked him profusely then sang a little song, which he welcomed graciously. 'There are many children like that,' said Beaupuy sadly. 'These forests are a revelation. What a pleasure it was to see that shine in her eyes, and all for one or two coins.'

William thought about the coins hidden in his room. He had often thought he should pass them on to the poor. But wouldn't gold coins attract attention, and what of his responsibilities?

'I will not let this war harden my heart,' said Beaupuy, straightening and touching his sword. From a nearby thicket came the sound of breaking twigs. 'My horse!' he exclaimed. 'I think I have found my horse!' They both moved fast, but the horse was nowhere in sight. 'Imagination is a wonderful thing!' he laughed as they carried on walking.

'Indeed it is,' said William. Then he spoke about Dorothy his sister in England and how he was missing her news. He spoke of his brothers. And he told Beaupuy about the baby.

121

'Good, good,' Beaupuy said kindly. 'You will soon be a father. There is much to celebrate in that. Death is so often with us, new life is inspiring. The wars will cease, then there will be peace and we can live. Life and liberty, is what we fight for.' He bent his head. 'Alas, there are swine who think different.' They walked on slowly. 'You have brothers,' said Beaupuy, gazing down at the thick grass at their feet. 'One is a lawyer, another a scholar, you say, and the third sails the seas. Ah, to have brothers like that.'

'Yes,' William said quietly. He sighed. 'I have very fine brothers and an excellent sister too.' For a moment or two they were silent. 'The talk at the Jacobin Club is stirring,' he said finally. 'I have seen today how so many are influenced by Robespierre.'

'Ah, yes,' said Beaupuy. 'He is a forceful fellow. There is a need for clear thinking however or our thoughts run amok.'

'You are right,' murmured William. There were people, he decided, who nurtured you and helped you grow, they were just like water and sunlight, nourishing the roots of your being. Beaupuy was one of those people. 'My uncles are not too pleased with me writing poetry.'

'Is that so?' The captain was thoughtful.

William shrugged. 'More or less.'

'You are creative, my friend,' said Beaupuy. He looked at William thoughtfully. 'God is shining in your eyes.'

William smiled at that. God shining in his eyes! 'I am all talk and writing. I don't really *do* very much,' he said awkwardly.

'But is writing not *doing*?' said Beaupuy, raising his eyebrows. 'The writing of Thomas Paine is highly respected in France.' He dropped his voice. 'Not Burke, of course. Though the man has helped abolish slavery and has aided many reforms, so why does he turn on the people of France who are only fighting for liberty?'

'He sees it as rebellion. He thinks it will end in disaster.' William sighed as he spoke.

'Ah,' said Beaupuy, nodding. 'He believes it is not thought through. It is important to think things through.'

He looked at Beaupuy searchingly.

'Emotions must be governed too,' said Beaupuy. He gazed at the sky as if questioning his own words. 'Must everything be governed, even our souls? So how shall we govern our souls, then?'

'Such interesting notions,' William murmured. He knew he could be reckless and fanciful. Now in the company of Beaupuy, who could magically transform what seemed like faults into virtues, his life made sense.

They found they had walked full circle. But the captain's horse was still missing. They were now on the edge of the forest, and Annette's home could be seen through the trees. 'Here, take my horse,' he said decidedly. 'I am almost home. I can walk.'

'I thank you, my friend,' said Beaupuy, staring at the obedient silent animal. 'I have a long way to travel.'

'Do the people at the club think me odd?' asked William, as he handed the reins to the captain. 'After all, I am a stranger, and easily identified as English.'

Beaupuy's eyes grew serious. 'They look at you strangely it is true. And I am sure you will be discussed. We are all talked about.' He made a gesture at the trees. 'Any tree in this forest might harbour a fiend with a pistol; we must always be watchful. There is much to be learned at the Jacobin Club. It is good to visit, though it is mainly the bourgeoisie who attend. There are other gatherings, of course, but they are held in secret. You will not be able to join them. They print and issue pamphlets. You will never know their whereabouts, given that you live with royalists.'

'Do they know that I live with royalists?' William spoke with surprise.

'Royalists are watched constantly. Many people hate them. The wealthy will do anything to keep their money in their pockets and the poor are right to be incensed, but we must not let the people turn into a mob, it can all too easily happen. We fight for the good of the poor that they might have a better existence.'

They crossed a bridge and walked on further for another few minutes. Then through the silence there came the sound of a gunshot. Beaupuy staggered forward, clutching his chest and groaning. 'God, I am done for! They have killed me!'

William dropped down by his side. He could hear the captain gasping and struggling for breath. Blood seeped quickly through the captain's fingers as he grasped the front of his tunic. 'At least it has missed my heart,' he moaned. 'The bullet has lodged in my ribs. I feel its hardness.' He strained to raise himself up.

'Don't move,' said William. 'You are bleeding badly.' His eyes searched ahead frantically. They were minutes from Annette's home. 'We are close to the house where I live; once we are there you will be safe.' He bid Beaupuy take his arm, and the obedient horse followed.

'*Safe* in the house of royalists?' moaned Beaupuy.

'They are good people,' William insisted. He took the weight of the captain's frame on his shoulder and they struggled onwards.

'I know this place,' said Beaupuy, as they arrived. 'I have seen the Mademoiselles who live here. Think carefully, my friend, for what you do now you may regret.'

William saw that Annette watched by the window. 'The captain!' she cried despairingly, opening the door. 'What happened?' Together they helped him inside and he fell on his back on the chaise longue, clenching his teeth in pain. 'Jean is upstairs' she whispered. William saw that she trembled. 'The man is so pale,' she said, 'it is a wonder there is any more blood in his body, he has lost so much.'

'Annette, why are you dawdling?' William said urgently. 'Go bring Jean!'

'Do you not know what it means to bring Captain Beaupuy to this house?' she whispered, turning her face to the stairs. The captain shivered deliriously, his eyes rolling. She went to the kitchen for cloths and bandages, then water to bathe his face with.

'The blood runs slower than before,' said William, noting it no longer seeped through the tunic, 'though he breathes less well. Please, Annette, do bring Jean. I beg you.'

'You are censured enough, my love,' she said, her voice trembling. 'Who can know of this man's intentions, his real allegiances?'

'Stop,' moaned Beaupuy, putting out a hand. 'Mademoiselle, I am no-one's enemy. I only seek justice.'

She opened his tunic and laid damp cloths against his ribs where the flesh was ravaged by the bullet. In the light of a nearby candle, the bullet glistened liked a jewel. 'It will have to come out,' she murmured. At that she took to the stairs and returned with the doctor on her heels.

Still as stone, Jean stood silent before them.

'It is Beaupuy,' said William. 'The captain was shot in the forest. Someone has tried to kill him.'

Jean went to him quickly. Beaupuy was becoming unconscious. William and Annette watched tensely.

'I am sorry,' William murmured. All the guilt he had felt that day was upon him. He had lied. He had betrayed Annette. But Beaupuy's life might be saved!

Jean looked at them confused. 'He has a deathly pallor,' he muttered. 'I do not think I can save him.'

'This man cannot die,' William insisted quietly.

Silently, Jean braced himself and rolled his sleeves to the elbow, then he glanced at William and Annette. 'The bullet is lodged in a dangerous place, it will be hard to . . .' He shook his head confounded. 'Raise him a little. He must breathe normally.'

William did as instructed.

The doctor talked on urgently. – 'Annette, fetch me my surgical tools from that desk. – I shall need a scalpel and forceps, and the catgut I keep in the drawer in my bedroom. – Bring everything!'

Annette went to the desk for his tools, then ran upstairs for the catgut.

'I need scissors to cut off this tunic,' Jean told William. 'And I shall need disinfectant too. – There is carbolic acid in the kitchen. – And the alcohol there on the dresser, get that.'

William brought scissors, and the doctor cut into the tunic, the scissors sliding through the blood soaked cloth, rasping where it had stiffened. The captain opened his eyes for a moment looking dazed. 'I shall try to remove the bullet,' said Jean.

'I thank you,' the captain said faintly. He grasped Jean's hand for a moment, then fell unconsciousness.

'Hold down his shoulders,' Jean said to William. 'He must be still.' He looked at his surgical instruments then arranged them quickly on a low table beside them. 'Annette, pass them as I point.'

After ten excruciating minutes he pulled the offending metal free, then knotted the last of the stitches. William and Annette watched in traumatised silence as the doctor examined the bullet in his forceps then dropped it into a dish. Colour rose fast into the captain's cheeks. Jean fell into a chair and sighed. 'Now we can relax.'

The terrible drama had now drawn to a close and they all fell silent. Annette gathered the pieces of blood soaked tunic. 'I shall burn them,' she murmured.

Jean nodded in agreement. 'He must stay where he is. We cannot move him.'

'But what shall we do?' said Annette. She looked down worriedly at the pieces of blood stained tunic in her hands. William gazed at the captain; it had been a traumatic afternoon.

'What's done is done,' said Jean. 'The fibrous tissues must knit together firmly, that will take some time, after that the captain can leave.' He washed his hands. 'But where can he go?' He looked perplexed, gazing out through the window.

'He will return to his regiment,' said Annette, throwing the pieces of tunic on the fire.

'But not so soon,' frowned Jean. 'The wound will take time to heal. We must hide him somewhere.'

For a moment or two they were thoughtful.

'He can live with Pierre,' Annette said straightening. 'Once he feels better, we can take him. Neither Jacobins nor Girondins will know where he is.' She met her brother's eyes then lowered her voice. 'For now we must move the chaise longue to a darker part of the room where the captain can rest and recover. Few people call on us nowadays. We can tell the family tonight when we are assembled, but no-one outside this house must know.' She turned to William. 'We can ride to Pierre's tonight and speak of our plans. I know Pierre will take care of him.'

Jean took the bullet in his fingers, then rested it in the palm of his hand, before dropping it back in the dish with a clink. The captain was breathing softly in what seemed like a profound sleep.

14

An Ending And A New Beginning

It was dark when they arrived at the château, William solemn and subdued, Annette fearful and anxious, Anton curious as to why they should visit at nightfall. But not a single word did he say as he dealt with their horses. Henriette, Pierre's maid, noting their late arrival had wondered at the strange proceedings. She had worked for Pierre's family since her teenage years, married, borne a son, suffered her husband's death from consumption, and lived in rooms at the back of the château for twenty-five years. It had been a successful arrangement and she had seen Pierre through many difficult times. She had seen him practise how to swordfight, watched him handle a pistol, and had enjoyed seeing him grow in knowledge at the Sorbonne. In the old days she'd gathered wild flowers from the banks of the Loire with his sister Clarisse, drawn them and pressed them, simple little pleasures she'd missed. To Henriette the château was home and she had known the family intimately. The death of Pierre's parents and sister had been a bitter blow for them all. It had been a comfort to have his Aunt Elizabeth's presence during those painful years, and it had been good to see Pierre grow strong. But the drowning still troubled him, and he gave the spirits of his family no peace, sometimes walking the house after midnight, when he would enter the library mumbling into the darkness as if trying to invoke their beings. After something like an hour, he would make his way back to bed, oblivious to it all next day. Of late though, his mind had been calmer, and the presence of William had helped him. Pierre had fought the burden of his pain, and it seemed he had profited from that. He was lighter of heart and less intense.

Henriette had risen just after daybreak that morning. It was now getting on for a week since Mademoiselle Vallon and Monsieur Wordsworth's visit. Why was Monsieur Pierre asking to see her? He had requested her presence in the library, he must speak, he'd said, about "a matter of great importance". It was most mysterious. Apart from herself and Pierre, there was no-one else in the house; the girlish young maid and her husband, the cook, had gone to Orléans for candles. It was a wet September day. Rain lashed on the windows and the branches of the trees in the grounds hung low and tired.

'We must shelter a very special guest,' Pierre said firmly, as he stood looking out from the library. 'He has been most unwell, and needs to go where no-one can find him until he is better.'

'Of whom do we speak?' said Henriette, standing on a stool and dusting a heavy chandelier. Whoever it was Pierre wanted to hide, the only safe rooms in the château were those in the East Wing. 'Monsieur', she said, still dusting, and in a quiet, measured tone of voice. 'You know where your safest rooms are, but do you want to use them?'

Pierre sat down and sighed. Henriette waited. There was a softer note in his voice now when he spoke about the East Wing. Two rooms lay behind the large oak door, one had been the bedroom of his parents and the other had been that of his sister Clarisse. Neither of the rooms had been touched since the drowning, and Pierre had tried to forget them. After so many years of neglect, Henriette feared they would be running with mice and insects. 'Monsieur,' she ventured quietly. 'Perhaps I should do some cleaning?' She waited. Only now, with the arrival of the poet from England and the attachment between him and the beautiful Annette, had the château begun to raise itself out of the earth and breathe new life. 'Monsieur Pierre . . .' she continued, this time a little bolder. 'Is it time to let in the daylight? The East Wing has been dark so long . . .' Still Pierre sat thoughtful.

'Yes,' he said, finally. Then he rose quickly from his chair with decision. 'One of those rooms will be for Captain Michel de Beaupuy! You see, someone has tried to kill him. He understands the fears of aristocrats and also champions the poor. For that he is sometimes distrusted. But he hopes the revolution will bring about a fairer society. We have to take care of him, Henriette, the man is important.' He went to a drawer in his desk and took out a key. Rain lashed hard on the windows. Lightning struck through the sky. Henriette straightened the drapes and dusted some books. 'The captain was shot in the forest and is coming here to recover,' said Pierre frowning and biting lip. 'We shall have to be careful . . .'

'Careful as a squirrel hiding a nut,' said Henriette, her tone serious as a prayer. She watched as he stroked the key with his finger. 'I wonder if your sister's drawings have faded,' she said abstractedly. 'I remember our pleasure as we pinned them up on the walls.'

'Yes,' he murmured. 'I remember it too. Come Henriette, let us go look.'

Henriette followed him in silence. There was much artistic talent in Pierre's family. She had often been amazed by the way his aunt might decorate a purse or a garment with the tiniest of coloured beads.

'I do not know if I am strong enough for this,' said Pierre shakily as they went together down the corridor.

'Monsieur, you are the strongest of men,' Henriette insisted, her duster clasped in her hands. They had come it seemed to a crossroads. Pierre gazed at the key in his fingers, then they looked at each with resolve.

'It is time,' Henriette said softly. She watched him as he turned the key in the lock and blinked the moistness from her eyes. 'I shall need you to help me with the windows, Monsieur, for they are bound to be stiff. We must open them to let in the air.'

They entered the purple room first. The musty odour of the past met them as they trod across the dusty carpets towards the long wide windows. Their glass was grimy, their curtains half perished. Pierre tore them down then rubbed the flat of his hands across the windows, thick with grease and dirt, the heavy rain clattering and streaming down the glass. The panes would need a thorough cleaning. They sneezed as they went about the room, lifting books and cushions that had lain there for years. Then they opened wardrobes and drawers. 'Dust, dust, everywhere dust!' he shouted, laughing. There was much to do, much to dispose of and much to save and love.

Next came another door, this time unlocked. As he turned the handle the door slid open to reveal a bundle of dolls on the floor, a small table and chair where a child might sit and play, a neatly made bed and a small selection of books in a bookcase by the window. A rocking horse seemed to be rocking slowly by a wall.

'It is only the pressure of our footsteps on the floor, Monsieur,' said Henriette, seeing Pierre was emotional.

There, on the wall by the bed, was a drawing made by his mother of Clarisse as a child. He reached for it and kissed it, his lips taking shape in the dust. For a moment or two he sat on the bed whispering his sister's name. *'Clarisse, Clarisse,'* he murmured, staring at the picture. 'You have gone beneath the waves with our parents – yet I feel you now, just as if you were here.'

Henriette, strong with purpose, stood resolute in the morning light, contemplating all about her. It would take a while to clean the rooms. The carpets would have to be scrubbed; fitting new ones might draw attention, the curtains would have to be replaced, and the bedding too, must be renewed. And the same would happen to the room awaiting the captain. She would enlist the help of the cook and his wife. 'Lazy old Time,' she whispered. 'Why has it taken so long for this day of deliverance?'

Pierre dragged the moth-eaten bedclothes from the beds, opened the drawers of the dressers and examined their contents, murmuring the names of the sadly departed as he went. Henriette braced herself ready for what came next and held back her tears. The dead could never return, except in those tenderly beautiful moments of dreams when the mind brought strength. They had opened the windows wide to the rain, that brought its sweet healing grace. The day was capable of great, magnanimous things!

15

Departures

Beaupuy had been at the château almost a month. 'Je dois partir!' he cried. 'I think I am going insane!' He'd spent a lot of his time reading books, or else gazing out on the grounds and forests from the windows. Fully recovered, he was fit and restless for his regiment, exercising every morning in his room, flexing his arms and jogging on the spot.

William had returned to his room at the château for there were deep concerns for his safety. On one occasion, he and Annette had returned to her home to find it bestrewn with their belongings. Many precious items had been stolen, including William's bag of coins. "It is as well we were out," Annette had reflected gloomily. "The loss of the money and a few valuable ornaments is nothing. Now though, my love, you must leave this house quickly." She had urged him to go to Pierre's château straight away. "Must we be robbed of everything?" he'd replied vehemently. "There is no other way," she'd answered despairingly. And she'd moaned for a while about the sad future of their child. "I shall come whenever I can, but we must not draw the least attention to the château."

During the time he'd lived with the captain they'd had many interesting discussions. Beaupuy had explained his way of thinking and how he had reached his opinions. And it seemed to William, there was a kind of divine balance in the way the captain's injury had brought Pierre to examine the wound in his soul and allow it to heal. A new found energy had flooded the house. As the colourful autumn leaves fell about the grounds with slow, peaceful movements in the glistening September light, the evils of war seemed distant and William had tried to write poetry. Though the terrible crack of the gunshot in the woods was very much alive in his mind, and he listened with Beaupuy each day for unaccustomed sounds. Today Beaupuy had ventured to join him in the library. He pointed through the window curiously. 'The rider who goes through the forest,' he said, 'he is heading for Paris, no? Do you know who it is?'

William knew very little about the comings and goings at the château, only witnessing Pierre dashing out to the stables and returning breathless. 'Strangers come constantly and leave without Pierre's knowledge,' said William. There were days when the cook left with Anton, returning the following day, though he had no idea where they went. But he trusted Pierre's discretion when it came to the captain's safety.

'Do I stop you from doing your work?' Beaupuy asked frowning. 'You are writing a poem?' He bent his head and looked in. 'Do you write of your lovely Annette?'

William sighed. 'No, I cannot. It troubles me to think of Annette. I hope she is safe. Revolutionary enemies are confused because of our love. Politics would tear it to shreds. He spoke quietly. 'Each minute I want to find a horse and gallop to Blois.'

'She is an excellent woman,' sighed the captain. He clasped his hands behind his head and stretched out his long legs. 'She has helped save my life. I will not forget.'

For a moment or two they were silent.

'I have felt free and happy in this house,' Beaupuy, continued, glancing about sadly. 'But duty calls me.' He gazed at William's writing. 'This writing you do — is it good?'

William gazed down at his work. 'I hope it is good eventually, just now it is only a fragment. The rest will come to me in time.' He spoke languidly. He was feeling quite desperate. Would he ever make money from his poetry? Would he ever even write it?

'When the poem is ready to be born, it will enter the world,' laughed Beaupuy. 'Just as a child grows in its mother's womb, the poem grows in the mind.'

'I think so,' William said tiredly. 'It can be quite frustrating.' The richness of his soul felt captive. He knew there were forces within him eager for freedom. He sat wringing his hands, anxious and irritable.

'Ah,' said Beaupuy. 'Your words are seeds waiting to be watered by your pen.'

'Oh yes,' said Pierre, entering. 'William's poems seed in the soil of his mind and are given life by his pen. It is a wonderful thing!'

'You have read these pieces?' said Beaupuy, looking at Pierre curiously.

'Some of them,' said Pierre. He gazed outside thoughtfully, looking towards the forest.

'You can read this English poetry?' said Beaupuy, astonished. 'I cannot do it myself; my English is far too poor.'

'Yes, I can read it,' said Pierre, over his shoulder. 'And for that I am grateful. But I have worked very hard at my English. My Aunt Elizabeth, of course, has always been helpful.'

'I saw you were reading English politics earlier today,' said Beaupuy. 'I am much impressed by your learning.'

'I do my best,' said Pierre, moving to join them at the table.

'And what do you write today?' asked Beaupuy, looking at William.

'There will be little poetry where the captain is going,' said Pierre, rubbing his eyes tiredly. 'Your writing will offer him solace. Let us hear it now on this bright September morning. – Speak the stirrings of creation!'

William stared down at his words. 'It is a part of something much longer,' he said. 'It wanders my mind but I haven't yet found it. It is called *An Evening Walk.*' He raised his face and saw that their eyes were waiting.

'Come, come, let us hear it,' said Pierre, casting out his arm as if the very room might listen.

William looked at them by turns. Moments like this were moments of pure exaltation. It was always good to read his poetry to those who were mindful. He lifted the page to the light and began:

> 'Fair scenes, erewhile, I taught, a happy child,
> The echoes of your rocks my carols wild:
> The spirit sought not then, in cherished sadness,
> A cloudy substitute for failing gladness,
> In youth's keen eye the livelong day was bright,
> The sun at morning, and the stars at night,
> Alike, when first the bittern's hollow bill
> Was heard, or woodcocks roamed the moonlight hill.'

"The moonlight hill!'" cried Beaupuy, clapping his hands. 'You can think of a moonlight hill in such dark and terrible times? How is it done?'

William smiled. 'It seems like a sort of game doesn't it. But I assure you it isn't. It's more like divine revelation I think.'

Pierre and the captain sat silent, thinking on the verse. Finally, Beaupuy sighed. 'You write of stars and moonlight, and the sounds of Nature. But I wonder if poems can really help us in wartime.' He shook his head and put his hand to his chest. 'It would be good to think so. But while we are thinking on a poem, might not a bullet enter our heart or a sword our back?'

For a moment or two, apart from the sound of a flock of birds rising from the grounds of the château, the library was silent. William gazed down at the verse. He hoped his poems might help transcend the horrors of wartime. Poetry might be powerless in times of conflict like these indeed. But where was the poetry of justice? Where was the poetry of truth, the poetry of love? Pierre and Beaupuy talked anxiously in heated French. Presently Beaupuy turned to him.

'My dear William, I have been too long away from my regiment.' He braced himself and sighed.

'They are defending the frontier on the Rhine,' said Pierre. 'I know these things from Anton.'

'Anton knows I am here?' said Beaupuy, looking alarmed.

'He knows of your bravery. Anton is a bold intermediary.' He looked at William. 'I know that you and Annette distrust him, but believe me when I tell you he is loyal. We are living through terrible days and a man must be brave enough to see them from every angle.' He turned his attention to the captain. 'You will leave tomorrow. You have a new uniform made by our tailor in Orléans. He too can be trusted. Henriette will bring it to your room tonight. I am giving you my best horse, and anything else you require.' Pierre looked at him sadly. 'This house will miss you, my friend.'

At dawn next day, William went to the library. Pierre was preparing a parcel for Beaupuy's journey. 'It is enough, no?' laughed Pierre. 'My maid has wrapped you a banquet!'

'I thank you,' said Beaupuy, solemnly. 'We must try to ensure that our fellow creatures have far better lives in the future. For that we battle.' He checked his sword in its scabbard, then pulled on his hat. 'Thank you for all you have done.'

'I trust you will have a safe journey,' said Pierre.

Beaupuy placed his hand on William's shoulder. 'I shall be far removed from your poetry, my friend, but it has been good to know you. Your soul is compassionate and warm, and in the rising anger of war, tenderness is too soon lost. I shall remember many of your words.' Then with a sad shake of his head he left for the stables, all his energies focused on the future, the dust of his past flying behind him with the thundering hooves of his horse.

There was a void in the house now; even the daylight cast melancholy shadows on the walls and furniture, while every creaking floorboard trembled with the captain's ghost. No fire had been kindled in Beaupuy's room that morning, and the sight of the cold grey cinders made William morose. Life at the château with Beaupuy had felt like a dream. Now they must face reality. Annette had arrived yesterday, and it appeared, he observed, that other visitors had also been to the château, for as he looked closer through the window he noticed that part of the shrubbery had been heavily trampled. Had she been followed? She'd grown easy with her occasional visits, sometimes even singing when wandering the long corridors. Other times she'd talked to him in fast, urgent French, difficult to catch, saying how their child would cry for its father when he'd left, and wondering if she could bear it. Then within seconds she would sink to her knees, insisting he should leave that day and that his safety was paramount. "You are English and I know they will come to find you," she'd wept. "They will think you are a spy because you love me." She feared Robespierre, and she feared what might happen if the Prussians invaded Paris. The revolutionaries would take ferocious action, she said, there would be vile slaughter and depravity. Then she would chant the Duke of Brunswick's manifesto over again, as if in a trance:

". . . . *to put an end to the anarchy in the interior of France, to check the attacks upon the throne and the altar, to reestablish the legal power, to*

*restore to the king the security and the liberty of which he is now deprived
and to place him in a position to exercise once more the legitimate authority
which belongs to him."*

Revolutionary Paris was now at the ready. The Paris prisons
were filled with counter revolutionaries whose lives were in
serious danger since the Duke's proclamations.

But Annette was powerless to alter what fate would deliver.
She had written to various officials, but the letters had never
been sent. William had found them on the desk in their room,
lines scored heavily through them. He admired her for helping
Beaupuy, and Jean for saving his life. But he knew that such
tolerance was over in France. Sympathetic sentiments in the
honest sense of a greater and more profound good were shrinking
to a kernel of hatred. Beaupuy's departure had forced them to
think on their position. The captain had gone to his cause and
his eagerness to leave for his regiment had only confirmed in
William the truth of his own position. He was endangering
Annette's life and must leave his beloved.

But what was to happen after that? The revolution was
advancing fast, each day different from the last. He felt torn
when he found her weeping, though she wept also for her family
and country as much as she did for them. There were times
when the poison of guilt pulsed through his blood like thorns.
Had he not made things worse by making her pregnant? How
would she cope with the baby? He ought to have thought about
that. But was it not right that Nature's fruit should multiply?
That Nature's love should have its time? And might not it all
go right in the end? Nobody knew what the revolution might
finally yield. Humanity was surely ingenious and must pit its
wits against evil. Today he felt deeply fatigued. Never in his life
had he known such painful indecision.

The next few days slipped by in relative peace. Annette would read, or else walk about the château thoughtful, while he tried to write poetry in the library. Pierre too had been silent and pensive, walking the grounds and staring at the sky as if it might offer him answers. But there were no answers; there was only confusion in the dark, hovering storm clouds. And the storm broke later that day.

As they ate together in the dining room, the sound of a rider cantering into the courtyard came to them loudly. Then came a deafening scream. The scream! William thought frantically. The scream is here! They ran to the window and saw Anton leaping from his horse. Within minutes he was up at the château banging on the door with his fists. Pierre went quickly, William fast behind him. 'What is it?' cried Pierre. 'What has happened?'

'The troops are here!' screeched Anton. 'There are fierce riots in Paris!'

William and Pierre looked at each other horrified. Annette came running. 'The manifesto has come to pass! There will be terrible violence and bloodshed!'

'What did you see?' Pierre asked Anton urgently. 'Was it as bad as expected?'

'Far, far worse!' wept Anton. 'It is the work of Satan himself! Paris has turned into hell!'

'Dear God!' moaned Annette, shivering. 'They are frightened of the Duke's armies. They will have opened the prisons and killed all the counter-revolutionaries.'

'They are butchered!' cried Anton, wiping his forehead on his sleeve. 'I cannot understand such viciousness.' Henriette brought brandy, which Anton threw down his throat in seconds. The cook came after her, followed by his delirious wife. ·

Anton trembled. 'I did not know what was happening. I was walking with my brother in the city, then all of a sudden there were torches blazing about us . . .' He clapped his hands on his ears. 'Muskets were blasting everywhere. – Ah, and those weapons – I swear they were made in their kitchens!'

William folded Annette in his arms, listening intently.

'It is too much!' cried Anton. 'France must have her revolution, but not like this!' He sat trembling with fear. 'My brother and his family fled, but I needed to return to the château to tell you.' He talked on tiredly, his damp hair tangled about his shoulders, his voice failing in the depths of his misery. 'A man was knocked over beside me, and they hacked off his head with an axe. I could not look, but I could hear him screaming and I could hear the axe at work, like the sound of a farmer hacking the head off an animal. It did not matter which side he was on, they were deaf to his protestations. – Then others were dragged from the prisons and stuck with knives like pigs – so many – so many! And once the blood had been drawn and the death rattle sounded in their throats, they were speared again, and again!' He shivered. 'Many were burned with torches, screaming and begging for mercy as their bodies blackened.' He looked about frantically, then rested his eyes on Pierre, who stared at him in stony silence. 'Monsieur Pierre, we must never underestimate the depths of human depravity!'

'What now?' whispered Annette, clinging to William and shaking.

Pierre spoke gravely. 'William must return to England, before he is carrion for the crows!'

Part Two

16

England

And so he had reached his homeland. He stood at the quayside watching the sea before him, his throat tightening with tears. When would he see her again – if ever? It seemed to have happened in a dream, all of them urging him forward. He had made the journey back as if in a nightmare and was lucky to have gained passage, for the harbour had been closely guarded. Without doubt, the truth of life was a mighty force to be reckoned with and had finally had its way. It was mainly a difference in his person he noticed most just now, particularly in his identity. He was the same, and yet he was different. The very sky that spread itself over England was the same as that in France, the air Annette continued to breathe without him, was still the same, though his inner world of hope and peace had been shattered. Now he must try to rebuild himself just as he had done in childhood, piece by painful piece. In his bag of things he had only his books and notes and his old repaired garments. Oh, that his mind might repair with one or two stitches. But such thoughts were not to be tolerated in the world of the mind. Feelings were stubborn, they were part of the soul, the eternal substance that could neither be touched nor understood but which brought him poetry from its birthplace. But there was no poetry here as he stood by the sea.

There was only harsh reality. The complicated forces at work in his mind were violent as the storming waves. He could feel the muscles of his face tightening as he turned to look for a chaise.

Well, whatever his fears he was home and had much to do. First he would visit Richard, his brother in London, and learn how the family had been faring during his absence.

As the chaise moved on, William's mind flooded with questions. Would Annette and her family be safe? Would Jean deliver the baby? Surely the child would be given their loving care, for was it not their very own blood? His heart ached for Annette. The savagery happening in France felt close as skin, the deaths, the maiming, the screams Anton had spoken of burned in his mind. Oh, cruel, cruel destiny! Was this desolate darkness in his soul the price of love? He could still feel her hands on his back, pressing him into the coach, still hear her voice begging him to leave. His whole body vibrated with the sense of loss. Honour, dignity, virtue, all those qualities he had once felt part of his being seemed to have gone. And he felt frustrated. But what use would he have been to Annette had he died in France? What use to his child? He didn't dare imagine the horrors Annette might encounter, or the fears his newborn baby might have to experience. He was a missing father. He was no father at all. He was nothing.

He was deep in thought for most of the journey until the day grew dark and the driver stopped at an inn. But the night seemed long and he could not relax, thinking he'd been followed from the harbour by a chaise close behind. He saw that it stood in the courtyard now silent and still in the shadows.

As he left next morning, he saw that the chaise had gone and sighed with relief. Until a mile down the road it reappeared from a bypath. Was it imagination, or was he being trailed? He forced himself to be sensible. It was possible others might have come from the harbour to make the very same journey to London.

Discipline, he told himself, he needed discipline! He had needed it in France and he certainly needed it now. He attempted to read but the chaise creaked and groaned and the road was bumpy. If he closed his eyes he saw soldiers arriving in Blois and doing what soldiers did when out of their minds. He tried not to think of anything.

Arriving in London midday, he wandered the streets lonely. He was back in the capital city, but everywhere felt unreal, the life he had come to was far removed from the life he had left in France. A cold shiver ran through him. Might those last moments of tenderness with Annette be all he had left to remember? He passed The Palace of Westminster, the seat of Parliament, where men had grappled for power since the thirteenth century, and the seat of the Royal Courts of Justice. 'Justice,' he murmured, 'moral correctness, ethics, equity . . .' All such concepts might be dashed to shreds in an instant when men grew murderous.

He braced himself. Here, in England, perhaps he could make some money and send it to Annette and the baby. But how would he do it? Dorothy believed in his poetry, as did his brother John. And he knew he could write something wonderful if he could only find somewhere to live and settle to work. He couldn't afford much rent, but if he lived frugally he could cope until matters got better. He would work his gift like the thunder and lightning worked a storm!

As he walked along the London streets in the cool September air, he felt like a different man, not the man who had crossed to France a year ago, naïve and hopeful. A new spirit had claimed him. Returning to England in the past he'd felt joyful, now though he felt despair at the thought of the mess he'd left behind.

He passed the café where he'd breakfasted with Priestley last year, though in the fading afternoon light it was difficult to see who sat there. He imagined talking with him now and wondered what their discourse might be after so much change. London felt unfamiliar, voices and tones were lower; whispered talk of the French revolution was everywhere. He glanced behind him as he went. Two hunched figures trailed him. Might they be men from that chaise, an Englishman returning to England from France was bound to arouse curiosity, if not suspicion. He lengthened his stride. He had little baggage, so turning a corner he ran.

After ten or so minutes, he needed to catch his breath and stopped in a doorway. Peering around it he saw that his clandestine companions were now out of sight, so he sprang forward and resumed running down the street. After several minutes he walked on steadily, trying to find his bearings. In his notebook he found the address of some lodgings a helpful fellow he'd left at the harbour had given him. If he couldn't stay there, he'd try somewhere else. The streets were becoming shadowy and the loud voices of drunks from the taverns entered the darkness. He walked on quickly. He would very much like to see Richard, but decided to visit him later when his thoughts were clearer, spending time with his older brother was often hard work. Surely he'd be pleased though to see he was safe back home? The thought helped him relax. Just one or two days alone and he knew he'd feel more collected. He must visit Dorothy too when he felt ready. But he didn't feel ready just yet. As a canon in Windsor, Uncle William fraternised with royalty. He could just see his look if he knew what had happened with Annette, and he imagined the furious scratching of pens as his uncles exchanged letters. It wouldn't be easy.

Finding the lodgings he knocked on the door and a pleasant elderly lady opened it. She could offer him accommodation, she said, and bid him follow her upstairs where he entered a small and pleasant bedroom. Putting down his bags, he fell into a chair and looked about. In some small way he was home.

A week later he went to see Richard. His brother's manner was taciturn and solemn, though it was only what William had expected. It was hard to tell if he knew about Annette or not. Richard looked him all over as they talked and drank tea. 'I've expected you,' he said. 'Dorothy said you would return, matters being so bad. She gives me your news.' He gave a slight cough. 'I would have liked a few more letters myself, actually.'

At that William raised his eyebrows. He had hardly expected Richard to go into a sulk, and had assumed Dorothy would filter out anything important; she had an expert understanding of her brothers. 'I knew Dorothy would apprise you of my intentions,' he said stiffly.

'Yes,' said Richard, looking downwards. 'But I am not Dorothy, am I?' He frowned. 'Dorothy tells me very little nowadays.' He braced himself, while giving William a glance of brotherly disapproval. 'You have caused us a lot of concern.'

William shifted about uncomfortable. 'But I am here and safe,' he said tentatively. Richard, it seemed, anticipated nothing but trouble from his younger brother and that is usually what he got. William sighed. He felt sorry that Dorothy got linked with his own indiscretions; it had happened since childhood. For a moment or two he remembered how it had been, how they'd wandered the woods as children, played together in the house on the spacious landing where dappled light danced in the early evening. But Richard was talking about law . . .

'Fox's Libel Act has now been brought into force,' said Richard. He strode about the room, his hands clasped behind his back. William watched and listened. Oh how his brother could pontificate! '*A Vindication of the Rights of Woman* has just been published,' Richard said taking a seat. 'Did you know about that? Mary Wollstonecraft is indeed an ingenious woman, and she dares attack writers like Fordyce and Gregory as well as philosophers like Rousseau, oh my life! Though I imagine

Rousseau might annoy her a bit. He argues a woman's education should be mainly to help her men folk.' He looked at William and smiled. 'He is certainly clobbered for that.'

'Well, yes,' said William, nodding assent. He thought about Annette. Complex feelings flooded his mind. Would Richard ask about France any minute? So far the hour they'd spent talking had been filled with the affairs of England, and the health of their uncles and Dorothy. Dorothy was healthier than ever, he said, and their uncles were thriving. It was good to know Dorothy was content. John too, appeared to be prospering and enjoying his life at sea.

'Draw up closer to the fire,' said Richard, 'there's a big draught comes from that door.'

William pulled up his chair, though he thought it was time to depart. Richard invited him to stay if he wished, adding by the way, it would save the family money. William decided he would stay in his lodgings a little while longer then think on it.

The next few weeks were spent writing and exploring the city. He did not write to Annette, fearing his letters might be seized, but he longed to know how she was. He wrote to Elizabeth and Dorothy again but he could not give them any address to reply to. They would meet very soon, he told Dorothy, and he would try to think of a suitable place in Windsor to have their rendezvous. His eyes wandered a lot to the window as he wrote, though all they met were buildings, and his conscience was no easier than before. One or twice he'd awoken to what he'd thought was the cry of a baby, but found it was just the mewing of the woman's cat roving the landing.

He spent most of his time reading all he could find about important world events, particularly events in France. He was overcome by shadows, shut out from the world.

All over Europe governments based on monarchies trembled,

determined to root out anyone who tried to topple them. There was much to rebel about in England, the enlightened poor expressed themselves fiercely in secret, nobles talked anxiously in their grand houses and clubs and writers were busy with their pens.

Many of the French nobility, who had now lost much-prized privileges, loathed the revolution. The Roman Catholic Church had also lost power, and the clergy had been pressed into an oath of loyalty to the state. Its transcendental influence lay in shatters. Robespierre claimed the constitutional government must constantly sustain the Republic and the guillotine fell hard and swift on the necks of any who opposed him.

'The news gets worse,' William murmured, folding his paper and staring at the fire. And it seemed the gulf between him and Annette grew greater by the day. But at least he had an address, though he doubted any letters would reach him. What was she thinking just now, he wondered, how was she feeling? He could not say how he felt himself any longer, not even in his letters to Dorothy. There were days when his heart hurt physically, days he felt tired and morbid and days he felt consumed with shame. But he tried to write poems and refused to succumb to his sufferings, for surely Annette suffered more.

He found himself staring at three potted plants on the windowsill. They were wilting and in need of water. He picked up a jug from the dresser and dropped a little water into each then pressed down the soil with his fingers. Their roots would be dry as old bones. And his thoughts fled to Lakeland where the wild flowers would be growing in abundance in the rich dark earth and streams would be racing down the mountains. He must get there soon.

He had just returned from a visit to West England and Wales with William Calvert, a friend of his from Hartshead. Calvert had inherited a large sum of money and had dealt with all the expenses, an extremely welcome act, William thought, since he was searching for somewhere to rent with Dorothy and watching his money. Was it fair though, he asked himself, to take her away from the comfort of the Rectory to live so frugally with him, possibly even in danger? He was dazed by his situation, but he'd enjoyed his time with Calvert and the pleasure of their conversations. "I must visit my Uncle Richard sometime this year," William had told him, "and my dear friend Elizabeth in Hampstead." He suspected his uncle Richard would want to know his future intentions. He sighed at the thought – if only he knew them himself! He wondered also, if Elizabeth had received any news. Her last letter said Annette had written twice, though the writing had appeared dashed off and was difficult to read; the content had indicated however, that she and Caroline were safe and well, which was mainly what he'd wanted to hear. Pierre had written but once, she'd said, and had suggested the letter might well be his last. Robespierre, he'd asserted, was blind to the demon he'd become. "He is severe and inflexible, and would have us all dead!" Pierre had told her. And he'd underlined the words boldly. The passing of The Law of Suspects at the end of 1793, had allowed Robespierre's power to burgeon into madness. Churches were wrecked and closed, clergy were beaten and deported, and thousands had gone to the guillotine. The sound of the tumbrels, Pierre reported, sent shudders down the spine of Paris. Clergy, aristocrats, ordinary middle class people, peasants who might be hiding Royalists, or seen as avoiding conscription, were all guillotined, while women sat clicking their knitting needles, watching as the heads of the victims thudded into baskets, soaking the hems of their skirts with blood. This, Pierre had written, was called "La Terreur!"

That morning there came two letters. One was from Richard with news of the family. Dorothy was missing him terribly, while John, he reported, had now set sail with the East India fleet to China. Their brother was shaping a history. 'Whilst I do nothing at all,' William murmured.

The second letter was a plea from William Calvert. His brother Raisley was seriously ill and unlikely to live much longer. Might William pay Raisley a visit in Penrith, he asked, for he himself would have to be away with his regiment? Poor Raisley, sighed William, no wonder his brother's writing was almost illegible. Raisley Calvert was only in his early twenties. He scribbled the address in his notebook and replied directly.

As he rode his horse to Penrith, William had an almost uncanny feeling that he too was close to death. He somehow believed he would fall off his horse and break his neck, all the poetry that lived in his soul gone, everything he was, gone – all his feelings, his loves, his hopes vanquished in seconds. For that is how it would be for Raisley. So it was for all living things on earth. He shivered. Life was a brief respite from nothingness, he thought hearing the splendid breath of his horse as it cantered over the hills. Everything that lived had to die, but how hard it was to accept that terrible silence.

'Thank you for coming,' rasped Raisley, as William stood by his bedside. 'I feel so useless . . .' Raisley was now in the strange wild country of fever and pain, where only fate knew the future. It seemed so tragic that a talented and pleasant fellow like him should suffer consumption. Raisley's nightshirt was soaked in sweat and he had very little flesh on his bones. Might love and caring help restore him to health William wondered. He found him fresh clothes, bathed him and read to him at night-time and tried to have simple conversations. He carried him food and drinks. But over the week Raisley was fading fast. His strained white face had resolved into a look of death.

This was how it happened, William reflected, death sucked you back into the earth, uncaring as a lion with its prey, so that all that remained were other people's memories, perhaps delivered through talk, or if the muse was willing through art, music or poetry. The housekeeper would come that morning at nine. She would boil up water, sweep out the house and provide clean linen. She was a cheerful, energetic woman and William was glad of her company. William Calvert would arrive in the afternoon.

The day drew on until there came the sound of a rider on the hill galloping up to the cottage. William Calvert fled in and went right to his brother's bedside. ''My brother, oh, you are here!' exclaimed Raisley, as the older man drew up a chair. 'Where am I? – Where am I going?'

'You are going to your freedom,' William Calvert said softly. 'And I cannot come with you.'

'But you are with me now,' said Raisley through his coughing. Then the strange laboured sounds of death came from his throat as he breathed his last.

Back in his London lodgings, Christmas came and went and William spent it alone. Another year was about to begin, another year without Annette. The winter had been cold and dreary, and the darkness had seemed interminable. 'Oh, for some light!' he cried to his small gloomy room. Each day he wanted Annette. In the still of the night he remembered that first tender evening, when he'd watched her brush out her hair. He remembered her body, strong and alive; he remembered her love and passion. – Had his letters reached her? Had she tried to reply? He was so impatient for news. Robbers looking for banknotes often attacked the mail coach, were his precious letters lying in a ditch or lost on the wind? He was constantly up and down the stairs enquiring of the landlady, 'Is there anything for me – anything, anything at all?'

Then came a letter from Elizabeth. He flung himself into a chair and tore into the envelope. His blood raced wild around his body! He turned the pages quickly. Robespierre's power was failing, she said. So many heads tumbling into baskets, so many deaths, the nauseating smell of fresh and congealed blood, had sickened the people of France. Pierre had reported people had even killed themselves to escape the authorities. It wouldn't be long, Elizabeth asserted, before Robespierre himself went to the guillotine.

The months passed by into summer. William went into roadside cafes to read what he could. News from France was slow, but he perceived that the French were weary of death. People speculated. – Robespierre would try to escape. He would simply disappear. He would be shot.

William felt his mind would burst; so much was happening and him so far from Annette. He wanted to touch her, to hold her, though he could only reach her in dreams. 'Where is she?' he murmured. 'What is she doing? Where is my life?"

17

Visiting Elizabeth In Hampstead

It was late in December as he made the journey to Hampstead. He hoped Elizabeth would be home. And perhaps there might be a special letter from Annette. He'd fancied he might spend Christmas with Dorothy that year, but their uncle had countless commitments at Christmas and if his nephew's presence proved awkward, then Dorothy might feel uncomfortable. He would leave it till spring when there was new life everywhere.

The wheels of the chaise were poor, the roads were wet and he ached from the effort of trying to stay in his seat. The horses laboured until they came to the top of a hill where the coachman drew up. William gazed about him. The highest point in London, Hampstead had wonderful views and a sweet smelling air. Once the home of wolves, only foxes slinked about now in the undergrowth, shy and scarcely ever seen.

Getting down from the chaise he looked for Elizabeth's address. It seemed like an age since she'd left the château for Rome, though it was scarcely any time all. There would be much to consider and talk about. As he opened the gate to her home he shuddered. What Anton had seen in Paris still haunted his dreams. He looked at what he'd said in his notebook:

"Such ghastly visions of despair, and tyranny, and implements of death and long orations with dreams, I pleaded before unjust tribunals, with a voice labouring, a brain confounded, and a sense, of treachery and desertion in the place that holiest that I knew of, my own soul . . ."

Much had changed. The king and queen were dead, executed by guillotine and Maximilien de Robespierre had now taken over. He shook away the thoughts and returned his notebook to his pocket. The elderly of France were weary and bewildered, only the young could cope with such violent change. Pierre's aunt was strong and had travelled the world, though she too had seemed exhausted when leaving for Rome. He'd known she wouldn't stay long. Looking ahead, he saw that candles burned downstairs in the house; it looked like someone was in.

A young bright-eyed maid welcomed him, and he saw that Elizabeth rested on a chaise longue. She put out her hands to greet him, but strangely he felt unlike himself as he looked at her. He felt remote and out of place in the large unfamiliar house where Elizabeth looked so at home. It was such a contrast from their life at Pierre's château. 'How wonderful it is to see you!' she said brightly, but he thought her breathing seemed laboured and she appeared to have aged dramatically. 'I enjoyed your letter,' she said as he kissed her.

'I was followed,' he told her quietly, as he found a seat by the fire. 'All the way here, I could swear it.'

She looked at him and frowned, then glanced outside through the window. 'I shouldn't worry too much,' she offered. 'I suspect they are watching me too; there were one or two curious eyes as I stepped off the boat. We are spies, you see. It's quite tiresome.'

'I'm glad you got that letter,' he said. The maid took away his hat and umbrella.

'Yes, it was good to know you were safe.' She settled to look at him.

He sat very close, waiting to hear the words that shone in her eyes.

'So what have *you* to say to *me*, William, for *I* have much to say to *you*?' She spoke playfully.

'Ah, you taunt me,' he laughed, though his voice was eager. 'I think you have news from France'

'Oh, I do, I do!' She glanced at the maid, a shy young woman of about twenty, who seemed to be awaiting instruction. William's eyes lingered on her face. What was it about her look? Could it be the eyes? Elizabeth gave her a nod and she went upstairs quickly.

'Thank you, Yvette,' said Elizabeth, as the girl returned with a letter. Elizabeth handed it over, all the time smiling.

His eyes sped quickly across the words, busy with joy, though he would rather be reading a letter from Annette, instead of a letter from Pierre.

'Well,' said Elizabeth. 'You see. Annette has given birth to a fine baby girl – *your* baby girl, William!' She tapped his arm with her fingers, her eyes glinting with tears. 'Congratulations, my dear!'

William sat dazed. 'She came into the world on the 15th of December,' he said shakily. 'And her name is Caroline.' Lifting his head, he said, 'I have a daughter named *Caroline* . . .'

'Yes,' said Elizabeth, emotionally. 'A divine little creature, it seems. And her star sign is Sagittarius. Sagittarians have natural exuberance and a strong sense of adventure. They are free spirits! That is how you would want it, of course, I know.' She took back the letter and the maid returned it upstairs.

William laughed at her words.

Elizabeth continued. 'She will be clever and ahead of all others in her thinking, and her heart will be all embracing; I know these things from my maid. She enjoys such mysteries.' She laughed a girlish little laugh. 'I am very fond of Yvette. She likes to think our behaviours are at one with the stars.'

'And perhaps they are,' William said abstractedly. He sat clasping his hands, filled with intense wonder. Would his child be safe in France? How had the Vallons received her? No doubt Leon would adore her. He hoped Annette would be happy, for he determined to return to her soon. He was with her now in mind if not in body. He was with them both. He had a daughter! What did she look like? What were her eyes like? Did she have hair? He longed to delight with Annette in their new baby daughter, but it could not be.

For a moment or two they both sat deep in thought. He closed his eyes, the heat of the fire on his cheeks, and imagined all manner of pleasures.

'You will have read in Pierre's letter, however,' Elizabeth murmured, 'that the riots are fiercer than ever and that the Jacobins are acting like wolves.'

'Yes,' said William, remembering his talks with Beaupuy and how hard it was to be fair in revolutionary France. 'But Pierre has friends?'

Elizabeth nodded. 'And I know they will help him.'

'And what of Annette?' His tone was urgent.

'She has a cautious and intelligent family.'

'Yes, that's good,' he murmured. The afternoon shadows fell softly about them. He gazed around the room. It was a large fine house Elizabeth lived in, close to the heath. The walls were a soft sage green, a colour that reminded him of the reeds growing by the Derwent, which he and Dorothy had tried to make papyrus from as children. Colourful silk cushions softened the chairs and chaise longue, while Persian rugs were spread about the shining oak floor. His eyes moved to a mahogany dresser, similar to one he had once seen for sale in Cockermouth while walking out with his father, a dresser with large brass handles and beautiful ogee bracket feet, almost the colour of blood. His father had liked it a lot. What would he have thought about his granddaughter, William wondered. It was hard to imagine how the gentle silent man might have felt. He imagined his father in the darkness of memory. He was not frowning, but neither did he smile. He too would have suffered the fear of what might happen to Annette and his newly born granddaughter. William stared at the fire. Did the dead live on, he wondered, always present, observing and watching, feeling and suffering with the living. He hoped they didn't, for the world was always at war. He returned his gaze to Elizabeth.

She straightened her shawl on her shoulders. 'France is now a Republic,' she said quietly and profoundly. She gazed down at her hands in her lap. 'And so it is done.' She spoke of the changes she'd witnessed there in the last twenty years. The most important thing in her life, she said, after her brother's death, had been to keep Pierre from harm and to love him. Now she felt helpless. She felt old and tired, she said, and could not bear the cruel forces that were now unleashed in her country.

The room grew darker. He hoped to arrange a meeting with Dorothy ere long, he said, and was eager to see her. 'I have no idea what she knows or doesn't, but I have sent her letters and tried my best to explain. I shall stay in my present lodgings a while and give her the address.'

Dorothy looked through the window murmuring sadly. 'Take care wherever you go, and with all you say. England has changed.'

18

Meeting Dorothy In Windsor

Spring was ending and summer was beckoning. The star shaped flowers of wood garlic lined his way as he rode his horse through Windsor. Pure white wood anemones mingled with green and white cowslips, while nearer the stream the purple bells of columbines and powder blue harebells flickered in the light breeze. Beauty, pure beauty. He took his horse slowly, glancing about rural Windsor as he went. Wearing the outfit made by the tailor in Orléans, all the way there he'd held on to his heartiest feelings, for it wouldn't be fair to croak like a toad, as Dorothy sometimes put it if he started grumbling. He felt exhilarated, knowing he would meet her very soon. The boy in him came through with the sunlight as he recalled their childhood together. He lifted his face to the breeze and stroked the neck of his dapple-grey mare. He had so much to say when they met.

Over the last few days, however, his emotions had resolved into a pain in his gut which had started to affect his digestion. That morning before he'd set out, he'd taken some salts to soothe it and to some degree it was easing. Dorothy's letter, as ever, had been warm and enthusiastic. She had written to Annette from Windsor, she said, and Annette had replied. He was eager to see the letter and hoped she'd bring it with her.

He gazed about abstractedly. Dorothy would no doubt know of his circumstances now. Ah, well, whether she told their uncles or not was entirely her choice, though he hoped she didn't. It was enough to have offended their politics let alone their sense of morality.

As he tethered his horse by the inn where they'd arranged their meeting, he wondered what she would think of him, all things considered. He knew that France had changed him, even fundamentally. He was quieter and felt much older. Just now his thoughts swam deep, and often in murky waters. He hoped there wouldn't be many people dining, conversations in England were awkward now and you never knew who was listening. Here outside it was quiet, though it was only late morning. As he looked through the window he saw to his pleasure that the inn was well near empty.

The room he entered was warm and cosy with a good roaring fire. It was a moment of great excitement when his eyes found Dorothy. She was seated at a corner table wearing her long black skirt and green woollen jersey, the very same clothes she had worn at Christmas in 1790 when last they'd met up. His heart flooded with old familiar feelings and he quickened his pace. As his footsteps sounded she lifted her head and smiled.

'You look so well, my dear!' he laughed, searching her eyes.

'Likewise,' she replied, with an odd new shyness. 'You are even more handsome than before.' She leant back in her chair and surveyed him slowly.

He smiled and sat down in the chair beside her, then he bent and kissed her cheek.

'Though maybe a little drawn . . .' she murmured.

'I'll bet,' he said biting his lip. He rubbed his eyes tiredly.

'I'm a full eight stone,' she added triumphantly. Her dark shoulder length curls half covered her plump cheeks.

'That's good,' he said, nodding approval. 'You mustn't get

skinny. I've warned you before about that.' He gazed into the basket at her feet. 'I see you've been gathering. – What have you got?'

She drew out a sprig of yellow jasmine. 'I intend to make a medicine for Aunt. She's been having palpitations. And I've a very nice dandelion root as well – an excellent specimen . . .'

He gazed at the plants as she laid them out on the table.

'I have quite a reputation,' she murmured.

'For causing mischief, I expect,' he laughed. Dorothy frowned.

'I do apologise, my dear,' he said, touching her hand. 'I didn't mean to sound flippant. I could use some of that medicine myself actually; I've had a hellish stomach of late.'

She looked at him concerned. 'You've probably been worrying. Or else you haven't been eating. You need to get proper food and sleep.'

'You're right,' he said vaguely.

'But I'm glad you're here,' she said, leaning against him fondly.

He could feel the warmth of her body on his arm. It was hard to take in. He was sitting in an inn with Dorothy, his sister, so grown and sensible and calm, so untouched by the terrors that had now become part of his mind. He took her hand and put it to his lips.

'I've been ever so concerned,' she murmured.

'Did you get my letters from France?'

She sighed and shrugged. 'Yes, but I had no address to reply to.'

He gave her a shamed look. 'I know. I'm sorry. But it couldn't be helped. It's all been so complicated. But now you have heard from Annette, you will know how things are . . .' His eyes searched her face, then again he looked at her basket.

'I haven't brought the letter,' she murmured. 'I thought it unwise. But you will know the contents anyway. It is all quite sad, my dear. But remember, it might have been worse.'

He sighed heavily and frowned. 'Well yes, I could have died, or Annette could have died, or . . .'

They sat silent for a moment. He was annoyed that she hadn't brought the letter. 'Do you think I'm a fallen man, Dorothy?' he asked, looking away. 'You do, don't you. I can tell.'

'You will see what you want, you always did.' She was thoughtful a moment. 'I liked the new poems you sent me.'

'That's good – but you didn't like the others?'

She played about with the plants on the table then put them back in the basket.

'You were rather critical in that letter, Dorothy,' he said dejectedly, 'and at a time when I needed your support. I dedicated *An Evening Walk* to you, though I do wonder why I bothered.' He heard her breathe in deeply.

'You have great work in you, William. I feel it and know it will come.'

'Well, it's good to know you have faith in me,' he said, though a little sullenly. He leant forward and warmed his hands by the fire.

'How could you ever doubt it?' she murmured. 'I know when a poem is your best and when it is not. You see,' she added assuredly, 'I know your mind.'

'Aye, I expect you do.' He sighed. 'I doubt my poems will suit the taste of the times though. Not yet. I need to acquire a following, create a taste people want, even yearn for eventually.' He straightened and swelled out his chest. 'I have decided that writing will be my life.' He saw she was smiling with approval. 'I doubt I shall fatten your purse with my earnings though, not for a while.'

'You have a calling,' she said quietly.

He talked on urgently, knowing she had touched the truth. 'Ideas, feelings, in art, need time to become a part of people's awareness, part of their everyday existence.' He gazed at his hands, as he often did when thinking. 'Take Milton, for instance, there wasn't much interest in his minor poems at first, yet look how we treasure them now. He gazed at the fire, murmuring:

> *'Untwisting all the chains that tie*
> *The hidden soul of harmony;*
> *That Orpheus' self may heave his hand*
> *From golden slumber on a bed*
> *Of heap'd Elysian flowers, and hear*
> *Such strains as would have won the ear*
> *Of Pluto to have quite set free*
> *His half-regain'd Eurydice.*
> *Thus delights if thou can'st give,*
> *Mirth, with thee I mean to live.'*

Her eyes were joyful. 'I do love Milton. I have some back at the rectory. Uncle buys me lots of books. You should see what I have, you'd be impressed.'

'I'm sure,' William said grudgingly. 'He wouldn't buy books for me, I can tell you. He thinks I'm a wastrel.'

'He doesn't understand you.'

He darted her a glance. 'Have you told him about Annette?'

She sighed. 'I had to.'

'I see.' He raised his eyes to the ceiling. 'And the baby?'

She answered with a soft smile.

'He didn't take kindly to that, then?'

'No. He and Aunt had an argument. I went out walking with the children. It was over though when I got back.'

'So she didn't exactly agree with him?' He gave a sigh of relief.

'Aunt has her own opinions. We haven't actually discussed it.'

William folded his arms wilfully and crossed his legs.

'They are fine people,' said Dorothy, seeing his look. 'If Uncle doesn't understand you, then let him alone for now. He will understand you in time.

'You are a good sister,' he said, suddenly serious. 'I hardly deserve you.' He saw that her eyes were sad. 'The baby will be well taken care of. I can vouch for that. Annette is intelligent and good. I love her Dorothy. I love her so much.'

'I know,' said Dorothy quietly.

'And I'm glad you've written to each other,' he said softly. 'She is just as bewildered as I am, and every bit as unhappy.'

'Why can't she come to live here?' Dorothy pleaded. 'Oh William, I long for that cottage! Annette could live with us, and the baby. We could help each other.'

He touched her arm gently. 'I've thought about that, myself. Truth be told though, life has its own plans.' He frowned tiredly. 'And we know so little about them.'

'I read about those massacres.' Dorothy shuddered. 'Thank goodness you're home.'

For a moment or two they were silent.

'I think we should order some food,' he said finally. He glanced about for a waiter.

Dorothy murmured, 'Morphia, P.B. forty minims, wine of antimony, thirty minims, citrate of potass, forty grains, syrup of orange peel, three drachms, water, sufficient to make five ounces . . .'

'Five ounces of what? – Are you chanting a spell?' He laughed, happy and content in her company.

She smiled. 'It's a recipe for some medicine. I mustn't forget it. I got it from the wife of a farmer. – Have you come on a horse?' She glanced outside through the window.

'I have,' he said. 'I've borrowed her. She is tethered by the trough.'

The waiter came and they ordered food and drink.

'I'd like to buy a horse of my own,' he said, sighing at the thought. 'I'd be paying at least sixty guineas though for a mare like that.'

'Uncle pays more,' she said thoughtfully.

'Oh, Uncle would, only the best for Uncle William, of course.' He sat wringing his hands. 'I have to start earning some money, and quick.'

'Then stop writing poetry and do something else,' she said, feigning nonchalance.

He gave her a steady stare.

'Now that wasn't nice, was it? You have chosen to become a poet, dear brother, and a poet you are. It won't make you rich. Not yet. But yes, you have a calling, and you cannot answer to it croaking like a toad.'

Apart from the sound of the fire crackling before them, the room was silent.

'You will write, and your work will mature,' she said in earnest. 'You will discover the beauty of its forms. They will come to you in all their glory for the world to enjoy.'

'Is that what you believe? I mean really, deep in your heart?' His sister said such wonderful things. 'Are there enough words, metres, cadences, heaven knows what, to deal with these fires inside me?'

'Of course,' she said quietly. She spoke with certainty, her cheeks flushed with excitement. Again, she went into the basket and brought out a small parcel. 'For you,' she said grandly.

'Scones!' he said opening the package, and smiling with pleasure. 'I'll get through this lot in no time. How kind of you, Dorothy, thank you.' He pushed the scones deep into the pocket of his frockcoat.

'I enjoy baking and cooking,' she said happily. 'Uncle and Aunt are wonderful people. They're the best.'

'You admire Uncle William, don't you,' he murmured.

The waiter brought tea and hot dinners, steak pie and potatoes and carrots.

'But of course?' She frowned confused. 'Why shouldn't I? I believe he helps teach what the human soul can rise to.'

'You believe in everything he stands for.'

'He has helped a great many people.'

'I expect he has.' William braced himself and poured out the tea. 'He will think it foul what the French have done to their king.'

Dorothy bent her head and sighed.

'Louis had absolute power, and absolute power corrupts,' William said flatly. He did not want to disturb her, but he did feel strongly about what the revolutionaries fought for. What he did not like were extremes.

'You sent me a copy of that letter you wrote to the Bishop of Llandaff . . .'

'That's right I did. I didn't care for that pamphlet.'

'He argued against the execution of King Louis. He has a right to say how he feels.' Her tone was adamant. 'How could you write him such a letter?'

William wiped his mouth with a napkin and heard her out.

'You even called yourself a republican.' Her features tightened with emotion. 'Why did you need to do that?'

'You haven't shown that letter about, have you?' He looked at her concerned.

'I would hardly do that now, would I?'

'That's good, because I didn't send it in the end. But I thought what he'd written disappointing. Must a republican be against democracy? I have always maintained – and I believe with Rousseau – that a good education is the best way to answer these questions. An informed opinion is vital.'

'My dear,' she said softly. 'You are far too passionate sometimes. Perhaps you should become a politician.' She raised her eyebrows and smiled at him wryly.

He remembered suddenly those last few hours with Annette and the pain of their parting. 'Oh Annette,' he murmured.

'I asked her to come to live with us in England,' said Dorothy, seeing his distress. 'When I see the happiness in the eyes of my aunt and uncle and their family, I remember how we lost our parents and were forced to live apart.'

'She will never come to England,' he sighed. 'The king has been guillotined. The queen has been guillotined. They would probably have guillotined me if I hadn't got away!'

'Annette must come to us,' Dorothy whispered adamantly.

He shook his head sadly. 'No, and she would not want to. She will fight it out until the end.'

'But can't we get the baby?'

'Never. Annette's family will be watched every second. I'm surprised you received her letters.'

They sat for one or two minutes, finishing their meal.

'Christopher tells me he intends to take Orders. – Did you know?' said Dorothy.

'Ah, good old Christopher, eh? What a dear brother, he is. Well, God has enough of our family's blood, I think.

'I shall beg God to pardon you in my prayers,' said Dorothy with a look of reproach. She glanced at the window. 'Oh see! There were starlings before in that tree, and now there is a dove. Perhaps it is an omen. Do you remember the doves in the woods at Penrith? There were ever so many.'

'I do,' he laughed.

'I think Mary is a dove,' Dorothy murmured. 'She is always so calm and sensible. If she hadn't been there in Penrith, I might have gone mad.'

'Mary, dear Mary,' he murmured. 'How is she?'

'Oh, strong as ever.' Dorothy threw out her hands. 'And lucky too, she never has a day's illness. – Do you still get those headaches.'

He nodded. 'But only when I despair.'

'Then best not despair,' she said firmly.

'But I can't just cut off my feelings. To do that would be a sort of suicide. You are right, though, I cannot return to France, I cannot help Annette and our baby just yet, but I must still feel for them Dorothy. You do understand, surely.'

'Of course you must, but there is little point in despairing. I'm sorry, but I can scarcely bear it when I see you unhappy. While you were away I feared for you constantly. You didn't have to fear for us.'

'But you were never far from my mind.'

'I'm glad,' she said quietly.

For a moment or two they were thoughtful.

'So when did you last see Mary?' he asked, looking at her straight.

She smiled and drew a breath. 'Just recently. She knows I am with you today.'

'I see. And did she . . . Did she send me any message?'

'There you go,' said Dorothy irritably. 'My dear, can I give you some advice?'

He looked at her and narrowed his eyes.

She spoke coolly. 'You had better not upset her.'

'When did I upset her?' he said, with a curious look. He moved about uncomfortable. 'Now this is getting difficult, my dear.' He spoke in a tone of annoyance. 'You had better explain.'

Dorothy held his gaze. 'You scarcely said a proper goodbye when you left. She cares for you deeply, you know.'

'But I did in a way,' he said, after a moment's thought. 'We walked out together at Christmas. She knew I was leaving for France.'

'You were friends at school. But now she is a grown woman. And there is something in your look that isn't fair.'

He dropped his head broodingly. 'I think you know what I mean,' Dorothy said quietly. 'It isn't fair to Annette. There is something strong between you and Mary, something sprung from the English soil. Its root goes deep.'

He frowned thoughtful. 'I see, my dear,' he said straightening. 'I am well and truly admonished.'

19

New Year In England And The Godwin Circle

There was a strange silence all about him as he read that evening in his lodgings, as if a part of him had departed. He felt oddly abandoned, belonging, it seemed, to the silence of churches, which he had sometimes entered, staring at the stained glass windows and enjoying their ethereal beauty, their colours spirited in the sunlight, their patterns wandering the floor; he belonged to the silence of night-time when he would wander beneath the dark night sky, walking for hours, stirring the peace of resting animals and startling birds from their slumber, such was his lonely existence.

Spring passed into summer. He perceived from his reading that the French were growing weary of death. They made up stories about Robespierre – he was caught in a web of his own making, his power was failing, he would try to run away, or he would simply disappear without trace. It was said he had tried to kill himself with a gunshot, but the bullet had only shattered his jaw. Now he was wearing a strange contraption to support it. But Robespierre, they asserted, could not escape his fate. The merciless finger of Time was pointing his way. He had thrown himself down before The Committee of Public Safety, pleading for mercy:

"Deputies of the Right, men of honour, men of virtue, give me the floor, since the assassins will not!"

But no-one was listening to the great orator now. And on the 28th July, 1794, at thirty-six years of age, Maximilien de Robespierre had been taken to the place of execution where the bandage was ripped from his jaw and his head was severed by the guillotine. Word passed fast around the world. Robespierre was dead, and the new authorities in France had forcibly declared that anyone advocating terror now would be seen as one of his followers and suffer in consequence.

In London William felt restless. He had missed his intense exchanges in France, and his thoughts returned often to the voices of those he loved. He desperately needed conversation, and good fortune had it that his lodgings were near to the home of the celebrated writer, William Godwin. Godwin was known to have well-known authors visiting his home where they discussed the matters of the day and kept abreast of what mattered; perhaps he should pay him a visit.

He reached down Godwin's book, *An Enquiry Concerning Political Justice and its Influence on Morals and Happiness.* The book had made him famous. William had found it in a second hand bookshop in London earlier that month, an excellent bargain he'd thought, since it was only recently published. It was quite possible though that someone had felt uncomfortable with it, he reasoned, for Godwin was often controversial, arguing that governments perpetuated ignorance and dependence, rendering a people powerless. Politics, Godwin asserted, would one day give way to a greater morality as truth triumphed and displaced government rulings. His book had caused something of a stir and he'd created a labyrinth of trouble for himself, as anyone did who dared to appear revolutionary.

As he leafed through the pages, William recalled the heated discussions at the Jacobin Club in Paris. He'd enjoyed them a lot, but who had guided them, and what were people saying now? It was all about choices. But how were those choices made – only through debate, surely? English minds had been stimulated now by the writings of thoughtful people. Mary Wollstonecraft, who William knew Godwin admired, had recently published *A Vindication of the Rights of Woman*, a book Richard, his brother had talked about last time they'd met. It incensed Wollstonecraft how women must so often keep silent and could not voice their opinions. And rightly so, thought William, no-one would ever have silenced Annette or Dorothy.

As he donned his frock coat, he doubted he'd see Wollstonecraft at Godwin's, for she, too, had excited much controversy. She and Godwin were quite a pair to be reckoned with. Godwin's belief in universal benevolence was vigorously argued about in London. Seemingly stern and austere, he was known to be a cool orator, as well as an excellent essayist, and there were many who said he had a sensitive side that he kept well hidden. And what man didn't? thought William as he found his umbrella and stepped out.

The sound of the heavy brass knocker echoed through the large house with the peculiar hollow sound that came on dull damp days. He could hear footsteps in the hall.

'Wordsworth!' cried Godwin with a laugh. 'And about time too!' He looked him over warmly. 'I was wondering when you would find us. I knew you were back in England. – Upon my word, how glad I am you still have your head! – My dear Wordsworth, come in!'

William handed his things to the maid. He touched his face.

'Yes, my head is still on my shoulders I think,' he laughed. 'And how are you, dear Godwin?

'We are all very well in England,' said Godwin good humouredly. 'The French are arriving here constantly though like deranged birds.'

William walked along with him broodingly.

'I believe you have published some poetry?' said Godwin.

William glanced at him hopefully. 'That's right.'

'You must tell us how it is going,' said Godwin. 'Montagu is here.' He glanced outside through the window. 'Awful weather. Anyway, there is still some daylight. Remember what Paine said about leaving your door unanswered after dark when there were folks about who didn't like you.' Godwin laughed, though his eyes were serious.

'So who doesn't like you?' said William. He smiled at Godwin wryly.

'Oh, oh!' laughed Godwin. 'Don't tell me you haven't heard? I am one of the branded!'

The olive green curtains at the end of the hall were opened wide, but the hall still appeared gloomy and the paintings that hung there were shadowy. The many brass ornaments standing about on dressers were without lustre, though it wasn't yet noon. Two candles lighted the hallway. Godwin took him to the dining room where a man sat at a table, a small child seated beside him.

'It's Wordsworth,' said Godwin.

The man got up to greet him, then pointed to a seat beside him. Montagu had quite a reputation for speaking his mind regardless. He was his own worst enemy. He had studied Law at Cambridge and was a good friend of Godwin's. William discovered as they talked, that he'd been having it rough lately. His wife had died. He'd had to take care of his little son on his own, and it didn't help when you were having problems with money. Basil had been declared bankrupt. A bankrupt lawyer was a very sad fellow indeed.

'It's good to see you,' said Basil smiling, though his eyes were weary.

'We must eat,' said Godwin, standing by the boy. 'This scamp is Basil junior. He is scarcely three years old, yet he is canny as an old fox!'

William sat down. The boy appeared to be playing with a small ornament, a rather splendid looking fly captured in amber. He brought it up to his eye, then banged it down on the table by turns.

'It won't come out,' laughed William. 'However you try, that fly is staying right there.'

The boy was defiant, banging the fly down harder.

'Here, give it to me,' said his father, putting out his hand. But the child withheld it.

'You are not taking it home,' said his father. 'Though we won't have a home to go to soon,' Montagu said despondently. 'I fear we shall be out on the streets ere long.' He shook his head and sighed. 'Oh yes, Wordsworth. We have nothing but the coats on our backs. I ought to have had an inheritance, but it has somehow deserted me.'

'Ah, yes,' William murmured. 'It happens.'

'Oh come on Montagu, it isn't as bad as all that,' said Godwin, smiling.

William gazed at the curly haired boy at the table, who appeared to have the face of a girl . . . *a girl called Caroline perhaps* . . . His heart leapt as he thought of it. They were about the same age. Did his own little child run about the room and play like that? Did she do as she was told, or was she like her father doing whatever she fancied? He wasn't sure he liked the idea of her doing whatever she fancied; it was far too dangerous.

'Do not disgrace yourself!' Montagu cried to his son. 'Where are your manners? – Now give me the fly, I demand it!'

The boy delivered the fly into his father's hand, then went beneath the table to hide.

'It's the best place for him,' Montagu whispered, glancing across at the fire. 'He rather likes flames. He sees such amazing things in the fire. A child's imagination is wonderful.'

'And so it should be,' said Godwin.

'I see you have Wollstonecraft's book,' said Montagu, nodding at the dresser.

William saw Godwin frown. That he did not want to talk about Mary was obvious, there had been so much scandal surrounding her. Her affair with Gilbert Imlay, an American speculator and author, whom it was said she'd pursued in earnest, had been talked about all over London. Totally enamoured, she had fallen pregnant by him. It was evident however, that Mary's love was unrequited.

Godwin's manner was defensive. 'She is a bold writer,' he said assuredly. 'And a very fine woman.' He sat down beside William and peered at the child beneath the table.

'The woman is a wonderful thinker,' Montagu added. 'I found her book most moving.'

'She writes from her heart,' sighed Godwin, heaving his considerable chest.

The maid came in with a large plate of pie.

'Ah, my maid makes a splendid meat pie!' Godwin said genially. 'You will enjoy it, I promise you. Do help yourselves.'

The maid went to bring cutlery and wine glasses and little china plates.

'Cut a piece for the child, will you, Montagu,' said Godwin. 'He might come out of his den. And do have a drink of that wine there; it's an excellent vintage – good for a rainy day.'

'I believe Wollstonecraft has set your heart a flutter, Godwin,'

Montagu smiled, as he cut into the pie. 'You are quite romantic in truth aren't you; however you try to disavow it.'

'We often surprise ourselves,' said Godwin. 'Mary is a very special woman; a man cannot help but fall in love with her.' He rubbed his nose and glanced at William. 'How is your sister? Does she still live in Forncett with your uncle?'

'She does,' said William. 'They have some interesting guests, too. She met Wilberforce, you know, and I believe she liked him.' He could feel the child tugging at his boot lace beneath the table. 'She found him invigorating company. He has worked tirelessly towards ending the slave trade, of course. He actually gave her money to pass on to the poor. Yes, Dorothy was quite impressed.' William took a forkful of pie into his mouth. It was a very good pie, though there were few who could equal Dorothy when it came to baking.

'Was she attracted to him then?' asked Montagu. He widened his eyes for more.

'What?' said William, with surprise. 'Dorothy attracted to Wilberforce? Oh, I doubt it, but she does like a man who can think.' He pondered on Montagu's words.

'Would she marry him?' Montagu badgered.

William moved about uncomfortable. 'Might you see to your boy, Montagu,' he laughed, lifting up the tablecloth and glancing at the child beneath the table. 'He has managed to take off both my boots, and I shall need them to get back home in.'

Basil Montagu got down and called to his son.

'I have him,' said William, finding the tiny hands clasped about his knees. The curly headed child surfaced and gazed at them confused.

Godwin rang for the maid. 'Please take Basil to the kitchen,' he said.

'No, no!' screamed the child. 'Not kitchen!'

'And I have no wish to have him there, either,' said the maid firmly. 'He ruins the order in my cupboards. And what's more, sir, I have placed a mousetrap by the door. Now you wouldn't want him snapping off a finger, would you?' She stuck her chin firmly into her neck and folded her arms.

Basil Montagu looked sternly at his child. 'Behave yourself,' he said. 'Or else.'

'Or else what?' said Godwin. He gazed at Montagu and waited.

'I'm not sure . . .' said Montagu scratching his head and frowning. 'Oh, if only his mother were alive. I cannot cope with him myself.' He gazed sadly at the ambered fly. '"*Preserved forever in amber, a more than royal tomb . . .*"' he murmured.

'You are still quoting Francis Bacon?' said William, shaking his head with wonder. Montagu had a reputation for quoting Bacon.

'There is little I encounter in life that does not bring him to mind,' Montagu said admiringly.

Having been back to the kitchen, the maid brought a plate of sweetmeats and put them on the table. 'There,' she said. 'He's been trying to get them all morning.'

'But is it good to teach my son, that if he is bad, he will be rewarded with a plate of sweetmeats?' said Montagu, looking bewildered.

'Now let us be fair,' said Godwin. 'The child has hardly been bad. Mischievous, curious perhaps, but never bad. I hope he will learn many good things in his life, and in the proper way. The most desirable way of learning, to my mind, is that a pupil shall want to learn and be curious. Only through wanting to know can a child become independent. Pupil first, master second.' He spoke with passion, his eyes fixed on the boy, his expression warm and serious. 'Schools, I believe, are places of control. Very bad. National education can encourage the acceptance of certain given arrangements that I do not . . . Hmmm.' He waved a finger in the air. 'Such arrangements can be a danger to freedom of thought.'

'And therefore strengthen the State,' said Montagu, frowning.

'Yes,' said Godwin. 'The mind is always capable of improvement. An individual surrenders the best attributes of man, the moment he resolves to adhere to certain fixed principles.'

'Perhaps he has eaten too many sweetmeats,' said William, seeing that the child looked queasy.

'You sit around dreaming up your morals and principles,' the maid said curtly. 'But real life, sir, is harder than what you write about in books.' She stood for a moment, gazing at the floor then went to answer the door. She returned with a note.

'We shall be all by ourselves today,' said Godwin, folding the paper. He glanced at the window. 'Look at that wretched rain!' They watched it battering the windows.

'It's lucky I arrived before it started,' said Montagu. 'Especially, since I had to bring Basil. I had to, you see. I've no-one to watch him.'

'He's an excellent child,' said William.

'You like children then, do you?' said Montagu with interested eyes.

'Aye, sometimes,' said William, smiling.

For a moment or two all three of them gazed at the child.

'Well, you can have him if you want,' said Montagu. 'I mean just for a while, of course, until I get back on my feet.'

William stared at the boy. 'I might take you up on that,' he mused, stroking his chin thoughtfully. They were all silent for a moment. 'I'm looking to rent a cottage with Dorothy. I think she might like a child about the place. She would probably miss the ones she takes care of at the rectory.' By now young Basil, seated on his lap, had put his hand into William's top pocket intent on drawing out his pocket watch.

'He has certainly taken to you,' said Basil.

179

'Wordsworth has an even temperament,' said Godwin. 'Children are sensitive to temperament.'

'So is something wrong with my temperament?' Montagu asked indignantly.

Godwin shrugged. 'Your temperament is different from Wordsworth's that is all I am saying. I am not judging you Montagu.'

'Take care he doesn't break the watch, Wordsworth,' said Montagu looking disgruntled. 'He is capable of taking it to pieces.' Then he leant forward and whispered in William's ear. 'I think I have a plan, my friend. And you might just like it . . .'

Retiring to bed that night, William decided that despite his training as a lawyer, Basil Montagu was a fellow of unbridled emotions. Somehow, through a stroke of bad luck, he had managed to lose an inheritance. Indeed, a bit of bad luck! Money ran away from you as fast as the streams on the hillside sometimes and you could never catch up with it. Rumour had it though, that Montagu and his father, the Fourth Earl of Sandwich, didn't get on. It was said that Basil had married against his father's wishes and it had caused much bother. Good for him, thought William, a man should marry as he wants, or what was a marriage worth? Montagu's wife, however, had sadly passed away, and her loss had obviously depressed him. What hypocrisy, on the part of Montague's father though, thought William, allegedly the Earl enjoyed dubious pleasures and cared nothing for his own reputation. One rule for him and another for Basil it seemed. Dukes, earls, lords, bah! Who did these people think they were that they should set their faces at the world as if they were gods when a lot of them were rogues!

Meeting Montagu at Godwin's house though had been quite serendipitous. He, himself, was searching for a cottage for him and Dorothy, and Montagu needed someone to care for his boy. He had offered to pay towards his keep as well, saying Basil was always hungry and could eat them out of house and home. Things were looking up financially. William had received a timely inheritance of £900 from Raisley Calvert, for looking after him during his illness. He had sadly died from consumption at 21 years of age, a terrible tragedy, but William wouldn't remember him wasting away, he would remember him in the fullness of youth, laughing and brimming with life, not the haggard man in Penrith with the tortured features.

And Montagu's 'plan' might prove to be a magical concoction. He'd been tutor to the brothers John and Azariah Pinney, sons of John Pretor Pinney, a wealthy plantation owner living in Bristol. The men lived with their father, who had built a country mansion for the eldest, but John hadn't wanted to live there and Racedown Lodge stood empty. The Pinney brothers were rich enough not to care. It was doubtful though that anyone would wish to rent it, thought William, since it stood at the top of a very steep hill in Dorset. It was a good big house though, Montagu said, with a garden and an orchard. Dorothy would like the orchard . . . Added to that, Montagu believed they might get to live in it for free, for Pinney would surely be happy to have someone inhabit it . . . William had written to Dorothy that evening and would post the letter next day.

Several weeks passed by. Then came Montagu's letter. William opened it quickly.

"My dear Wordsworth, John is indeed, more than happy for you to occupy Racedown Lodge, and asks only that you keep good fires and see that it is regularly aired. I propose you write and take up his offer straight away. – And Wordsworth, you have truly impressed my son! He speaks of you so freely each day and promises to behave should he live with you. Though I own, he is all but a baby. A thousand times thank you! I can assure you,

my friend, he will not run wild or slip away, and I am able to offer you fifty pounds a year for his keep. It delights me to think of it, and I have a much lighter heart as I write to you!"

This important exchange was transmitted to Dorothy without delay.

"I fancied something special might happen for us soon!" she wrote excitedly. "How I rejoice at the thought of us sharing a home together – a garden, and an orchard too! – Have you had word from France? Uncle thinks we have much to worry about in England. His friends are saying it is likely we will to have to reinforce our coastal defences and train volunteers, for there might be a French invasion. Thank goodness our Navy takes care of us in mainland Europe. Uncle believes that food could get scarce, but we can grow our own vegetables at Racedown and eat the fruit from the trees. And I would be glad to take care of little Montagu. What a delight! How does he look? Please tell me!"

20

Racedown Lodge

As the chaise sped over the Dorset downs in the afternoon sunshine Dorothy chatted with the child. He was a bold energetic boy, and would take some managing, she thought. What a tale he told of his father's chastisements over simple trifles. 'And I try so hard to be good,' he said mournfully. William gazed across the downs. It might have been a time of happiness, but the troubles in France never left him.

The house looked dark and lonely as the three of them stood outside staring at the three-storey building. '*So big,*' murmured Dorothy.

William glanced at the chaise as it went down the hill. 'We'll get plenty of exercise with that slope,' said William. 'What a climb. I do like the views though.'

'Can we really live here for free?' Dorothy said curiously. 'It doesn't seem possible.'

'Well, I've been given this bunch of keys,' William replied, shaking them before her and looking slightly confused. But he smiled as if he were pleased. 'Come on then, better go in.' He found the key for the lock and they entered, but before they could move the boy was away exploring.

Dorothy looked about quizzically. 'It's a bit far away from the world . . .' she said worriedly. 'And it feels sort of deserted.'

'What, like another planet?' he laughed, hearing the boy racing around the bedrooms. They went upstairs to find him.

'These rooms are lovely,' said Dorothy. 'We must write to Uncle and tell him what it's like.'

'I don't know where we'll post the letter,' said William. 'Somewhere right down the hill I suspect.' From the windows, they gazed at the fields and woodland. 'That countryside beckons,' he said wistfully. 'I need to get out.'

The next few weeks were warm and sunny and Racedown Lodge was beginning to feel like home. Breakfast being over William went to sit in the garden. His latest poem, *Incidents on Salisbury Plain,* wasn't working as he wanted and that day he felt tense. He wrote. He crossed out. He wrote again. Who was she, he wondered, this poor lost girl he must work into his poetry? Was she Annette? Was she Mary? Would guilt and sorrow pursue him for the rest of his days? He murmured as his pen scraped the page:

> '. . . *There was a youth whom I had loved so long,*
> *That when I loved him not I cannot say.'*
> *Mid the green mountains many . . . and many a song*
> *We two had sung . . .*
> *When we began to tire… of childish play*
> *We seemed still more… and more to prize each other:*
> *We talked of marriage . . .*
> *And I in truth did love him like a brother,*
> *For never could I hope to meet with such . . .'*

The child came across the garden with Dorothy, clapping his hands and dancing.

'The parsley's done well,' Dorothy said heartily. 'It's grown so fast. You were right about moving it.' She stood for a moment looking abstracted. 'The farmer's wife, Betsy, says rioters have pelted the king's coach with stones, a large one smashed through the window and almost killed him.'

'I never heard about that,' William said frowning. He put down his pen and faced her. 'It'll be treason next to say anything against king and country.' For a moment or two they were thoughtful. 'We could do with one or two visitors,' he said glancing about. 'We're learning nothing up here.' The Pinney brothers visited now and then, but they rarely had guests at Racedown. Hedgehogs, badgers and foxes sidled up by the door or else scratched about beneath the windows but that was the extent of their company.

Days followed days, weeks became months and soon it was autumn.

'*Le chien, le chat, le cheval . . .*' William's finger stayed on the picture of a horse as Dorothy entered the parlour. 'I'm teaching Basil "animal French", he said, obviously pleased with their progress. The child, enjoying his lesson, tugged on William's sleeve.

'He's bound to be lonely out here. I thought I might take him to the farm down the road. The farmer has children . . .' Dorothy said, looking at the boy sadly. 'There's a lot going on down there.'

'I dare say there is,' William replied, rubbing his face tiredly and wondering how long it would be before he could find some proper employment. Dorothy's words flowed on. The farmer's wife had befriended her and Dorothy had given her home made bread in exchange for fresh eggs, usually returning light-hearted. But underneath it all he did not think she was happy. He looked down at the pictures he'd drawn for the child that morning. He wasn't very skilled at drawing; his cat looked ferocious as a tiger. 'It's lonely for all of us up here. I'm desperate for news,' he said, tensely.

'But the views are worth a lot, I suppose.' She spoke quietly, frowning.

'Aye, you suppose. I'm not so sure I do. We might be on a hill, but there are not so many folks who'll want to walk up it, and it's bad for coaches as well. We might have to look for somewhere else.'

'And they'll charge us too. No, we must make the best of it, William. We're here for a good while longer and that's a fact.'

'Facts are stubborn things, my dear.' The thundering tread of a herd of cattle pursued by a sheepdog came from behind the hedges. Ah, it wasn't so bad really, he decided, he got the odd visit from members of Godwin's circle, which was always welcome. For a minute or two, he contented himself with the thought. Dorothy hovered beside him, sorting out clothes for ironing. He met her eyes; they were strong, capable and shining. 'I was hoping John might come to stay for a while when he's home from sea, but I doubt it, and Kit is trying to get closer to God by the second. God help us, we'll be there soon enough as it is.' He carried on teaching the child, *'la chèvre, le cochon, l'oie . . .'*

Dorothy put the iron on the stove.

'I ought to be getting the rest of those apples from the trees,' said William, glancing outside.'

'Betsy told me there's been a lot more smuggling at the coast. Those coves and caves are perfect for hiding things in.'

'What's a smuggler?' asked the boy, looking at Dorothy curiously.

'It's a sort of thief,' William said vaguely. 'There are a lot of them about.'

He got out his pen and ink. He needed to write to his friends in London. How long, he wondered, before government authorities started to open their letters. He hadn't heard a word about Annette in ages. He must write to Elizabeth, see if there had been any news. And he needed to work on his poems . . . Facts were stubborn things, indeed, but not half as stubborn as poems. He had much to do. Basil ran off to find his spinning top, singing as he went; the child seemed content, but there were times when his tears had wetted Dorothy's face and he'd needed her arms close about him. But much good reading and writing could be done, William concluded. And they would make best use of their time.

As the months went by, every once in a while the Pinney brothers called and brought newspapers. No echoes answered to the tread of visitors at Racedown sometimes for weeks. But there was many a patter of animal feet near the house. He hoped sometimes, on opening the door at night time, that he might find Annette, hollow eyed and bedraggled, as if she had travelled over land and sea to find him, a sad forsaken ghost, desperately seeking him out. But there was only the silence of night.

All in all, they were happy at the lodge and the boy grew strong. 'He likes to sit beneath the tree at the foot of the orchard,' said William. Dorothy was filling a pie dish with plums. William continued. 'He has a friend there, he says, who arrives every day and brings him nice things to eat, adding of course that sometimes he's hungry, because we don't feed him properly. Oh, he lies like a little devil!' They both gazed at the boy, who looked innocent as an angel just then, sleeping softly on the carpet. 'He has an excellent imagination, and it will no doubt help him in life if he does not let it devour him.' He rubbed his eyes and looked outside. 'I think I need a walk.'

'But I'm preparing our lunch.' Dorothy looked at him and sighed. 'Where will you go?'

'Not far,' he said vaguely, 'just across the fields.' As he spoke, he felt bad. His thoughts were not to be shared with his sister. Just then they were all of Mary. As he pulled on his boots, he wondered if Dorothy knew. There was such a terrible distance now between him and Annette, and he feared he had lost her for ever. Mary was a special friend he could talk with in a way he couldn't talk with Dorothy. Did he love two women? His heart told him he did. Each day he struggled with his feelings, but he found no solace.

He stopped by Maynard's farm to talk with Betsy's husband Michael, who had just passed the lodge with his cows. They were now herded in a field. William sat down on a dry stone wall and gazed at the fine looking cattle.

'A vet came to look at 'em,' said Michael, pulling shut the gate. 'Them cows'll not be gettin' smallpox,' he says, 'because they've all been sick wi' the cowpox an' it's made 'em stronger. Can ye believe it?'

'Aye?' William said curious. 'I shouldn't fancy either myself.'

'I've to tell him if I see any signs though,' Michael continued. 'He's left his address with the missus.' He glanced at another field as he talked. 'I want these cows in that field over there. But they know what I'm up to ye see. An' they don't take a blind bit o' notice o' the dog 'ere. He's getting' that soft, I can see I must train another.' He put down his fork and placed his hands on his hips, staring at the cows. 'They like this field but there's good buttercups an' daisies in t'uther. I just can't budge 'em today!'

'Would you like me to help you?' asked William, getting down. The cows were lowing and restless.

'That's good o' you, sir, but it's best if you don't. They're typical bovines that lot. As likely as not they'll sit down. Or they might just go for ye. Oh aye, it's been known.' He scratched his head. 'Ye never know wi' cows, they're crafty.' He took a horn from his belt and blew it loudly.

'Farewell then, Michael,' said William. 'And good luck!'

The morning air was warm and there was scarcely a cloud in sight. He went through the gate and crossed the road. Then he climbed a stile and listened. Was someone reciting poetry?

> *'How are ye gone, whom most my soul held dear!*
> *Scarce had I lov'd you ere I mourn'd you lost;*
> *Say, in this hollow eye, this heartless pain,*
> *Fated to rove thro' Life's wide cheerless plain –*
> *Nor father, brother, sister meet its ken –*
> *My woes, my joys unshared! Ah! Long ere then*
> *'The tear which mourn'd a brother's fate scarce dry –*
> *Pain after pain, and woe succeeding woe –*
> *Is my heart destin'd for another blow?*
> *O my sweet sister! And must thou too die?*

'Good day, sir,' William said curiously.

The speaker seated on the grass threw aside his reading as William climbed down from the stile. 'What? – Oh, I am done with good days!' he cried. He was unshaven and grubby with long black curls hanging about his face. William saw in an instant it was Samuel Taylor Coleridge, a well-known writer and orator who he'd heard once or twice in London.

'I believe you are William Wordsworth,' said Coleridge. 'I've seen you before. I was just relaxing. This grass is as soft as a king's chaise longue.' He laughed at the sky. 'But who would sit on a king's chaise longue these days?'

'Who indeed,' said William, getting down beside him and gazing at Coleridge with interest. 'And you are Samuel Taylor Coleridge. I heard you lecture in London some time back, an excellent talk it was, too.'

'Was it?' Coleridge grunted. 'I probably needed the money.'

William replied with silence. They gazed together at the sky. Coleridge continued.

'I've been through it Wordsworth. Oh, yes.' He shook his head and waved a finger. 'One or two things are bothering me, as well.' He mumbled for a moment, as if to himself. 'One of them is that I don't know where to go to next.' He spoke flatly and nodded. 'I am certainly not going back.' Birds circled in the sky above them. Coleridge trembled with feeling. 'Oh yes, I've been through it.'

'Come, come, my friend, we have all been through it,' said William, 'especially the French.'

Coleridge looked at him sharply. 'Oh undoubtedly.' He straightened. 'I believe you were amongst them just recently.'

William bent his head. 'Ah, yes, I had to leave.'

They were both thoughtful for a moment. 'We knew it would come,' said Coleridge. 'We all knew in England. France has been wickedly served.'

'By its leaders, you mean?'

'By fate,' said Coleridge. He spoke in dramatic tones. 'We are apt to think we can outwit it, but we can't. So many wigs, so many rings, so many heads so far removed from their owners. Ah, nauseating stuff.'

'Now Robespierre is dead, also,' said William, his voice falling to a whisper. Where was Annette that minute? What was his child up to? He waited for Coleridge to reply.

'It was inevitable,' said Coleridge with a sigh. The smell of the earth rose about them. Coleridge tore out a handful of grass and pressed it against his nose. 'Very good! You can imagine why cows want to eat it.'

'The grass is tired though now. See how it bends,' William said abstractedly.

'I know the feeling,' said Coleridge, shaking his head at the thought.

'I read about your play,' *The Fall of Robespierre,* said William.

'Pooh!' said Coleridge, making the grass into a ball with his hands and throwing it down the hillside. 'You no doubt read that dastardly piece in *Critical Review.* Damned unfair, it was, and anonymous at that. You need to read the play, my man. Read the play!'

'Yes, reviewers can be mean. The horror is recent, of course. It is always difficult to write about anything so close.'

Coleridge sniffed and drew himself up. 'Well, somebody has to write about it. God, how I hate reviewers! Have they any idea how difficult it is to write a play like that? Damn the lot of 'em!'

'I doubt Southey was particularly happy either, since I believe you wrote it together.' From the look on Coleridge's face, William wished he hadn't said it.

'He wouldn't let them think so,' said Coleridge flatly. 'You know what Southey is like.'

William looked sadly at Coleridge. He was a man of medium build with busy, intelligent eyes. His knowledge was immense and his poetry was highly respected. How could he be so miserable? 'It's a good day to be out walking,' he said to him genially.

Coleridge spread himself out on the grass and rested his head on his hand. 'I am not *walking,*' he said. 'I am *running.*'

William laughed. 'Have you committed a felony?'

'I hope not,' said Coleridge, biting his lip, and it seemed, suppressing a wince. 'I have escaped my wife.' His voice fell low. 'And the baby too.' He pointed to a hare speeding down the hillside. 'See how it goes! Now wouldn't you like to clear the ground like that? What divine pleasure!'

They watched the hare leaping the rocks until it was out of sight. 'But why did you want to escape your wife and baby?' said William, surprised; it hurt him even to think of it. He knew Coleridge was married, but he wasn't aware of a child. How could a man want to take flight from his child?

'Oh, I needed some peace,' Coleridge moaned. 'I can't write a thing in that house. If my wife isn't moaning, the baby is crying. It's impossible.'

For a moment or two they were silent. William picked up a sheet of paper Coleridge had cast on the ground. 'Is this what I heard you reciting?' He gazed down at it curiously.

Coleridge put out his hand. 'Oh, don't look at that. For what it is worth I have got away with my life, though my dear sister did not.'

They gazed together down the hill. Autumn thickets and woods stretched for mile upon mile before them. 'It can't be as bad as all that,' said William.

'It probably isn't,' sighed Coleridge. 'I am prone to exaggeration. It is one of my faults. Well, it isn't a fault of *mine,* not exactly; it is more a fault of my mind. My mind is not *me,* you see.' He screwed up his face as he thought. 'It is only *a part* of me.'

'Your sister?' said William, still curious.

'Yes, Ann is the woman in the poem.'

'You were obviously fond of her.'

'I adored her,' Coleridge sniffed. 'You have no idea.'

'I think I have,' William asserted. 'I too have a sister, a dear and excellent creature, who is very much adored, and happily very much alive. We lost our parents in childhood and had to part company. But we have found each other again and live in a house nearby.' He pointed to the way he had come, suddenly aware as he did so, that he was talking happily in the face of Coleridge's pain. 'Please forgive me,' he murmured.

'Oh, don't be sorry for being happy,' Coleridge laughed. 'I am always miserable about something. I used to be in the army, you know, a very unpleasant business. I ran away from that too. I am always running away!' He laughed again. 'I claimed I was insane.' He rubbed his nose. 'It's probably true actually. I got married. What better proof could you have than that? Live with your sister, my friend, but do not live with a wife!'

'Your work gives you solace, does it not?' said William.

'My poetry – ah that. How would I live without my poetry?' He pressed his lips tightly together as if in determined silence, then opened them again and continued. 'I made a friend of it in childhood. My brother Frank thumped me on the nose and I fled from the house. A bully, that's what he was. There were ten of us children. I didn't think anyone would notice I'd gone, but they were all out searching.' He ran his hands through his hair. 'By then it was too late. Some metaphysical monster had hold of me. Now it is with me for good.'

'But do you not love this *monster?*' William asked incredulous.

'Love it?' said Coleridge, frowning. 'Well, I suppose I might in a way.'

William stopped him. 'Enough, dear Coleridge,' he said rising. 'I fear you are quite unwell. You must reach for . . .'

'For what – the poison? Oh, yes, I should reach for the poison, if I did not do so already ...'

'"*Poison?*"' William stared at him concerned.

'Chatterton reached for it, most successfully too. He was very soon out of his suffering.'

'Yes, poor devil,' said William.

'Those vile publishers,' Coleridge murmured. 'They robbed him, that's what they did; they robbed him! He poisoned himself with arsenic, an agonising death too.' Coleridge pulled a bottle out of his pocket and to William's horror drank of it deeply. 'Imagine killing yourself, all so you wouldn't starve to death.' He wiped his mouth with the back of his hand. 'Oh don't worry about this, it's only whisky.'

William saw that Coleridge had started to tremble. 'Do you want me to go and bring a horse?' he said.

'"*A horse?*"' laughed Coleridge. 'I'd be bound to fall off.'

'But you say you have been in the army. Did they not train you to ride?'

'Now that was a bit of a problem . . .' Coleridge whispered, as if disclosing a secret. 'And I have not yet recovered from it either. I am half sane most of the time and completely insane for the rest. When I am completely insane, I go out walking. The countryside cares nothing for sanity and neither do I.'

William leant against the wall leisurely, but his thoughts were busy. What could he do for Coleridge now? Perhaps he should take him to the lodge?'

'You are kind to be concerned about my health, Wordsworth. Seriously though, I assure you, I am quite alright.'

'Where is your home?' William watched Coleridge put on his boots and return his papers to his knapsack.

'I reside in a house with a woman who does not like me – oh, miles from here.' He pulled his bootlaces tighter and gritted his teeth.

William continued to watch him. He could not leave him as he was. He looked exhausted and his mind was wandering. 'Please come back to my house,' he said. 'We're to eat cold mutton and potatoes. You are quite welcome to join us. The orchard has delivered us an abundance of plums this year; my sister was baking a pie when I left.'

Coleridge looked down the fields, then swung his knapsack on his shoulder and stood. 'I have travelled from Nether Stowey. First I took a chaise, then I walked and found myself here. Last night I slept here by the wall. – I am rather hungry to tell the truth and that plum pie sounds delicious.'

'Then come,' said William. They both climbed over the wall, then waded through the ferns and grasses. 'Does your wife know your whereabouts?'

'She won't even care,' Coleridge said flatly. 'I simply depart. She'll expect me back within the week though. That's how it goes.'

They walked in silence for a while, gazing at the farmers' cottages below in a haze of autumn sunlight. 'We men are such fools,' murmured Coleridge. 'We try our passions at this and that but we waste ourselves mostly.' He slapped his hand on William's back and smiled. 'I thank you heartily, Wordsworth. It is good you are here. I believe heaven has sent you!'

Dorothy and the child were waiting for William in the kitchen. The smell of fresh plum pie pervaded the air as she pulled it out of the oven. They'd had such a plentiful harvest of plums that year. Some were for chutneys, others for preserves, and others they'd eaten fresh. Having brought mutton from the larder and put the pie on the table, she went outside and scattered some crumbs for the birds. But where was William, he ought to have returned by now. Just then there came a rustling from the hedgerow, and he emerged from the bushes with what looked like a tramp from the hills.

'I have brought us a guest, my dear,' he said. The stranger straggled behind him.

Dorothy stared in disbelief. Her brother liked talking with hobbledehoys, but he had never brought one of them home, it was quite a surprise.

'This is Samuel Taylor Coleridge, the writer and poet,' William declared grandly, casting out his arm. 'We met on the hills. He has travelled from Nether Stowey.'

Coleridge bowed to her lightly. 'You are indeed a lovely lady,' he smiled, 'Your brother has kindly invited me to lunch. I do not wish to impose . . .'

Dorothy smiled awkwardly. *Samuel Taylor Coleridge!* She was wearing her old brown dress and needed to tidy her hair. 'Not at all Mr Coleridge,' she said. 'You are welcome to join us. How nice!' As she looked at him she wondered why he looked so unkempt. 'Shall I boil you some water?' she asked tentatively. 'Perhaps you would like to freshen up.'

'Miss Wordsworth, I thank you,' he answered. 'Yes, I fear I am rather dirty.' He rolled up his sleeves and sat down.

'I am honoured to meet you,' said Dorothy, filling a pan with water and setting it to boil on the stove. 'William has told me a lot about your writings.'

'Oh?' said Coleridge with a wink. 'Well, so long as his talk is good.'

'Oh yes,' said Dorothy, glancing at William who leant against the wall watching. 'It is always good.' She went to a cupboard and brought out a bowl to put water in for Coleridge.

'There are lots of spiders about,' said Coleridge, gazing at the ceiling. 'They're everywhere you look. I like spiders. Their webs always amaze me. They create such beautiful worlds all by themselves.'

'They must watch that the birds don't go and peck them out,' said the boy, seated at the table.

'Aye, and there are spiders eat birds as well,' said Coleridge, nodding at him and smiling.

'Only in Australia,' said the boy loftily. 'Never in England.'

'Oh, I wouldn't be too sure,' said Coleridge, feigning to see one in a corner and pointing a finger. 'That one there would eat you alive if it got you!' He laughed loudly. 'We must all be careful that the birds don't come a pecking at us, mustn't we, young fellow? Nature is a cruel beast.'

'Nature is also good and inspiring,' said Dorothy. She poured warm water in the bowl and set it beside him. He washed his face and hands, then sprinkled water on his hair, all the time sighing and anxious.

William sat down. 'The struggle for survival is one thing,' William added, pondering. 'But its essence can be wholesome. We must seek out the best it can give, and learn. – Nature is innocent and wild, and in wildness is wonder and freedom, and I believe great joy, for that is how we are in the unfettered part of our spirits.'

Coleridge stared at him. 'If you know the pathway to joy, dear Wordsworth, then map it out for me, will you, for I would very much like to get there.'

'Nothing is perfect,' murmured Dorothy. She took away Coleridge's bowl and threw the water on the garden.

'Yes, I believe you are right,' said Coleridge when Dorothy returned to the kitchen.

'Beauty is perfect I think . . . at least for a time,' murmured William. 'We must hold it in our hearts and save it.'

'Or capture it in poetry,' said Dorothy.

Coleridge sat glancing about. 'It's a big place you have here,' he said. 'Three storeys?'

William explained how they had come to live at Racedown by courtesy of John Pretor Pinney a man from Bristol. 'Not a bean do we pay him in rent.'

Coleridge laughed. 'Oh, I know Pinney. He won't have a clue that his son's let you live here for nothing. Once he finds out, he'll want business.'

Dorothy and William glanced at each by turns. Coleridge was chortling.

'I trust you won't speak of it to anyone,' William said sternly. 'We're just settling in, and we have little Basil to consider. Pinney's son John is a fully grown man. I should think he can please himself what he does with his house.'

'I promise to be silent as the grave,' said Coleridge, nodding and suddenly serious. 'But he's bound to get wind of it somehow. Pinney knows plenty of people.' He sighed and frowned. 'We writers, you know, can't find peace anywhere. The government is convinced we are spies; it's becoming something of a nuisance.'

'I haven't seen anything strange,' Dorothy murmured. 'We only have farmers around here.' She gazed at Coleridge abstractedly.

William saw that Coleridge's coat was too big, and that one of the buttons was missing. His outrageously wild hair made him look mad. He had taken a book off the shelf. '*The Maid of Orléans*,' said Coleridge, with an interested look. 'And in French too.'

'I have it translated, if you would rather read it in English,' said William. 'My friend Pierre in Orléans is good at translating.'

'No, no. I much prefer it in French,' said Coleridge, returning the book to the shelf. He went to sit at the table. William began slicing the mutton and laying it out neatly on a plate. 'I intend to enjoy your company though just now,' said Coleridge, 'and this excellent lunch!'

Dorothy gave William a serious look, then excused herself quickly. She returned with a letter. 'A boy brought it this morning,' she said, handing it to William anxiously.

Seeing the hand was Annette's, he went outside to read it. After five or so minutes, he came back and sat down at the table. 'Annette and Caroline are well as can be,' he said pensively. 'Caroline grows strong. But of course, the wars continue . . .' He put the letter in his pocket. He had none of Annette's possessions, he did not have her substance, but at least he had some of her words. 'She says very little, but that is how it must be.'

'I'm thankful there's a letter at all,' said Dorothy. 'And the boy brought it right up the hill.'

Coleridge, who had fallen asleep at the table, woke up with a sudden jolt, full of apologies. William resumed the business of slicing the mutton. The exhilarating scent of autumn came in through the open window. And William remembered walking by the Loire with a woman he had loved with a passion. But the long shadows of Time were advancing towards him.

21

Life With Coleridge

It was autumn, 1797. Coleridge was often at Racedown. His mind, Dorothy asserted, was a treasure trove of knowledge and fun. His private life at home, she argued, was his own concern, for who could know what went on between husband and wife. There were days he arrived at nightfall, tired and unkempt as a beggar, talking to the point of exhaustion, finally falling asleep on the chaise longue sometimes rising up in the night and shouting accusations from the dreadful depths of his dreams. But he was soon up and about again as the sunshine of his soul returned to him. William and Dorothy took him just as he was and he was welcomed with open arms. Dorothy's activities, her talking and cooking, even her brews, interested Coleridge greatly, which gave her immense pleasure as he followed her about with his questions. Other days, he liked to read William's new writing, immersing himself totally, and proclaiming that William was indeed, a genius. – "Your soul inhabits the universe Wordsworth, like a god!" he would cry. "You arrive at truths by intuition!" He also brought work of his own, but was deeply sensitive to criticism, uncertain of his own brilliance, Dorothy said. She claimed she could see it trembling in his features whenever he recited his poetry. If ever he made her angry, she would leave him to argue with William and march upstairs to her bed. But disputes didn't last long. There was much to say, much to imagine, and much to write.

Coleridge though, had been unusually absent. Dorothy sat by the fire with her sewing, while William shaved upstairs. It was ten thirty in the morning. Every so often, he glanced through the window at the trees. It occurred to him achingly as the autumn leaves floated by the window that Annette might now be in the arms of another, for the ways of love were complex and she must have been lonely. Would he love her any the less he asked himself, if it were so. No, he decided, he would not. But it was a dark place he went to having to think it.

He tried to think better and applied more soap to his chin. Just then he was alerted by the sound of a carriage clattering into the courtyard. Coleridge arrived on foot normally and Dorothy hadn't mentioned any guests, who could it be? He finished his shaving and patted the towel across his face. Had Pinney sent someone to evict them? He pulled on his shirt and did up one or two buttons, all the time peering through the window. Then, as if in a dream, Mary stepped down from the coach, to be greeted by Dorothy who ran to her laughing. He listened to their jubilant voices as they walked to the house. What would he say to Mary, he wondered, confusedly. He felt roused and excited; it had been so long. He saw she had two bags of luggage and a hatbox; it looked like she intended to stay.

As he made his way down the stairs his mind was awhirl. Mary Hutchinson was indeed a good looking woman. 'Mary, my dear, how lovely to see you,' he said, kissing her cheek. 'I had no idea you were coming. See, I am hardly decent . . .' He fastened the remaining buttons on his shirt and breathed in deeply. He was talking too fast. He felt exposed, like his young impulsive self again, vulnerable and awkward. Always mistress of herself, Mary stood listening and interested, looking him over with a calm, familiar fondness.

'We wanted to surprise you,' laughed Dorothy. She took away Mary's coat and hat, then found her a comfortable chair.

'And heaven knows you did!' laughed William. Heaven knew a lot. Just as his soul had desired, Mary had come.

'You have no idea how I've missed you,' said Dorothy. 'And how are the others?'

Mary, radiant, smiled at them both. 'Everyone is well. They have changed, of course, but they are well.'

'And how have they changed?' asked William, knowing he too had changed, and wondering if she'd noticed the furrows in his brow and his now greying hair.

'They have settled into the tedious role of being adults,' she said. Her vivacity changed into a wistful sigh. 'Nothing worse though, my brother works hard on the farm.'

'I did wonder about Tom,' said Dorothy, taking a seat beside her. 'Farmers are finding it difficult. I'm surprised how people who are rich around here can drive them such a hard bargain. – We take care of little Basil Montagu now. I told you in my letter. Today he is playing with the farmer's children on the hill. They are quite delightful.' She glanced at Mary's luggage by the door. William went to collect it. 'In the room that looks over the orchard!' she called as he took the bags upstairs. 'Mary can see the fields from there and the window is easily opened!'

'You will probably have the pleasure of meeting Coleridge, the poet,' said William, returning. 'He often pays us a visit. You will like Coleridge, I'm sure.' He smiled wryly. 'He has the curious habit of falling asleep while talking, so do be ready for that.'

'But he picks up where he left off,' said Dorothy defensively. 'He brings us news and we talk about poetry.'

Mary listened attentively, looking by turns from Dorothy to

William, happy and content. William looked at her steadily. He watched her flashing eyes as she listened to Dorothy. It seemed she had adopted Dorothy as a sister since childhood. Mary had always been there, a part of the noise and fluster of their lives, even the long silences. And Dorothy was right, there was something more than friendship between him and Mary, something that stirred his blood. He stood there troubled, looking at this bright young woman he had known all his life, so thoughtful and clever and kind, and always so loyal.

Dorothy went to brew tea in the kitchen, then brought out cake and plates, and they sat by a low table next to the fire. 'Without our knowing it,' William murmured, 'our clay is subtly moulded and we are made into new people.'

'But there are things we must *never* forget,' Mary added quietly.

'Yes,' said William, 'of course.' He felt suddenly tense. His world was fast and passionate, and perhaps it was irresponsible. But he would not reproach himself for that. He would not scorn the free spirit he'd been born with.

For a moment or two they were silent.

'Dorothy likes to make notes,' William said, glancing across at her journal on the table. 'She writes about things from the woodlands and people she talks to.'

'But I only make *notes*,' she smiled, looking at her brother with pride while pouring out tea. 'William makes *poetry*. I would never pretend to be a poet.'

They all three talked of the past, melting it seemed, into the airy substance of memory, filled with childish fears, beautiful moments of joy, precious times when they had all felt secure together. Splendid were the stories they recounted; deep was the laughter they shared. Though nothing was said about France, and Mary did not enquire. For William now, France seemed far away, somewhere deep in his mind across a great sea of despair, where a child cried, "Father, where are you?" And a woman cried, "William, I love you!"

The days went by and the countryside fell into the plaintive strains of September, melancholy, tender and wistful. In the soft pulsating air, the three of them went out walking, enjoying the clear blue sky and the rich vegetation undergoing metamorphoses. William too was undergoing a metamorphosis. The man he had been was walking away, step by silent step, and another was taking his place. He felt oddly weak in his bones, as if he were being remade. And he was.

Dorothy, sick with a headache, stayed home that day and William and Mary walked in the woodland without her. The tension between them was strong. He felt awkward, as if all his reserve had left him, his emotions were naked, there were words he'd wanted to say, but Dorothy's presence had saved him. Alone with Mary in the open air his spirit felt raw and exposed. But he knew the words would have to come, it was now their time. 'Basil tells me he likes you,' he found himself saying.

She laughed. 'He's canny. If there's something he wants to know, then I give him an honest answer. That's if I have one. If I don't, then I say so. He seems to think every question he asks has an answer.' Her mood became pensive. She lowered her voice and looked away at the still silent countryside. 'Of course, it doesn't. I've tried to explain. It perplexes him a little, but he learns.' They came to a part of the path overrun with ivy. It glittered about them in the sunlight. 'Strange how some things take over,' she murmured. 'See how the ivy embraces those trees so closely. I fear it suffocates and strangles. I have never liked ivy.'

'Yes, Nature can be very selfish,' he sighed. 'Precious growth can be strangled if something has the power to do it.' It was good to be out with her like this, he thought, the golden gorse flaming, the trees swaying, the sky so wonderfully clear, and she so warm and alive.

'The autumn will leave us and the winter will replace it, then the spring will surprise us as ever,' she said, treading the ferns at their feet. 'Don't you think it's odd that we never see flowers opening?' She turned to him curiously. 'I've often wondered about that. It's as if it happens in secret.' She laughed, softly at her words. The sun came fast through the trees in long white lines and she shaded her eyes with her hand. 'First you see the rosebud, then suddenly there is the rose. And the rose looks beneath her eyelids and whispers, 'But you will never see how I do it!'

They went through a gate as the bells of a nearby church chimed three. Here, he thought, in that hour, was the very essence of happiness, unmarred by hopes for the future, just the simple pleasure of now. He wanted so much to tell her how he felt, to ask how she felt about him. Dare he feel love again so soon? Dare he? His first feelings of love, other than for his family, had been the love he had felt for Mary. But he had thrust it away and gone to hide in the hushed dark undergrowth of the woods. He had brutally torn himself away. But there had been an echo in his mind that had never ceased sounding. Now it was loud in his ears. But he was not ready for the power his heart was urging. 'Did Dorothy tell you?' he said quietly.

'Tell me?' There was a slight tremor in her voice.

He paced the grass then stopped. He couldn't pretend with Mary. He looked at her straight. 'About me. – Did she tell you what happened in France? – Did she say I . . .' His throat tightened. 'Do you know that I . . .'

'You have a right to live as you wish,' she said, raising her eyes to the sky.

'Have I?' he said loudly. His tone was angry. He leant against a tree. 'But we can't just do what we want! People have *responsibilites.*'

'I see,' she said flatly, in a cold tone of voice. She looked down and tried to sound nonchalant. 'Are you saying you are not responsible?'

He bit his lip anxiously. 'No, I am not. I hurt people, Mary.' The words came quick and hard. He had left a woman in France with a child that was his, an innocent girl roamed Blois without a father, all because of him. He covered his face with his hands.

'Is there something you want to tell me,' she said softly.

He looked at her weakly. Must he sob out his tale like a child? Must he lose all dignity? Perhaps he must. Mary as ever was calm. How he would like to have shared his pain with her now, he knew she would ease it. He opened his mouth to speak, but the words wouldn't come. The light flew about the trees then danced at their feet. He felt as if the whole of Nature was with them. 'I would like to tell you . . .' He saw there were tears on her cheeks. 'Mary, I'm not what you think,' he faltered.

She breathed in deeply and tried to smile. 'How do you know what I think?'

For a moment or two they were silent.

'Do you want to know what Dorothy has told me?' she said, finally.

He waited.

'She has said . . . Not because she needed to confide . . . Not because she is weak, but because she . . .'

Still he waited.

'Because she thinks we are part of each other, you and me.'

He met her eyes and waited for more. She looked confused as she talked. 'And I think . . .'

He saw she was struggling for words.

'She sent me a letter . . .'

'Ah, did she?' He stared at her, waiting.

'I burned it.' She spoke quietly and coolly.

'A very bad letter, then?' He sighed.

'Not bad, just sensitive.'

'And have you and my sister discussed it?'

'Briefly. But what is there to say?' She shook her head sadly.

Again he waited. He knew he must prompt her for more. He wanted her words so badly. 'Did the letter upset you? Could you scarcely believe what you read?' Again he paced, his hands deep in his pockets. 'Tell me, Mary! For pity's sake tell me how you felt! You see how I am.'

'I am over it now,' she murmured.

'Over what?' He stared at her astounded and afraid. 'Over *me?*' He knew how she cared, how she had always cared, and how he had always known.

'Is she beautiful?' said Mary, awkward and hurting.

He looked at her, and she lifted her eyes to his own. Sunlight fell on her tear stained face. Her lost despairing look cut him to the quick. 'Oh, Mary . . .' He dropped his voice to a murmur. 'Yes, she is beautiful. She's an incredible person too. But it should never have happened. I knew how things were in France. I was selfish and thoughtless. But that's how I am.' He threw out his hands.

She spoke faintly, choking back her tears. 'You are not selfish for loving. You cannot be with her now, and she cannot be here, there is war between our countries and who knows how long it will last or where it is going. You are young and alive. At least forgive yourself for that . . . You have a child, a little girl, that's wonderful.'

He reached for her hands and held them. 'Still such tiny fingers,' he laughed. 'They have scarcely grown.'

'Do you love her?' asked Mary. Her eyes flashed boldly.

He sighed and looked away.

'Of course you do.' Mary's voice was shaky. 'You will marry her one day. When the wars have finished, you will find each other and get married.'

He drew a breath and straightened. 'I received a letter – oh, some time back. I was lucky to get it. Little reaches us normally. She was well and busy. She is working for the royalists.'

She looked at him curiously.

'She didn't say much about *us* . . .' he faltered.

'But that's inevitable,' Mary said solemnly. 'We can have no idea what it is like for her. But I'm sure she will wait for you, however long it takes. If you were mine I would wait forever.'

With a rush of emotion he put out his arms.

Quickly she pulled herself away. 'Do you suppose I will just let you *use* me?'

He stood before her bewildered. 'Is that what you think?'

'Yes,' she said softly, her voice failing as she spoke. 'I doubt you gave me a single thought in France.

'And did *you* think of *me*?'

'Oh, yes,' she said boldly.

'And what did you think? he returned sharply, catching her eyes.

She spoke in a low, soft voice. 'I thought I had lost my heart forever. I wondered if I might become insane . . .'

A cold chill ran through him. 'I did not know. Dorothy didn't tell me.'

'I didn't confess my feelings. Why should I, it isn't my way. And anyway, what could be done?'

'And now?' he faltered. 'What now?'

For a moment they were both silent.

He stood before her wretched. 'I'm sorry, Mary,' he whispered.

'Sorry for what?' she sighed. 'For not wanting me?' She gave a little laugh.

He lifted his face miserably. 'It isn't true! – I *did*. I have always wanted you. You are part of me, Mary, just like Dorothy says. You are part of my childhood, part of everything I am!' He moved towards her. 'Mary, things happen *in secret*.' He saw she was weeping quietly. He felt numb. What had he done? He had wanted her saved just for him, kept for himself as in amber. He damned himself cruelly and gritted his teeth. 'Please don't weep,' he said. 'I can't bear it.'

She braced herself quickly. 'You need a holiday, William. Look, why not come to the farm at Sockburn with Dorothy. Come whenever you can. Tom would love it, and bring Coleridge too and his family. We have plenty of room.'

He nodded and smiled, glad of the better spirit. 'Thank you, that would be good,' he murmured. But he brooded for the rest of their walk. The still peace of the countryside was in direct contrast to the feelings that rushed through his blood. They walked some more, not touching, not speaking, but with more understanding than before.

Mary left just after lunch next day in her heavy woollen coat and her pretty red hat in the rain. She'd hurried down the path to the carriage. He was still annoyed he'd upset her. She had become quite morose and they'd had little to say to each other that morning as she'd climbed in the coach. But what was done was done. He gazed through the window, wondering about her journey in the pouring rain and when he might see her again. He went to sit by the fire.

'Do take a breath and stop sighing,' said Dorothy. 'Whatever you've said, I'm sure it was all for the best. What a pair you are, but I don't know how I can help.'

But he wanted Mary beside him. She had stirred his heart into life again and now she had gone. – And where, oh where, was Coleridge? Perhaps he had done with the Wordsworths. Did he make friends and discard them when he got bored; he was certainly known to be fickle.

It was early afternoon and they were resting, when there came a rap on the door. William got up and opened it on an extremely wet Samuel Taylor Coleridge. 'Where have you been? I fancied you'd forgotten us,' William said frowning.

'What? Forgotten you? Impossible!' Blustering in, he fell into his favourite chair.

Dorothy fussed him as always. He must remove his coat; it was soaked. He must take off his shoes. Did he want something to eat? Did he want something to drink? She stood awaiting his words. Coleridge was always the heart of her concerns when he visited.

'I knew you'd wonder where I was,' he said, rubbing his hair with a towel. 'But I've been carried away with other people you see, completely swept out to sea!'

Dorothy's eyes widened. Coleridge was often histrionic when disturbed. What had happened?

'Dorothy, my dear, please don't look at me like that,' he said. 'I would never have forgotten you.'

'Well, I hope not,' said Dorothy, shrugging.

'Let me explain,' said Coleridge, calming and clearing his throat. 'Wordsworth, stop pacing the floor. – Come and sit down.'

Dorothy poked at the fire, watching the flames abstractedly. 'Relax, dear Coleridge,' she said. 'Everything is quite alright. As a matter of fact, we've been very busy ourselves. Mary Hutchinson, a friend who I have talked about before, has been staying. She has left us this very day.'

'Ah, has she, I hope she had a jolly good time. Well now, I have been with a Mary myself.' Suddenly he fell thoughtful. 'Now let me tell you of my meetings in London and what I have discovered.'

They fixed their eyes on him and waited.

He gave them a wink. 'I have much to report about Godwin. – Oh yes! He is very busy with his pen. And very busy with Mary Wollstonecraft too, oh, what a woman! I hope she has got that Imlay out of her system.'

'Did you talk about Imlay in front of Godwin?' Dorothy said, looking dismayed.

Coleridge ran his hand about his chin. 'I'm not sure,' he said, thoughtfully. 'Anyway, what does it matter? Godwin is a man of substance. And now he has the woman for his own I doubt he would care a jot if I mentioned Imlay.'

'But there's little Fanny to think of,' said Dorothy sadly. 'You must always think of Imlay's daughter. The poor little dear has been dragged from pillar to post.'

'Ah, little Fanny,' said William, suddenly wistful.

'Godwin will take care of her, I'm sure,' said Dorothy, assuredly. 'He is an excellent man, and from all accounts he admires Mary Wollstonecraft greatly. *A Vindication of the Rights of Woman* is a wonderful book. – However did she write it?'

'Oh, he admires Mary,' said Coleridge changing his position in the chair and gazing at the fire.

'To admire a woman's intellect can often arouse her passion,' Dorothy said quietly. 'I am sure they are good together. Quite perfect I should think.'

William saw that Coleridge exchanged mischievous glances with Dorothy. He did not like their intimacy. She laughed with Coleridge in a way she didn't laugh with him. She had even danced with him, prancing about the room to *Comin' through the Rye*. He was jealous; he couldn't deny it.

'I doubt she cares in the least for Imlay now,' Dorothy continued.

'She ought never to have cared for him at all,' William asserted. 'He hardly seems worth it. Those terrible suicide attempts, it's as well she got through them, for life, it appears, is better for her now and good.'

'She was very lonely and unhappy,' said Dorothy.

'Well, now she is married to Godwin,' said Coleridge flatly. He sniffed. 'Him having criticized marriage and all, now he has gone and done it.'

They all sat thoughtful.

'So where else have you been?' asked Dorothy.

William saw Dorothy stared at Coleridge as if studying him acutely. Would he ever leave Sarah, his wife, he wondered, for good? A cold fear ran through him. What if he fell in love with Dorothy? She would certainly love him back . . .

'William, are you tired?' asked Dorothy, tapping him gently on the knee.

'What – no, not at all.' He rubbed his eyes and straightened. Sitting between him and Dorothy, Coleridge was like a ghostly presence, half in one world, half in another.

'He's thinking about *me* taking laudanum,' growled Coleridge. 'He must always berate me. He thinks I've taken some today. You shouldn't make assumptions Wordsworth. I'm a little excited, that's all.'

'You will run into trouble with that laudanum Coleridge if you take any more. But who can advise you?' said William.

'Well, I'm certainly in trouble now,' said Coleridge, drawing a deep breath. 'I didn't run into it either. It has sort of run into me, oh yes, it has gored me!' He stuck both fists in his stomach and made an agonised face.

How dramatically Coleridge delivered himself, thought William. He was a totally different spirit himself. Or was he? He wondered if Coleridge might actually be a part of himself, a spirit of his own that belonged to him, along with the trees and waterfalls out in the countryside. Were people just parts of each other? 'So what is it?' he asked, talking in a relaxed tone of voice.

'I have made my wife pregnant,' Coleridge said quietly. 'She is breeding, yet again. There now, what about that? We shall soon have another baby. I ask you, what am I to do?' Coleridge's features whitened as he spoke.

'As I was saying,' Dorothy interrupted, unsteadily. 'Mary

Hutchinson has been with us. We thought you might have called, but you didn't. I think she was disappointed. Anyway, now she has gone.'

'So it seems,' said Coleridge, tapping the arms of his chair. Whenever Coleridge was with them, William felt Coleridge belonged, whenever he wasn't his ghost wandered the rooms as if in waiting. They could not bear his absence.

'So what did you do with this Mary, then?' asked Coleridge.

'Just ordinary things,' Dorothy said nonchalantly. 'The same as we do with you.'

'God forbid that anything is *ordinary* with me!' Coleridge exclaimed indignantly. He brushed back his hair with his hands and Dorothy caught sight of a bruise on his brow, purple and mysterious. Perhaps he had fallen. Walking across the hills in stormy weather was often hazardous. She glanced at William. Coleridge sat for some minutes, gazing at the ceiling and murmuring, then he closed his eyes and fell asleep.

The week continued less dramatically. There were days all three of them went walking with the boy, other days William walked out with Coleridge alone. Such days they talked poetry, soft as the hush of stone, loud as the highest wind, excited and glowing as the stars. Annette and his life in France were fading for William into a life imagined rather than lived. From time to time he was aware of Annette as pure exultant joy rushing his blood, distinct, fiery and alive, but a joy he could not reach. The last letter he'd received from Elizabeth claimed Pierre's staff had departed and his vineyard was withering. Annette and Paul no longer visited the château, she said, and Pierre never visited Blois. The vital part of himself, William realised, that had lived there and loved, was dying. He was twenty-seven years old, but he felt much older, he had witnessed so much, experienced so much and had felt so many emotions. Whenever he walked out with Coleridge, they glanced about cautiously, for there was now much tension in England, and they were constantly sitting on walls and writing things down. Ideas flew between them like comets. Dorothy too brought her own compositions which she added to her diary each day. "Three persons with one soul," Coleridge called them, and they cherished their trinity as if it were a gift from heaven. "You must come to see us at Nether Stowey!' Coleridge said one evening. 'Well, that's if you want to, not if you don't, obviously. Sarah would be glad of your company and Hartley can play with Basil. Anyway, my friends, do give it some thought.'

William glanced at Dorothy, who looked confused. For a moment or two Coleridge stood with his back towards them, his hand on the latch. 'We'll expect you Saturday,' he said finally. With that he left.

22

The Visit To Nether Stowey

Coleridge had talked at length about the beautiful coastal walks around Nether Stowey and they'd entered Dorothy's dreams. She'd imagined herself with William, walking across the fields to the beach, listening to the breakers crashing on the cliffs, buzzards and seagulls wheeling and circling above.

She gazed from the window of the chaise, straining her eyes in the yellow autumn sunlight. In the foothills of the Quantock Hills were the remains of castles and prehistoric sites. Castle Hill, Coleridge had said, led to a place called The Mount, from which the whole village might be viewed, wonderful to see in springtime, carpeted with buttercups and bluebells. But there were things about Nether Stowey, he did not like. Bear baiting and cock fighting were known to take place around The Mount, and there was the curious tale of a giant who lived in a cave, frightening travellers as they passed with his hair-raising cries. Coleridge thought he'd seen him one evening while returning to his cottage, an enormous fellow standing in the road, waving his great arms and intent on mischief.

Dorothy had packed pies and preserves for their visit and William had carved a small wooden animal for Hartley to play with. As the chaise came to a halt, they saw that Coleridge's home was a quaint thatch roofed cottage.

'You are here at last!' cried Coleridge, dashing towards them. 'And the weather was on your side all the way, lucky people! – Oh, everything is always on your side Wordsworth isn't it! And what about that new fustian jacket and those striped pantaloons? Is it Beau Brummell who visits us?'

William glanced at the doorway as they all walked up to the house. Sarah was nowhere in sight. Little Basil, silent and good, glanced about for Hartley.

'You must see the bay tree I've planted,' said Coleridge excitedly. 'It thrives a lot better than I do. I have one or two fruit trees too that bring us lots of butterflies in summer.' He talked on quickly in his normal feverish way. 'You might like a walk to Porlock sometime. It's probably too far for the child, but he can always stay here with Sarah and Hartley. We've put you in a room where there are views of the coastal hills and a scent of the sea. And a grand little room it is too. Sarah thought Dorothy would like it.' Coleridge covered his face with his hands. 'Oh, what a morning! Like a tempest it was. Thankfully it's over. I hope she's in better humour when we go in. She is subject to weeping, I'm afraid.' He shrugged. 'Of course, it is all about me.'

William noted a tremor in Coleridge's voice. He glanced warily at Dorothy, then smiled wryly. 'Is she happy for us to descend on you all like this?'

'Well, your room's all neat and ready, and she's prepared you some food, so I expect all is well.'

'I hope so,' said Dorothy worriedly. 'Believe me, Coleridge, I do not wish to upset her.'

They followed him into the house.

The cottage was warm and homely with simple unpretentious furnishings. Pretty yellow cushions were thrown about the sofa and chairs, and a red patterned rug lay across the floor by a welcoming fire.

'Ah, here is Sarah!' said Coleridge, as she came down the stairs. 'And the little rascal on her arm is mine. Or so I am led to believe.'

Sarah's skin tightened with annoyance. The child was about two years old.

'He's just a baby,' Basil whispered to Dorothy. 'How can I play with a baby?'

'Hush,' said Dorothy, frowning at the boy.

'I trust your journey was comfortable,' said Sarah. 'The roads can be bad after rain. We've had a lot of rain in . . .'

'Oh, for pity's sake, Sarah,' sighed Coleridge. 'Why are you grumbling about the weather, the last few days have been grand?' He smiled at Dorothy.

'But sometimes the rain lasts for ages,' said Sarah. 'It's as if the skies are weeping and will never stop.'

'See what I have to put up with, Wordsworth,' said Coleridge, clapping his hand on his brow.

'I've brought Hartley a toy,' said William. He pulled it out of his pocket.

Sarah put the child on the floor and he scrambled across to the toy, stroking the little bird William had made him.

'I never made a toy before,' said William looking amazed, and enjoying the child's pleasure. 'Those wings were very hard to carve.' He squatted down beside him, watching with wonder. 'I do believe he likes it.'

Sarah bent down to the child, murmuring into his ear, and the child clapped his hands. Her long dark hair fell about her face, rich, strong and magnificent. William thought her quite beautiful.

'And I brought you something for the larder,' said Dorothy. 'Just a small box of pastries – they are all quite fresh.'

'Thank you,' said Sarah, kissing Dorothy's cheek.

The women, thought William, seemed to have made a connection, though he did not feel he had connected with Sarah himself. He felt she resented him. It was probably because Coleridge kept leaving her to visit them. But Coleridge would never be still. If he did not come to see them, he would have gone to see somebody else. It was easy to see there was a gulf between Sarah and Coleridge, a sad, desperate gulf, filled with pain and shame, for it seemed they abused each other badly. They stood in a room full of books. William was keen to take a look.

'That poetry we're working on, Wordsworth,' said Coleridge. 'We'll not do much writing in here. Hartley rules I'm afraid. If he doesn't get his way then he'll scream the place down. It sounds like murder.'

Sarah came back from the kitchen where she'd gone to brew tea. 'We rent the cottage from Tom Poole, a local tanner,' she said. 'He lives across the way.' She spoke softly and smiled. 'He is very kind and generous.' Settling the baby on her hip, she took Dorothy's arm. 'Come, let me show you your bedroom.'

William and Coleridge followed them upstairs with the luggage. Sarah's skin thought William, as the sun embraced it from the window, was white and powdery like the bark of a young birch. She was elegant, slow and secretive, moving like cold winter sunlight. A nervous woman, with a wistful look in her eyes, there was a mystery about her like the quiet of an underground stream. He could see that on occasion it might burst out of the earth.

'The road can be noisy with horsemen,' said Sarah, seeing Dorothy gazing outside.

'I can't move the road, my dear,' said Coleridge flatly.

Sarah got bedding from the cupboard. 'We have a housekeeper sometimes, but we manage on our own mostly. I think your beds will be warm enough though, but here are some extra blankets in case. The child will sleep by the window in the bed over there. Tom Poole brought it last week. We hoped you would come.'

There was a single bed to each side of the room with a thin purple rug between. Green damask curtains hung at the windows, while a number of amateur watercolour paintings relieved the cold white walls, and a writing table and chair stood by the window.

'Dorothy makes notes, my dear,' said Coleridge to Sarah. 'I believe she keeps a sort of journal. You ought to keep a journal yourself, don't you think?'

Sarah smiled wryly.

'Though I know what she'd write about,' said Coleridge, churlishly. 'Me and my villainous practices!'

'Poor you,' said Sarah dryly. 'Why I bother about you at all, I do not know. – Oh dear, where has it gone?' She fell to searching about the beds frantically, then the floor.

'What have you lost?' asked Coleridge, shaking his head with irritation.

'Please shut the door,' she said fretfully. 'Hartley will fall down the stairs.'

'What a wasted imagination,' Coleridge murmured, picking up the baby. He looked at Dorothy and William. 'I think we've finished up here, let's go down. Damned if I know what she's after.'

Sarah's search had obviously been successful, for after a while, she came downstairs and joined them, looking more cheerful.

'Have you found what you lost?' asked William.

She touched the band of gold on her finger. 'It was my ring. It somehow fell off. I have lost some weight recently. I do at the start of a pregnancy.' She gazed at her hand. 'My fingers are thinner. – Which reminds me, I must get us some food.'

William got up to look at Coleridge's books. 'You have many good books on theology,' he said, peering at the titles. 'Are you really leaving the Ministry?'

Coleridge looked at him reproachfully. 'You know my reasons, Wordsworth.' He sighed, bracing himself. 'We have often discussed it. – And anyway, you were not too happy yourself about taking Orders, if I remember.'

'You are quite right,' said William.

'We cannot continue to interpret the Bible literally in defiance of science,' said Coleridge in a tone of exasperation. 'We have to think harder.'

Dorothy and Sarah went to prepare food in the kitchen while Basil played with the baby and his new wooden toy.

'Dorothy has some excellent ideas,' said Coleridge, stroking his chin. 'She is quite amazing.'

'Indeed, she is,' said William quietly. Coleridge was far too frivolous with Dorothy, and she with him. Even today, in the presence of his wife and child, he had placed his arm around her shoulder and smiled at her as if they were lovers. 'She is very vulnerable too,' added William. 'But I shall always be there by her side.'

Coleridge laughed. 'You feel you have to protect her, do you? I wonder who from?' He leant forward and whispered, 'Yourself, perhaps?'

William eyes narrowed with annoyance. 'Damn you Coleridge! – How dare you!' He sat seething with resentment until time took hold and put him in a better frame of mind.

The tension in Coleridge's home was often disturbing. William and Dorothy could see how the couple suffered and didn't know what to make of their complicated silences. Coleridge would stand about miserable. Sarah would retire to her bedroom. And there were days when Dorothy and William had thought they should leave. Though Coleridge would beg them to stay. How would they cope once they had the new baby, William wondered? They had such an unhealthy way of being and it appeared to have grown into a habit. If it was war the two of them wanted, then they were well matched, William decided. If Coleridge glared at Sarah, Sarah glared back. If Coleridge tapped his foot irritably, then she tapped hers. And so it continued. They each carried their anger as if nursing a hideous demon. And it was very much alive and well. They all tried to talk about politics and life. Though it seemed Sarah's life didn't happen. She was out on a limb. He wondered what she and Coleridge would do if they did not quarrel, for the quarrelling held them together.

But there were better, happier times, when Coleridge was tender, singing to Hartley and clasping his wife's hand. At such times it seemed their pains might be banished for good, though it was naïve to believe it. William felt they enjoyed their mercurial relationship and concluded it was Sarah's pride that was hurt because Coleridge kept wandering off, either to visit friends, or to climb some silly mountain, she said, all on his own, and when he was at home he was difficult. "I have reason to think he is changing," Dorothy had said to her hopefully. "Do not ask too much of him, my dear. Just wait. I do believe he'll get better."

Why Dorothy held such a belief, William couldn't imagine, for it was hardly likely Coleridge would change in the least, he was far too lost. His genius grew from some tremulous bud of sensitivity that had urgent, relentless demands, uncaring and utterly independent. Coleridge maddened everyone he met. He even maddened himself. But for Sarah it was all so crucial, for she nurtured him from the bosom of her soul and each time he hurt her she suffered.

But William reasoned Coleridge's needs could never have been contained in the small family unit at Nether Stowey. He and

Dorothy though, had done the right thing, he decided, in coming to see them; Dorothy had listened to Sarah's frustrations and believed she had eased her fears. She was married, she'd told her, to a man with so many minds he could scarce know who he was from one day to the next. She must grip her feelings and govern them, Dorothy had urged, or they would surely destroy her. All well and good, thought William, but Sarah wasn't Dorothy.

But Dorothy could be deeply sensitive too, William pondered as he sat alone in the parlour. He recalled how Coleridge could cause his sister to tremble, just with his smile. He was glad he didn't suffer like that, for Coleridge suffered greatly, sitting about with his head in his hands or else striding the hills angry. William reflected that his own private pain was a deep secret in his heart. He did not trouble Dorothy with his own depression, or anyone else. Dorothy didn't suffer depression, but she did get headaches when she worried, and had to lie down. But perhaps she hurt more than he knew. If she did, it was rarely evident, she always had something to do, mending a collar or a cuff on his shirt, repairing the lace on some dress, or else writing up her notes. Her observations were wonderful and there were times they brought tears to his eyes with their piercing perception.

He began to emerge from his thoughts and gazed about the lonely room. Dorothy and Coleridge were out walking, Sarah was taking a rest upstairs with the baby, and Basil was asleep on the floor. The house felt unusually peaceful, the fire crackling and the afternoon sunlight falling on the child from the window. He was holding *The Alchemist*, a comedy by the playwright Ben Jonson, who had published some powerful writing, and another fellow who had suffered a difficult marriage. For a while he had offered his services to the army and had spent some time in a regiment, reportedly having killed in combat. And he had spent some time in Newgate prison, as well! Oppression and misery were always at a writer's door. Jonson was a colourful fellow surrounded by much controversy. *The Alchemist*, which Coleridge had recommended, on account of it being hilarious and with an excellent plot, satirised human gullibility. With its fairy rites and the promise of forging a philosopher's stone for use in all manner of farce, the play was most entertaining. He put it aside and braced himself, then went to the door to look out. Where could they be? He wanted to go over the work they'd done that holiday. In spite of Hartley and Basil's commotion about the house, they'd managed some excellent writing. But he'd have to get back to Racedown tomorrow. How handy it would be to live closer, he thought. And he thought again about Coleridge's words at breakfast that day: "How do you fancy a mansion, Wordsworth, with deer in the grounds and the taste of the sea on your tongue?" Dorothy's eyes had widened. – "But where is it?" " Oh, quite nearby," Coleridge had sniffed. "Splendidly furnished too, and plenty of room for guests." "I am not wealthy, Coleridge," William had replied flatly, though keenly attentive. They were getting weary of Racedown Lodge; the hill was something of a treadmill and they felt cut off, also the elder Pinney had discovered they were living there for free and might turn them out. "Oh, I doubt the owners would ask for much rent," Coleridge had said, nonchalantly. "I can speak to Tom Poole if you like. He knows all about it. Alfoxden House has been empty for a while. It's someone's inheritance, but they don't seem to need it." "Another one of those," Dorothy had sighed. But her eyes stayed fixed on Coleridge. "My dear," she'd murmured. "Do continue . . ."

William had said to declare their interest straight away. The owners might indeed be generous, he thought. Since the French Revolution the rich were becoming more benevolent having witnessed the results of greed in torrents of blood. Just then he heard footsteps on the path. Coleridge and Dorothy were back, laughing and talking. What went on, he wondered, that caused Dorothy such excitement and made her laugh like a girl. There was something special between Dorothy and Coleridge that was all their own and from which he felt excluded. It was beautiful, yet it was a thing that set itself up against him in a way, didn't she see it was a sort of betrayal to link arms with him and laugh so loudly?

They all ate a quiet supper together and it was more or less decided they would rent Alfoxden House, in fact they would go and take a look at it tomorrow, William said, on their journey back to Racedown.

The carriage passed by hills, blazing with yellow gorse and rushing with silver streams, then rattled through thick tall woods, finally meeting the crystal lakes, Coleridge had spoken of which were reaches of the Severn Sea.

'It's there!' cried Dorothy, pointing. 'I can see it through the trees.'

They could see the building through the parkland. Beech and holly trees flanked the approach to the many windowed mansion that looked out on the Quantock Hills. There was a large garden to the front and another garden to the side where a small herd of deer grazed quietly.

William's hopes rose high. It was certainly a lovely house, quite perfect for Dorothy to live in, and with a mere two miles between them, he and Coleridge could carry on their work with ease. And would it not be better for Sarah, if Coleridge could return straight home after their labours and not have to stay with them? To William their poetry was integral to his life and spirit; it was where his soul focused. And Coleridge's too if he would let it. But a lot of the time he would not, he forgot to bring important pieces forgot important discussions, scattered his genius to the winds.

They wandered outside, peering through windows and ambling around the gardens, the child running freely through the trees. It was all very impressive. Tom Poole, Coleridge had said, was a man who liked to be helpful. He was widely read, entertaining the likes of Hazlitt and Lamb. It would be good to join such a crew, thought William, and expand his ideas. Coleridge had said that Poole had an excellent library and lent his books out freely: "He is a good and candid fellow, a liberal Englishman who has travelled widely and very much applauded round here. He is guardian of so many children whose father's have sadly died, it is little wonder he is loved."

'Can we live here?' asked the child.

'I do believe we can,' said William. They would await Coleridge's letter with interest, the matter was resolved.

23

Lyrical Ballads

The rooms at Alfoxden House were big and chilly, but fires would warm them in winter, William thought as he went round examining every nook and cranny. It was coming to the end of summer; soft, drowsy light gently wandered the house. In such a place, with so much space, Coleridge could bring his family and stay overnight and the rent was a mere trifle. The lease would be only for a year, but much could be done in a year with the right attitude. The still and lonely abode felt wary and watchful. They went to look around the grounds. Straggling deer fed peacefully beneath the trees. Glorious flowers were plentiful. The gardens bristled with gardenias, heavy looking flowers with soft creamy heads and strong exquisite perfumes, growing beside purple hydrangeas and red geraniums. The deer, which seemed quite tame, did not scatter when called and intrigued the child who went closer.

'Do not make them afraid,' urged William. 'They are good, innocent creatures.' The deer stared back through large other worldly eyes.

Back inside, they investigated further. Every room was filled with elegant furniture. A gate leg table in English cherry shimmered in one of the sitting rooms beside a grand mahogany bookcase packed with interesting books. A writing desk, he knew he would use, stood by the window. The whole house was dusty, but that could be resolved in minutes, Dorothy said light-heartedly.

These rooms need airing,' said William. 'I saw some firewood by the door. – Now, where is the tinderbox?'

The kitchen cupboards were a wonder to Dorothy, filled with beautiful tureens and crockery and big heavy pans, while from the window upstairs, and most delightful of all, was an excellent view of the sea. There would be many more walks with Coleridge . . .

As the weeks went by, the house emerged as a home. Coleridge came often with his family, when Hartley would run along the thin winding paths through the trees, Sarah walking behind, her head bent low, her bonnet obscuring her face, her silk skirts rustling in the undergrowth. William and Coleridge worked on their poetry, while Dorothy and Sarah sat quietly together, the children sleeping.

Sometimes William sat alone outside in the dusk when thoughts of France overwhelmed him, or he would pace the grounds thinking, gazing at the evening star. It was 1797, would the wars never cease? The English government feared the French more than ever and suspected spies at every turn. Dorothy had heard strange movements by the windows at night time outside, she said. William said it was an animal; a fox, a deer, a hedgehog perhaps, daring too close. But Dorothy insisted they were spied on. She'd seen faces at the windows, she said, and figures running off into the shadows. William admitted to sometimes hearing peculiar sounds himself when walking the woodland, not animal sounds, but more like the movements of humans, and he would freeze on recalling the day in the forest with Beaupuy. But the faces Dorothy had seen at the window were probably just locals, he'd said, wondering who lived in the house.

Coleridge brought guests from London, and the neighbouring community were bound to be curious. The empty mansion had been a mystery. The locals had invented stories about it, stories about murder, stories about ghosts and now stories about spies! Of late there had been a couple of peddlers at the door hawking needles and pins, looking them up and down strangely and going off murmuring.

He thought about Annette. He thought about Mary. And he thought about Caroline. Each time he pulled on his boots to take a walk, he knew he would think of them all. But he could not solve the complexities confounding his mind. And he could not stop the torments he felt in his soul.

1797 passed into 1798. And now it was June. Alone in the parlour, Dorothy opened her journal and looked down at her notes. Oh, the pain of great ideas, she thought as she dipped her pen in the ink. Her most sensitive feelings were her children, it was a bit like she thought giving birth might be, until she wrote her thoughts in her journal, she did not see the full glory of their beauty, the subtle turn of a phrase, the rhythm and music of her language. She wrote about people, she wrote about plants and animals, she wrote about the seasons and the sea, and she wrote about the weather, for the weather always held sway, many a planned walk could be foiled by its antics. She read what she'd entered that January:

"January 20th 1798. – The green paths down the hill-sides are channels for streams. The young wheat is streaked by silver lines of water running between the ridges, the sheep are gathered together on the slopes.

January 23rd. – Bright sunshine, went out at 3 o'clock. The sea perfectly calm blue, streaked with deeper colour by the clouds, and tongues or points of sand; on our return of a gloomy red . . ."

They had lived in Alfoxden House a year, the lease was up and now they must depart. How she would miss the flowers and shrubberies, the gentle deer, the tall shimmering trees with their multitude of birds, the ferny knolls and waterfalls and the Quantock hills. It had been good to live close to Coleridge and see him more often. But what was to happen now? William was lying in, tired from a late night writing. Basil played in the garden, gathering stones and leaves to take to his bedroom. But he would have to return to his father now; it was time. Last night there had been a family of foxes in the garden. The vixen had walked across the lawns slowly, her three well-fed cubs waddling behind. How she admired such creatures, such splendid, proud, independent animals living in the wild. But she could not live with William out in the wild. Must they beg shelter from friends? William had talked a lot about returning to Lakeland. Is that what they'd do?

She closed her eyes wondering what to write that day. The journal didn't know everything. Not *everything*. She did not write of her brother's anxieties. Nor did she write of how much she would like to see Annette, to touch little Caroline and kiss her and let her know she had an aunt in England who cared. But what a strange caring it was; like caring for a fictitious character in a book, not a real person at all. But it was all the caring she could offer. What did the little girl look like? Did she have curls like her own? She wondered what it would be like to have a child of her own, and if she'd be a good enough mother.

Sarah had given birth to another baby boy and his name was Berkley. Berkley's lungs, Coleridge claimed, were even more powerful than Hartley's for he needed constant attention and their life in the little cottage was more frantic than ever. Dorothy hoped he was now back safe in his home. He'd left Alfoxden House in the early hours of the morning that day after talking with William. The energy of their book was devouring them both. Without doubt, it would be unique. It would manifest the voice of ordinary people, William had asserted loudly as Coleridge walked out into the darkness. – "It will light the way for a whole new age of poetry! And its name will be *Lyrical Ballads*", he'd said, for a lyric was a musical poem, and the way the rustics delivered their stories was like listening to music. "'*Lyrical Ballads!*'" Coleridge had called out from the night. "Hallelujah to *Lyrical Ballads!*"

Dorothy understood that the true voice of poetry for her brother rose from the dark earth; it was a verdant, homespun language. Coleridge though, brought a different voice, a strange, visionary voice, a voice from the ether, which William pondered on, biting his lip and frowning, and which sometimes made Dorothy tremble with its intensity. She looked at the scattered pages on William's desk. How hard he and Coleridge had laboured. "They'll tear us to pieces!" Coleridge had cried, almost insane with tiredness. "Your name is nothing, Wordsworth. And as for mine, it stinks!" It was new work, it was different, and it was daring, thought Dorothy. It would probably make people jealous. There were poets who didn't understand her brother's genius. He didn't understand it himself, but his strange wisdom, his knowledge of the old dark earth he walked on, was at one with his soul. He belonged to the elements, to the stars, and to her.

Pulling on his knee breeches upstairs, William was thoughtful. He didn't want to go back into lodgings and have Dorothy return to the rectory. He racked his brains for a solution. What would happen to the writing he did with Coleridge? It must not pass into oblivion! It didn't do Coleridge the least bit of good barging out at the dead of night irritable. Inside he was a tortured soul. His words came to birth shrieking and screaming sometimes, filled with an awful power, the voices of heaven, even the voices of hell. William hoped it wasn't too long before Coleridge returned. The poems needed work. He wanted to know more about *The Rime of The Ancient Mariner.* What was he going to do with that damned albatross? He could hear Dorothy moving about downstairs.

'Coleridge sounded unhappy last night,' she murmured, as he joined her. 'I heard the two of you arguing.'

'Aye, we had a bit of a set-to. I expect he'll be here tomorrow though. He'd a problem with some verse.'

'Of course,' she murmured. 'What's it about?'

'Oh, something to do with a bird. He'll sort it out.'

'So long as I'm not in the way . . . I could go out walking if you like.'

'Not at all, my dear. He likes to have you around. I don't need to tell you that now, do I?'

And William talked on about the ballads, Dorothy listening intently. There was much to do. William went out into the garden, came back and sat in the kitchen staring downwards as if in a dream. It was almost as if time stood still. Nothing was more important than the *Lyrical Ballads.* He mumbled poems to the floor, sometimes smiling pleased, sometimes frowning, as imagination took hold of his senses.

Next day Coleridge arrived at the house, his hair tousled, his eyes bleary and sleepless. 'You'll not be happy with it, Wordsworth!' he cried. He clasped a bunch of papers to his chest, then cast a page before William. Dorothy sat silently sewing.

William read through the poetry, then lifted his head slowly. Coleridge held the rest of the poem close, watching William intently.

'This is all about guilt and punishment,' William murmured, without looking up. 'What are you up to?'

'There's redemption in it as well,' Coleridge protested. He lifted his shoulders then dropped them with a sigh. 'Oh, read it properly, Wordsworth!'

'So what have you done with the albatross?' asked William quietly. 'This tells me nothing.'

Coleridge cried out painfully, 'I do not know if that albatross is alive or dead. It plagues me even in my sleep! – Bah! I knew you wouldn't like it.'

'Am I not to criticise?' sighed William.

'I need to believe in what I write, Wordsworth!' said Coleridge.

'And you don't?' said William.

Coleridge, shaking with anger, was silent.

'I have to say what I think,' said William flatly. He put out his hand for the rest of Coleridge's poem. 'You wouldn't want any less from me, would you? Let me look at some more.'

'I'll write the poem as I want!' Coleridge thundered. – 'Yah, Cottle and his cavilling. Archaisms indeed! The poem comes as I feel it. You, dear Wordsworth, want the pure, innocent idea, as if you could pluck it from the earth like a delicate flower. I, my friend, want the airy mystery of the great celestial spheres!'

'Well, let's not quarrel about it, Coleridge,' said William poking at the fire. 'If we're going to publish a book together we must do it in the right spirit. But do please tell me. – What has happened to the albatross?'

Coleridge clutched the pages of his poem tightly. He would not hand them across. 'Right,' he said quietly. Listen and I'll tell you.' He bent his head and began:

> *'And a good south wind sprung up behind;*
> *The Albatross did follow,*
> *And every day, for food or play,*
> *Came the mariners' hollo!*
>
> *In mist or cloud, on mast or shroud,*
> *It perched for vespers nine;*

Whiles all the night, through fog-smoke white,
Glimmered the white Moon-shine.

God save thee, ancient Mariner!
From the fiends, that plague thee thus! —
Why look'st though so? — With my cross-bow
I shot the albatross.'

William rose and stood before him. 'So you killed it?' He folded his arms and gazed at the floor frowning. For a moment they were silent. Dorothy watched confounded. 'It's good. I like it,' William said finally. He nodded at Coleridge seriously. 'There is bound to be mischief now, of course. The unseen forces of the universe will have to get even! The spirits will avenge!'

Coleridge's lips twitched as he nodded back. 'It'll be ready for Cottle within the week, and he'd best not be moaning or I'll be shooting him as well!'

'He still isn't happy about us publishing the book anonymously,' said William.

'We'd see a thousand new moons before we'd satisfy Cottle,' said Coleridge, flatly. 'He must do as we say.' Attempting to change the subject, Coleridge went to the bookcase and ran his eyes across the books. 'Hume wasn't *that* original, you know,' he murmured, furrowing his brow. 'I believe he stole that essay on miracles from a sermon by South.' He turned and gazed curiously at a page of poetry on a chair. 'What's that?' he asked, pointing.

William reached for it. 'It's *The Ruined Cottage.* I was doing some work on it earlier.'

'I like that poem very much,' said Coleridge. 'I will be pleased to hear it when you're ready.'

William braced himself. It was always good to get Coleridge's support. 'A little more editing and I'm there.'

Coleridge gave a little shudder and brought down his eyelids.

'Are you unwell?' asked Dorothy, rising from her chair.

For a second or two Coleridge swayed. The pages of the Mariner floated like autumn leaves to the floor. He grasped the back of the chair and sat down. 'Everything is a little unreal today,' he said weakly. 'But I am denied the visions I seek. The words and images are too far away . . .' Then he fell into a chair and slept. Basil, seated on the carpet, lifted his eyes and gazed at Coleridge then bent again to his play.

24

Mary

That month a letter came from Mary inviting them for a holiday on the Sockburn farm. And a very lively letter it was. William felt relieved no end. His letters to her had been warm, while hers to him had been guarded. In consequence, he thought he had lost her. He wrote back quickly. It was as if new music had begun to play in his soul. The sight of Mary's handwriting filled him with hope and all his thoughts were clearer. He would find a cottage with Dorothy very soon; it was simply a matter of time. *Lyrical Ballads* would be published and the reviews would be spectacular. He rode on the crest of a wave. And now it was time to leave Alfoxden House, and to say goodbye to little Basil also, a carefree, intelligent child who now returned to his father eager and smiling.

It was mid September when they made their way to the farm. William and Dorothy sat musing on the Autumn scenery about them, the sound of the boy's chatter no longer enlivening the air, their thoughts intense, the clattering wheels of the chaise the only sound in the otherwise hushed countryside. Dorothy knew that her brother was in love with Mary. He had visited Elizabeth twice that year but had returned despondent. Nothing had been heard from Annette.

Gentle orange light fell about the chaise as it advanced north-east. The Sockburn farm was in a lovely location, the river Tees winding its way about it and plenty of English countryside to roam and enjoy. The last of the summer flowers were now bowing out and the ferns were withering into a deep brown sleepy softness. Coleridge had declined the invitation. It was quite beyond reason, Sarah had asserted, for him to think of taking a holiday just now. There were matters to deal with at home.

But *Lyrical Ballads* would soon make a dignified entrance into the world, William reflected. And he had added another poem, a special, glittering, magical poem he had at last achieved. The words of *Tintern Abbey* exulted in his soul!

Arriving near the Hutchinson farm they spotted Tom in a field, gathering dried stems of corn and performing some of his regular autumnal tasks. William called and Tom waved back. 'I have to gather these in before the rain!' he shouted. 'I'll be there in ten minutes!'

William leapt down from the chaise and stood by the gate, while the driver took Dorothy on ahead. Tom came across the field and they walked along the path to the farm. There was a shocked autumn stillness on the land all about them. 'Does anyone come to woo her?' asked William earnestly. He glanced at Mary's brother sideways and smiled.

'Mary?' said Tom, with a laugh. 'What do you think? I can't say no.'

'Anyone *special*?' William asked warily. He brushed back his hair with his hands, as ever he was looking shabby. Then he gazed up at the sky. Not a single bird to be seen. The quiet of an English autumn always moved him.

'But don't get too worried,' Tom said laughing. 'Whatever your questions, you must put them to her yourself. She'll answer honestly. I know what's in her eyes though. And I know you're there every day. You should see how she loves your letters.'

William frowned and looked downwards. 'Does she? I'm glad.' He braced himself. 'You know what happened in France though, don't you.' For a few seconds there was silence. 'I'm not exactly a saint, Tom. I suppose she's told you.'

'She has,' said Tom flatly. 'It upset her at first, but not now. A man has to love as love finds him.'

William smiled thoughtfully. He had tried so hard to still his passion for Annette. But he had kept it bound so long; he felt he had killed it. How could he call himself a poet if he tried to kill his deepest feelings just because they hurt? He sat down on a heap of hay and sighed.

'I'd best walk on,' said Tom. 'The hens'll be waiting for their seed. See you at the farm when you're ready.'

A week passed by and William and Mary often went walking alone, but it was only what the rest had expected. What had occurred in France was complicated, and no-one could tell how long the wars would continue. Life and death, Tom had remarked sagaciously, would always have its own way.

One day in the middle of the week, Sara Hutchinson was cleaning the floor in the kitchen, when she saw that a stranger had arrived at the farm, standing by the door with her brother. Better to see him, she blinked in the bright sunlight. 'I have come uninvited,' said the figure, talking with Tom. 'But I hoped I might stay for a while. The fact of it is I am rather depressed.' The man's eyes searched about the yard. 'I know that Wordsworth is with you.' As yet, Sara Hutchinson did not meet his eyes.

'The Wordsworths have been with us a week,' said Tom. 'Dorothy and William are both in the sitting room. Ah, Mary is returning from her work in the stables. Here she is!'

'Mr Coleridge?' said Mary. 'We were talking about you this morning and here you are! William felt sure you would come.' She glanced at Sara. 'This is Sara, my sister.'

Coleridge bowed lightly, first to Mary then Sara. 'Good day,' he said cheerily. 'I hope you are both keeping well.'

'Indeed we are,' said Sara, rising from the floor. 'And you?'

'I wasn't so good, but now I am feeling much better,' laughed Coleridge. He pulled off his knapsack and flung it down on the floor. Then he wiped his brow with his neckerchief.

'You are more than welcome, Mr Coleridge,' said Tom. 'You might have brought your wife and children; the youngster would have liked the harvesting . . .'

'Oh, oh, oh,' said Coleridge, looking away. 'I am sure you are right. Hartley would have loved it. Thank you Tom, your heart is in the right place. But I fear my own has fled.'

Tom, a ruddy-faced fellow with bright red hair, brushed hay from his breeches, inviting a scowl from Sara as the grass littered the floor. 'Let's hope a little holiday will help you feel better, Mr Coleridge,' he laughed. He looked downwards. 'You've made a grand job of this floor, my dear. I hope we can keep it clean now you've scrubbed it.' William came out of the sitting room.

Sara Hutchinson dried her hands on her apron. The sun shone on her thick brown hair, softly tied in a bun at the nape of her neck. She put out her hand.

Coleridge shook it warmly. 'I am pleased to meet you, Sara.'

'You do not look as I thought,' said Sara, curiously.

'Oh dear,' said Coleridge, a little perturbed. 'So how should I look?' He gazed down at his well-worn boots, the laces knotted and broken. His frockcoat was stained and torn. He laughed loudly at the ceiling. 'A tramp I am and a tramp I'll be, hey ho and fiddle di dee!' He stamped his feet on the floor, disturbing a couple of horses tethered by the door. 'Well, you may rest assured, my dear, it is I, Samuel Taylor Coleridge, for better or worse!' He looked sideways at William, who now stood quietly beside them. 'I suppose you think I should look like Wordsworth, eh? – Oh yes, what I would give for that torso, those shoulders, that fetching image!'

'Don't be an ass,' William whispered, sighing.

Coleridge's eyes explored the kitchen with interest. Baskets of fruit and vegetables were placed against walls. The smell of baking bread came from the oven, while the strong aroma of cinnamon and stewing apples came from pans on the stove. Everywhere was bright and clean and the scent of sweet new wood rose up from freshly sawn logs in a corner beneath shelves of conserves.

Dorothy came next and greeted Coleridge warmly.

Tom invited them all to take a seat around the large rustic table which was laden with all manner of cheeses, fruits and meats. Sara still stared at Coleridge. 'Shouldn't you be with your wife, Mr Coleridge?' said Sara, vexed by his carefree manner. 'You have a family.'

Coleridge's face reddened. 'Ah,' sighed Coleridge. 'I am quite a rogue it seems. But you do not know the whole of it, my dear, so better not judge.'

Tom brought a large pot of tea to the table.

'Well then, Tom,' said Coleridge. 'You have two very different sisters. One is gentle, while the other is . . . well, rather impudent I think.' He smiled at Sara wryly.

'I would reserve the word "impudent" for children,' said Sara, tossing her head. 'Did I touch a raw nerve, Mr Coleridge?' She put her hands to her hair and fixed back some pins, though her eyes stayed firmly on Coleridge. 'I speak my mind, Mr Coleridge. It is a luxury to wander as you do, forgetting your wife and family and scribbling out poems.'

Dorothy, sitting by William, gave a little cough.

'I would like Mr Coleridge to stay for a while,' said Tom. 'Do make him welcome, Sara.'

Sara scowled. 'I have been scrubbing the floor for an hour. After I have eaten I must collect the eggs from the hedgerows. Then I must milk the cows. While you, Mr Coleridge will probably just sit writing poems.'

'I am sure Mr Coleridge will lend us a hand, my dear,' said Tom, pouring out tea. 'Do you expect him to help milk the cows?'

'Perhaps,' she murmured.

'I have never milked a cow in my life,' laughed Coleridge, piling slices of ham on his plate.

'Then you will have to be shown,' said Sara curtly. 'It takes but minutes to learn.'

'Then learn I shall,' said Coleridge, delightedly. 'Or it seems I am doomed.'

'I have never been able to master it myself,' William added vaguely.

'You have to trust your instincts, Wordsworth,' said Coleridge. 'If a cow is for milking, then milk it you must.'

'William has helped us a lot,' said Mary. 'He has done his share of collecting eggs and the like. We might go for a ride tomorrow, weather permitting.'

'Well, there are horses at the ready by the door. Use them as you like,' said Tom, pointing to the open doorway. 'You too, Mr Coleridge.'

'Coleridge doesn't ride,' smiled William.

'No, I don't,' said Coleridge flatly, filling his mouth with food.

'You must trust your instincts Coleridge,' said William, fixing his eyes on him and smiling. 'If a horse is for riding, then ride it you must.'

'*Touché*,' smiled Coleridge. He shook his head and sighed. 'The thing is horses don't like me. And I have to say, if I were a horse, I wouldn't let a human near me. Whatever must those creatures be thinking when we take the poor devils to war? I can never understand why they don't stampede and be done with it. They fall on the battlefield as easily as autumn leaves. It is quite horrific.'

Dogs barked loudly in the yard. Mary got up to attend to them and William followed.

After they'd fed the dogs, they walked across the gravel yard together to a wooded area nearby and climbed down a bank. Little tired leaves flew about their faces in the soft afternoon breeze. 'Do you remember the autumns we shared as children?' William said wistfully.

She turned to him and smiled. 'Of course, I remember it all.'

For a moment or two they were silent. 'I'm sorry about that with Sara,' Mary said, frowning. 'She was rude to your friend.'

William laughed. 'Oh, on the contrary. She is a plain speaking woman, and why not.' He gazed ahead, thoughtful. 'It will do him no harm.'

'She spoke harshly, but I think she likes him.'

William shrugged. 'Oh she'll like him. In spite of his foibles Coleridge mesmerizes everyone. Ah, the man does as he wants.' William's voice fell low. 'But he suffers too . . . He is always running away.'

'But what does he run from?'

They checked their pace on a wet part of the bank.

'From himself, probably.' He offered his hand and helped her over the stream, then they walked on silently enjoying the autumn woodland. He wanted to stop and take her in his arms, but the process of love was tortuous, he would have to be careful. They were both quite fragile. 'Mary?' he faltered. 'I . . .' He saw she was waiting. 'You know what I want to say, don't you.'

She looked away quickly. 'Do you really want to say it?'

He could hear the ache in her voice. 'I do,' he said quietly. 'We must say what has to be said.'

She stopped and faced him. 'You are going to talk about *her* aren't you, the woman in France. It is a choice between her and me. You have a child over there with its mother – Oh, the pain and torment of it all.'

He gave her a long look. Had it really been as bad as that? He had known great passion in France with Annette, and Mary had seemed far away. Here though, now, he felt changed. She was close and he wanted her. He had known her smile, the flash of her eyes, her energy as she'd dashed through the woods, he had thought it wonderful just to be near her, to laugh with her, talk with her, unfasten her clothes from the thistles . . . He gazed at her, helpless with feeling. 'It is you I care for now. I want to have a wife. And I want that wife to be you.'

'And your child in France?'

'I can never be a proper father to Caroline.' He sighed guiltily. 'Nor a true husband to Annette. It just isn't possible.' He cleared his throat and tried to continue, stopping her with his hand on her arm as she again turned away. 'I love *you* Mary – I have always loved you.' The words as they came were nervous and clumsy, not the bold proud words in his mind. He drew her towards him. 'Marry me,' he said urgently. She lifted her face and he brushed her cheek with his lips, breathing softly in her ear. 'I want to be with you, always.'

'And I with you,' she said painfully. 'But what is to happen?' She trembled slightly as he held her. 'Will you go to France when you are able, is that what you'll do, will you leave me and go to Annette? I have always thought it.'

How lonely and vulnerable she seemed in her distress, he thought. 'I shall have to go over sometime,' he said, biting his lip and frowning. 'But only briefly. I need to see Caroline . . .'

'And Annette?' Again, she drew away, and he paced about frustrated.

'Yes, I have to see Annette, of course.' He threw out his arms. 'Who knows – perhaps she is married. I have no idea of her circumstances or what sort of life she is living.' For a moment he hung his head and his voice fell low. 'Or if she is living at all.' He knew that Elizabeth heard nothing now from Pierre. But he vowed to visit Hampstead soon. His heart though, did not stir for Annette now, but it still stirred for his child and he needed to know she was safe.

'And what if . . . What if you . . .' She stood before him trembling slightly.

'Do you think I will love her again, when I see her?' he said quietly. He kicked a stone down the path. 'I will not,' he said flatly. The dark, trodden grass by his feet looked tired and weary.

Mary's voice came loud as she ran towards him. 'If you want me, my love, you shall have me, so it will be!'

25

A Lonely Dorothy

Back at the farm, Dorothy dried away her tears. She had seen at a glance how it was. Sara had been so bold, so daring, though she scarcely knew him! And after all, was he not married with children? Sara Hutchinson cared not a bit about that, Dorothy reflected resentfully, she was very different from Mary. She had stolen Coleridge's heart with as little guilt as a magpie stole a shining object for its nest, and Coleridge shone like the sun.

She went to the mirror and let down her hair. It fell thick, strong and dark, not so dark as Sara's but lovely enough. She saw though, that her shoulders were hunched as if she might curl into a foetal position, back into her mother's womb. Oh, to be back in her mother's womb, she thought, so safe and warm, and start life over again, never to lose her siblings, for her mother not to die, or her father to lose his way on the hills . . .

She straightened and listened to the silence about her, hoping to hear the voice of her mother in the stillness. Once, just once, she had heard it. She listened hard and waited, but she heard nothing. She gazed again into the mirror, a delicately made woman with a brown sun-tanned skin and small inquisitive eyes. She knew she had deep feelings; unique treasures nobody knew anything about. Such treasures she gave to her brother, and she knew they inspired him to write. But she had other treasures too, treasures she might have given to Coleridge, and oh, so wholesomely!

She braced herself and returned the pins to her hair, gazing at her form through the mirror. She had a fine, comely figure. More than that, she knew she could talk with Coleridge in a way that Sara couldn't. Sara could never have talked about poetry like she did, and however much they'd flirted, she, herself, would never have stepped between Coleridge and his wife, or done anything to damage his family. Despite Sara's sarcasm about him neglecting his family, her laughter and glances revealed a monstrous hypocrisy. Dorothy chilled. The fire had burned low. She piled it high with logs and sat still in the silent room. Poor John, she thought, thinking of her brother at sea. He had confided before leaving, that he too loved Mary, but that he'd known she would marry William when the time was right. It had surprised Dorothy that his emotions had been so strong. She recalled the morning when he'd come to find her in the garden, sad and confused. She hoped he hadn't gone to sea simply to escape a painful love as many men did. Each day she prayed he'd be safe. At that moment Coleridge ran in.

'Where is she?' he demanded. 'I can't find her!'

'Who do you want?' Dorothy asked, poking the fire steadily, though she knew too well who he wanted.

'Sara – I must find her!' he cried.

'She is milking,' said Dorothy quietly. She picked up her book and turned a few pages. 'Everyone is out. William and Mary are gathering strawberries in the field. Tom is collecting eggs. And I believe Sara is milking.'

'How long does it take?' he asked, almost painfully.

'It depends how heavy the cows are,' said Dorothy. She rose to inspect a ham she was roasting in the oven. Coleridge followed.

'It took her an hour yesterday,' she told him over her shoulder. She turned to him and stared at him hard. 'Why don't you go to the milking shed and find her? Help her milk the cows, learn how to do it yourself, then she'll be finished much sooner.'

Coleridge's heavy eyebrows came together quickly. 'Is she always so busy?'

'So it seems. A farm is always busy. But a couple of farmhands are arriving tomorrow to assist with the harvest. They will no doubt help with the milking too, then Sara will have more time.' She spoke coolly and gazed outside through the window. 'Go then, Coleridge,' she said, waving him off. 'Go!'

Coleridge turned and ran across the yard.

Reaching the milking shed, he saw that half a dozen cows awaited milking. Seeing that Sara sat busy on a stool, he sang as he approached:

> *'It was on a fine summer's morning,*
> *The birds sweetly tuned on each bough,*
> *And as I walked out for my pleasure,*
> *I saw a pretty girl milking her cow;*
> *Her voice so enchanting, melodious,*
> *Left me quite unable to go,*
> *My heart it was loaded with sorrow,*
> *For cailín deas crúite na mbó.*
> *Then to her I made my advances;*
> *"Good morrow, most beautiful maid,*
> *Your beauty my heart so entrances!—"*
> *"Pray sir, do not banter," she said;*
> *"I'm not such a rare precious jewel,*
> *That I should enamour you so,*
> *I am but a poor little milk girl,"*
> *Says cailín deas crúite na mbó.'*

Sara turned to him and laughed. 'Except it's autumn, Coleridge, had you forgotten? – Summer indeed!'

'Ah, so it is,' said Coleridge. He stood by her side watching. 'The seasons escape me once I'm with you, my dear.'

'You have come to serenade me, have you?' she smiled. 'You sing very well Mr Coleridge, but you must not fluster the cows, they are not familiar with singing.'

'It is an Irish milking song. I'm sure your cows enjoyed it. And it is perfectly fitted to you, sweet maid. I fancy their milk will flow all the quicker because of it.'

'It's a very nice song,' said Sara, stopping and stretching her arms. 'I'm feeling quite tired. But there is help arriving tomorrow, we can scarce keep up this week.'

'I've tried to help where I can,' said Coleridge scratching his head. 'But dealing with cows isn't quite my thing, they are rather like horses, don't you think?'

Sara shook her head and laughed. 'They are not in the least like horses, any more than a goose is like a hen. Come; let me show you how to do it.' She rose. Finding him a seat by one of the cows she went for a pail. 'Now listen.'

Coleridge waited bewildered.

'The cows have been left too long,' she said sighing. 'It might be difficult.'

Still he waited, uncomfortable.

'There,' she said, her fingers grasping the udders. 'You must place your hands on the udders like this.'

He watched and did as she said. The cow grunted and kicked. 'A most unpleasant business,' Coleridge whispered. 'I have lived all my life and I have never milked a cow. Even if I were starving I could not do it.'

'You can, and you will,' said Sara determinedly. 'Think carefully.'

'For you, my dear, anything,' he said, attempting to smile.

'Pay attention!' urged Sara. 'Neatly, smoothly, with long smooth strokes – try harder.'

Coleridge worked at the udders, and gasped at the sound as the milk fell into the pail.

'There,' smiled Sara. 'Now, ensure each udder is empty before you start on the next.'

'I think I can do it,' said Coleridge triumphantly, concentrating now and serious.

'It isn't mathematics,' laughed Sara. 'You are only milking a cow.'

'I do believe it is happening!' said Coleridge, delighted. They laughed together loudly.

The afternoon drew on.

Bringing the last of the pails to the kitchen, Sara turned to him. 'I know you are miserable,' she said quietly.

'Do you?' sighed Coleridge. He looked at her surprised. For a moment or two they were silent. 'Well, you are right.'

'It's a shame about you and your wife . . .'

'Is it?' he said, frowning. 'But we shouldn't have married in the first place.' He turned to her in the dusk. 'Now, if I'd married you instead . . .'

She shook her head and smiled. 'No, no, Mr Coleridge, you are not the marrying kind. You should never have married at all.'

Coleridge breathed in deeply and straightened.

'You are very different from William,' she said thoughtfully.

'Oh, I do not deny it,' said Coleridge, a little annoyed.

'I know that William would make an excellent husband,' she said flatly. 'He'll have lots of children.'

'Is that so?' said Coleridge, biting his lip. 'Such thoughts have never entered my head, though I suppose you are right.' He could not be frivolous with Sara on matters of marriage. She had a powerful, independent spirit. But there was a quality about her he wanted, an essence he needed, an iron will that might guide him, which he could not find in his wife.

It was an autumn of brooding and lamenting, as autumns generally were Coleridge reflected as he sat on his own by the fire. Everyone else had gone out. He'd hoped to catch up on his reading, but he hadn't got far. There was something the matter with Dorothy and it bothered him. She'd been acting strangely that morning and he didn't know why. The atmosphere in the house of late had caused him to catch his breath and he wasn't feeling well either. He knew he should return to Nether Stowey. But he was trying not to think about Sarah and Hartley, for it gave him a terrible headache then he needed to lie down and rest, or worse still reach for the laudanum. He'd been working through a section of Emmanuel Kant's *The Critique of Pure Reason*, though not a word had entered his mind. He stood and read it out loud:

> *"By means of outer sense, a property of our mind, we represent to ourselves objects as outside us, and all without exception in space. In space their shape, magnitude, and relation to one another are determined or determinable. Inner sense, by means of which the mind intuits itself or its inner state, yields indeed no intuition of the soul itself as an object; but there is nevertheless a determinate form [namely, time] in which alone the intuition of inner states is possible, and everything which belongs to inner determinations is therefore represented in relations of time . . ."*

No good, his mind stayed stubborn. Putting it aside, he went to the window. The geese in the yard sat still and close, the horses tethered by the door of the barn were motionless and staring into space and the three dogs lay silent. The scene looked just like a painting by Paulus Potter. He braced himself. It was all very odd. Had he entered some transcendental reality? It was quite possible, for such was the make of his mind. Reality, dreams, he didn't know one from the other some days and moved about clumsily like a creature without bearings. He remembered the months of loneliness he'd suffered at school when he wasn't allowed to go home and must live in desperate isolation. He recalled how he'd invented spectres and images for company, whole worlds of his own that lived and had space in his mind, so much so that he had almost brought them into being, the source, he'd decided of his great love of philosophy.

He returned to his chair. Was thinking philosophically a means of escaping reality, he wondered? Was it just like doing mathematics, a safe and pleasurable experience, removed from life's tribulations? But philosophy was different, he reflected, mathematics offered solutions, while philosophy left you drifting, or else going round in circles, arriving at the same conclusions and getting nowhere. He sometimes sat thinking for hours, trying to find solutions to problems in the end unsolvable. But thinking about them was fun. And he was often applauded for his thoughts, which was always a bonus.

It was almost 11 am; the morning would soon be over. Wordsworth had better get a move on if they were to take that walk they'd promised themselves that day. The others knew what to expect however if they walked until dark and went further than they'd said, then they would stop at an inn and return next day. They needed to talk about the *Lyrical Ballads* in the fresh open air; it was quite a different experience from talking in the house where the walls could move in and stop you thinking. Wordsworth had noticed it too, though there was nothing much Wordsworth didn't notice, and he too got annoyed, though he liked to say different. Blasted reviewers! The Lyrical Ballads had been as good as strangled at birth! Even in his stormiest moments though, Wordsworth affected nonchalance. What he didn't know, though, was that his eyes gave everything away. He had done today what he always did when things disturbed him; he had gone to sit in the woodland and communicate with Nature. They would prepare another book, he'd said, another *Lyrical Ballads*, with some new poems, and a powerful Preface that explained the poems to the readers. He did not fear the readers, he'd said, not at all! He'd been quite decisive. They were both in agreement to fight for their art. And they would. But where was Wordsworth now? He'd promised to return within the hour. And everyone else had disappeared.

William thoughtful and brooding was almost back at the cottage. He quickened his pace. A wind was up and the trees were creaking about him. He wondered if he should cancel his stroll with Coleridge, for it seemed there was a storm in the offing. 'Oh, the book, the book!' he murmured. How many had Cottle sold? Just enough, most likely, for a handful of nasty reviewers to tear the poems to shreds. His small poems had been battered and bruised, and things had been said he had no intention of remembering. 'But *Tintern Abbey*!' he called to the wind. 'They dare not touch *Tintern Abbey*!' He had always feared that *The Rime of the Ancient Mariner* might injure the volume, and it seemed it had, the old words, and the strangeness of it all had made it hard to understand. In the next edition, Coleridge would have to replace it. And he would write a proper Preface too, something that told of the source of the poetry and the furnace from which it sprang.

He buttoned his coat and pulled down his hat. He had taken longer than intended and Coleridge was bound to be irritable. As he approached the barn, he could hear the sound of the roof rattling. Tom would no doubt bring out his ladders tomorrow and fix it, or he would offer to fix it himself. But what would he do about Mary? Lovely, precious Mary. He wanted to marry her. He'd proposed and she'd as good as accepted. But where would they live, and how could he tell Annette?

'Ah, Wordsworth!' Coleridge called as William entered the parlour. 'I thought you'd got lost.'

'There's a strong wind out,' said William. 'And there's a storm brewing too.'

'I never knew a wind to bother you before,' Coleridge frowned.

'I don't like storms,' said William flatly. 'I think of what happened to my father . . .'

'The poor reception of our book has disturbed you.' Coleridge gazed at the floor as he spoke. 'But I doubt the wind has an opinion.'

Coleridge went for his coat and buttoned it slowly. 'I don't think there's going to be a storm,' he said casually. 'Imagination, my friend, imagination!'

For a moment or two they were silent.

'Don't disappoint me Wordsworth,' Coleridge murmured. 'I need your strength. Don't become a broken vessel like me where it all leaks out.'

'You wreak havoc on yourself,' William sighed, sitting down.

'I don't have your talents,' Coleridge said flatly.

'You have a great many talents of your own,' William murmured.

'You have such perspicacity . . .' Coleridge said, biting his lip. 'What I would . . .'

'What do you mean?' William looked up.

'You know what I mean,' said Coleridge, slowly pulling on his gloves.

William frowned confused. 'I'm not sure I do.'

'It's the way you go about things,' Coleridge said sighing. 'You see, you *do* go about things, Wordsworth, don't you. Let's face it. You don't just throw yourself into them as I do. You acquire what you want by stealth.'

'Do I?' William raised his eyebrows curiously. He shook his head and sighed.

'The women for instance . . .' Coleridge continued. 'Mary, Dorothy, Sara – oh the whole damn lot of 'em. You have them exactly where you want them.' He shrugged. 'I suspect Sara is in love with you.'

'With *me*?' William frowned. – 'I think you mean Mary? Or I hope so.'

Coleridge waved away his words. 'Oh, I know about Mary. No, I mean Sara.'

'Don't talk nonsense,' said William. He screwed up his face irritably. 'Oh Coleridge, this is such rubbish.'

'Ah, but it's true.' Coleridge stared at him. 'See how she serves you first at table, always before she serves me. See how she looks at you when you speak. See how yesterday she ran for you when the hen got caught in the wire. She ran for *you*, Wordsworth, not me. – Oh, ho, and let us not forget, you have a mistress in France, my friend.' His voice fell low. 'And also a daughter.' Coleridge laughed briefly. 'And you've escaped the nuptial bed! My God, you are clever.'

'Go to blazes!' cried William. 'You can take that walk on your own!'

But Coleridge talked on quickly and moved in closer. 'I believe you would have them all if you could, one for this, another for that . . . And what's more, I believe they'd all be happy to serve you.' He went to William, who now stood by the window gazing out. He put his hand on his shoulder and whispered in his ear. 'You even have me.'

'Aye, and you have me,' William said sighing. 'And yes, you are right; I would have my loves about me always if I could; however we might serve one another. Love is the fulcrum on which the whole of our happiness depends. Destroy it Coleridge at your peril.'

Coleridge gazed down at his boots. Did he still have time to pick up his life, he wondered, or had he walked right over it years ago and left it behind?

But the two men understood each other well. And they were often of the same mind, which could sometimes be irritating when they saw things differently. Disagreements, however, were common. 'I don't care if it rains,' said Coleridge.

'And neither do I,' said Wordsworth. And so they went off into the woodland.

'Dorothy told me you'd talked about leaving us this week,' said William as they walked. – Is it true?' He waited. It always disturbed him that Coleridge talked more intimately with Dorothy than with him.

'Yes, that's right.' Coleridge looked up at the sky.

'Will you return to Nether Stowey?'

'That was my intention,' said Coleridge, with a long sigh of despair. 'I'm not sure Sarah will be there though. I think she'll have gone to see her family. But she'll not stay long; they've a job getting on.' For a moment or two they were silent. 'I doubt she'll return to Nether Stowey either,' he said finally.

William gazed downwards as they went. It was hardly surprising. Coleridge's marriage was fierce and destructive; he was just like an imprisoned demon, but with a crafty way of getting out. Though he always had to return, for it seemed he was afraid of something. He must take the laudanum to cope, for then he was safe in his dreams. Coleridge was breathing heavily as they went uphill. 'I think she'll leave me,' he moaned. His voice cracked with emotion.

William felt there was a new fragility about Coleridge, painful to see. It seemed such a wretched prospect if Sarah were to leave him. They stood for some minutes resting their backs against a tree. The wind had fallen. 'I doubt she'll leave you, Coleridge,' said William. 'So much has happened between you. Fate has tied you together in some awkward knot which I fear there is no undoing. It is rather like a Greek tragedy.'

'A tragedy indeed,' sighed Coleridge. A squirrel came out to look at them then quickly scaled a tree.

They walked on slowly. 'But you need to give her more consideration,' said William, in a serious tone of voice. 'You can't just do as you want. There are consequences.' He frowned as he spoke then turned to Coleridge who met his eyes quickly.

Coleridge smiled. 'Indeed,' he said quietly.

'Sara told me you'd declared your devotion to her earlier this week,' said William, calm as he could.

'Ah, well, Sara isn't to be trusted is she?' Coleridge said shaking his head. He braced himself and drew a breath.

'It is you, my friend, who can't be trusted,' said William sighing.

Coleridge shook a finger at William vigorously. 'Ah Wordsworth, anyone with half an eye can see what's happening with you and Mary, yet you already have a family in France. You have captured Mary's affections like the dawn captures the day. – But I ask you, supposing you still love the other? What then? There is no knowing how a man really feels about a woman until she is standing before him. I warn you, my friend, the minute you are with your lover in France you will want her. Then what is to happen to Mary?'

'No, no,' said William emphatically. 'Our countries are at war,' He threw out his hands in a gesture of hopelessness. Then he stood for a moment, thoughtful. 'There is a part of me that will always remember Annette. And Caroline holds us together. But I know I love Mary and we intend to get married.'

Coleridge shrugged. 'You are going to marry Mary, and the French woman will be all but a ghost?'

William glanced around at the woodland, the idea of Annette being a ghost made him shiver. For all he knew she might be dead, she had compromised herself by loving him. He felt though she would still be living, most likely assisting the royalist cause, risking her life, but sensible enough not to lose it. A surge of tenderness ran through him, the feeling of a dream.

'You criticise me for all manner of things, yet you are blind to faults of your own,' Coleridge said quietly.

'I see my faults only too well,' William retorted. 'I know I fall short. But . . .' He shook his head confounded. 'I have written to Annette. This isn't how I wanted it. – Oh, how we tear ourselves to pieces. But there is often no other way. Some things, I know . . . and this is certainly one of them . . . are better said in person, but since that isn't possible, I have put the words on paper as best I could. It really was the most painful of letters to write . . . I posted it several days ago, though I doubt she'll receive it.' They walked on silently a while. But they had walked too far and needed to get their bearings. Stopping to look at the map, they decided to stay at an inn. 'Sara cares for you, Coleridge,' William said quietly. 'Rather more than she should.' He folded the map and returned it to his pocket. 'She has said so to Mary.' He waited.

'There's an inn at the bottom of this slope,' Coleridge said, dismissively. 'But we need to get past those cows. I do hate cows!'

They had both slept well and eaten a fine cooked breakfast. It was a crisp dry day, and it was warm. Fresh and revived, they walked mile after mile, talking about poetry and the belief that the *Lyrical Ballads* with their heartfelt tales about ordinary people would throw a new and unprecedented light on the art of poetry.

After a while Grasmere rose in the distance. The grey silk stone of the town, plundered in times gone by from the great Helm Crag, glittered in the morning sunlight. 'It's the loveliest place I ever saw,' said William in earnest. 'I shall live there with Dorothy and Mary! Come Coleridge, let's run! There is such a thing as flying to fate when it beckons so splendidly!'

They ran down the slope, leaping heathers and ferns, climbing over dry stone walls and hastening through woodland. After another fifteen minutes, they came within feet of the village.

Stopping to speak to a local, they enquired if he knew of a cottage for rent in the area. He pointed. 'Something over there I think, above Nab Scar . . .'

Their frock coats flying they both went fast up the hill.

Dorothy's mind was filled with questions when William returned to the farm. Where had they been? What had they seen? Was there anything of note to report? And why wasn't Coleridge with him? William told her of a house he had found for rent in Grasmere, previously known as *The Dove and Olive Branch Inn*, 'a fine solid house', he said, which could make an excellent home. He had searched out the landlord, a John Benson of Grasmere, he said, and made enquiries. Everything was in their favour. 'At five pounds a year we can easily afford it!' he told her heartily. Dorothy listened enrapt. Compared to what they'd been used to, she would find the rooms quite small, he said, but they'd suffice. The walls were whitewashed and clean and the flagstone floors were straight and easy to walk on. But whatever else, it stood in a sublime spot. How could it not be perfect? He and Coleridge had gone around the orchard three times, he said. 'All kinds of fruit lay wasting on the ground half eaten by animals and insects. And I noticed a vegetable patch . . .'

'It sounds like we might grow the broccoli and beans we've talked about,' Dorothy said with approval.

'Just let me get my spade in that earth,' said William. He paced the floor clasping his hands as if he held dreams inside them. 'I can probably get some plants off Tom . . .' he murmured.

'And we can dig some up from the fells,' Dorothy said brightly, 'primroses, daffodils, all manner of beauties.'

'What luck,' he murmured. 'What luck!'

Dorothy was looking through the window.

'The cottage will make a wonderful home for all three of us,' said William.

'All *three* of us?' Dorothy said abstractedly.

'Yes, Mary, will live with us too. That is what we decided, is it not?'

'Did we?' she said, turning and looking gloomy.

His sister's feelings for Coleridge unsettled him. She went to the fire and riddled the logs, staring intently at the flames. He could see she was hurting. 'After we are married, Mary and I will take the downstairs room for our own. It used to be a room to drink in, so it is bound to have some merry spirits. – Come Dorothy, please don't be dismal.' He tried to laugh, but Dorothy's face stayed stern. He heard her sigh. 'I fancy we shall have some interesting visitors, too,' he said hopefully.

'So who will visit us?' said Dorothy grimly.

'Well, Coleridge, of course, and John our brother . . .' He went on quickly. 'Walter Scott and de Quincey too, I hope, and lots of others.'

For several minutes they were silent. 'Coleridge left,' he said finally, seeing her anguish. 'He said he was going home. We parted up the road.'

'Just like that,' she said softly.

'Well, that's how he is.'

'And so he has returned to Sarah?'

'Who else?'

'Did he tell Tom he was leaving?' she said of a sudden.

'I have no idea,' he said exasperated. 'I don't know his every thought.'

'Well, we shall have to find out,' she said, moving to the door swiftly.

'But you knew he intended to leave,' William added annoyed. 'It was you who told me earlier. I am sure Tom would know too.'

'I see,' said Dorothy, straightening her dress and her hair. 'He didn't say anything about leaving today though.'

'He is married, Dorothy,' William said sternly. 'He has no business at the farm. His place is with Sarah and his children. Coleridge will do as he wants, now please, my dear, no tears.'

Dorothy sat down heavily nursing her frustrated misery, trying to find some peace in her soul for the coming night.

26

The Beaded Purse

Autumn passed and it was very soon December. The weather was bitterly cold as they made the journey to Grasmere, which made it seem longer than ever. It was early evening when they arrived.

They pulled the last of their belongings from the carriage and carried them into the cottage. 'You'll feel easier now,' said William. He felt they'd been saved. He did not know what from and was glad to have missed whatever the experience might have been, but the terrible feeling of homelessness was no more. 'Courage, courage, that's what's required,' he said triumphantly. He was thinking of the orchard too and the things they would plant in the gardens.

'It's a charming little place,' laughed Dorothy. 'How clever you were to find it.'

'I was lucky,' he said. 'You can't say more than that. I just came across it.' But he was glad of her happiness. She was like a child at Christmas, he thought, she was so elated.

'I knew I would love it,' she said, looking about. The woodwork, dark with age however, seemed tired and sombre and had accumulated much stale polish, but that could be easily remedied, she declared brightly, a little vinegar and water would soon do the trick. William told her the rooms needed airing and they should open some windows, but they would have to wait for better weather. Their main objectives that evening were to light a fire and find themselves somewhere to sleep. They had several good warm blankets and one or two pillows; it could all be accomplished without fuss. 'We'll have an excellent breakfast in the morning,' said Dorothy, wandering the kitchen. 'The farmer gave me bacon and eggs.' They went along the tiny corridors, in and out of the bedrooms and the downstairs rooms. Delicate beams of evening light made a dappled effect on the floor so that the place seemed sprinkled with stars.

'Very good, very good,' said William. 'It is all quite perfect.'

The little house felt cramped at first and there was much to be done, but it gave them pleasure to think how they might improve it and the walks they could take in the vicinity. One evening he wrote to Coleridge:

"Grasmere, 1799.

My dearest Coleridge

We arrived here last Friday, and have now been four days in our new abode without writing to you, a long time! But we have been in such confusion as not to have had a moment's leisure . . . D is now sitting by me racked with the tooth-ache. This is a grievous misfortune as she has so much work for her needle among the bedcurtains etc that she is absolutely buried in it. We have both caught troublesome colds in our new and almost empty house, but we hope to make it a comfortable dwelling. Our first two days were days of fear as one of the rooms upstairs smoked like a furnace, we have since learnt that it is uninhabitable as a sitting room on this account; the other room however which is fortunately the one we intended for our living room promises uncommonly well; that is, the chimney draws perfectly, and does not even smoke at the first lighting of the fire. . . .D is much pleased with the house and appurtenances the orchard especially; in imagination she has already built a seat with a summer shed on the highest platform in this our little domestic slip of mountain . . . We do not think it will be necessary for us to keep a servant. We have agreed to give a woman who lives in one of the adjoining cottages two shillings a week for attending two or three hours a day to light the fires wash dishes etc etc. In addition to this she is to have her victuals every Saturday when she will be employed in scouring and to have her victuals likewise on other days if we should have visitors and she is wanted more than usual. We could have had this attendance for eighteen pence a week but we added a sixpence for the sake of the poor woman, who is made happy by it . . . Rydale is covered with ice, clear as polished steel, I have procured a pair of skates and tomorrow mean to give my body to the wind . . ."

New Year came in fast, and right on its heels came February. It was February 1799. William liked walking in February. It was a time when seeds were awakening and making their way to the light, a time when the sharp white cups of snowdrops trembled in the sharp sunlight and daffodils were beginning to arrive by the lake. Dorothy wrote in her journal each day about what she saw and experienced. The gracious and genial mood of Grasmere, the rugged rocks, and the sweet smelling scents and tastes in the air entranced her. They had acquired some furniture from here and there, and *The Dove and Olive Branch Inn* had now been named *Dove Cottage*. The February trees in the orchard were damp and still, but within them came the promise of spring. With this view, William and Dorothy talked intensely about what to do with the fruit once it arrived and what they would grow in the garden. In his wildest imagination he had visions of Caroline, lovely as her mother, strong and eager for life, running by the Loire, Annette wandering through the flowers. But an essential part of his soul had dimmed and he knew it could never be lighted. He must talk with Elizabeth soon . . .

The weather was fair and the horses were strong as the chaise rattled on to Hampstead that fine spring morning. He had much to relate to Elizabeth and was determined to talk about Mary. But what sort of talk would it be? She was bound to feel loyal to Annette; after all she had seen her grow up. And she had also seen her in love. And was it not due to her that he and Annette had come together? Their love had blossomed and grown in France and Elizabeth knew that Annette had borne a child, his very own daughter. But it seemed like a long time ago. Thoughts of the revolution still seized him and made him miserable. Before the advent of the guillotine he'd been fiercely republican, but the natural balance of human sensitivities had been badly damaged by that monstrosity, and far too many had gone to their deaths in the tumbrels. Change belonged to the young, indeed. But the young were tired and desperate. Such thoughts sped through his mind as he travelled. But what would he say about Mary. He needed to say how wonderful she was, how he had found such harmony with her in his pain, and more than that, how she had helped him piece together his soul.

Soon he was standing by Elizabeth's door. The young maid opened it smiling as brightly as ever.

'William, how are you?' Elizabeth called as he entered. 'I believe you have moved to Grasmere?' She was seated on the chaise longue and beckoned him over. The maid stood about, waiting for his coat and hat. Again, the girl intrigued him. Those eyes! What was it about her eyes! She took his things and he sat down, looking about. 'Can you bring us tea, my dear and a little light refreshment!' called Elizabeth as the girl went out.

'Yes, we have a nice little place, Elizabeth, but big enough for one or two guests. I hope you are well.' William settled into a chair by the fire and gazed at the flames.

'Well enough,' said Elizabeth. 'But I know no more about

Annette than you do.' She spoke despondently, playing with the collar of her dress and looking more anxious than usual. 'But we must not sacrifice ourselves to worries, must we.' She straightened. 'It's an abstract thing isn't it, imagination going wild.' She shrugged and smiled.

He sighed. 'Indeed,' he said quietly, though suddenly sad. 'There are other things I need to tell you,' he faltered. He felt tense and uneasy. She gave him a curious look but did not speak. The maid came back with refreshments and they both gazed at her in silence as she poured out the tea. What could it be about her look that so intrigued him, he wondered. The thought plagued him.

'Did you get a letter?' Elizabeth asked him softly.

He braced himself and took a drink from his tea. 'No, nothing.' He tried to think of what to say.

'Me neither. There are days I brood on it too much and must take to my bed.' She did not travel nowadays, she said. Her life was all in her head. 'Yvette brings provisions. I rarely step out of the house and it disturbs me to think on the future. I have had nothing by way of news from Pierre, and the nothingness grows bigger by the day.'

'It does,' said William. His energies seemed to have left him. He sat hanging his head. He felt weak. The memory of the dead man rising from the lake came to him again and he shivered. In his mind he heard the scream.

'But what do you wish to speak of that makes you so nervous?' she asked. 'I do not expect such angst from my bold young friend.'

Her tone made him restless. He changed his position in the chair. 'Oh, how can I say it?' he murmured, bending his head. But it had to be said.

'You can try,' she said solemnly. She waited.

'I am in love . . .' he said quietly. He looked up slowly to see her response. She was bound to despise him, he thought. But her face was calm and her eyes widened with kindness. He continued. 'Her name is Mary. I have loved her since boyhood.'

Elizabeth listened attentively. 'I see,' she said, gently.

"Mary," he smiled. As her name passed through the air it seemed to belong. 'You see, Annette has gone. Not gone from my mind, but . . .'

'Gone from your heart?' Elizabeth offered. She frowned. 'It was bound to happen, my dear. And I believe Annette would want it.'

'Would she?' he said, startled and searching her face. But his feelings for Mary were strong and he could not govern them. His voice sounded hollow like a voice from the past. 'Thank you. I would like to think she'd understand. It has been so long . . . Mary and I are to marry.'

Elizabeth held his gaze. 'I'm glad,' she said softly. 'I have sometimes felt guilty about you and Annette. After all, it was I who introduced you. I ought to have known she would fall for you, William.' She smiled her tender smile. 'And that her beauty and cleverness would capture you. I knew it deep in my heart, but I allowed it to happen.' She sighed and shook her head. 'And your child runs innocent in France, a child who knows nothing of the dreadful politics that drain the blood from our loves.' She called to the maid and requested she bring more tea.

'Merci, Madame,' said the girl. She gave a little curtsey and spoke some sentences in French. 'I have almost finished the book,' she said proudly.

'Already?' laughed Elizabeth. She turned to William. 'Yvette likes to read. She makes her way through my library fast as a falcon.'

'You are French?' said William, still pondering her eyes.

'I believe I am,' she said wistfully. 'I love the French language, but I have lived here most of my life.'

'Her French is excellent,' said Elizabeth, with a sort of possessive satisfaction. 'Yvette grew up in a nunnery. – I am sorry, Yvette . . .' She turned to her curiously. 'I have never enquired of your history. You see, some of the maids who have worked for me are French émigrés and do not like to be questioned.'

'Oh no, do not be sorry,' gasped the girl. 'Why should you think about the past, when now is so cheerful?' She turned to William. 'My history is strange but not sad. It belongs with the nunnery. The nuns were my mothers. But the ones who found me on the beach were old and have died.' She gazed at the flames in the fire, darting and dancing, then spoke as if deep in thought. 'I know so little of my origins. There were a lot of foundlings at the nunnery. We made up stories about our families. Sometimes we made each other laugh.'

The girl stood before them enjoying the exchanges, her thick dark hair in a loose plait falling down her shoulder. Her olive skin shimmered in the firelight. 'There was nothing to tell the nuns,' she murmured. 'Everything was lost when our vessel crashed on the rocks . . . Even my memories. I had only the clothes I was found in. The nuns gave me my life. What can be more important than life?' Tears formed in her eyes. 'I was the *sole* survivor . . .' She drifted for a moment into thought. 'I wonder sometimes if I might have had family who were drowned in the shipwreck.'

'*Dear God,*' Elizabeth whispered. She leant forward and beckoned the girl towards her. 'Come here, my dear. Tell me about this rescue. Sit by my side.'

William and Elizabeth waited. 'Not too fast,' Elizabeth murmured. 'Tell me your story from start to finish slowly and carefully.'

The girl went to sit by Elizabeth as requested. 'I was spared,' she said softly. 'Our vessel sank and the rest of the crew were drowned. We did not discover the name of the boat or the names of those who were lost. It was always a mystery. The nuns told me boats often collided with rocks in that wretched place. There were few, if any, survivors from such disasters.'

William listened astonished. A hope sped through his mind.

She continued. 'The nuns said I talked to them in French but I do not remember. I try to remember my life before the shipwreck, but I have only odd little flashes.'

'These *flashes*,' said William. He leant forward, searching her eyes intently. 'What do the flashes show you?'

'I will try to tell you,' she said, taking a breath. 'But I have to go slowly, my mind invents sometimes.' She gave a nervous little laugh. 'It likes to tell me I had a family in France, a grand house to live in – oh, such a beautiful house . . . I had parents, and a brother . . . It tells me of happiness, of love and laughter. So much laughter. I do not know what my name was. The nuns called me Yvette. I would sit beneath the trees at the nunnery, and sometimes . . . sometimes in the evening light I thought I saw my brother, a handsome, smiling boy . . .' Her voice trembled as she spoke.

The girl looked awkward. 'I know it is sensitive, my dear,' said Elizabeth blissfully, but it is good to talk about it now. It is as if I am listening to the seraph! This is wonderful.'

Yvette bent her head. 'Yes, I am quite content. Living in this house I have felt . . .'

'What have you felt?' Elizabeth urged. 'Tell me what you have felt for perhaps I too have felt it. Do you feel . . . Do you feel *a bond*? A bond that is more like . . .'

'Oh yes,' said Yvette. And the words burst out in a flood. 'I am only your maid, I know. But my imagination is like a beautiful bird in flight, it will visit places I long for; make of people what it wants.' She laughed at her words. 'But oh, how I suffer for that!'

'Such splendid suffering,' murmured Elizabeth.

William stood and paced the room. What could he say? Yes, the girl was surely Clarisse.

Yvette put her hand in her blouse and drew out a tiny heart shaped purse secured on her neck with a ribbon. She touched it with familiar fondness. 'See it is embroidered with beads, and the beads still shine. The nuns said it was tied on my neck when they found me. I think . . . I think I was loved.' She took off the purse and passed it across to Elizabeth. 'Perhaps you would like to see it?'

'Oh, I know it well . . .' Elizabeth said emotionally as her fingers slid about the tiny pieces of glass and stone. 'Indeed you were loved,' she said softly. 'I made you this purse a long time ago.' She gazed at the tiny glass beads, worked into soft spring flowers, glistening in the firelight. She traced the patterns with her fingers. 'You were loved very much, and still are.' She looked up slowly and spoke shakily. 'My dear . . . I am your aunt.'

An uncanny silence filled the room.

'Ma tante?' Yvette whispered. She screwed up her eyes in disbelief. 'How can it be?'

Elizabeth continued. 'And what's more, yes, you have a brother, a brother in France. His name is Pierre, and how he pines for his sister! – Oh, Yvette, this is a blessed day.' Her eyes moistened with tears as she drew the girl into her arms. 'A whole new world awaits you when the wars are done with. How well this purse has served you. It is the very heart of your family!'

27

The Warmth Of Hope

It seemed Elizabeth's discovery had given her a second youth. William laughed, as he read through her letter that morning. She and her niece had written to Pierre. When the wars had ended, they would make their way to Orléans, she said, and Clarisse would meet him. William would join them too, and could see Annette and Caroline! It would all be marvellous.

He handed the letter to Dorothy. Letters – letters, filled with stories of hope. He admired the determination of letters, their sheer unflinching capacity to surge into the future. Clarisse, Elizabeth reported, claimed she'd awoken from a long deep sleep and with great eagerness of soul longed to see her brother. William remembered the château and the way Pierre had grieved.

'What does Yvette look like?' asked Dorothy. 'You say she has eyes like Pierre's, but I haven't seen either.' They indulged themselves with all manner of possibilities, and the warmth of faith. Perhaps it could all come right; the wars would end very soon, Pierre would meet with Clarisse and they would live at the château together.

The second edition of *Lyrical Ballads* still awaited its Preface and William had been up throughout the night trying to perfect it.

He had also written to Annette, but it was more like a list of thoughts rather than a letter, and he doubted it would ever be sent. There was a serious quietude in him, as if his very being had entered an unknown season. Aching all over from too long sitting, he decided to walk out into the orchard and listen to the sounds of dawn.

The door creaked as he opened it. He made a note in his mind to attend to the hinge, then closed it as quietly as he could. He didn't want to wake Dorothy, though he could hear the rattle of a cart on the road already and the farmer calling his dog. 'Do farmers ever go to bed?' he whispered.

He roamed about the orchard, strangely aware of the steady crunch of his feet on the dew filled grass. 'A good space to grow some cucumbers here,' he murmured, squatting by a place where the sun shone strongly. He touched the soil with his fingers, then gazed all about him. 'And perhaps some peas over there . . .' He went across to the apple tree; it yielded excellent fruit and they'd had lots of apples that year. His musings went on until he found himself back in the house.

'Did I wake you?' he asked. Dorothy was tending the fire.

'Do put a comb through your hair, my dear,' she said as she turned to him. 'Have you witnessed an apparition? You've been up all night. You won't think half so well if you're tired.' She stirred the fire and watched it burst into flame. 'Please take some rest. Coleridge is coming today, remember. Or so he has said in his letter.'

'Morning or afternoon?' William said, yawning.

'Oh, don't expect precision from Coleridge,' she shrugged. 'You know him better than that.'

'I see you have sewn some lace on your collar, my dear,' he said.

Dorothy touched her white lace collar with a little smile of embarrassment. 'Yes, it was just in my sewing box. I thought I should use it.'

'And rightly so,' said William, raising his eyebrows and nodding. 'A very pretty collar it is, too. I'm sure Coleridge will like it, he notices things like that.' He gazed at her sleepily. 'You are quite right, I must rest.' He touched the back of his neck and winced.

'Neck ache again?' She went for a bottle of oil in a cupboard and poured some into her palm. 'Now open your shirt,' she said. 'I'll give you a massage, then you can sleep.'

He did her bidding and she worked the oil into the muscles at the back of his neck. 'Better?' she asked.

'Very much,' he sighed.

After returning the oil to the cupboard, she went to wash her hands. Then she glanced at his writing on the desk. 'I see you've been working on the Preface for *Lyrical Ballads*.'

'I have,' he murmured, screwing up his eyes drowsily. 'I think it's done.'

'Go and lie down,' she emphasized, 'and I'll read it.' He climbed the stairs tiredly. Dorothy felt nervous. It had taken so much of their energies, and she'd unfortunately hung on to every word they'd said. It had given her a lot of headaches. She might have been holding a white hot coal as she read it, it was almost holy.

"... It is supposed, that by the act of writing in verse an Author makes a formal engagement that he will gratify certain known habits of association; that he not only thus apprises the Reader that certain classes of ideas and expressions will be found in his book, but that others will be carefully excluded. This exponent or symbol held forth by metrical language must in different eras of literature have excited by different expectations: for example, in the age of Catullus, Tereance, and Lecretius, and that of Statius or Claudian; and in our own country, in the age of Shakespeare and Beaumont and Fletcher, and that of Donne and Cowley, or Dryden, or Pope. I will not take upon me to determine the exact import of the promise

which, by the act of writing in verse, an Author in the present day makes to his reader: but it will undoubtedly appear to many persons that I have not fulfilled the terms of an engagement thus voluntarily contracted... they will look round for poetry, and will be induced to inquire by what species of courtesy these attempts can be permitted to assume that title. I hope therefore the reader will not censure me for attempting to state what I have proposed to myself to perform . . . The principal object, then, proposed in these Poems was to choose incidents and situations from common life, and to relate or describe them, throughout, as far as was possible in a selection of language really used by men . . ."

She read for a full fifteen minutes, then went to the mirror and pinned up her hair. Reading by the fire had reddened her cheeks. They also glowed from the excitement of knowing Coleridge was to pay them a visit. He'd been silent about Sara since leaving the Hutchinson farm. Had he forgotten her? What woman in Sarah Coleridge's position would put up with Coleridge's behaviour, and at such a price? Yet what woman could harden her heart against him either?

'Did you read it?' asked William later when he came downstairs.
'Not all of it,' she told him awkwardly.
For a moment they were silent. He waited, observing her closely.
'My dear, why is it so long?' she asked finally, smiling and with a slight frown. 'It is good,' she said hurriedly, 'very precise, and . . .'
He took a seat by her side. 'I have fought with those words, Dorothy. Not a single sentence would give way.' He shrugged. 'My readers must see what I'm doing with the poems. I must guide them to a new way of thinking. Anything new is controversial.'
'Of course,' said Dorothy. 'But I do not want you to demean yourself by explaining your every thought. Why should you?'

'*Demean myself?* You do say the strangest things.'

'You needn't explain your genius, my dear. I don't think you can.'

He rose and went to the window. 'I think it might rain,' he said gloomily.

Dorothy sighed. 'You *will* marry her, won't you?' she said. 'You are bound to.'

'What?' He turned with an enquiring look. It hurt him to see her unhappy.

'You will marry Mary.'

He buried his face in his hands. 'But you know it, Dorothy,' he said wearily. 'We've discussed it. You know what will happen.'

'But what about me? Am I to live in some rude dwelling on a hillside with only shepherds for company?'

'Oh, Dorothy,' he moaned. 'We shall all live together in this cottage. No-one will abandon you. Mary loves you.' He went to her quickly. 'Please don't despair. In any case, I can't marry Mary yet. What have I to offer? . . . And I need to talk with Annette before I . . .' He broke off speaking. What would he say to Annette? How could he let her know how he felt about Mary?

28

Time And Tide

It was autumn 1801. The fruit from the orchard was now gathered in, small sweet pears, bright red apples and large purple plums. William had raked up the leaves for compost and the soil had been prepared for bulbs. He enjoyed growing fruit and vegetables and seeing the flowers blossom by the winding pathways and much had been accomplished in a short space of time, he thought. He was fond of the cottage interior, too, for every corner had a presence entirely its own. Also, he thought with relief, the second edition of *Lyrical Ballads* was at last in print and had gone out into the world, and the world had given its blessing; for that he was glad.

Coleridge and Sarah now had another baby boy and had named him Derwent, the name of the waters of William and Dorothy's childhood, and a name they loved. And Coleridge had reported that the child was "walking", with a curious emphasis on the word, as if walking were a means of escaping. He had now moved his family to Keswick, which made for easier journeys to and from their homes. The air, the sun, even the wind and rain, were charged with a sense of fecundity. But William knew such harmony could not last. Sarah had been to see Dorothy that week, sobbing the same old grievances.

Coleridge had gone to London to work for a newspaper. "He says we are penniless," she'd wept. William and Dorothy had despaired. Coleridge working for a newspaper? He was sure to hate it.

On second thoughts though, perhaps he wouldn't, William decided. There was a great deal of news to write about just now and Coleridge wrote with passion. He had written a lot of letters himself that year, so many he couldn't keep count. He had written to the leader of the Whigs. It was important to look into the deteriorating lives of country folk, he'd said. Charles James Fox was a powerful orator, a man who advocated liberal reforms and could go on a foray like a whirlwind. As a matter of fact, he was writing him something just now. He drew it out of a drawer and looked it over:

> "… *It appears to me that the most calamitous effect, which has followed the measures, which have lately been pursued in this country, is a rapid decay of the domestic affections among the lower orders of society. This effect the present Rulers of this country are not conscious of, or they disregard it. For many years past, the tendency of society amongst almost all the nations of Europe has been to produce it. But recently by the spreading of manufactures through every part of the country, by the heavy taxes upon postage, by workhouses, Houses of Industry, and the invention of Soup-shops etc. etc. superadded to the increasing disproportion between the price of labour and that of the necessaries of life, the bonds of domestic feeling among the poor, as far as the influence of these things has extended, have been weakened, and in innumerable instances entirely destroyed. The evil would be the less to be regretted, if these institutions were regarded as only palliatives to a disease; but the vanity and pride of their promoters are so subtly interwoven with them, that they are deemed great discoveries and blessings to humanity. In the mean time parents are separated from their children, and children from their parents; the wife no longer prepares with her own hands a meal for her husband, the produce of his labour; there is*

little doing in his house in which his affections can be interested, and but little left in it which he can love . . ."

'Absolutely,' he said to himself. 'I hope he reads it!' Dorothy was singing in the kitchen. And with a sudden quick painful remembrance, he thought of Annette's sad song . . . *"The pain of love lasts a lifetime . . ."* 'Must it be so?' he murmured. Thoughts of her swept through his mind. And for a moment he held her lovely face in his palms and remembered her smile. He remembered her scent, the feel of her skin against his lips. 'How I adored you!' he whispered. And for a moment the love returned to him, but it did not stay.

It seemed though now, that a visit to France might be possible, and he felt both anxious and excited by the thought. Interesting events were afoot. Napoleon's armies were weary of war, and he'd been made to parley a treaty to temporarily halt hostilities. And the following year, in the spring of 1802, the definitive *Treaty of Amiens* was signed between Britain and France. Oh, such a divine treaty! News spread fast. Elizabeth had written that all was well at the château in Orléans, though Pierre's wealth had been greatly diminished. Annette, she said, had been working hard for the royalists and living a dangerous existence, while Paul had almost been executed for an alleged involvement in an attack on Leonard Bourbon, a deputy in the National Convention. Pierre though had claimed that Bourbon was intent on trouble, and a liar to boot. Paul, she said had been working in Orléans as a lawyer and had somehow got involved. Bourbon alleged he'd been attacked and had only been saved by a coin in his pocket that had caught the edge of a sword. Paul had been forced into hiding.

William went walking. And so he would meet with his daughter! Françoise, Elizabeth had written, would deliver Caroline at an appointed time to a place he knew by the Loire. –

How would she look, he wondered, this girl, who was his own flesh and blood? Would she look like Annette – might she have her eyes and manner? Or might she look like him or Dorothy, or one of his brothers? He steadied himself against a tree, tears falling down his face. It was so long ago! He had never yielded again to that sort of passion. He had yielded to other kinds of passion, but not to that wildness, that absolute rawness of spirit that had taken possession of him then. And yes, he had served it, raw and wild as it was that utterly fathomless ecstasy he had known and loved. That week, he and Dorothy would make the journey to Hampstead to meet with Elizabeth and Clarisse, and from there they would sail to France. Elizabeth, Dorothy and Clarisse would stay with Pierre, while he himself, would take up lodgings in Blois. He sighed away the pain of the past then took the path to the cottage.

Elizabeth stayed close by her niece through the crossing, as if the girl were a kind of apparition and might vanish any moment from sight. Dorothy, too, stood near, while William's complex feelings seemed to shriek with the sound of the gulls flying about them. Much had changed since last he had crossed these waters. He was better off financially for one thing, and it seemed, too, as if the dog-tired family debt was about to be paid. The Earl of Lonsdale was dead and his heir had agreed to honour his obligations. William felt glad that he could offer Annette some financial assistance in the future. As he gazed at the sky, the white skeletal clouds of August were like the trailing hair of celestial beings guiding them on to their fates. – And oh, how he needed guidance!

Reaching their destination, they all disembarked. Pierre had sent out a carriage for the women. "To Orléans!" the coachman had shouted, and they were out of sight within minutes. William stamped his feet on the earth of France, the very same feet on the very same land he had walked ten years ago in so many moods. He had changed so much, he reflected. No doubt Annette had changed too. He hoped she'd explained to their daughter the way it had been, the beautiful way it had been. Would the child appreciate how it was? Would she forgive him? He would write about it in verse when the poetry was ready. Not yet. The cruel severing of his love for Annette had made a part of him lame, and he had no way of knowing what damage had been done to her. It had been to him both torture and joy to love her – but what had it meant to Annette? He half hoped she might have a lover, even another child, anything other than that cruel, sacrificial allegiance love could demand of its captive. Better he met Caroline on her own at first, Françoise had said, and see Annette later at their home. Something, William discerned, was falling into place, but he had no way of knowing its shape. And now Pierre would see his sister! What an extraordinary moment it would be.

The lack of communication from Annette, however, concerned him. But the silence would soon be broken. What would it contain, he wondered, how would it sound? Would it be ferocious and volcanic, or would it be gentle and light as a mountain breeze.

He stood listening to the voices about him; serious voices, cheerful voices, voices from many nationalities. His heart beat fast as he waited to return to his past. But he could not feel his old spirit, that fierceness bounding through his veins. He still loved the ordinary people, the peasants, the farmers, the poor who he knew he must speak for, though he had seen in England a much better answer to France's turmoil, a more realistic freedom . . .

'You are wanting a chaise, sir!' a driver called to him in French.

'Ah, yes,' said William, roused from his thoughts. He braced himself and got in. 'Take me to Blois!'

The wheels of the carriage grew louder as they travelled along denser clay. Then all of a sudden he heard the barking of dogs and into his nostrils came the metallic smell of blood. Carcases burned all around him while shouts and screams burst into his ears. 'But what can I do?' he called. 'I am only a visitor from England!' Waking quickly from his sleep, he wiped the perspiration from his brow.

The driver stopped and a man in a long black cloak got in and settled in the seat opposite. His large bloodshot eyes stared as if at nothing. 'Where are you going?' asked William. A wind was up. The clatter of the chaise on the lonely road made for a sense of desolation.

'"*Going?*"' said the man, his voice deep and unearthly. 'I am going nowhere.'

'Then why do you travel?' said William, feeling chilled.

'Because I am bound to do so,' murmured the stranger.

'But *why?*' William persevered.

'I know nothing of why or wherefore,' the man said distantly. 'I only dream.'

There was nothing in his eyes, thought William, nothing but the memory of night, with its deep unfathomable darkness and glittering stars. 'Who are you?' he whispered.

'My name is Jean-Jacques Rousseau,' was the haunting reply.

William sat stunned. '"*Rousseau*"? – But Rousseau is dead!'

After another few minutes, the carriage came to a halt and the stranger stepped out. He stood for a moment adjusting his cloak, then strode out into the mist.

William alighted from the chaise at the appointed place. Then stood for a while listening to the song of the water as it lapped the banks of the Loire. Sunlight streamed through the trees and the branches danced with the light on the river in a soft warm breeze. A colourful array of wild flowers trembled by the path. Time passed languidly as he gazed at the scene before him. But he throbbed with memory as the young and vibrant energy of his earlier feelings came to him again. Must he bid them farewell? – No, no, not yet! He would give them the homage they deserved, at least for now. For *now* belonged to Annette and Caroline, did it not?

But for the sound of his breathing and the gentle lap of the water, the warm, beautiful valley was strangely silent. He strained his eyes to look for Pierre's vineyard but the woods obscured it. He wondered if it was wasted like so many others, or might still be a working estate. – Suddenly, from the top of the hill he heard the clatter of a coach. – She is here! he thought, Caroline, my daughter, is here! His heart pounded. He sank back behind a tree. How many minutes before he beheld her face?

The coach came to a halt, and he could hear Françoise talking in her high-pitched French, the words too fast for him to hear, answered by the excited chatter of a girl, who then sped down the hill, calling to the trees, 'Father, Father, where are you? You have promised to meet me!'

Then where the bank lifted up to the road, he saw her, the wind blowing her long dark hair about her face. 'Père! Père!' she called, her voice echoing as if her spirit had left her body. He held his breath, hearing her laugh as he approached her. She gazed at him trancelike. How strong and alive she looked against the rich blue sky of the valley!

'Etes-vous mon père?' she asked incredulously, coming towards him slowly, and cautiously looking him over.

'Yes, I am your father,' he said, his voice unsteady. He could scarce catch his breath. She was beautiful and curious to him, her bright brown eyes flashing, her gentle mouth smiling softly and her young arms reaching out for him.

'I knew you would come,' she said earnestly.

Why was he so afraid, he wondered? He wanted to draw her towards him, to hold her and feel her breath on his cheek, to touch her hair and meet her bold brown eyes. But he could not. His throat tightened with tears.

'Will you not kiss me?' she said, throwing her hair behind her shoulders, and straightening. She looked at him sideways and narrowed her eyes as if trying to read his thoughts.

He bent towards her. She offered him her olive skinned cheek and his lips brushed against her skin. The smell of her was sweet and good, like the first scent of spring.

'Will you fix my shoe?' she asked him, looking down at her foot.

He could see that one of the buckles was undone and that the shoe hung loose on her stocking. He knelt before her to secure it.

Françoise, who had walked a little way down, watched all the while. 'He has brought no horse!' called Caroline.

'Non, no,' answered Françoise. 'Your father has come on the water.'

'But you *will* have a horse very soon, no?' said the child, taking hold of his hand and examining his strong fingers. 'Then we can ride together.'

'She has talked a lot about riding with you,' called Françoise. 'She is an excellent rider like Annette.'

The reference to Annette made him glance up, though Françoise averted her eyes. 'I shall hire a horse straight away,' he said assuredly. 'And I promise you Caroline, we shall ride together this week.' Her name as it passed his lips, sounded different here in France than it did in England. He laughed at his happiness. The child knew him. Annette had done well.

'Only an hour!' called Françoise, climbing back into the carriage. 'Then I shall return. – Go now and walk with your father!'

They walked together by the river and she talked in excited French, punctuated by very poor English. Much was lost on his ears, though he heard the tones of her emotions, the happiness some things occasioned, the irritations of others, as she frowned and pouted and occasionally stamped her foot. But he did not want to stop the waterfall of words, for it was quenching a long endured thirst. She shook her finger at the sky. 'I am very angry. My tutor has kept me too long with my lesson. How silly. My English is good and I wanted to be with you.' Her bright eyes flashed with emotion. 'I can learn English from you, Papa, can I not?'

'Indeed you can,' he smiled. 'You can learn as we talk.'

Suddenly, there was a piercing shriek from the river.

'See!' cried the child, pointing. 'It is a crow! The black swans nest by the water. A bad dog stole into their nest last week and the swans attacked it. It was horrible to see them fighting. The swans are vicious while nesting.'

He watched her as she shaded her eyes with her hand, trying to look against the sunshine. The female swan flapped and screeched at the determined bird. 'How many days can you stay?' she asked him eagerly. 'Maman says you will leave us and return to England.' She gave him a forlorn look.

'Maman is right,' he smiled. 'But I intend to stay for a month.' It seemed such a meagre length of time, he thought, as he said it. 'But I shall see you a lot before I go. And I hope you will come to see me in England too. You have family there. My sister Dorothy, your aunt, is with me in France. She is staying at Pierre's château. I shall bring her to Blois to meet you.'

They emerged through the trees to a familiar place where he had often sat with Annette. They found a spot amongst the wild flowers and settled in the grass.

'I still have the baby clothes you bought with Maman,' she said, sighing as she spoke. 'The day will come when I shall have a baby of my own. I am saving the clothes for then.'

He shivered with sadness. *The baby clothes?* Oh, how he had loved that day when they had gone to buy them. His heart tightened with memory. 'I am glad they are saved,' he murmured.

'Maman tells me you have touched them.' She lay on her back, her long hair falling about her. 'I love them for that.'

Just then he was unable to speak.

'How glad I am that you are here!' she cried, suddenly bursting into tears. 'I cannot bear for you to leave us! Oh, why must you leave us?' She covered her face with her hands and slowly sat up.

'I would like to stay longer,' he said, half glad of her sadness. But her emotions were free and honest, and he delighted in her loving directness. He saw that she recovered quickly, drying her eyes and smiling. He dared to take hold of her hand. 'I have work to finish back in England, my dear, but I shall visit you again before long.'

'But you must see Maman before you go!' she cried. She clutched his arm urgently. 'I know she is eager to see you. She talks of you often and takes long walks by the Loire, thinking of how she loves you.'

'Does she?' he murmured, starting at her words. 'I do not want her to forget me.'

'She will never forget you. How could she? Promise me you will see her. Please promise!'

'I have come to see both of you,' he said. He plucked at grass and stared about.

'Today?' the child beseeched him. 'Please see Maman today!'

'Of course,' he laughed. 'That is my intention.' He had written to say he would visit Annette later that day – had Françoise not told her? But Françoise still acted strangely and had gazed on him coldly. But he did not know the perils she had known in

The Terror. Her face had looked tired and her dark hair had turned grey.

He talked with Caroline another half hour, telling her about his life in England, why he had left her mother so quickly and how it had broken his heart. She said she understood, screwing up her face at the horrors of the revolution and speaking in her fast emotional French from the depths of her young heart. 'I forgive you everything, Papa. The whole world forgives you!' He told her about her uncle John at sea, and in his own struggling French, told tales to arouse her laughter. They talked some more until the sound of the carriage on the road alerted them. Oh, such a precious hour!

He looked at her again and embraced her. The air felt cold and the waving grass had darkened. The sun had gone behind the clouds. The child talked on until they reached the top of the hill, then she climbed inside the carriage and was gone.

It humbled him, the way she had trusted and loved him, and he secured that trust in his soul. She had not spoken of any other man in her mother's life and neither had he asked.

After another half hour, he stood by Annette's door, wondering how it would be. He had arrived at a place he had dreamt of for the last ten years, yet he could not say how he felt. All words were absent. He was here at the time they had decided, standing in the spot he had envisaged; yet he could not move. He was about to meet with Annette again after so many hopes and dreams. Had she seen him arrive, he wondered, would she open the door any minute? It was as if a musical offering were about to be played, a thing long rehearsed though wearied now of itself and worn as a beggar. For all those years he'd been a father. Yet he had not felt like a father. Not until meeting and talking with Caroline had the full reality of it come to him. To search for family characteristics in her features and to find them, to find again her mother in her movements and smile, had filled him with joy. He had great admiration and respect for Annette that his daughter appeared so untouched by the ordeals the Vallons must undoubtedly have suffered. He struck down the knocker and waited.

Grey and tired it was Paul who came to the door. There was an eager welcome in his eyes. 'William – How glad I am not to have missed you! I have to go out. We have so looked forward to your visit!' They shook hands warmly. 'So many years! Come; let me pour you a drink.'

'I am glad to see you are alive and well,' said William in earnest.

The house inside was gloomy and still as if even the furniture had drawn away from the world. But Paul's usual grace had not abandoned him; he smiled and poured drinks, asked about Dorothy, asked about Elizabeth and Clarisse, and remarked with wonder how strange it was that they had found each other so accidentally. Paul talked of his experience with Leonard Bourbon and the alleged attack he'd been involved in. Apart from the sound of their talk, the house was still and silent. 'Annette isn't here,' he said frowning. 'She was summoned to a meeting.' His eyes turned towards the window then back to William. 'But I know she will be here very soon.'

'I'm glad,' said William, for it had passed through his mind that Annette might try to avoid him. He felt as if he stood on the edge of a precipice, ready to leap into darkness, for it was all darkness now with Annette, he could not see her in his future. Paul lit candles about the room. The thin flames flooded his features leaving them in shadow by turns. William saw that his hair was streaked with a bluish silver colour, like the scales of a fish.

'I cannot tell you how relieved we were by the Treaty,' said Paul. He passed William a glass of wine then took a seat beside him. 'So many have died we can scarce take count.' He shook his head; ashamed it seemed, for the monster France had let loose. 'Many have lost hope for mankind,' he murmured.

William looked at him and held his gaze. 'Such a terrible thing,' he murmured.

'You too?' said Paul, with surprise. 'And you always had such sanguine expectations.'

'I do remain hopeful,' said William shifting about uncomfortable. 'But goodness cannot be happy just for its smile; kindness finds its services are unsought. It is we who make it so.'

'Best not to think on it too much,' said Paul, taking a long drink of wine. He rose and went to the window. 'You look well,' he said, over his shoulder.

'Life has been good to me,' said William.

Paul sighed and turned.

'I do not think Annette would have liked me to be always depressed,' William continued, seeing that Paul was unsettled. 'She would have insisted I get on with my life.'

'Of course. So what have you done with this life, then?'

William answered with silence.

Paul drank deeply and emptied his glass. 'I must leave you, my friend. I'm sorry.' His shoulders rose and fell. 'There is always some conflict to attend to.' He breathed a hopeless sigh. 'That tyrant, Bonaparte!'

'Such is the way of war,' murmured William. 'To some he is a great leader.'

Paul gave a shrug. 'He makes promises with his enemies, but he does not keep them. What sort of leader is that? I believe he is very much feared. It is interesting how fear can turn into love if it is politically expedient to do so.'

William rested his head on the back of the chair and closed his eyes.

'Please forgive me,' said Paul quietly. 'You are speaking your mind as always. It is one of the reasons my sister has always loved you.'

'"*My sister has always loved you.*"' The words rang out in his mind. How good it was to know that he had always been loved. But he could not answer to that love. He would try in time through poetry. But he wondered where the beautiful thoughts and words he had shared with her lived, in the very heart of the Almighty perhaps, where all things were sacred and unfathomable. He gazed about the room, remembering. Paul looked older. He was bound to look older himself. – And Annette, dear Annette, who had been subject to war and tyranny so long, what about her? 'How is she?' he asked quietly.

'She is well. – You saw Caroline, I believe. Françoise told me. I am glad it worked out.'

'Yes, we spent a blissful hour by the Loire.' The child had made him feel decent and honourable, not selfish and bad. In her own warm-hearted way she had helped redeem him. 'She is a loving creature,' he murmured, more to himself than to Paul.

'Indeed,' said Paul. 'She has so much love in her heart it worries me.'

William saw pain and frustration in Paul's features. There was much to fear for the child, but the concern ought not to have been Paul's. 'Do not worry about the love she has in her heart,' said William. 'It can only be good for her, surely?'

'It is possible to love too much,' Paul said flatly. 'It can drown you. Françoise and I have talked about it often.'

'Françoise scarcely acknowledged me today,' said William, in a tone that made Paul look up.

'I believe Françoise has an aversion to men altogether. Do not judge her too harshly. She has many problems. And in any case, she is a private person and not at all like Annette. Reserve is a habit with Françoise, ever since childhood.'

William watched the sun going down through the window.

He saw the sycamore he knew so well near the door, much higher now and virtually strangled by ivy. He saw the stones of the path to the door glittering in the last of the light, the path where he had struggled to the house with the wounded Beaupuy. So many memories came with the ticking of the clock. Paul stood up and went for his coat, then dallied before him, buttoning it slowly. 'I hope I shall see you again,' he said, putting out his hand.

Alone in the room William sat thoughtful, looking about. He did not feel his conversation with Paul had gone very well. Paul hadn't asked him how long he intended to stay, nor had he asked about England. Did he think that he brought bad tidings? – Just then he heard footsteps on the path by the door, footsteps his soul knew well. Panic mounted inside him. How would he greet her? What would he say? He rose slowly as the door opened and she entered.

In the hazy light he saw her, and the ghost of his love rushed forward to embrace her. Oh, how it hurt to constrain it! 'Annette?' he whispered.

'William,' she returned, her voice stronger than imagined. 'Is it you?'

With her voice came the memory of wet satin slippers drying by a fire, damp resplendent tumbling hair spread across a pillow . . . And yes, he wanted her! His heart quickened with pain. 'Oh, Annette!'

In the dimness of the room, she went to the chaise longue and sat down. She spoke softly. 'Do you remember how it was?'

'Of course,' he whispered, his nerves failing as he moved shakily towards her. 'My dear Annette . . .' The voice that came from his throat spoke from another time, but how strong and unshakeable it was when set in the present, and he fell on his knees at its mercy. For a moment or two there was silence. He saw that her hand moved across the chaise longue slowly, as if with the movement of memory.

'Poor, poor Beaupuy, we could not remove the bloodstains,' she said sadly. 'We tried so hard but they would not go away. That is why the chaise longue stays in the darkness here.' She gave a light little laugh. 'Life is senseless, yet we are forced to take it so seriously.'

He listened, afraid to move closer. She clung to the shadows.

'Jean saved the life of the captain,' she continued, in an almost inaudible voice, 'and now they are both dead.'

'"*Dead?*"' he gasped, straightening. 'Jean and Beaupuy both dead? – But how did it happen?'

She spoke tiredly. 'I asked Pierre not to tell when he wrote to England. What good would it have done to tell? Jean was shot in the forest, shortly after you left.' She sighed. 'What irony.'

'Cruel irony indeed,' William whispered.

'It happened at night time,' Annette said calmly. 'It was instant. He was going to help a wounded man. Such was the nature of my brother.'

For a moment they were both thoughtful. He chilled at the thought of a bullet finding Jean in the forest just as a bullet had found Beaupuy. 'And Beaupuy?'

'Beaupuy was killed at war. I do not know where he died, but we heard of it.'

William sat down and rested his head in his hands. Jean cared nothing for the politics of those he healed. And Beaupuy cared only for the welfare of others and serving the cause of freedom. 'The world asks too much,' he said quietly.

'We do,' said Annette, her voice firm and strong. 'Did we not bring it on ourselves this misery, this madness?'

He listened, drifting back into his old familiar way of listening to her emotions, the music of her voice. Beaupuy had died for what he believed in. Jean had died on the way to a wounded man, determined to offer his services as a doctor. What more could both men have done? He listened as she talked. Her voice and form seemed ethereal.

She changed her position on the chaise longue, and he made a gesture towards her, but she moved away quickly. Could he not *see* her, just for a second? He longed to see her! Why must she hide in the shadows? Apart from the occasional rustle of her dress, the room was silent. He wondered what she was wearing and how she was looking. 'How have you been?' he asked softly. 'I wanted to come to you. I have thought of you often . . .' His voice trailed off to a murmur, the words seemed false and absurd. It was true, he had often thought of her, but his feelings had changed as the thoughts had dimmed and other thoughts had taken their place. Was it betrayal? No it was not. Love did not wait, and he loved Mary Hutchinson deeply. Now their marriage was inevitable. But how would he tell Annette that the man who was here with her now in her home, was not the man she had known, that he had grown into someone else? He waited for her answer.

'We have to survive,' she said, sighing. 'We are all weary. I am constantly watched. They have searched this house all over to discover my activities. Now and again I am careless. I left a list on the table of the people I talk with. The revolutionaries came and grabbed me roughly in the way that they handle men.' She laughed lightly. 'But I often get my way. I can charm them, you see. It is true I have hidden people here – oh, many. And I have taken food to the Royal Army. They were hungry.'

He listened with a kind of numbness. It was the first time he had really thought of her as a soldier. She had helped the royalists. She would. But how far had she gone to get her way? 'How far did you charm them, Annette?' he asked quietly.

She spoke loudly and boldly. 'As far as I must. – I have had to save lives.'

For a moment they were both silent.

'The fact of *you* made it easier.'

'The fact of *me* — but how?'

'You have friends here, William, revolutionary friends. I needed to use them.'

'What do you mean?' he whispered.

She told him how she had lived, the terror in the hearts of her friends and family, the way they had been forced to depend on each other, fearing for their lives. She still remained in the shadows, her voice thin and waiflike, in a tone of sadness. 'You saw our daughter. I am glad.'

'Yes, and thank you.'

'She tells me she loves you. She says you are her friend.'

He braced himself and sighed. 'Well, a father ought to be a friend, of course. You have worked hard for her to have me in mind. It surprised me.'

'But why should it surprise you? I have loved you, William. Our daughter will love you too.' She left the chaise longue and went to the bureau nearby. Lifting the lid she brought out a wad of letters. 'These are the letters I wrote to you. But of course, they were never sent. Why send letters to a man who is in love with another?'

He rose from the chair, confused. What had Elizabeth told her? What did she know about Mary?

'I hate that it is true,' she whispered, her voice trembling with emotion.

'I would like to have known how you felt,' he murmured.

She laughed loudly. 'I see! I did not know how I felt about it myself at first. So I did not write. I was suffering so much in my country that the death of your love was just another horrible death. I put it with the rest of my pain.' She went on, her tone less painful and a little more tender. 'It came to me finally that I could not retrieve your love however I tried. The time was too long, and I was too far away, or I know I would have taken it for myself. I would have wrenched it out of your heart with my bare hands!' Her breath trembled with her words. She was silent for a moment, then with great feeling, she murmured, 'But what else could you do, my precious, with that mighty love of yours, other than give it to another? It would have killed you to keep it prisoner.'

Here they sat in the dismal room in the late afternoon dusk, the dark trees through the window seemingly frozen in time.

'I would have known anyway,' she said, defeatedly, 'without Elizabeth's letters. Such knowledge comes on the wind.' At that moment the letters she held fell to the floor and scattered. 'William, oh, William!' she cried. She went to him and buried her face in his chest. 'Our love has died through want of living!'

'Hush, my love, hush!' he whispered, his heart heavy with confusion. He breathed her essence in, the scent of her hair, the scent of her skin. He could feel her shoulder blades through her thin cotton dress, sharpened as if to weapons. She had lost much flesh. 'Annette, I have missed you so much!'

'And I you,' she sobbed.

He held her tightly. But his mind was decided. He would return to Mary and marry her. 'You know I shall always care for you,' he said, struggling for words.

'I do,' she said. 'We shall always care for each other.' She lifted her face and looked at him.

'Oh, my dear, what happened?' he cried. In shocked amazement, he ran his finger down a scar on her cheek.

'No, do not look!' she shivered, pulling away quickly. 'The blade of a sword caught me. The man intended to frighten me, but the weapon slipped. It is nothing.'

'Which man?' he asked angrily.

'He was a soldier. He is probably dead by now. He was a poor swordsman, no?'

He touched her arm and made her look at him so he could see her scar more closely, a sharp straight line down her cheek.

'You see,' she whispered. 'I am no longer your beautiful Annette.'

He fell into a chair wretched. 'I should have been with you!'

She sighed. 'No, no. You would probably have died. It isn't your fault. And anyway, the scar will be gone in a year. Each year it fades. I might have had my throat cut or gone to the guillotine. I tell you the scar is nothing.'

'My poor, dear Annette,' he said helplessly.

'Not so,' she laughed. 'I have Caroline, and our daughter is happy. Life will get better. – I believe you are here for a month.'

'Yes.'

'Then we shall see each other again and the three of us will walk together. I would like that a lot.'

'But I have much to explain . . .' he began.

'No, no,' she urged. 'I know those things already. You will marry this woman in England. You will have lots of children and be happy. I am sure she is lovely.'

He knelt for the letters on the floor and she stood before him watching. He returned them slowly to her hands, then she went to put them in the bureau, carefully, neatly, touching each with her lips. It hurt him that he did not care what they contained. Picking them up from the floor, he had felt like an impostor, an intruder, not the man he had once been, to whom the letters were written.

'Now you must go,' she said quickly. 'Enough of talk for today. We will say more words tomorrow.'

She went to open the door, and he walked out slowly on to the gravel path. He heard his feet crunching on the stones. He saw his shadow on the wall. Yet somehow he did not feel there, he felt far far away. He was lost in feelings and memories. He stopped and turned. She watched from the window, her arms folded, her figure proud and strong. In the fading light he could not see her fully, but he imagined her with that loving look that connected them both in his mind and which he knew he would see forever. He turned again and walked away.

Sources Of Extracts Used

'The Prelude', William Wordsworth, 1888

'An Evening Walk', (Addressed to a Young Lady),
   William Wordsworth, 1793

An abstract of English and Foreign Literature, Volume 22

'On Reading an Account that his only Sister's Death was Inevitable',
   Samuel Taylor Coleridge, 1791

'Pretty Maid Milking her Cow,' Thomas More, traditional Irish Folk-
   song circa 1779

Emmanuel Kant, Critique of Pure Reason, 1787

Letter from William Wordsworth to Samuel Taylor Coleridge,
   Grasmere, 1799.

Preface to 'Lyrical Ballads' (1802 version) William Wordsworth

Letter to Charles James Fox, William Wordsworth, 1801